Revelations

Laurel Dewey

THE
STORY PLANT

The Story Plant
The Aronica-Miller Publishing Project, LLC
P.O. Box 4331
Stamford, CT 06907

Copyright © 2011 by Laurel Dewey

Cover design by Barbara Aronica-Buck
Author photo by Carol Craven

ISBN-13: 978-0-9841905-5-3

Visit our website at www.thestoryplant.com
Visit Laurel Dewey's Facebook page at www.facebook.com/
pages/Laurel-Dewey-Author/200115782067

First Story Plant Paperback Printing: June 2011
Printed in the United States of America

To my husband David.
It's no secret that I love you deeply.

And to my mother, Priscilla, who is now with me in Spirit.

Acknowledgments

My gratitude goes out to Lieutenant Wayne Weyler of the Mesa County Sheriff's Department in Grand Junction, Colorado who helped with research and story accuracy.

Thanks to the transformative work of Bert Hellinger and his book *Acknowledging What Is*, which was the impetus for the subject matter in this book.

To Jan Rupp, for her friendship and invaluable understanding of the family constellation.

To Carol Craven, for always catching the light to grab the perfect shot.

Kudos to Peter Miller for helping make the Jane Perry series a success.

As always, many thanks to Lou Aronica for his dogged determination and belief in Jane Perry. Without you, none of this would be possible.

If we could read the secret history of our enemies
we should find in each man's life sorrow and suffering enough
to disarm all hostility.
— Henry Wadsworth Longfellow

Losing an illusion makes you wiser than finding a truth.
— Ludwig Börne

When we try to avoid what is unpleasant, sinful, and confrontational, we lose precisely what we wanted to keep, namely our
life, dignity, freedom, and greatness. Only he who confronts
the dark forces and accepts their existence is connected to his
roots and the sources of his strength.
— Bert Hellinger

CHAPTER 1

Jordan Copeland ran like a monster through the rain-soaked woods, chased only by his demons.

The darkness fell in on him—and within him—as he fought the choking sensation in his throat. It was just like forty-one years ago. But this time...*this time*, it was deeper, darker and more profound.

Sweat beads bled into the fat raindrops that covered his long, oilcloth, olive green duster. The full moon traversed between the clouds, emitting fleeting glimpses of the world around him—a stand of trees, the rushing, unforgiving river, his log cabin on stilts. Nearly out of breath, he took temporary shelter under a leafless oak.

That's when he smelled it. *Death*—sudden, stark, shattering and without dignity. Death, with vacant eyes staring back, the silver cord cut between the worlds.

Jordan crouched down against the tree trunk, burying his head in his chest. The hard rain heightened the sharp, pervasive, oiled odor of his duster. Lifting his head toward the heavens, his wide-set blue eyes and elongated forehead felt the brunt of the icy pellets. His grey beard was laced with mud and rain that quickly hardened into frosty threads. The roar within was deafening. He clamped his large, calloused hands over his ears, as the syncopated beat of his racing heart pounded in his head. *Not again*, he thought. *God... not again.*

The pressure around his throat increased. Forty-one years ago, he had youth on his side. He could run harder and longer. But now, his fifty-nine-year-old body was broken by a life unraveled. If he didn't keep running, he knew he'd black out. Jordan felt the walls of his narrow world caving in. The sound of the rushing river thirty feet away, drifted into the distance.

He pressed his hands harder against his ears. For a moment, he heard nothing—just sweet silence and peace. Then, a second later, a stabbing pain sliced across his heart. He pulled his hands from his ears and pressed them against his chest, bracing himself against the oak tree's trunk. The relentless storm sent waves of freezing rain across the inky landscape, raising the water of the thunderous river. The pressure around his throat increased until each breath became a life or death fight. *Run*, he thought. *Run hard and escape.* Yes, it was the same detached terror from forty-one years ago. He was able to sprint like a champion then, but it didn't do him any good. The end result was still a life of suffering and loneliness.

The storm subsided. Jordan sucked in a deep breath, the primal grip on his throat suddenly releasing. The knife-like pain in his chest mellowed to a dull throb. He could handle that, he figured, as he glanced down to his chest. The moonlight swept across his hands, revealing crimson streaks of blood. *But from what? From where?* Jordan regarded his oversized hands, as if they belonged to another. It made no sense. *Dear God.* It was happening again. But this time…this time, the terror was carving into his gut. *Think, dammit, think.* But as hard as he thought, he couldn't remember how he'd arrived at this spot—under the oak tree, dying for breath, and bleeding.

The demons moved closer, their claws whipping toward him like the lines of the fly fishermen that stalked the river's edge. Rising to his towering height, Jordan's eyes flared into a wild gaze. His wet, tangled salt-and-pepper mane slapped against the soaked duster. Spinning from one side to the other, Jordan exposed a warrior's sword that only he could see. The rage inside flared into a conflagration as he slashed and cut the demonic tentacles that coiled around him. *They won't win this time.* A generous sweep of his blade slaughtered the last of the fiends and sent them back into the underworld.

Crack!

Jordan turned toward the still echoing sound. The taste of death prickled on his tongue—bitter and sour.

Roar!

They were coming for him and he was cornered. Hunted

like a rabid dog, Jordan wasn't going to give up without a fight. Taking a step backward, he misjudged the embankment and plunged down the muddy, clay-laden slope. His ravaged body absorbed every rock and fallen tree while the pain consumed him. He was back on the cement floor of the jail cell forty-one years ago, getting the shit beaten out of him by the guards. "Fucking killer!" they screamed with a brutal punch to his face. "Child killer!" they grunted with each kick to his kidneys.

A high-pitched squeal shot into the night air as Jordan's body hurtled toward the water's edge.

CHAPTER 2

"Jane?"

Jane Perry stood staring outside the office window. The spring rain swept across the Denver landscape as the somber grey dusk enveloped the city. It was a fitting backdrop to the jarring statement she was still attempting to grasp. Jane wrapped one arm around her chest, her fist balled. Chewing the thumbnail of her other hand, she felt the syncopated pounding of her heart. The rain fell with renewed fury as her world narrowed and darkened.

"Jane…why don't you sit down?"

The doctor's voice sounded as though it was filtered through a wall instead of a few feet away. *Breathe*, Jane thought. But breathing was dangerous. Sucking in too much life might burn it up too fast. Everything would need to be measured from now on. *Jesus Christ, what a way to live.*

She turned toward the doctor, still in suspended animation and noted that the woman had a look of finely tuned compassion on her face. Jane wondered how many years it had taken to hone that visage so that patients would feel safer in her presence. Even with the news, Jane's cynicism was still alive. "So, what's the protocol?" she asked, in the same tenor she used when entering a crime scene.

"I'd like to do another cone biopsy," the doctor responded flatly.

"I thought you already determined it to be..."

"The pathology suggests a possible Grade II cervical intraepithelial neoplasia. It looks to be confined to the basal third of the epithelium..."

The words swam through Jane's head like sharks during a feeding frenzy. Each multisyllabic word gnashed into the other, creating a chaotic drone. She knew she'd get a second opinion, but this *was* the second opinion.

"Suggests?" Jane interrupted with an edge to her voice. "Is it or isn't it cancer?"

"There appear to be premalignant dysplastic changes but there are also abnormalities in the biopsy that are inconclusive..."

The sharks resumed their multisyllabic feast. *It's fucking insane,* Jane thought. Life had been going along at a nice, uneventful pace for over a year. She was now *Sergeant* Detective Perry, sharing duties with her former boss, Sergeant Morgan Weyler. They were an odd, yet highly effective team; Jane with her gruff, penetrating approach and Weyler with his eloquent, restrained demeanor. Together, they'd solved a few high-profile Denver homicide cases, washing away the tragic stain that had dogged the Department two years ago. After nearly four decades of shallow breathing, Jane had finally been able to exhale.

Now that old voice in her head started spouting the mantra again—*Life is a struggle and then you die.* All the books she'd read in the last fifteen months on everything from Buddhism and the mind/body connection to esoteric meditation and higher consciousness were a waste of time. Faith and trust were incomprehensible now. It was easy to have faith and trust when life was chugging along at a happy pace. Now, *right now*, when she needed them most, Jane's abject fear devoured them whole.

"So, we do another cone biopsy and then what?" Jane asked.

"It all depends on what that biopsy concludes. Typically, if it confirms severe cervical intraepithelial neoplasia, there's an eighty- to eighty-five percent chance that it's a squamous cell carcinoma…"

"*English*, dammit!" Jane insisted, her patience wearing thin.

"We can do a few things," the doctor related, undaunted by Jane's tone. "We usually perform a loop electrical excision procedure and conisation in which the inner lining of the cervix is removed and examined…"

"*Electrocution*?" Jane asked, shifting her weight uncomfortably in her cowboy boots. "That sounds medieval."

"It's basic protocol. The pathology will determine what stage we're looking at. Early stages may involve radiation and/or a hysterectomy."

Jane noted a cold, rather calculated delivery of her options. She was reminded of the unemotional banter standing across from medical examiners over the years, as they rattled off a perfunctory list of data that led to the death of the poor son-of-a-bitch filleted open on the metal table between them. It was one thing, Jane considered, to discuss a dead man's outcome in a detached manner, but to use the same cadence with someone who still had a pulse felt insensate to Jane. "Isn't a hysterectomy a bit aggressive?"

"Cervical cancer is aggressive, Jane." The doctor glanced at Jane's open file on her desk. "I know the idea of a hysterectomy at the age of thirty-seven can be difficult to wrap one's mind around, but the fact that you can't conceive a child anyway… takes a bit of the concern out of it."

Right, Jane thought. *Wasn't using my uterus anyway, so what the hell?* She slid into the single chair opposite the desk and felt the butt of her Glock bite into her side as she dug her elbow into the arm of the chair and dragged her fingers through her shoulder length brown hair. Her leather jacket issued a soft *crick* as she sat back and looked the doctor straight in the eye. "I don't get it. I think I've made some significant changes in my life.

I'm eating better…sort of…I took up running two years ago. I even completed a three-month yoga course that my boss signed me up for." Jane still had a penchant for calling Weyler her boss even though they were now on equal footing. "Good God, I've been sober for fifteen months and nine days. Doesn't that count for something?" Jane instantly realized that it was both absurd and desperate to think you earned points and dodged death for choosing sobriety.

"Lifestyle changes that improve health benefits are always positive," the doctor offered.

Jesus Christ, she thought. *There must be a manual these physicians follow, filled with pithy, mollifying statements that sound good but mean nothing.* She couldn't stand it any longer. "What in the hell are you talking about?" Her voice raised several octaves as she leaned forward and slammed her fist onto the doctor's desk. "*Obviously*, it made no difference, given your diagnosis!"

"You can't put a price on sobriety, Jane."

Fuck! Another Hallmark card contribution. Jane promised herself if the doc's next statement was, "You have to name it and claim it," she was going to dive across the desk and strangle her.

"You *are* a smoker, Jane," the doctor gently put forth. "That's one of the ten behaviors that put you at greater risk."

Great. Somebody made a list. Somebody *always* makes a goddamn list, Jane deduced. We've become a nation where we respond to lists and studies. Out of studies you get lists and out of lists you get people who chat about the lists as if the list was absolute. "Yeah, of course I smoke," Jane said nonchalantly, realizing that a cigarette would taste pretty damn good right about now. "Cigarettes are the reformed drunk's best friend."

"Cigarettes are also a significant risk factor for cervical cancer, not to mention…"

"Yeah, I get it."

"Multiple partners…"

Jane regarded the doctor with an arched eyebrow. "That's

on the list?" The doctor nodded. "Define 'multiple.'" Jane stated, pretending for a moment that she was talking to her across a dimly lit table in Denver Headquarter's tiny interrogation room.

"That's difficult to say. It's more pertinent whether a partner had an STD."

"Well, let's see, I haven't had a *partner* in the religious sense for two years. And *he* was pretty fucked up on drugs. Are fucked up partners with drugs on your list? Before that, I could count my *partners* on one hand and still have a finger or two available. So, I don't think I fit the multiple-partner profile." The doctor flipped the page on Jane's report. Across the table, Jane could read her name across the top line: *JANE ANNE PERRY. Who in the hell was that?* she thought. She was Sergeant Detective Perry. *That* was a name she could answer and relate to—not Jane Anne Perry. Jane Anne Perry died a long time ago. "What you else you got on that list, doc?"

"Long term use of birth control pills…"

"Since pregnancy has never been possible, the Pill was never an issue," Jane countered.

"Multiple pregnancies."

Jane shook her head and a disparaging half-smile crept across her face. "This is your list?"

"Genetic history of cancer…especially the mother." The sarcastic grin quickly left Jane's face. "That's actually a formidable risk in comparison to the others," the doctor stressed, sitting back in her chair and holding Jane's gaze.

Jane swallowed hard. It had been twenty-seven years since she had witnessed her mother, Anne, take her last violent breath before collapsing in a pool of blood and vomit. The memory was as fresh as ever, as was the invasive stench of death that Jane could never shake. "She died of lung cancer and never smoked a cigarette in her life." The randomness of life suddenly struck Jane. What was the point of changing one's lifestyle if it all came down to an arbitrary spin of the wheel? You might as well build a meth lab in the bathtub and have anonymous sex.

"It doesn't matter the type of cancer she had. It matters that she *had* cancer and died of it. Between that and smoking, you are at a much higher risk."

"She never lived..." Jane's voice softened as she turned toward the office window. The rain was quickly turning to snow as it pelted the glass. "She existed."

The doctor flipped through Jane's file. "She died at 35."

Jane turned back to face the doctor. "Is that supposed to be significant? I've lasted two years longer than my mother so my clock's ticking?"

"Genetics...our family history plays a major role for all of us." The doctor closed the file and leaned forward. "You can't ignore your DNA, Jane...your bloodline."

"What are you saying? That I'm doomed to repeat my mother's history? I don't buy that, doc. I'm nothing like her. She was compliant...she was fragile...she had no gumption, no fight. She was always a broken woman. Cancer was a gift because it got her out of a life that she chose to crawl through."

"So, you're saying that strong, tough people like *you* don't die of cancer?"

Jane sat back. She'd painted herself into an idiotic corner. "I'm saying...that I don't believe blood defines my life...or my death." She realized her hand was shaking. Suddenly, there was a strange sense in the tiny office—a heaviness that had not been there a few minutes earlier. Jane shifted with purpose in her seat, hoping she could shake off the unidentified impression that lingered around the edges of her chair. But instead, it hung even tighter.

"Did your mother take DES when she was pregnant?"

Jane felt outside of herself. "What?"

"DES. It's a synthetic estrogen that was used between the 1940's and 1971. Women were given it to prevent complications, especially with a history of premature labor..."

Jane tried to push herself back into her body. "I'm the oldest. She wouldn't know if she had a predisposition to premature labor so why would she take the drug?"

The doctor pursed her lips. "She could very well have taken it if there were complications during the pregnancy…"

Jane's head was spinning. "There were no complications when she was pregnant with me."

"How do you know?"

"I would have heard about it. Trust me," Jane responded curtly.

The doctor took a breath. "DES-exposed daughters have an increased chance of developing dysplasia in the cervix, usually around twenty to thirty years of age."

The strange, wraithlike heaviness sunk around Jane's body, almost demanding to be acknowledged. "And I'm thirty-seven," Jane stressed.

"It's not absolute. Since you don't fit into the profile completely, all other mitigating possibilities should be considered."

"She didn't take the drug."

"She didn't take it because you *know* she didn't or because you don't want to believe she took it?" In an unconscious, almost trance-like manner, Jane gently brushed her fingertips across her forehead, repeating the motion continuously. "Are you all right, Jane?" Jane stared into nothingness, her hand continuing its soothing rhythm across her forehead. "Do you have a headache?"

Jane suddenly noted the odd, uncharacteristic movement of her hand. She crossed her arms tightly against her jacket, a slight disconnect engulfing her. "I'm fine." She was aware of how distant her voice sounded.

"It's absolutely normal to feel anxious." The doctor reached for her prescription pad. "I can write you a script. It'll take the edge off."

Jane let out a hard breath, struggling to ground her scattered senses. "Doc, I came out of the gate with an edge. I've self-medicated for years to take the edge off and the result has been an extremely sharp point that almost cut the life out of me." She could feel that comforting, familiar grit return as she stood and faced the doctor. "I'll take a pass on your happy pills."

Jane stormed out of the parking garage in her '66 ice blue Mustang and was met with a battering mixture of rain and snow pattering across the windshield. Checking the car's clock, it was 6:30 pm. In a little over twelve hours, she'd be back at the doc's office with her feet in the stirrups as they sliced another chunk of tissue out of her. A few years ago, her plan of action would have been simple: go home, get piss drunk, pass out, wake up, nurse the hangover and plod through her day. She may have given up the bottle, but Jane hadn't given up her need to escape.

She gunned the Mustang onto I-70, easily passing three cars before stationing in the fast lane. Tomorrow was Friday. Next week was spring break. *Perfect.* She hadn't taken any time off save for the two days when her younger brother Mike got married barefoot in Sedona. *Yes, yes,* she thought. The escape plan was coming together perfectly. Jane unconsciously reached for her American Spirits, deftly lifting one of the slender cylinders out of the pack with her teeth as she changed lanes to pass a truck going the speed limit. Slamming the car's lighter into place with the heel of her hand, she continued to formulate her unplanned temporary departure. She'd wake up tomorrow, get the biopsy done, go to the market and stock up on enough food and DVDs to last a week, then return to her house and hole up like the old days—sans booze—until she got the phone call with the test results the following Thursday. She liked her plan. It was a classic Jane Perry mixture of *fuck you* revolt and sanctioned hooky. The car's lighter clicked. Jane pressed the pedal to the floor, passed an eighteen-wheeler and slid back into the fast lane. She drew the lighter to the tip of the cigarette when the reality of the moment came into focus. "Fuck," she whispered, and her plan quickly deflated.

It was only right that she leave a note for Weyler at DH.

It also didn't hurt that it was 7:15 pm when she squealed into police headquarters at 13ᵗʰ and Cherokee. Weyler was certain to be home by now, feet propped up on his ottoman, watching whatever PBS had programmed.

Getting off the elevator on the third floor, Jane quickly entered the homicide department and took a sharp right into her office. She snagged a blank sheet of paper out of the fax machine, scribbled a few sentences and signed her name. Before turning off the light, she grabbed a stack of paperwork from her cluttered, dusty desk, tucking it under her arm. *Goddamned Protestant work ethic,* she scolded herself.

A quick look around the Department showed no one. She walked into Weyler's office, placing her letter in the center of his pristine, uncluttered desk. It would be a stealth departure, Jane assumed, until she spun around and smacked into the 6' 4" frame of Sergeant Weyler.

"Jane," Weyler said with ease. "Just the person I'm looking for."

CHAPTER 3

"Boss!" Jane stammered. "I thought you'd left."

Weyler sidestepped his way around Jane and crossed to his chair. "I was on a long call to an old friend." He slid a yellow pad filled with handwritten notes across his desk and spied the folded sheet of paper. "What's this?" he asked, unfolding Jane's letter.

Jane never planned to be standing in the room when he read her hastened note explaining her abrupt weeklong leave. "It's...a..." It was uncharacteristic for her to stumble like this. She respected Weyler too much to bullshit him but she also wasn't in the mood to explain herself in person.

"'Boss?'" Weyler rejoined, reading the heading on her note. "Why do you keep calling me *boss*?"

"Habit, boss," Jane said, distracted, and feeling like the proverbial fish in a bowl that was about to be shot. "Let me explain about the note…"

Weyler slid the letter onto his desk in a nonchalant manner. "Sorry. Can't give you any time off now."

Jane's back went up. A second ago she was hesitant. Now she was pissed by Weyler's offhand attitude. "I have more time on the books than anyone in the Department! I'm just asking for a week…"

"I've already committed you to a case. Well, *both* of us, actually."

Jane felt the walls caving in. That all-too-familiar edge began to creep up. *God, a cigarette would taste damn good right now.* "I really need this time off…"

"Is someone dead or dying?" Weyler stared at Jane, waiting for her answer.

For a moment, Jane wondered if Weyler could read her mind. *Dying.* His words yanked the freshly formed scab off the news she'd received just an hour earlier. "I…" She was at a loss for words.

"Because someone *else* is," Weyler stated, taking a seat in his plush, leather office chair and motioning for her to sit across from him.

Jane reluctantly sat down. "We work in homicide. Someone's always dead or dying."

Weyler drew the yellow pad toward him. "But *this* one is way outside the norm. Goes against the statistics."

Jane hated the fact that Weyler knew how to play her so well. She loved cases that dwelled outside the box and made her think. She took the bait. "What stats?"

"A fifteen-year-old boy was kidnapped…after what appeared to be his attempted suicide."

The thought briefly crossed her mind that some poor kid

was having a worse day than she was. "He tried to kill himself…"

"By hanging. On a remote bridge."

"And then someone kidnaps him? What are the odds of that?"

"Million to one."

"Make it two million to one, given his age. Fifteen-year-old *boys* don't get kidnapped. They're full of testosterone and attitude…"

"His name is Jacob Van Gorden. He goes by *Jake.*' Even though he's fifteen, he's small for his age," Weyler offered, checking his notes.

"So what? *He's fifteen*! He's a *boy*! Fifteen-year-old boys run away, hop a train…"

"Hop a train?"

"You know what I'm saying. The suicide wasn't real. Jacob…Jake obviously set it up and ditched town."

"That's what everyone thought. But here's where it gets interesting. The family and police are being sent odd clues as to the boy's disappearance."

"Asking for ransom? Come on! The kid's in on it. He's pimping his family to get attention and some money."

"No request for money, Jane…just odd deliveries of statements to the family."

The day was quickly catching up with Jane. She pinched the skin between her eyes. "You said a remote bridge? Didn't know Denver had any of those left."

"It didn't happen in Denver. This occurred up in Midas."

Jane let out a tired puff of air. Midas, a town of less than 10,000, was located about 90 minutes northwest of Denver. "That's a tad out of our jurisdiction!" She was preparing to volley another lob for a week off when Weyler spoke.

"They've got their eye on a local guy…Jordan Copeland. Name ring a bell?" Jane shook her head. "Way before your time, I guess. It was a huge tabloid story back in the summer of 1968." Weyler filled her in on one of the more infamous murder cases of the late 1960s. It had "sensational" written all over it. Copeland was eighteen and found guilty of killing his next-door neighbor, a mentally retarded, thirteen-year-old boy, Daniel Marshall, in the backyard of his home in Short Hills, New Jersey. For no particular reason, Copeland shot the kid in cold blood with his father's rifle and then hid the boy's dead body under his bed for several days before the smell gave him away. "He did thirty-four years hard time," Weyler added. "Got out of prison seven years ago and settled in Midas about two years back."

"If they think Copeland did it, then why are we getting involved?"

"They don't have enough evidence to hold Copeland... even though his behavior is pretty damn strange. They took everything they needed from him before letting him go—handwriting sample, blood, hair, DNA. Bottom line...time's ticking away. This all went down five days ago. The family didn't jump on it because they thought it was a suicide."

"With no body?"

"Figured he slipped out of the noose and fell into the river. But the day after the disappearance, the family started getting the strange notes."

"How come no news coverage?"

"Family insists on keeping it low key. So does the town."

"Wait a second. What happened to whoring yourself across primetime TV to get help? Maybe Copeland dumped the kid across state lines..."

"This is Midas, Jane. People don't move to Midas, Colorado to get attention. They move there to blend in and live a quiet, unexposed existence. The family and the police chief want to respect those wishes. The last thing they crave is a goddamned media circus. Can you blame them?"

Jane certainly had been part of media circuses. Too many times, she'd reluctantly played a pivotal role in high-profile cases and had the spotlight directed her way. She hated it and rejected all offers to cash in on her celebrity—except once, almost two years ago, when she agreed to an appearance on *Larry King Live*. The owner of the local coffee joint still gave her a free refill for that. "If they *like* this Copeland asshole for it, why don't they have some cops sit up on him to watch his moves 24/7, harass him, see if the weird notes stop arriving and then pummel him into a confession?"

"They're short staffed. You have the police chief, his secretary and a few deputies."

"Midas is one of the wealthiest small towns north of Denver. They can certainly afford to hire out extra help." Jane noted Weyler's expression. "Oh, shit. *We're* the extra help?"

"I pulled this file on Copeland." Weyler stated, ignoring Jane's annoyance and handing her a slim, olive green folder. "We'll learn more when we get there tomorrow."

"Tomorrow?"

"I told Bo I'd be there tomorrow."

"Who the hell is Bo?"

"The police chief. We're old friends. Came up together on the job as rookies," Weyler slightly hesitated. "I owe him this."

"Owe him what?"

"Long story. Bottom line is...he's retiring in less than two weeks and he'd like to leave his job with this case put to bed. Suffice to say, he's calling in his chips and I'm going."

Jane had never heard Weyler talk like this. "Chips?" What connection could an urbane, refined Black man like Weyler have with some small town police chief to make him jump so fast to his tune? "Boss, what in the hell's going on here?"

"File this case under *mutual aid,* Jane." His tone was succinct and unwavering.

Jane's understanding of mutual aid was that if an outside jurisdiction had information on a case or could help through means of better equipment or manpower, they could be brought in to work with the acting police department in charge of the case. Midas had plenty of money, thanks to the scores of wealthy people who flocked to the mountain town and paid hefty taxes on their multimillion-dollar homes. "So, what do *we* have that they can't get somewhere else?"

"Me," Weyler declared. "And you," he quickly added. "But mostly, me."

Weyler's evasive tone was unusual. Jane was quickly piqued. "Getting back to my week off…"

"This is something I need to do, Jane, and you're coming with me."

"For what? Shits and grins?"

Weyler leaned across his desk. "Because I need someone who can think outside the box while I'm working inside it. But I'm also bringing you along for your inimitable tact, composure and sweet demeanor." He smiled and stood up, latching the yellow pad under his arm.

The day was just getting worse for Jane.

The trip to Midas was set in place, but not without a few choice omissions on Jane's part. If Weyler insisted on keeping secretive about why a two-bit police chief was "calling in his chips," she figured she'd keep her Friday morning doctor's appointment a secret from him. Before leaving his office that night, Jane arranged to pick up Weyler at Headquarters the following day and drive her Mustang to Midas. He balked at the idea, preferring the comfort of his roomy sedan that blended into the scenery rather than visually shouting its arrival. But Jane's classic coupe won the coin toss.

Until then, Jane had pressing business to attend to back at her house on Milwaukee Street. She cleaned every cigarette pack out of her Mustang, emptied the ashtray and shook the butts off the floor mats. After collecting more packs from her leather satchel and backpacks, she zoomed around the house and found every cigarette in and out of sight, and stuffed the heap into a plastic trash bag. Just to make sure she wouldn't cheat, she hauled the bag down two blocks and deposited it into an alley Dumpster. Yeah, that would solve her problem—like she couldn't get in her car and drive five blocks to the store and buy another carton. Jane knew it was just a game, but the fact that she was making up the game's rules somehow made her feel in control again. That all went out the proverbial window when she got home and found a single, unwrapped pack of fresh cigarettes in a kitchen drawer.

She set the single pack on the dining room table and plopped down on the couch. The overhead light shone down on the cellophane wrapping, allowing the pack to take on a heightened sense of appeal. She looked at the clock. It was 8:30 pm. When did she smoke her last cigarette…5:30 pm? It was right before she headed into the doctor's office. She wished she could remember it more clearly so she could have the sweet, nostalgic memory to fall back on when she was desperate for a hit of nicotine. How long had she previously gone without a cigarette? Maybe eight hours. But, of course, she was *asleep* during those eight hours. Jane stole a glance at the clock again. 8:31 pm. *God, this is torture.*

Jane tossed together a quick shrimp stir-fry, the entire time stealing furtive glances to the solo, alluring cigarette pack on the table that had taken on a provocative life of its own. This was her demon and she had to fight it. In order to push the emotion of the moment to the back of her head, she turned to logic and the comforting "If/Then" scenario. It went like this: If you do this, then that will happen. If you bang your head on the wall, then your head will hurt. The "If/Then" association always gave Jane a modicum of reassurance, offering a black-and-white action/reaction she could rely on. If you smoke cigarettes, then you get cancer. If you take care of yourself, then you live. Jane added more extra virgin olive oil to the stir-fry and stirred the over-cooked shrimp with greater vigor. But what if you only really started taking care of yourself at the age of thirty-six? Then what? Then…you *might* live. "Fuck," Jane muttered. She hated nebulous equations. The reliable "If/Then" had always made her feel safe. But now there was a rupture of grayness—a defined flaw in her black-and-white presumption.

Jane carried the searing fry pan to the dining room table, slapped a newspaper down as an impromptu placemat and set her laptop in front of her. The opened computer served to temporarily obstruct the view of the still-tantalizing cigarette pack. Drawing the slender green file on Jordan Copeland closer, she tested a bite of the stir-fry and opened the folder.

The top document was a black-and-white mug shot of Copeland, dated July 7, 1968. The stats showed Copeland to be eighteen years old, by only a few days. Although the photo wasn't in color, Jane easily determined that Copeland had pale, blue eyes—the kind of pale blue that almost appeared iridescent. *Penetrating...almost hypnotic.* In reading one of the many esoteric books she'd inherited from her friend, Kit Clark, Jane recalled a passage that referred to *the psychic eye.* Supposedly, there were people born with a distinctive eye that was described as intense and enigmatic. It was an eye that couldn't be ignored and drew one in to its gaze without the least effort. Jordan Copeland had such an eye. The paleness of his eyes was even more defined against his dirty, olive complexion.

Turning the photo over, Jane uncovered a newspaper clipping from the *New York Times,* dated August 10, 1968. A large photo above the story showed what appeared to be a cleaned-up Jordan moving through a crush of reporters on the courthouse steps, accompanied by his exceptionally strained-looking, upper-crust grandparents. But when Jane read the caption, the couple was identified as Jordan's sixty-one-year-old mother, Joanna, and his sixty-eight-year-old father, Richard. "Huh?" Jane grunted to herself. A quick mathematical calculation showed that Jordan's mother was forty-three when she gave birth to him, while his father was fifty. Certainly not typical, Jane surmised as she scooped another mouthful of shrimp into her mouth. Just when she was considering that Jordan was an "oops baby" after a line of older siblings, a cursory read of the accompanying article revealed that Jordan was an only child. "*What?*" Jane said aloud, wondering if anyone else found this odd back in '68. Jordan's parents were obviously one of the tonied elite—his mother's painfully trim, bony frame dressed in a classic Chanel wool tweed ensemble with matching gloves and hat, and his handsome father outfitted in a smart suit reminiscent of something Cary Grant would model, complete with a modest ascot. They could have been headed to a day at the country club rather than a somber walk toward the courthouse with their felonious son.

Jane wanted to read more. She turned the page to where the story should have been continued and found nothing. Obviously, whoever copied this particular article off the old microfiche archive, failed to note there was more of it. Jane shook her head in frustration. How many times had she been forced to go back and find the missing pages to articles? Too many. And this one wouldn't be easy to track down.

The next newspaper clipping in the short stack was dated, *October 13, 1968* and featured a sensationalized headline: *SCANDAL AND SHOCK IN SHORT HILLS—COPELAND FOUND GUILTY OF MURDER*. The tabloid-like story told of Jordan's conviction after the jury deliberated for only two hours. The sole photo was of Jordan's parents driving away from the courthouse in their Bentley, both of them appearing grim and stoic. Amongst the throng of reporters surrounding their car, Jane noted an irate group, holding up signs that read, *GO TO HELL, CHILD KILLER!* and *COPELAND NEEDS TO DIE!* Clearly, this was a case that had elicited vitriol and retribution.

And now, more than 40 years later, the same SOB was being fingered for another missing boy in another wealthy enclave.

"Shit," Jane muttered and closed the folder. Too worn-out to attempt an Internet research, she slammed her laptop shut only to find the single pack of cigarettes still upright and staring back at her. It was too much. She grabbed the pack and quickly unwrapped the cellophane. *Sweet seduction.* The arousing aroma of unlit tobacco teased her brain. It was the aromatic foreplay before the tactile pleasure of feeling the naked, white paper stroke her bottom lip. That would lead to the erotic moment of lighting the tip and inhaling that first, comforting yet electrifying hit of pleasure that would numb her mind and allow her brain to slow down. Just the thought made Jane's heart pound harder. Her lighter hovered less than an inch from the cigarette tip. Instant gratification was a second away.

Then an overwhelming sense of gloom sucked the bliss from the moment. She threw the lighter across the room, flicked the unlit cigarette onto the table, ceremoniously dumped the remaining nineteen down the kitchen sink's garbage disposal and flipped the switch. *Life is a battle.* That much, Jane believed. *Struggle is part of life.* So in keeping with that belief, she carefully slid the remaining single cigarette back into the pack and secured it in her leather satchel. She didn't have to do that, but she felt comfortable walking the hallways in Hell. The hard, brutal way was a familiar road she'd traveled often. She needed to keep the temptation at her fingertips so that she could never relax, never feel too complacent. There was no edge with complacency and Jane Perry required a jagged edge in order to function. Everyone needed to meet his or her Waterloo—to endure a great test of character that would lead to a final and decisive, often negative culmination. That solitary, sensuous, slender, aromatic roll of tobacco was Jane's Waterloo and she would fight it with the same intensity that she fought every other battle in her thirty-seven years.

She ambled down the hall toward her bedroom, walked into her closet and began tossing shirts, jeans, sweaters and an extra pair of roughout cowboy boots into a large duffel bag. Jane figured the trip to Midas would be three days max, so she packed accordingly—two long-sleeved, nearly identical blue poplin shirts, one pair of jeans, underwear, her faded *Ron Paul for President—2008* nightshirt and some toiletries. Her mind wandered through the day's events, resting on the sobering visit with the doctor. *"You can't ignore your bloodline, Jane."* For some strange reason, those words resonated in her cluttered head.

What did the doc mean by that? she questioned. In the end, was she doomed to be the sum total of her bloodline? That was an ominous predicament, given her violent, sadistic father who stroked out and her weak-willed, capitulating mother who died prematurely of cancer. Did a tattered bloodline hold one hostage to its whims and fate or was there a way to break free and chart a new course? Standing there in her cramped closet, she resolved to ignore her twisted family roots and tortured past. At that moment, it was the only possible way she could survive her future.

Jane was just about to turn around, when the whiff of gardenias gently wafted across the closet. As suddenly as it blossomed, the scent died. *Odd*, she thought. The dominant aroma in her closet, home and car was American Spirit cigarettes. There were no fresh flowers in the house; no scented candles or soaps that could transmit such a fragrance that Jane associated with doddering, blue-haired ladies. Besides, her olfactory senses had been weakened by twenty-three years of hardcore chain-smoking. She'd heard that when you quit smoking, your sense of smell and taste returned with a vengeance. But it had only been less than four hours since taking her last hit of nicotine. Certainly those senses weren't re-emerging this soon.

She scanned the middle shelf of the closet. Suddenly, a distinct heaviness set in around her. It was the same weighty feeling that swelled around her chair when she was sitting in the doctor's office. The air grew thicker, like sticky honey against a cold spoon. Her feet felt wedged into the carpet. An icy shiver cut through her body. Each breath seemed a bit more difficult to take. God, was this the cancer setting in? Was this some tentacle on a tumor that had reached a blood vessel and was strangling the life from it?

Jane lifted her head to the top shelf and noticed a large boot box in the corner. Written in black marker across the front were the words: *PHOTOS FROM HOUSE*. Next to it was a smaller box with the words: *KIT'S/MISC.* in red marker. The scent of gardenias swept through the closet again, this time lingering a little longer before disappearing. *Yes, it has to be something in one of those boxes*, she thought.

Jane slid the box of photos off the shelf and lifted the lid. A jumble of black-and-white, and color photos were inside— all recovered from her father's house two years ago when she cleaned it out. She'd never once looked inside the box, preferring to shove the images as far away as possible. Now she was staring into a muddle of memories; hundreds of eyes jockeying for her attention. A seeming innocuous photo on top showed her and Mike, her brother, competing in the annual ski race that Denver PD used to host in Breckenridge, Colorado. Fifteen-year-old Jane stood next to her puny, eleven-year-old brother on a pair of downhill skis that had seen better days. What the bright sun and reflections of the snow masked was the black-and-blue imprint of her father's fingertips where he'd grabbed her neck the night before during a drunken rage. Jane turned the photo over and dug into the pile. She brought up a black-and-white photo dated *1969* of her father and mother standing in front of the famed Broadmoor Hotel in Colorado Springs. In the photo, her father, Dale, draped his arm stiffly around her mother's shoulder. Anne Perry had the same sullen, lifeless gaze on her face that Jane always remembered. It was a portrait of sustained suffering. Turning the photo over, Jane noted the words, *Honeymoon*. She shook her head in disgust. The marriage started well below the curb and descended from there.

The scent of gardenias grew. Jane sunk her hand under the mass of photos and felt the edge of a folded document. She lifted it out of the box and discovered her parents' marriage certificate. She opened it to watch a photo and yellowed newspaper clipping drop to the floor. Retrieving them, Jane was somewhat stunned to see a posed, black-and-white portrait of her mother, still serious in nature but minus the haggard eyes. A dewy glow emanated from her skin as her perfectly coiffed brown hair had nary a strand out of place. Looking at the clipping, there was the same photo reprinted and a brief announcement that twenty-two-year-old Anne LeRoy of Willcut, Colorado, was to be married to Dale Perry of Denver, Colorado. *LeRoy. Yes, right,* Jane mused. Before Anne became cursed with the Perry name, she'd been a LeRoy. Just seeing the name of Anne LeRoy in print seemed to project an entirely new image of her mother. Anne was infused with a French lineage. Of peculiar interest, though, was that on the back of the portrait photo, someone had written, *Anne LeRóy* with a sharp accent mark over the *o*. While Jane couldn't be certain, it looked like her mother's handwriting.

Her mother's hometown of Willcut, Colorado, was as small town as you could get and had long ago been absorbed into Jasper, Colorado, which sat on the rim of Larimer County north of Denver. Reading that yellowed engagement announcement, Jane sensed a strange incongruity between the photo and the text. This somewhat fresh-faced, chaste woman named Anne LeRoy was going to marry a cop named Dale Perry. Did she think she would be moving up in the world by doing such a thing? Did she feel he would make her life better? Maybe so. But by the time the grim honeymoon photo was snapped, she certainly learned that she'd made a terrible mistake.

The gardenia scent lingered, almost becoming cloying to Jane's senses. She replaced the box of photos back on the shelf and removed the second box titled, *KIT'S/MISC.* Jane knew this would be anything but normal viewing as her friend was a believer in all things metaphysical, esoteric and New Age. Jane tossed off the lid, expecting to find a spilled bottle of gardenia essential oil. Instead, she discovered a mishmash of items including incense burners, ear candles, a few mood rings from the 1970s, a bag of *sacred dirt* from Chimayo, New Mexico, a small satchel of stone animal totems and a deck of tarot cards. Jane fondly recalled the bag of animal totems that had played a freakish, pivotal role in her life 15 months ago. At Kit's urging, Jane drew a stone from the bag and uncovered the snake—"the symbol of radical transformation," as Kit so enthusiastically exclaimed. That stone had indeed signaled a shedding of the old skin for Jane Perry and was subsequently tucked underneath a mat of grass next to her father's headstone. As much as Jane didn't want to believe in all the *boojey-woojey*—New Age crap as she called it—there was no denying the palpable significance of how that silly stone led Jane to solve a headlining kidnapping.

The aroma of gardenias sunk around Jane, shouting its presence. Jane lifted the deck of tarot cards out of the box and set the box on the carpet. "Fucking ridiculous," she muttered as she slid the rubber band off the deck. She didn't have the guts to inquire as to her demise. But she just wanted to know…know something…what that *something* was, she wasn't sure but she needed an answer to…

Jane didn't think she'd moved her hand, but the deck of cards slid away, cascading downward and sprawling across the carpet. Every single card fell face down, save for one. Jane picked it up and stared at it. A drawing of a middle-aged woman with flowing hair and ribbons of light encircling her body emerged from the center of a blue lotus flower. A single word bordered the card: *MATER*. Jane's negligible education in Latin decoded the translation: *MOTHER*.

Abruptly, the scent of gardenias evaporated.

CHAPTER 4

The noonday whistle ripped through the seam of silence. At least, that's what it sounded like to Jane when her alarm clock rang at 5:15 am. With one hand, she slapped the OFF button while the other hand covered her ear. It took a few seconds before the reverberating echo drifted away, leaving her in stony, sweet silence. Jane had experienced this acute sense of sound after a night of hard drinking and then the expected pounding head and sick stomach accompanied it. But this...*this* was entirely different. It was as though her auditory function had suddenly shifted into the realm of a dog's aural ability. Jane lay on her back and listened. She heard a slight *tick-tick* of a clock, but the one beside her bedside was a digital. The only clock with a second hand was located in the kitchen, down the hall thirty-five feet and around a corner.

Jane threw back the covers and traced the *tick-tick* sound to the kitchen clock. It didn't make sense. Last night, she smelled gardenias as strongly as if she'd been standing in a field of the heady flowers. But there were no gardenias in her house. Now, sound had become sharper. *Logic...use logic,* Jane urged her weary head. She'd stopped smoking exactly eleven hours and fifteen minutes ago. It was reasonable to believe that things would taste stronger—she'd heard that ad nauseam from people who had successfully quit tobacco. But hearing and smelling things that were distant or weren't even present? It made no sense.

There was a distinct brutality to how Jane felt—*exposed, vulnerable.* She knew the dance quite well as her battle with the bottle proved nearly impossible to beat. Addiction was a sadistic lover; at once, enveloping you in its arms and then making you beg for mercy. It urged her back repeatedly and then slammed her against the wall, trapping her soul. Each time she gave in and returned, she was less in control; less able to dig herself out of the chasm that held her with sharp teeth. Now that battle would be waged with the nemesis of nicotine. While sobriety had been a hard row to hoe, Jane was beginning to wonder if giving up cigarettes would prove even more difficult.

Noting the time, Jane figured that she could get in a thirty-minute run before leaving for her 7:00 am doctor's appointment—an early time given to her as a favor from her doctor. She'd been good about keeping up her daily running routine for over a year and a half. Her legs were toned and the sagging skin under her arms had developed into muscle. Jane deduced that she'd have to ratchet up the exercise routine since there was that inevitable gain of at least twenty pounds when one quit smoking.

Outside, the late winter air was crisp and inviting. Spring was in the air, but winter was still clutching onto the fabric of the Denver landscape. Patches of snow and ice pockmarked with pebbles and dirt lingered against north-facing lawns. Jane pulled the collar of her fleece jacket closer to her throat. Darkness still traced the streets as the orange glow from the streetlamps illuminated Jane's path. This would be the first test of many for Jane Perry. Her usual habit—albeit an odd habit, given the healthy aspect of running—was to light a cigarette on the porch and take three good drags before dipping the glowing ember into a can of sand that stood next to the doormat and setting off for her run. It was a comforting nicotine sacrament and this was the first morning that the ritual would be retired. Just the thought of that loss made Jane's irritability jack up another few notches.

Even though the cloak of night had not given way to the dawn, Jane easily navigated down Milwaukee Street. A resonant hum grew apparent to her, accompanied by the aroma of a dryer venting the distinct odor of a fabric softener circling inside the tumbler. It wasn't until Jane ran another two blocks that she located the house with the humming dryer. *Two blocks.* How could twelve hours of not smoking cause such a bizarre effect?

When she returned to her house, she started her morning coffee, adding her usual four heaping tablespoons of the espresso blend to the coffee filter. But upon sipping the brew, not only was the temperature searing, the taste was overpowering. She checked the filter to see if there was a problem but nothing looked abnormal. Jane could now add two more acute senses to her newfound, overly active body.

An hour later, Jane was seated in the doctor's waiting room, wondering why the carpet suddenly smelled so pungent. Even though she was the first appointment of the morning, the doctor was still not on time. Her irritation grew with each passing minute. Her thoughts turned to fifteen-year-old Jake Van Gorden and her impatience piqued. The more she thought about the drive to Midas and the plausible conclusion that the kid was a runaway and the strange notes sent to his parents were his way of getting his parents to pay attention to him…well, it wasn't what she needed right now. Jane Perry needed to hole up and hide away. That's why she didn't hesitate to whip out her cell phone and call Betty, one of her dependable connections in Denver who oversaw a group of runaway shelters along the I-25 corridor. Jane figured that Jake would most likely catch a bus and go south toward Denver, ending up at a shelter when he got hungry or tired.

"J-A-C-O-B," she spelled it out to Betty on the other end of the line. "Goes by *Jake*." The more Jane filled her in on the whole situation—including the noose on the bridge to look like a suicide—the more Betty agreed with Jane that it went against the norm for fifteen-year-old boys to be kidnapped.

"Has he got a girlfriend?" she asked Jane.

"No idea."

"Well, if he's a runaway, he took his girlfriend. Or he's meeting a girlfriend somewhere…or maybe a friend on the Internet…"

Jane's head spun with the various angles, none of which she felt like pursuing. Betty agreed to put the word out and call Jane back soon. Yes. *This is progress*. As Jane slipped her cell phone back into her leather satchel, she enjoyed the fleeting power of circumventing protocol in order to take care of Jane Perry.

The nurse finally arrived and ushered Jane back to the far room at the end of the hallway. After taking a few notes and asking the same damn questions she'd asked Jane less than ten days ago, she handed Jane a paper gown and directed her to the white table with stirrups. She assured her that the doctor would be right in, but she didn't appear for another ten minutes. It was just enough time to ratchet up Jane's tension. She closed her eyes and imagined taking a long, hard, satisfying drag on a cigarette, hoping the visualization would allow her anxiety to abate. But all it did was make her body crave a hit of tobacco.

When the doctor finally strolled in, Jane was met with a usual "how you doing?" chatter that was meant to create some sort of cozy connection between the two of them. But Jane tuned her out. She was more aware of the stainless steel tray singing as the doctor swung it closer. The overhead light demanded to be heard. The sharp aroma of disinfectant stung her nostrils. The clutch of the speculum groaned. The cold knife cut with judgment. Everything around her came alive within her raw, unfiltered, sentient awareness. Jane closed her eyes, desperate to tune it out. But her mind cried, *Life is a struggle...and then you die.*

Weyler stood waiting at the corner of 13th and Cherokee in front of Denver Headquarters. Never one to dress down, he looked dapper as usual in his navy suit with the imperceptible pinstripes. He rolled his oversized suitcase with the discreet monogram *M.E.W.* toward Jane's Mustang. Jane unlocked the passenger door and flipped down the seat so Weyler could deposit his suitcase in the backseat. The first thought Jane had was that he had packed a lot of clothes for a few days. The second thought was, *M.E.W.?*

Weyler lowered his lanky, 6' 4" inch frame into the passenger seat, chafing at the narrow entrance of Jane's classic car as he dragged his briefcase onto his lap. "I suppose what it lacks in leg room it makes up for in visual appeal," he groused to Jane, shutting the heavy door.

Jane floored the Mustang, turning right onto 13th Avenue and raced toward Speer Boulevard.

Weyler hung onto his briefcase and secured his seatbelt. "For a woman who doesn't want to go someplace, you certainly are going there fast."

Jane lifted her lead foot off the gas and turned onto Colfax.

She grabbed her mug that held four shots of espresso and three teaspoons of sugar and took a generous swig. "I just don't get it, boss. Midas is out of our jurisdiction and…"

"I told you…"

"Yeah," Jane abruptly interrupted as the dancing image of a cigarette teased her mind. "What does some former co-rookie, pissant police chief from Bumfuck, Egypt have over you?"

"Bo Lowry is a friend. And that's all that's important right now." Jane let out a loud breath of exasperation as she peeled the Mustang onto I-25 Northbound. "If you don't mind my saying, you are *much* more direct this morning than normal."

Jane gripped the steering wheel. "I quit smoking," she offered, her voice tense.

"*When?*"

She stole a look at the clock. "Fifteen hours, thirty-six minutes ago."

"And how long have you smoked?"

"Over twenty-three years."

"And you just decide out of the blue that *now's* a good time to quit?" Weyler sounded wary.

"Yeah. Why not? Life was going along too damn well. I figured it was time to inject some torture." Her mind focused on the single cigarette ensconced in her last pack of American Spirits.

Weyler shifted in his seat and looked out the front window. Reading his body language, Jane knew he was growing apprehensive of spending much time around her. "They say the first three days are the worst."

"Is that right?" Jane took another healthy sip of her espresso.

"I heard once that you shouldn't drink coffee when you quit smoking because the two are usually interconnected."

"Yeah, well. Ask me to quit smoking *and* coffee simultaneously, and somebody's going to end up being shot."

"I guess nicotine is tougher to kick than heroin."

"Maybe I'll take up heroin to get some perspective."

Weyler chuckled at Jane's retort. "You're going to find that your senses wake up. Smell and taste will be much more acute."

"Oh, Jesus, you have *no idea*, boss. I can smell the buttons on your shirt." Jane changed lanes to flow into US Highway 36. She was just about to tell Weyler about alerting Betty regarding Jake and the runaway shelters when he spoke first.

"You have a chance to look over the file I gave you last night?"

"Yeah. Some of the continuing pages were missing. I'm going to have to go the library and play puzzle maker. Did you check out Copeland's parents?"

"His parents?"

"Yeah. His mother would have been forty-three when she had him. Dad would have been fifty."

"What's that got to do with anything?"

"Jordan's an only child. His parents were the epitome of the East Coast country club set in the sixties."

"So?"

"So, that type didn't make a habit of starting a family at forty-three and fifty."

"Where is this going and how does it relate to Jake Van Gorden?"

"I don't know," Jane mused, her eyes canvassing the tawny landscape that framed the highway. "It's the little things, you know? People are always looking at the elephant in the room and I'm always looking at the peanut." As Jane drove further, the landscape became deafeningly bland. She was reminded that winter and spring in much of Colorado were bookends that held desolation, isolation and death. The low-lying areas were asleep, devoid of anything green. For five to six months, one lived in a brown and tan world, interrupted only by the powdered drifts of snow that reminded Jane how life could freeze and kill, and do it with impunity.

"Have you spent any time in Midas?" Weyler asked, reviewing a few pages of information he'd stashed in his briefcase.

"No. You?"

"No. I've kept up on it over the years because Bo ended up there. Obviously, the town likes the lack of interest. You know how some Colorado towns have reputations?"

"You mean like the *trustifarians* in Telluride, the freaks in Nederland and the disenchanted in Crestone?"

"Exactly. For some reason, Midas attracts people who have secrets."

"How do people find out about it?"

"Not sure. Maybe word-of-mouth. Maybe rumor. But the town's a magnet for all of them. Move there and your secret is safe. There's lots of rich kids who are black sheep. It's got *more* than its fair share of East coasters with no idea where they want to be or who they want to be. They just know they don't want to be found out."

"Copeland's an East coaster. Is that why he chose the town?"

"I don't know."

"After doing thirty-four years of hard time, he can't be rolling in greenback."

"Bo said something about a trust fund he lives on. Must be pretty sizeable because he lives about a mile outside of town on ten wooded acres by the river. In fact, it's just down a bit from the bridge where Jake tried to hang himself. Once a year the trustee of the fund flies out to check on Jordan, deposit the funds into his account and make sure he's staying out of trouble."

"Was the trustee informed of Jordan's possible involvement with Jake's disappearance?"

"Yes. Bo mumbled something about that. The guy's due out next week."

Jane shifted lanes, passing a semi. "I need more info on Jordan's background."

Weyler shuffled through a short stack of neatly clipped pages he'd copied from a couple crime databases. Weyler read from the page. "'Copeland was fine until the age of eight when he started to exhibit severe isolationist behavior traits.'"

"Any history of killing small animals?"

"None. Just an intense desire to not associate with others."

"Why would an eight-year-old boy suddenly decide to be alone? There's gotta be a trauma trigger. What happened to him at the age of eight?"

Weyler glanced down the page, searching. "Nothing's referenced."

Jane's edginess crept closer. "I can't believe somebody didn't ask that question. It's a fuckin' no-brainer." She shook her head in disgust and slowed down as the speed limit dropped to 55 mph. "So, from age eight to eighteen when he's arrested for shooting his next-door neighbor Daniel Marshall and stuffing his body under his bed, what's Jordan doing?"

"I guess going to school and suffering the slings and arrows of puberty like the rest of us."

"No friends?"

"No one, according to the docs. No one except Daniel and he's thirteen and mentally challenged."

"They called it *retarded* back then."

"They call it *mentally challenged* now."

"Fucking PC talk." As if on cue, they entered the outskirts of Boulder, a bastion for eco-freaking, Prius-driving, hemp-wearing, left-wing-leaning individuals. "Soy latte, boss?" Jane remarked with a sarcastic tip of her head toward a coffeehouse named *The Eco Café* where they served coffee in cups that were so quickly biodegradable, they started decomposing before you finished drinking the brew.

"You really do need to take it down a notch, Jane. Keep this up and you and Bo are going to mix like gasoline and fire." He eyed Jane more carefully. "There's something else going on with you...something besides quitting smoking..."

Jane had briefly forgotten about her ominous health problems until Weyler reminded her. His comment felt like a sucker punch. She turned away, not wanting to reveal any emotion.

"What's going on, Jane?" Weyler's voice was concerned.

"Does Jordan own a car?" Jane responded, shifting to her "all business" tenor.

Weyler realized pressing her further was pointless. "No car."

"So, if he did kidnap Jake Van Gorden, did he walk him down to his place from the bridge and stash him somewhere on the property...like he stashed Daniel's body?"

"Bo said they did a fairly intense search at the house and around the property."

"There had to be more than his past conviction for probable cause to search."

"Does wandering on the road, covered in mud and with bloody hands, generate probable cause?"

"Jesus. Okay, but they released him. The blood had to be his own."

"It was. The question was—why was he looking like that within a day of Jake's disappearance? Coincidence? If so, bad timing for it. Bo wonders if maybe this is a two-man-or-more operation and Jordan's involvement was to draw Jake into the web."

"You said there are a bunch of notes or clues?"

"Right. No ransom. Just odd, non sequitur deliveries to either Jake's parents' house or Bo's office. We'll see them when we sit down with Bo..."

"Jordan doesn't need the money but he's also not looking for attention. What's his motive?"

"Maybe it's just part of his sickness."

Jane reached the outside edge of Boulder and started up the long highway that led to Midas. "'Is he a Frequent Flyer?'" Jane asked, referencing someone with a history of being in and out of jail. Weyler shook his head. "Okay. You know as well as I do that perps typically re-offend a lot sooner than seven years after they get out. And if their arrest history prior to going to prison is zilch, like Copeland, the chances of recidivism go down."

"You know my feelings on statistics."

"Right. It just takes one person to slant the chart." Jane let out a tired breath. "One stat I do know is that the odds of a kidnapped kid showing up alive after five days missing are pretty slim. So if Jake is dead and Jordan's got a part in it, he'll never see the outside world again."

"Maybe that's exactly what he wants. Maybe between prison and freedom, the former is safer for him."

Forty-five pensive minutes later, Jane wound the Mustang off the highway and into the town of Midas. After one block of service stations and several restaurants, they arrived on Main Street and a sign that declared they were 7,200 feet in elevation. The main drag had a wide-open feel to it—oddly exposed for a town so steeped in secrets. Sidewalks were well swept of debris and showed no signs that snow had fallen just a few days before. Wealth obviously bought swift attention from the town's public works department. Even though it was a Friday, the streets were nearly bare of traffic and people. Jane mulled that everyone was probably tucked away in their homes—either counting their money or keeping a low profile.

It was obvious to Jane that Midas was a place where even the most severe euphemistic *economic downturn* wouldn't cast a shadow down Main Street. Destructive outside forces like a pesky global recession simply weren't allowed to penetrate the tenuous façade. There was a tangible eeriness that Jane felt as she drove slowly down the street. It wasn't like the haunted vibe she got when she visited Creede, Colorado, or the outright fusion of contrasting vibes she felt driving through Peachville. No, Midas was different altogether. Midas felt like a town holding its collective breath; at once on edge and at the same time aggressively protecting itself. There were no outward signs of community involvement. No banners that announced town events. There was none of the corny, albeit apropos, small town greetings, such as

Howdy or *Welcome!* on the town sign. Midas was a brick wall encased in a steel tomb.

Weyler directed Jane to drive to the middle of Main Street where the two-story, inconspicuous Midas Town Hall was located. She parked in front, having her choice of seven open spaces. The only action around Town Hall was the sight of two men on ladders installing cables and what looked like a wireless Internet antenna. As she locked the car door, the sickly sweet scent of gardenias surrounded her. Jane glanced at the flower boxes outside Town Hall expecting to see them awash in the ivory flower. But the only thing they held was dirt. Strangely, the aroma was even stronger standing outside in Midas than it was the night before when she first detected the fragrance in her closet. It hung closer to her, almost suffocating her with its intensity.

"Something wrong, Jane?" Weyler asked.

"You smell gardenias, boss?"

"No."

"*Seriously*?" Jane said irritated. "You can't *smell* that?"

"Bo's waiting for us, Jane. Come on."

Inside the front door, Jane and Weyler walked into a tiny seating room. An exceptionally round-faced woman sat behind a wall of security glass. As quickly as the scent of gardenias flowered, it abruptly ceased. But Jane's heightened sense of smell still kicked into gear as she noted the pungent chemical bouquet of wood shavings, varnish, paint and glue—all leftover from the recently installed security window. The old, battered carpeting beneath their feet had been cut at the corners, in preparation for removal. Behind the glass, Jane watched several workers moving tables, removing antiquated Selectric II typewriters, pulling wires out of the ceiling, drilling holes in the walls and negotiating their way around a pile of large unopened boxes that looked to hold computers and high-tech equipment. It was clear that a massive remodel and overhaul of the place was in progress. A fine coating of drywall dust and ceiling debris drifted off the window when Weyler tapped his finger against it to get the receptionist's attention. She turned toward him, obviously unaware of their presence due to the ambient noise. He held up his badge and announced that he and Jane were there to see Bo Lowry.

"Hang on," she mumbled, seemingly unacquainted with the buzzer that needed to be depressed in order to let them inside the office. She pressed it and Weyler pushed the door but it wouldn't budge. The woman, clearly overwhelmed by the technical revamp, depressed the button again—this time with more impatience. Weyler pushed harder and the door released. The woman pried her chubby frame out of her new chair with the tags still on it and led them through the maze of dust-laden boxes, freshly constructed desks and computer tables, as she yelled across to a worker to "rewire the buzzer for the front door...*again!*"

Turning one corner, she pointed toward a windowed office cloaked in half-drawn, yellowed Venetian blinds. "He's in there," she said, out of breath from the thirty-foot promenade.

Weyler rapped his knuckles against the closed door and opened it. "Hello, old friend!" he said in a genuine cadence.

The sweet smell of cigar smoke bit into Jane's nostrils. A large man with a gut that hung well below his belt buckle swung his scuffed cowboy boots off the desk and put down his cigar. "Well, Christ Almighty, am I happy to see you!" Bo enthusiastically shook Weyler's hand and patted him hard on his back. "Goddamnit, Beanie, you couldn't have gotten here a minute too soon!"

"Bo, I'd like you to meet, Sergeant Detective Jane Perry."

Bo's gratitude quickly shifted to distaste. "No, no, *no*, 10-74!" he said waving his chubby hand in the air. "I asked for *you*, Morgan! *Only you*. Get her the hell *outta* here!"

CHAPTER 5

"God, I forgot how much I love that small town charm!" Jane sardonically responded after Bo's less than enthusiastic greeting.

Bo's face was turning five shades of red as he painfully spun toward Weyler and guided him around in a confidential pose. The juxtaposition of the two—with Weyler's tall, lanky frame and Bo's squatty, porcine physique—reminded Jane of Mutt and Jeff. "Beanie, I told you I wanted this under the radar. I ain't fiddle fuckin' around! What in the hell were you thinking?" Lowry's voice sounded like he ate gravel and ground glass for breakfast and chased it with a cup of hot, spent ammo.

Weyler put his arm around Bo's shoulder and spoke in a soothing manner. "You're out of here in less than two weeks, Bo. We need all the help we can get and Jane is one of my best."

"We don't want TV cameras and publicity here!" Bo retorted in a gruff stage whisper. "And *she*..." Bo jabbed his thumb behind him toward Jane, "tends to attract that nonsense! *And,* I heard she's a loose cannon! Jesus, Beanie, I need someone with a slower heartbeat than her."

Jane hated the media coverage she'd drawn in the past two years more than anyone. But she also hated being referred to as "her" and talked about as if she wasn't standing in the same room. And why in the hell was Bo calling Weyler, *Beanie?* "Well, fuck me!" Jane said under her breath, with indignation. "I don't need this shit." She turned toward the door.

"Jane!" Weyler snapped. "Close the door and sit down." He turned to Bo. "She's staying. I'm staying. And we're going to figure out this damn case. So, let's all take a deep breath and try to work together."

Jane closed the door and meandered to an empty chair in front of Bo's desk. Weyler slid into the seat next to her as Bo readjusted the sinking waist on his trousers, zipped up his standard issue police chief's jacket and walked with an unsteady gait to his beaten-down office chair. He plopped down hard into the seat, wincing almost imperceptibly. The cluttered room was hot and stuffy. Jane removed her jacket and scanned the disorganized office. Sure, there was the building remodel but she figured that Bo's office space had probably always looked like the aftereffects of a tornado. His desk was littered with paperwork, a cluster of old coffee cups, opened and unopened files, pens, and dried rinds of oranges that were beginning to petrify. There were also three mismatched lamps, all with a thick coat of dust on their shades, and a myriad of sandwich wrappers and Styrofoam containers that held some kind of food that was eaten during the Clinton administration. A wooden sign—at one time displayed on the wall—now lay across a stack of papers. It read: IT IS WHAT IT IS.

Two file cabinets stood to Jane's left, both topped with another pile of papers and files bursting with even more documents. A calendar was taped to one of the file cabinets. Large black Xs filled the dates that had already passed. The square eleven days from that date was circled in a thick red pen. Behind Bo's desk was a large window that overlooked Main Street. In front of the window stood a strange assortment of file boxes, each a different color and each marked with either a !, ?, a thumbs up and a thumbs down drawing. The patchwork chaos made no sense to Jane. For her, sitting in this office was like inhabiting the center of Bo Lowry's brain—an unbalanced place, indeed.

"Looks like you have your hands full with the remodel," Weyler offered in an attempt to inject a neutral statement.

"Yeah, we're charging feet first into the Twentieth Century," Bo snorted, obviously not happy with the whole upheaval.

"Don't you mean Twenty-first?" Jane asked.

"I got bad knees. I can only handle one jump of a century at a time," he snarled, his liver still spitting bile knowing that he had to deal with Sergeant Detective Jane Perry. He took a puff of his cigar. "It's what the new police chief asked for. He's one of them young, *techno* boys. It's costing the town a bundle but they don't care. Throw enough money around and you know what it buys."

Jane wanted to say, "Whores, silence and beauracracy" but decided against it.

"Too much goddamn technology for my blood! They try to tell me it's all 10-8," Bo grumbled, using old cop talk for a good piece of equipment, "But it's all over my bald head." He tapped his pudgy fingers nervously on his cluttered desk. "Everybody *texts* and *emails* these days! Whatever happened to callin' somebody up and actually *talkin'* to them?" Quickly, he sat up in his swivel chair, waving his hand toward the activity on the other side of his half-opened Venetian blinds. "That's not my style, Morgan. See what I'm sayin'? They start usin' all these fancy *techno* words and I can't figure heads or tails what they're talkin' about. Makes what's left of my hair hurt." Jane sensed an uneasy edge to Bo's voice. Fear crept in at the corners of his tenor.

"You still have seven or eight good years in you, Bo," Weyler offered. "You're not that close to Social Security."

"Hell, Beanie, I could have a massive stroke, completely paralyzed, livin' in a wheelchair, drool drippin' down my chin and unable to speak my own name and these fine people would still keep me around!"

"Then stick around for another few seasons," Weyler stressed.

"10-74, my friend," he said, using the 10-code for the word, "No." "*It's time.* I see the writin' on the wall. I'm old hat." Bo ran his fingers across his sparse comb over. "Eleven days and I'm outta here. Day after Easter. Jesus resurrected and so will I! I can't wait to retire. I'm gonna sleep for weeks. I love to sleep. The only drawback is, you can't enjoy it fully since you're unconscious." Jane wasn't sure if Bo was nuts or just pleasantly eccentric. He turned away, letting out a stiff breath. "You know, Vi's cuttin' out too. She's sixty-five. Takin' the dole and ditchin' this place."

Weyler turned to Jane. "Vi has been with Bo since his first day in Midas. She's his right arm…"

"Right arm, left arm, right leg, left leg, ears, eyes and lungs," Bo quickly interjected, his breathing sounding shallow to Jane. "I couldn't see my way clear without her!" His voice was desperate, like a man clutching onto a sinking life rope.

"What are you going to do?" Weyler asked.

"Florida coast," Bo touched the edge of a bright yellow folder on his desk. "Warm, you know? Lookin' forward to it." Jane watched as he pulled a page over the yellow folder, covering it completely. It was a gestural extension of shame—a literal *covering up* of what he was saying. Bo's mind seemed to drift momentarily.

"I didn't think you liked the humidity *or* the ocean."

Bo looked up at Weyler, lost in a private moment. "Yeah, well, we all gotta make the hard choices in life, Beanie." Jane noted that Bo continued to call Weyler "Beanie." Obviously, it was a term of endearment but what did it signify? Weyler might have been considered a beanpole in stature in his youth when Bo and he were FNGs…"fucking new guys." Jane noted a moment of sadness coming from Bo, only to be quickly buried and replaced with a *back to business* approach. "I got a shit pot of crap to go over with you." He spoke only to Weyler, making a point to ignore Jane with his body language. He proceeded to unearth sundry pieces of paper—all protected in clear, plastic evidence bags—and a book, also placed inside a clear bag. "The day after little Juice Box's disappearance, his folks found this in their mailbox." Bo handed Weyler a book, clearly leaving Jane out of the discussion.

"Little Juice Box?" Jane questioned in a confused manner.

Bo wedged the cigar into the corner of his mouth. "Juice Box Jake Van Gorden," Bo replied, never looking at Jane. "I look at him and I think of a juice box. Small kids drink them. Jake is small for his age. He's like one hundred and twenty pounds and a song. It follows. You got a problem with that?" Bo snuck a chary eye toward Jane.

Jane wasn't sure if the song was a *short* song, but she wasn't about to ask Bo to decipher his odd verbiage. "No problem, Bo. It's perfectly normal." Her tone was laced with sarcasm.

Bo looked at Weyler. "You put up with this shit from her?"

Weyler would have none of it. "Getting back to the clues?"

"Inside that book was a *sympathy* card," Bo handed the card to Weyler, "sealed and addressed only to BAWY." Jane reached for it but he laid the white envelope encased in a plastic evidence bag on the desk in front of Weyler.

"Been dusted for prints, I assume?" Jane asked, irritated.

"Yes," Bo replied in an over-the-top manner, "and we found nothin' so he wore gloves when he touched it. Same thing with the book."

"Find any DNA on the envelope flap?" Jane wasn't about to back down.

Bo let out an exasperated sigh. "10-74. It's a peel 'n' stick flap."

"Whoever did this knew his DNA could be found on the flap from his saliva and thought ahead of time to buy self-sealing envelopes," Jane rejoined.

Weyler considered it. "You only do that if your DNA's in the system. Otherwise, it doesn't matter."

"So, somebody with prior convictions, somebody smart and someone who likes to plan things out."

"Why don't you get a pad and write all these ideas down," Bo said in nasty tone, "so we can make a long list and then we can solve this before lunch."

That was it for Jane. Between jonesing for a cigarette and dealing with Bo's dismissive manner, she'd reached her maximum capacity for arrogance. "Listen, I don't want to be here anymore than you want me here!"

Bo jerked the cigar out of his mouth. "*That* is the exact attitude I saw comin' down the pike!" He yelled, pointing over Jane's shoulder. "There's the door, little lady!"

"*Enough!*" Weyler insisted.

"Boss, I can't work with this!" Jane's voice sounded almost too desperate.

Weyler realized he had to take a stand. "Bo, here's the deal: either you back off Sergeant Perry and try to maintain civility or we walk. What's it going to be?"

The blood drained from Bo's face. He suddenly looked like a big kid being disciplined by the principal. Taking a nervous puff on his cigar, he moved uncomfortably in his chair and gestured with his chin to the book and card in Weyler's hand. "So, see, that's the first clue," Bo said, reluctantly acquiescing.

Weyler handed Jane the envelope. The letters on the front, BAWY were written in a hesitant hand. "This looks like the way a kid writes who is just learning to hold a pen," she mused.

"Could be right handed and he purposely used his left to disguise his handwriting," Weyler offered.

"Yeah. What is a BAWY?"

"Maybe an acronym?" Weyler considered. Now it was Bo who was left out of the discussion.

"If it is, I've never heard it." Jane tried to sound it out. "Be Aware..." She shook her head. "It's anybody's guess."

Weyler slid the card out from the plastic bag and opened it. "'So sorry for your loss. *JACKson* sends his regards.'" Weyler compared the shaky printing from the outside of the envelope to the inside of the card and was confident the same hand wrote both. "The boy's name is Jake. Why is he referring to him as Jackson and emphasizing the *Jack*?"

Bo nervously shuffled through the papers on his desk. "Let me see here." Spotting a bright green sheet of paper, he grabbed it and handed it to Weyler. "I had Mr. Van Gorden write down the boy's full name. That's what they gave me."

Jane took a gander at the page. It read: *JACKSON JAKOB VAN GORDEN*. Her thoughts immediately turned to the misspelling of *Jacob* she'd given Betty earlier that morning. "Does he call himself Jackson?"

"10-74," Bo said gruffly. "Parents told me that was his given name but he hated it and went by the shortened version of his middle name."

"What's the book?" Jane asked.

Weyler handed it to her. "*You Can't Go Home Again* by Thomas Wolfe."

"See, *You can't go home again* pretty much tells me what the kidnapper is planning for Jake," Bo surmised.

Jane was beginning to feel into the person who had kidnapped the boy. Her prior assessment of someone who was exceptionally smart and a planner was becoming more evident now. Wolfe's book wasn't exactly fluffy pulp fiction. Written in the 1930s, Jane remembered reading it in a college lit course. The main character in the book, George Webber, is a writer who pens a successful novel about his family and hometown. However, when he returns to that town, he is shocked by the rebuke and outright hatred that his family and friends feel toward him for exposing their lives to strangers. The story then shifts to Webber's life as he leaves his hometown and ventures around the world in search of his true identity. In the end, Webber returns to the United States and rediscovers his reality with both sadness and love. It's about a man coming to terms with himself, his family and his purpose. And in Jane's mind, it had to have a hidden meaning that the kidnapper was eager to convey in a veiled, intellectual manner. She slid it out from the plastic bag and thumbed through the pages, finding page 243 freshly dog-eared. "Did the book come like this?" she asked, showing the page to Weyler.

"10-4," Bo affirmed. "See, that's also where the card was stuck in the book."

Jane factored that it's one thing to just slide a card into a book and quite another to make sure that others notice the page by turning down the corner.

"What came after this?" Weyler asked.

"We got the next clue here at the office in the form of a

voicemail message." Bo then hollered out toward his office door, "Vi! Can you come here? And bring in Copeland's file, would ya?"

Jane turned and saw Vi opening up a file cabinet, finding a folder and tearing off the top page that was stapled to the outside of the folder. *Odd*, Jane thought. But what was even stranger was that Vi took the top page and slipped it into her top drawer before heading into Bo's office.

She nodded toward Jane and Weyler with a short and to the point, "Hey!" Vi's wavy salt-and-pepper hair was cut in a no-nonsense style and fell just below her ears. She didn't wear any makeup but she didn't need to as her skin was surprisingly vibrant and youthful for her sixty-five years. Her 5' 5" frame was solid and grounded, fully in charge of whatever needed to get done at any given time. Jane could tell that she and Bo shared an *understanding*. His demeanor clearly became more relaxed when she was in the room and he was, strangely, more than happy to let *her* control the events.

"Vi," Bo said succinctly, "Morgan Weyler and Jane Perry from Denver."

"Nice to meet you," Vi said, "What do you need, Bo?"

"I can't remember how to use this damn thing," he groused, pointing to the phone. "Wanna play them the voicemail."

"Sure." With insouciance, Vi maneuvered her way around the clutter and, after pressing a few buttons, entering the voicemail code and releasing the SPEAKER button, a computer-distorted voice could be heard loud and clear.

"Do you know what it's like to feel as if you're two seconds from your last breath? *DO YOU*? It feels just like this…" There was a scratchy sound on the phone as if something was brushing against it, followed by the whimpering and pleading of what sounded like a very young male child from across the room. That lasted all of ten seconds and abruptly stopped before the scratchy sound against the phone reappeared and the distorted voice of the kidnapper spoke again. "He pounds on the window and you do nothing." *Click.*

Bo was visibly shaken by the recording. "You…wanna here it again?"

Vi replayed the sickening message. Jane timed it using the second hand on Bo's wall clock. It was thirty seconds exactly, short and untraceable—not that Midas had the ability to trace a call when the kidnapper left the message. But for Jane, it was a new aspect of the man's personality. He knew the drill and he knew that it took at least forty seconds to trace a call if a live system was up and running when the call came in.

"We checked the incoming number," Bo said, resting his cigar in an ashtray. "It's one of them throwaway cell phones." Jane added another element of the kidnapper's personality to her visual list. *Methodical.* "Well?" Bo asked Weyler. "What do you get from the message?"

"He had to remove the voice disguiser in order to get the sound of the boy screaming," Weyler offered. "That's the scratchy sound you hear right before the boy screams and then right after when the last sentence is distorted again."

"But the boy sounds like he's six or seven the way he's whimpering, not *fifteen*," Jane argued. "And the screams just stop suddenly on cue before the guy re-fits the disguiser and starts talking again. Wouldn't there be whimpering and screaming in the background *during* the whole message for better effect?"

"Hell, it's a not a goddamn Hollywood movie here," Bo said, irritated.

"No, Jane's got a good point," Weyler nodded. "It's too rehearsed. Too planned out. And the kid *does* sound much younger than fifteen."

Jane felt finally vindicated. "Like I said, Jake ran away and he's pimping his parents with this shit! Look, I called…" She was just about to mention her conversation with Betty at the runaway shelter that morning when Bo interrupted.

"But if it's a setup, the kid's not askin' for money!" Bo argued. "So, if there's no ransom, what's the point of all this?

Scaring the shit out of your parents?"

"Maybe so!" Jane replied. "Maybe he's trying to teach them a lesson…"

"10-74. That ain't Jake's style, see! He's a quiet kid, a little offbeat perhaps. If I had to describe him in three words, I'd say, scrawny, shy and…artistic."

Jane noticed that when Bo said the word *artistic,* there was another word he wanted to use but chose not to. "What do you mean by *offbeat*?"

"He's got a *ponytail* 'bout seven inches long," Bo emphasized this statement with an exaggerated roll of his eyes. "Usually stuffs it inside these hats he likes to wear. You know? The hats from the 60s that those fellas in the Rat Pack used to sport."

"Fedoras?" Weyler asked.

"Yeah, them. 'Round here, it's either ball caps or a cowboy hat, but not *fedoras.*" There was a slight mocking tone to Bo's voice. "Nah, Jake's the *sensitive* artist type. I mean, come on, *he's got a goddamn ponytail.* No matter how pissed-off he might be at his folks, he's *not* gonna go this far! He'd draw a picture before he did this!"

"What kind of stuff does he draw?" Jane asked.

"When we searched his room, we saw a bunch of sketch pads with doodles all over them. Nothin' with guns or monsters. Just harmless doodles." Bo turned to Vi. "Didn't we start a file on little Juice Box?"

Vi nodded and left the room momentarily to grab Jake's file.

Jane sat back in her chair, furtively glancing over her shoulder at Vi. Amazingly, she repeated the same pattern of removing the file from the cabinet, ripping off the sheet on the front of the file, securing that sheet in her drawer and then returning to Bo's office. She handed the file to Bo.

"See what I'm talkin' about," Bo stated, laying several pages on his cluttered desk.

The drawings were hardly what Jane would call *doodles.*

They were well-executed drawings, mainly of cars, dirt bikes and fedoras. However, in the corner of the last page was a small but precise drawing of pretty girl's three-quarter profile. Jane recalled what Betty at the runaway shelter mentioned about Jake leaving town to meet a girl. "Who's that?" Jane asked, pointing to the girl on the page.

Bo turned the page around. It didn't take him long to respond. "That's Mollie. Jake's girlfriend. Daughter of the Methodist preacher in town. He and his wife also own the B&B you two are gonna be staying at. Jake was real smitten with Mollie."

"Was?" Jane asked.

"Yeah, see, she broke up with him two weeks ago. He took it real hard."

"A reason to want to hang himself on the ol' bridge?" Weyler proposed.

"Or a reason to set it up like a suicide and then run away to gain sympathy," Jane countered. "Did you find a suicide note in his room or at the bridge?"

"No," Bo answered curtly.

"Well, if the suicide was spur of the moment, he might not have left a note. But most kids…most people…leave notes… *if* this is real. And you have to admit, the chances of Jake being kidnapped *while in the process* of attempting suicide is stretching the plausibility factor off the chart! We cannot categorically rule out that Jake is not involved in his own disappearance."

"Well, I can tell you he wouldn't be sending his folks this!" Bo exclaimed, signaling Vi to hand him the third clue. "This was also left in the Van Gorden's mailbox." Bo placed an 8½ x 11 sheet of paper shielded in a plastic bag in front of Jane and Weyler. On it, was the full-color figure of an eight- or nine-year-old boy that had been cut out of from a magazine. Based upon the clothing and the vintage red baseball cap on the kid's head, Jane thought it looked like it came from an from an old magazine advertisement from the 1950s or 1960s. The figure was glued on the page to give the impression that the boy was being dragged by his arm. The other arm had been artificially extended and highly exaggerated with a pen drawing that gave the impression that the flat of the boy's palm was pressed against a surface. Below this, were letters cut out from various magazines that spelled the sentence: *THOU SHALT NOT STEAL INNOCENCE!* Bo laid the large envelope, also protected in plastic, next to the page. The only writing on it was the cryptic *BAWY* in the same unsteady hand. In the upper right corner was a lone, uncancelled, twenty-five-cent stamp with an old Packard on it.

"It was hand delivered to the Van Gordens, right?" Jane asked. Bo nodded. "So, why put a stamp on it?"

"Why did Jeffrey Dahmer pick up only certain boys to eat?" Bo cracked. "The criminal mind is complex!"

Jane thought back to the sinister voicemail message. "'He pounds on the window and you do nothing.'" Jane repeated as she pointed to the exaggerated extension of the palm on the third clue. "Doesn't this look like a palm pressed against glass?" Jane held her hand up in the air to mimic the drawing.

"Maybe when he grabbed Jake," Weyler interjected, "he threw him in a car and Jake was screaming or pounding on the glass trying to be heard."

"What car?" Jane asked.

"The one on the bridge that left a stain of antifreeze. The peckerwood must have a leak in his radiator. We got tire tracks, which proved we can rule out smaller cars. We figure we're lookin' for a truck, van or SUV. That narrows our search from 1,000,000 to 500,000."

"How do you know the car that was sitting there has any connection to Jake?"

"We have to make an ass out of you and me, and *assume* it does. This is an old bridge that's hardly used. You don't see cars just sitting there…waitin'…"

"What do you mean by *waiting*?"

Bo let out a tired puff of air. "One witness came forth. A woman walkin' her dog. She said she saw a black vehicle sittin' on the bridge. Couldn't see the driver and, no, she didn't get a license plate."

"Black vehicle? Black what?"

"She's *a woman*," Bo stressed, as if Jane wouldn't understand. "I asked her what the make was and she looked at me like a pig looks at a wristwatch. I was lucky to get the color of the vehicle out of her and even then, she said it could have been dark blue."

Jane realized her next question was absurd, but she had to ask it. "There wouldn't possibly be any security cameras on that road or outside town hall or the Van Gorden's subdivision so we could see who's dropping off these clues or identify the vehicle?"

"These yahoos are settin' up cameras all over the damn town. But that's on the QT. 10-4? There's none in the subdivision yet. They put one outside the door here but it works about as good as the front buzzer. As for the road, we got a couple speed photo cameras out there by the bridge but it only takes a photo if someone happens to be speedin'. There was one photo on March 22nd but there was no vehicle on the bridge and no sign of Jake in the photo."

"You have more clues?" Weyler asked.

"Oh, yeah. The hits just keep on comin'." He turned to Vi. "Wanna play 'em *numero dos*?" Vi punched in the codes on Bo's phone and then depressed the SPEAKER button. "This one came in after-hours on the same day as the other voicemail and the creepy cut-out of the kid with the red ball cap."

There was the stark sound of what sounded like a young boy whimpering again in the distance, followed by the scratchy interlude and the distorted voice of the kidnapper. "He *cried like a baby* and will never be a real man." *Click.*

Bo shifted in his chair, clearly in some sort of discomfort. "Nice, eh? I'd like to see this peckerwood hangin' by his goddamn nuts!"

Now it was Jane's turn to shift uncomfortably in her chair. "Wait a second. There's not a word wasted with this guy. He used the word *cried* instead of *cries*. That doesn't make sense when we just heard the boy actively crying in the background. Wouldn't Jake *still* be crying when he leaves the message? So the guy should have said, 'he's *crying* like a baby.'"

"You a part-time lawyer?" Bo asked. "'Cuz you just took an ax to split a hair."

Jane leaned forward, pressing her index finger into Bo's desk. "Why is he telling us something obvious? We can *hear* the kid crying. Of course, the kid conveniently *stops* crying right before the kidnapper makes the final statement."

"What in the hell are you sayin'?"

"She is saying," Weyler interjected, "that the kidnapper is possibly playing both roles on the phone. He takes the disguiser off the phone, moves away, does the crying jag, puts the disguiser back on and says a message."

"Thank you!" Jane declared to Weyler. "Which brings us back to the idea that there is no kidnapper and this is all Jake's elaborate set up. That's why I called…"

"You don't know Jake, lady!" Bo bellowed. "*I do!* Vi knows him, too. He's not involved in this!" Bo slapped another plastic covered drawing in front of Weyler and Jane. A crinkled blank page in plastic was attached to it. "Or this!" He slammed another plastic sheeting on the desk that held a smaller piece of paper. "*Or this!*" The final clue hit the desk, another protected sheet of 8½ x 11 paper. "This one," pointing to a sexually graphic drawing of a young boy around eight or nine years old in bondage, with his pants around his ankles, "is *not* something Jake would draw!"

The other two were handwritten in the same hesitating and somewhat childish scribe. One was an odd riddle:

Name this classy car.
Seven letters.
The first four spell what you do before going on a trip.
The first three spelled backward is something you take on that trip and
wear on your head.

The last clue was written in all capital letters:

I BEARED MY SOUL AND STILL YOU IGNORE ME???

"His parents got the sicko drawing with the blank sheet of paper," Bo added. "The last two were delivered under the mat out front. This one," he pointed to the *I BEARED MY SOUL…* clue, "showed up this mornin'!"

Jane stared at the graphic drawing of the young boy that implied sodomy. She'd seen a lot of perversion directed at children in the early days when she worked four hard years in assault but this sketch somehow seemed more explicit. She felt deep down in her gut that what was drawn on that page had indeed already occurred. Now, the idea of Jake being a runaway was starting to feel less likely *if* his "scrawny, shy, sensitive, artistic" description was indeed valid. And yet, the more Jane scanned the clues, the more she felt that there was a deeper *implied* message as well as an actual and quite *valid* threat to Jake's family. She began to regret her knee-jerk phone call to Betty at the runaway shelter. It was now clear to her that this case would require some intense thought, and intense thought usually involved a pack of cigarettes. She pinched the skin between her eyes hard, realizing that she had never worked a case without nicotine fueling her adrenal glands. Suddenly, the idea of making any headway on this case seemed beyond comprehension.

"You got a problem?" Bo's voice broke the silence.

Jane pulled herself out of her self-imposed mind fuck. "I'm good," she said succinctly.

Bo searched his desk. "I got a fax somewhere around here from a *profiler* at Quantico…" Vi spotted the sheet on his desk and handed it to him. Jane immediately noted a strange apprehension in her movement as she put the fax in Bo's hands. Bo pursed his lips as his eyes scanned the page. "Oh, hell!" he tossed the page toward Weyler, "I don't have to read the goddamn thing again. See, I got it memorized. Suspect is a male

Caucasian, thirty-five to fifty-five years old, educated, social outcast, dissociative disorder due to early childhood trauma. Prefers to operate alone, rather than work with an accomplice. Based on handwriting, is exacting and seeks retribution for past wrongs. Likes order. Wants his message to be clearly heard. Has an overwhelming need to prove himself."

Weyler finished reading the page. "You've still got a photographic memory, Bo."

He turned his head slightly to Vi. "10-4. I sure do." He shifted in his seat. "I called up the feller in Quantico and told him to let me know what kind of coffee the son-of-a-bitch likes so when I pick him up, I can have a cup ready."

"I thought you liked Jordan Copeland for this," Weyler asked.

"Oh, yeah. Trash Bag is definitely the *numero uno* pervert on my short list."

"Trash Bag?" Jane said.

Bo leaned forward, looking weary as he explained himself. "I look at Copeland and I think of a trash bag...a big brown plastic trash bag. A human *blivet*...ten pounds of shit in a five pound bag. A walking, two-hundred-and-fifty-pound dingleberry...*a trash bag*. It follows!"

Jane stared at Bo, speechless. Jake Van Gorden was a *Juice Box* and Jordan Copeland was a *Trash Bag*. The visuals were stunning.

"Vi, why don't you set up the video of Trash Bag's interview with me." Vi worked her way around the crowded office to a small monitor near the file cabinet. Jane noted how antiquated the system was versus what Denver Headquarters had installed. "Beanie," Bo said to Weyler, "you give her the background on Copeland?" Weyler nodded. "What the paperwork don't tell you is the high and mighty son-of-a-bitch he's become! He don't talk like a common criminal. Nah, he's *educated*. He got himself not one but *two* college degrees while sittin' in his cell."

"What in?" Weyler asked.

Bo leaned forward to make his exaggerated point. "Philosophy and *esoteric* psychology. Our tax dollars at work! When I got wind that Copeland was comin' to live here two years ago, I 'bout shit a brick. In the five years he'd been out at that time, he'd lived in no less than *six* places. Got run out of *all* six places. One of the towns he lived in, a bunch of teenagers damn near beat the crap out of him. It almost became an annual event to kick Jordan's ass. Can't blame 'em. Nobody wants a goddamn child killer or 'Chester' livin' 'round them?"

Chester was a word amalgamation of *child* and *molester*. "I didn't know Jordan molested Daniel Marshall," Jane offered.

"He didn't," Bo stated. "But you know as well as I do that child killers can graduate to molesting…especially when they've had thirty-four years to sit in a cell and think on how they want to get back at society."

"So, Jordan picks a town known for its secrets, in hopes of getting better treatment?" Jane deduced.

"Maybe, but livin' here ain't no guarantee people like him will be safe," Bo tartly replied. "I'm partly responsible for his two year streak livin' here and not gettin' a weekly beat-down. Let's get one thing straight: *I don't like Jordan Copeland*. He's got a stink on him like cat piss on shag carpet. But my job is to protect the citizens of this town and that's what I do. I've protected that child killer ever since he moved his sorry ass to Midas. People here keep to themselves but that doesn't mean some citizens didn't fantasize about tying him to the bumper of a trailer and taking him for a scrape down the road, or burnin' down his little log cabin on the river…"

"Is that why he lives outside of town and doesn't drive a car?" Jane asked.

"I don't know. I'm not his real estate agent. I'm just the guy who's hired to make sure we don't find him tits up, DRT on the side of the road."

Jane hadn't heard the cop term *DRT* for *dead right there* in a long time. "So you've protected him for two years," Jane said.

"I protect everyone in this town. *Everyone*. People don't move to Midas to live in the spotlight. They come here to lay low and live out their lives in peace and quiet. And it's my job to make sure they *get* their peace and quiet!"

"Do you keep their secrets?" Jane asked.

Bo was caught off guard. "What the hell kind of question is that?"

"One that could use an answer!" Jane wasn't about to back down.

Bo stood up, leaning his large gut over his desk. "I *protect* people!"

Vi put her hand gently on Bo's back to calm him down. "Bo..."

Bo retreated and sat back down, cringing as his large ass hit the chair. He snapped up his cigar and puffed several times on it. "You got that tape cued up, Vi?" Vi nodded. "Let 'er rip."

Vi depressed the PLAY button. The video between Jordan Copeland and Bo Lowry began. They sat across from each other at an empty table. Jordan appeared seriously disheveled. His straggly, curly salt-and-pepper hair was matted with cakes of dried mud; his grey beard and mustache sported the same filthy look. His face—although mostly hidden by his beard and mustache—looked ravaged by time and regular beatings. The crystal, enigmatic, nearly translucent blue eyes that stared back at Jane from the mug shot in 1968 were now dim, clouded by prison and a grim, lonely existence. He wore an oilcloth duster that brushed his mid-calf and was draped with threads of mud. While she couldn't be certain, Jordan's large hands looked to still have the remnants of the blood Weyler mentioned. As a whole, Jane had to admit that Jordan Copeland did indeed look like a giant human trash bag.

"It don't look too good for you, Jordan," Bo's voice rang out tinny on the video. "Where'd the blood on your hands come from?"

Jane watched as Jordan's body language reflected complete

condescension mixed with distrust of Bo. It was the way he pulled his shoulder away from Bo and the manner in which he glanced across the tiny room when he spoke to Bo instead of looking him in the eye.

"I told you," Jordan stated in a *been here before* tenor, "I was running outside along the riverbank and I fell."

"That explains the mud, Jordan. That don't explain the blood."

"Well, I know it *don't.*" Jordan's voice turned demeaning. "I can't tell you where the blood came from…"

"*Can't* tell me or *won't* tell me?" Bo yelled.

"*I don't know,*" Jordan replied in a surly fashion. "I must have cut myself when I was running."

"Why were you runnin' in the middle of a goddamn rainstorm? At *night?*"

Bo motioned for Vi to put the tape on PAUSE. "See, the thing is with ol' Trash Bag here, he's hardly ever *inside* his dingbat cave. He prefers to roam the woods around his property night and day." He raised a judgmental eyebrow. "Reminds me of someone who's been over-vaccinated!" Bo motioned for Vi to start the video again.

"Why were you runnin', Jordan?" Bo repeated the question to Jordan on the video. Jordan sat motionless. "Did Jake slip out of the noose on the bridge and fall in the river? Did you find him, Jordan? You pull him out of the river? Was he dead? Or did you kill him like you killed that poor little, retarded Danny Marshall forty-one years ago?" Jordan turned his body away from Bo. "You hide Jake's body on your property? *Are we gonna find that boy's dead body under your goddamn bed?*"

Jordan looked like he wanted to jump across the table and kill Bo. Instead, the convicted felon just sat seething, his eyes purposely turned away from Lowry. "I…blacked…out…by… the…river." Jordan said, in measured syncopation.

"*Blacked out?* Well, you sure picked one helluva time to do that, Jordan!"

Jordan collected his thoughts and turned to Bo. "I am the ruler of shovels. I have a double. I am as thin as a knife. I have a wife. What am I?"

On the tape, Bo sat back in his chair. "What in the hell are you jabberin' about?"

Jordan let a smug snigger.

Bo looked at Weyler. "He's just a bubble shy of bein' level, eh, Beanie?" Bo asked Vi to fast forward to the section where Jordan is given a polygraph. "I was hopin' that if I went knee-to-knee with him, I'd get a confession. But that was a big ol' 10-74. So, we put him on the box." Bo looked at Vi. "Ready?"

Vi nodded and hit the PLAY button again. Jordan was strapped to a lie detector. Across the table, a polygraph expert asked him questions and jotted down notes.

"Is your name Jordan Richard Copeland?" the man asked Jordan.

"Yes." Jordan answered quietly.

"Do you live in Midas, Colorado?"

"Yes."

"Do you have a beard and mustache?"

Jordan shifted slightly in his chair. "Yes."

Jane watched the tape carefully. The first questions were controls, used to ascertain a baseline response line that, when stressed, could determine a possible lie. The way that skilled criminals "beat the box" is to use the control questions so that the peak comparison values on later pertinent questions—questions that can determine guilt or innocence—don't equate. This could be done a variety of ways: inserting a tack into your shoe and pressing your toe on it during a control question, squeezing your anus together on the question or varying one's breathing techniques to create artificial stress. It was for this reason that Jane watched Jordan more closely when he shifted in his chair when he answered "yes" to a simple question about his beard and mustache.

"Are you the son of Richard and Joanna Copeland?"

"Yes." Jordan stared straight ahead, his voice extremely modulated.

Jane leaned closer to the monitor, looking for a *tell* but the poor quality of the video didn't allow for reading the minutia.

The questions continued with the expected, "Did you kidnap Jake Van Gorden?" "Did you have any knowledge of Jake Van Gorden's kidnapping?" and "Are you connected in any way with Jake Van Gorden's kidnapping?" The clincher came in the form of "Did you kill Jake Van Gorden?"

Bo motioned for Vi to shut off the video, thanked her for her help and then told her she could go. "So, see, between the fact that he beat the box and we didn't find any dead bodies inside his little log shack or around his property, we had to cut the Trash Bag loose." He sucked a hard drag off his cigar. "I could pick him up again on some trumped up charge. You know, aggravated mopery or P.O.P.O., but if I can't get him to sing, it's a goddamn waste of time!" Jane recognized P.O.P.O. as *Pissing Off the PO-lice*, a sometimes-common charge used by cock-of-the-walk cops who like to flaunt their muscle with a perp they don't like but don't have enough ammo to hang. Bo set the cigar in an ashtray, leaned forward, clasping his hands together and looked at Weyler. "This is a tough one, Beanie. Ain't no way to *Gomez* this case away."

"'Gomez?'" Jane said, incredulously. "I've never heard that one."

Weyler turned to her, a sly look on his face. "Really? It's an old school term."

Bo shared a private glance with Weyler.

"My dad was a cop," Jane offered. "I heard them all. But I never heard to *Gomez* something away."

"Yeah, well, maybe you ain't as smart as you think you are!" Bo chortled in a satisfied manner. "Back to ol' Trash Bag, it's worth mentionin' that no clues were delivered while Jordan got his three hots and a cot. I also think it's a tad odd that we got a bunch of clues that make no sense and one of them is a riddle and this yahoo is jammerin' on about *I am the ruler of the shov-els.* I hear that shit and I'm thinkin' he's dug a hole on his property and buried the kid's body!"

"He's testing you," Jane stated.

"Excuse me?"

"He's an East Coast elitist and he doesn't suffer fools."

Bo's face suddenly became extremely hard. "You sayin' I'm stupid?"

Bo's defensiveness was over the top. "Of course, not. Jordan is a smart guy but *people* are what scare the hell out of him. So he uses his intelligence to set himself above others and create distance so he doesn't have to interact."

"So, the riddle about shovels is just a coincidence…bein' that a clue sent to us is *also* a riddle?" There was a nasty edge to Bo's voice.

"Maybe he's just messing with your head. Besides the Van Gordens, how many people know about the clues?"

"Oh, the whole goddamn town!" Bo said, leaning back in his chair and taking a quick puff on his cigar. "See, I have the local paper print 'em up on the front page every time one rolls in the door!"

Weyler cut in. "Bo, she didn't mean it that way!"

"Jesus Christ, you think that because we're small and understaffed that I don't know how to run an investigation?"

"I'm not trying to insult you," Jane defended herself.

"Well, it sure as hell comes off that way!"

Jane had only seen this kind of defensiveness in cops who were covering up for what they felt were other inadequacies—like dropping the ball and worrying about getting caught. The snappish responses were always a telltale sign to Jane that the cop in question wasn't as surefooted as he made himself out to be. "We didn't see the whole videotape. I'm just wondering if you used the kidnapper's clues as leverage when you were interviewing Jordan."

"No, I did not! The only people who know about the clues,

besides myself and Vi, are the Van Gordens and *they* only know about the ones that come directly to them."

"Why does Vi have to know?"

"*Why not?*" Bo was standing now, one fist on his desk supporting him.

Great. More defensiveness. Jane shook her head in amazement. "Jesus, what's the deal here? Are you and Vi a couple?"

Weyler grimaced. "Jane. *No.*"

Bo took a step back. "Goddamnit, Morgan! I don't have to put up with this shit!"

Weyler buried his head in his hand as Bo turned away, trying to control his emotions. "*What?*" Jane asked bewildered.

Weyler leaned over to Jane and spoke quietly. "Bo's wife of thirty years died last year of cancer. He's still...you know..."

"Fuck," was all Jane could muster. *Damn, do I need a cigarette.* Her cell phone intoned, signaling a text message. "Look, I'm sorry..." she stumbled. "I want to...*we* want to help you with this case." Bo was still not buying her *mea culpa.* "I promise you, I will honor your wishes to keep this whole thing under the radar..."

Bo looked at Weyler, gathering his thoughts. "Okay. *Under the radar.* I got your word?"

"You have my..." Jane was about to sign off on her guarantee when she snuck a look at her text message. It was from Betty at the runaway shelter and it read, *I MADE SOME CALLS. PUT OUT ON WIRE. GOOD LUCK!* As if on cue, a low rumble could be heard approaching the building. Jane looked out the large window in Bo's office that faced the street. There, lining up one by one in the available parking spots around her Mustang, were five Denver news vans. Within seconds, cameraman and newscasters poured out of the vehicles and headed toward the front room of the Town Hall.

Bo turned around in time to see the last guy lug a tripod out of a van and walk to the front door. "What in the hell?" he stammered.

"Betty..." Jane whispered to herself. "What have you done?"

Bo spun around, his eyes spitting fire at Jane. "*Damn you!*"

CHAPTER 6

There wasn't much Jane could do. Escaping out the back door of Town Hall was an option but not a viable one. No, the only thing she could do was reluctantly follow Weyler and Bo into the front room and onto the street where the assembled video cameras and rabid newscasters set up their shot. The cameras and attention focused on Bo, who stammered his way through the impromptu news conference as best he could. Flanked on either side of him were Weyler and Jane, who looked as if she were headed to the slaughterhouse once the cameras were turned off.

The Midas media blitz did attract minor attention from some business owners and citizens. Jane noted, in particular one clean-cut older guy, about fifty, with brown-and-grey hair observing her with an amused grin on his face. Every time she glanced over at the man, he was staring back at her, his eyes twinkling. *Do I know him?* The way he looked at her, there seemed to be some undercurrent of mild infatuation on his part. *God help me.* She quickly built an invisible yet impenetrable wall around her. Once the cameras stopped rolling, she half-expected the guy to approach her but he only smiled, got into his truck and drove down Main Street.

It was fortuitous as Jane figured the sooner she created some serious distance between herself and Bo Lowry, the better off she'd be. When she heard Bo mumble something about "We're just a few clowns short of a goddamn circus," she took that as her cue to beat feet.

Jane wound her Mustang around the curve that topped Main Street and headed left on a narrow, two-lane highway. The jagged red rock cliffs towered on the passenger side while the rushing river, replete with the frozen spring runoff from the snowpack, raced on her left. She factored that Weyler was, at that moment, doing whatever he could to convince Bo not to put out a contract on Jane for leading the Denver news network lemmings to Midas. However, in some ways, she couldn't blame the media interest. The story was provocative. It wasn't every day that a fifteen-year-old boy from a wealthy family went missing and inspired his kidnapper to send out a glut of bewildering clues that made no sense but, at the same time, seemed to be veiled, off-kilter threats. It was the kind of story that, once resolved, would be featured in any number of news specials and subsequent books.

It was clear to Jane that Bo Lowry was way over his nearly bald head and desperate to put this case to bed. Realizing he only had eleven days left before his grand exodus from Midas to the coast of Florida, Jane reasoned that Bo didn't want to leave the people who trusted him with an unfinished case that might involve the imminent murder of one of their own. No police chief wants to leave their job with lifeless loose ends dangling for the next guy. But the reality for ninety-eight percent of them was that they'd walk out the door and leave a few boxes of cold cases with their name on it—which would go from cold to frozen as more immediate issues flooded their desk.

As Jane drove down the two-lane road, the red rock on the right hand side gave way to a mile or so of snow covered clearings and the occasional gated service road. Her mind shifted back to Bo Lowry. He was an odd fellow, she surmised. A guy who other people say "ain't right" but put up with because of tenure or seniority. His penchant for talking in 10-code and using cop talk bordered on comical. But there were other observations Jane couldn't understand.

The calendar came to mind. Who marks a calendar with large *Xs*? In Jane's mind, the only people who mark the days off a calendar are the desperate and children under the age of six who are counting the days until Christmas. There seemed to be an overt edge around Bo; a distracted urgency to get out before something awful happened. And yet, his destination also seemed clouded in mystery and met with a less than excited expectation. As Weyler said, Bo was still seven or eight years from social security and obtaining a higher pension. He had an insanely secure job. Why not wait out seven or eight more years and then ride off into the sunset?

The yellow folder on his desk that he so clearly tried to obscure *had* to be connected to his departure. Jane considered what kind of presentations come in folders. She quickly came up with hospitals, assisted living facilities and investment opportunities. Jane crossed off the last option, as she didn't think Bo had enough financial acumen to navigate around that fiscal landmine—especially given the volatile nature of the market. But hospitals and assisted living facilities…yes, that sounded plausible. Bo did seem to have difficulty walking and she caught him wincing more than once when he sat down. Maybe he was sick…maybe terminally ill? It made sense. Of course, what were the odds of his wife dying of cancer last year *and* him contracting a deadly disease that would require a long distance relocation?

But there were so many other eccentricities Jane noticed. The boxes, for example—boxes with exclamation points, question marks and others. Who marks boxes with symbols? Then there was the flagrant ripping of the front page by Vi on both Jordan Copeland's and Jake Van Gorden's file. What in the hell weren't Jane and Weyler supposed to see? If they were there to help, wasn't full disclosure a given?

But there was something else that Jane noted—something another person might easily overlook or not even hear. And yet, it was akin to the peanut in the room that Jane tended to focus on rather than the elephant. Bo used the word, *see* a lot. "See what I'm sayin'?" or "I couldn't see my way clear without her," referring to Vi. Once or twice in a conversation was one thing but Lowry used the word so frequently that it revealed to Jane the way Bo viewed life. He was visually driven. He understood his world by what he saw and then created vivid visual images to reflect that reality. The fact that he chose for to call Jake "Juice Box" and Jordan "Trash Bag" further exemplified his visually driven perceptions. Why he called Weyler "Beanie" was still an unsolved mystery but Jane was determined to put that one to rest as soon as she could have a few private moments with her fellow Sergeant.

Jane was so deep in thought that she didn't see the infamous bridge on the left hand side where Jake allegedly went missing. She'd asked Weyler for directions to the spot before ducking out of the sidewalk news conference. Jane actually noted the speed-trap camera warning sign before she saw the bridge. She drove another half mile before locating a safe place to turn around on the narrow two-lane highway. An idea sprung to mind. She floored the Mustang and sped well past 60 mph on the 45 mph road, blasting past the first and second speed cameras located just across from the bridge. It was a test. She wanted to see if the damn thing worked *and*, if it did, how clear the bridge was in the photo. Her reasoning was cloudy but one of those back-pocket possibilities. If the photo proved to be sharp enough, she would strongly suggest that Bo discreetly replace the speed camera with a 24/7 security camera so the bridge could be monitored remotely. The idea had a dual purpose. The first was mundane. Due to the signage, drivers would still be under the impression that the camera would only click for speeders and thus, slow down at that point making it somewhat easier to distinguish vehicles. The second idea took into account human nature. Often, the kidnapper returned to the scene of his or her crime. Perhaps, with this seemingly brazen kidnapper, he would chose to leave a message or clue on the bridge. As much as Jane despised Big Brother and the monitoring of law-abiding citizens, installing a temporary rolling security camera at this location made sense.

After blowing through the speed trap, Jane turned around and headed back to the bridge, parking the Mustang at the edge of the somewhat rickety overpass. She got out of her car just as a determined gust of cold wind beat against her body. She raised the collar on her leather jacket and stood for a moment in the center of the fifty-foot bridge. She could see the rushing river between the cracks of the warped planks. The temperature at this location was decidedly colder, thanks to the freezing water below her feet, still clutching ice chunks along the banks. Jane's acute senses awakened again. The frigid air felt like a knife cutting her face. The sound of the river below seemed deafening and lawless in its intensity.

Thankfully, Jane had been able to bury her fear of her own death during her time in the office with Weyler and Bo. But now the trepidation was resurfacing with unrepentant vehemence. As she canvassed the area around her, the world looked as dead as she felt inside. Spring in the Colorado high country is like a coquettish tease; the young tart begging to show off her nubile physique. After the icy assault of winter, where the days don't rise above thirty-five degrees and the nights harbor a deathly frozen bite, spring whispers a promise of renewal and a better life. The monotonous haze of drab browns and grays, spotted with patches of the now gravel and mud-embedded snow, slowly give way to pinpoint shoots of green that struggle through the frosty surface. Gradually, the days warm and the world is reborn into a new life with endless possibilities. As bulbs burst into showy, seductive ribbons of eye candy, there's a sense that no matter how dark and dead the world can appear, underneath it all, there are formidable powers that demand to be heard and seen.

But as it is with everything that starts anew, there is the tendency to fall backward. Spring in Colorado is no different. Just when you think the bitter cold and snowflakes have left, the wind whips, the sun sinks behind a bank of clouds and everything that worked so hard to emerge, is covered by a blanket of white once again. The air warms again, melts the snow and what was meant to survive stares back with a steely strength that reminds even an agnostic that nature's soul purpose is to adapt, transform and endure.

As Jane stared out at the brittle landscape, still smothered in layers of dead leaves and brown snow, she felt a sense of despair and emptiness creep around her. The thought that she might be able to count her remaining springs and summers on one hand crossed her mind. Fear gripped her belly and she found herself holding her breath—only to let it out in short, shallow bursts. She stared into the void, cut off from the world circling around her. The isolation was tangible—a natural reaction of facing her mortality, coupled with a paralyzing dread that chilled her ability to think rationally. She could only see directly in front of her and the view was bleak. Her world was narrowing and the tunnel she was digging began to grow deeper and pull tighter.

Moments like this in her life could always be abated with the hit of nicotine. Jane turned back to her Mustang, focusing on the single cigarette hidden in her leather satchel that was patiently waiting for her, confident that her resolve would soon fracture. The motto of "one day at a time" that she'd heard ad nauseam at AA came to mind. With this addiction to tobacco, it was more like one minute at a time.

Jane closed her eyes and attempted to focus on that still point within her. It was a trick she'd learned from one of the esoteric books she'd read over the last year. It had taken her a few months to learn to ignore the chatter in her head and the world around her, but eventually, she was able to focus solely on that point where everything and nothing converge. Jane could feel herself almost reaching that place when that familiar perfume of gardenias washed over her. But *this time,* there was a defined vaporous presence attached to it. Jane opened her eyes and spun around, her heart beating like mad. The flowery fragrance engulfed her, seemingly attempting to own her as the awareness of another distant heartbeat stood next to her. Inexplicably, her eyes filled with tears and a soulful ache of grief clawed at her throat. Almost simultaneously, a throbbing pain grew in her pelvis. She pressed her palm against her lower belly in a failed attempt to ameliorate the excruciating sensation. She bent over, feeling as though she was about to vomit. The now sickly stench of gardenias overwhelmed her as the phantom tightened its hold against her body.

Is this the entrée to my impending death? she wondered. Were the ghosts of hell gathering and practicing their moves so that when Jane's life was over, they could move efficiently in a coordinated effort to snatch her soul? There was at once a weighty sense of loss, coupled with a burning rage of being abandoned. But there was nothing tangible that Jane could attach to that gut-wrenching feeling. Just when the terror and pelvic pain reached a blinding crescendo, the aroma of gardenias vanished. And with the scent, went the anguish.

All that was left in the aftermath was fear and the question of how a pain that severe could suddenly dissipate? Jane stood straight up, wondering what in the hell was happening to her body. *Is this cancer? Is this a glimpse of what I can expect in the months to come?*

It was too much to deal with. *Lock it out,* she instructed herself. Bury the fear and focus on anything but her inevitable death. Turning back to the bridge, Jane caged the uncertainty and funneled her energy into Jake Van Gorden and the bridge where she stood. Knowing that Jake Van Gorden came to this place to end his life and was then taken possibly by force, she let herself fall into the spaces between the chaos; the place where words previously expressed and feelings already suffered still hung like the stems of ice along the branches of trees in the nearby forest. She imagined the vaguely described "black vehicle" parked on the bridge, waiting for Jake to arrive. If the driver was waiting for Jake, how did he know that Jake was headed to the bridge? Did he stalk the kid and, if so, did Jake walk to the bridge to escape on a regular basis? *But what about Jake,* Jane thought. If you show up at a bridge with the clear intent of killing yourself and carrying only the rope needed to hang yourself, would you follow through if you saw a strange vehicle parked in such close proximity? Isn't the act of suicide inherently private? Jane deduced that either the vehicle was there and Jake saw that it was empty, or the vehicle had been parked there earlier in the day—long enough to leak antifreeze onto the bridge and stain it—and then watched Jake from another vantage point?

Jane crossed to the obvious stain of antifreeze on the bridge. Even the hard driving storm that night wasn't enough to erase the telltale mark. Her eyes shifted to the right side of the bridge and the threads of fresh rope that were still wedged in the upper wooden girder. Looking closer, just beneath the girder, she saw a pale yet fresh ink drawing of a dragonfly. Underneath, were the words: ILLUSIONS DIE HARD, followed by the initials, L.G. Did some passerby stop to reflect on Jake's disappearance and leave a heartfelt message behind?

She followed the girder down to the wide plank railing where Jake would have crawled up and stood, throwing the rope over across the overhead beam and preparing to die. *It took time,* Jane figured. There was time to think about what you were doing and time to change your mind. Maybe he *was* thinking when he stood up there. Maybe just the time it took to rethink his plan was enough for an opportunistic crime to take place?

Jane needed to stand in Jake's shoes. She hoisted herself up on the wide railing and carefully stood up with help of one of the diagonal support beams. Powdery orange rust that lay caked on the beam brushed against her poplin shirt, leaving a mark. Looking down at the roaring river, she imagined what it must have been like for Jake to stare into that water at night, with a raging spring storm pelting sleet against his skin. *If* suicide truly was his intended motive that evening, was he even aware of the frozen sting on his face? Had his thoughts caved in so deeply within himself that he could no longer feel cold or heat? Was he so numb that he didn't hear the kidnapper approaching? Did he get the noose around his neck? Was he willingly led off the railing or was there a struggle?

Jane held onto the diagonal support beam and studied both edges of the plank at her feet. Running her fingers along the wood, it was clear that there were fresh chunks of the old wood recently scuffed off the surface of the edge that faced the river. Her gut clamped down and she felt it, as if she were melting into Jake's desperate body. There *was* a struggle that night. He had put his head in the noose and he was in the act of snuffing out his young life. Jane connected hard with Jake's shock as he kicked his feet against the bridge in an effort to let go and then the sudden, expected interceding of someone else pulling his body back onto the plank and his soul back into his body. If this is how it happened, was the kidnapper actually Jake's savior? And did that savior salvage the boy's life only to turn around and use Jake as a pawn in a twisted game?

Jane stood up, securing her cowboy boots firmly against the diagonal beam. The persistent grief still hugged the bridge. She felt his despair and allegiance to death. *Allegiance*, she thought. *How odd?* But that's exactly how she interpreted what motivated Jake that night on that bridge. He was being led by the rope of another, convinced that this was the fate he was born to fulfill.

An abject sense of desolation wrapped its unforgiving arms around Jane. She had almost ended her life on her kitchen floor just a few years back. She understood the disconnected anguish that brought her to that moment. And then, for some unexpected reason, her thoughts suddenly turned to the young man so long ago; the one she loved without question but who couldn't see through his own pain to love her enough to not destroy everything they shared—including their addictions, pain and wound-bonding. *Did he hesitate before he pulled the trigger?* she wondered. Was her face in his mind's eye when the .38 slug sliced through his mouth and obliterated his brain? Did he still hover in the undone world between here and there, waiting for the light of God to let him in? And if it was Jane's fate to leave this world prematurely, would she find him in that murky fold of purgatory?

The thoughts bombarded her mind so completely, that Jane failed to see the darkened figure standing in the woods thirty feet above the rushing river's edge. He had been watching her, studying her and purposely moving his consciousness into hers for five focused minutes. He sought to inhabit her awareness because she had something he desperately needed—something that would serve his greater good. He wasn't sure what that *something* was; he just knew that the woman hanging onto the support beam on the bridge with the distant look in her eyes and the aura of death was essential to his survival.

His hand began to shake—imperceptibly at first but then growing with an intensity he couldn't suffocate no matter how hard he tried to hold his wrist still. The quiver only happened when he was close to someone or something significant. It was the way his body always alerted him to the fact that whatever stood in front of him and generated that reaction needed his immediate attention. He didn't know who she was, but he did know that he hadn't shaken with this kind of intensity in over fifty years.

He dove deeper into her mind, seeking a solid connection but she unconsciously fought him in her preoccupied state. But wait...*there...yes, there...*the current between them engaged. Now his hand shook violently as he willed his psyche to occupy every nerve ending in her body. She had his lifeblood in her grip and he was damned if he was going to let her get away.

As if the psychic stream between them was made visible, Jane turned, emerging from the dark recesses and saw him. There on the banks stood Jordan Copeland staring back at her, his hands shaking uncontrollably. The untraceable fuse ignited, jolting Jane off the railing and back onto the safety of the bridge. The minute her boots hit the beaten planks, she stood immobile, not sure of the disconcerting vibration that had bored into her flesh. Jane stared at Jordan, her senses simultaneously alive and hypnotized. She fought the merge, but those penetrating, enigmatic blue eyes sucked her into his desperate grasp.

"*Jane!*"

She spun around to the sound of her name. Sergeant Weyler stood on the rim of the highway in front of a borrowed patrol car with its engine running.

"I'm heading over to the Van Gorden's house to talk to them!" Weyler yelled above the din of the rushing river. "Follow me!"

Jane fell back inside her body. She turned toward the woods. But she already knew Jordan was gone.

CHAPTER 7

It was a short drive to Blackfeather Estates and the Van Gorden's stony house that sat tucked at the end of a cul-de-sac off a narrow winding road outside of Midas. Jane factored the distance was a little over one mile, an easy jaunt for Jake to make on a regular basis if he often escaped to the bridge. The unsettling experience on the bridge still vibrated around Jane. It was one thing to churn the memories so unexpectedly about the one who died long ago. But to suddenly come face-to-face with Jordan Copeland in such a disturbing manner and, without even a hint that he was right there and Jane didn't know it…well, she wondered if she was losing her ability to sense danger when it was that close.

There was definitely something unnerving about Jordan. He had a crazy Rasputin vibe from a distance—an intense, mesmerizing gaze coupled with that grimy, weather-beaten appearance. He was reminiscent of the frightening monster in the woods that wakes children from their nightmares and keeps them up with a flashlight under the covers. She figured that she'd keep her spontaneous unspoken sighting of Jordan under wraps for now just in case connecting with him went against some ad hoc protocol Bo Lowry instigated.

Jane parked her Mustang behind Weyler's borrowed patrol car half a block from the Van Gordens' cul-de-sac and got out, quickly scanning the area. From what little she'd seen of Blackfeather Estates, she didn't like. The affluent subdivision was another one of those made-to-order enclaves that had infested the Colorado landscape over the recent years. Developers typically bought up acres of ranchland or farmland, making the rancher or farmer multimillionaires and then ruthlessly carved one-and-two-acre plots out of the once rustic terrain. On those plots, they would build the ultimate fantasy Colorado *McMansions* with floor-to-ceiling cathedral windows, radiant-heated driveways, meticulous stacks of firewood all cut the exact same length, rock fireplaces big enough to hold two lawn chairs and a table, five-car, heated garages and wrought-iron designer mailboxes. Jane had to laugh at the pretreated siding so many of the houses chose; a factory-beaten stippling and shredding, known as "the old barn look." To her, the choice was ludicrous; an elitist attempt to pander to what they *thought* would make their estate appear *rustic*. These Colorado estates all felt the same to Jane— sanitized wooden boxes that stood like architectural eunuchs, devoid of that rough-around-the-edges western mettle.

As for the people who inhabited these ludicrous log lodges, Jane typically found them to be as facile and authentic as the made-to-order patina bear or eagle that adorned their manicured lawn. From their unscuffed, two-thousand-dollar Lucchese alligator cowboy boots to their ridiculous turquoise, silver-and-coral bolo tie and freshly pressed jeans, they were about as in touch with reality as they were acquainted with their automated dishwasher. Something told Jane that the Van Gordens wouldn't disappoint in this generalization.

"They always have to live up *above* town, don't they?" Jane grumbled as she and Weyler walked toward the Van Gorden's driveway. "That way they can figuratively and physically look down on the peons."

"You know, this whole idea of quitting smoking cold turkey...how about just tapering off instead?" Weyler gently offered.

"No, boss. There's not enough suffering in tapering."

"Try chewing on the inside of an orange rind. I heard that helps quell the urge for nicotine."

"Fascinating," Jane said dryly. "You hear that on your favorite PBS station?"

"Yes. A program on addiction."

Jane needed to change the subject. She touched Weyler's coat sleeve and stopped at the edge of the long, steep driveway.

"Your ol' buddy, Bo, is quite the character."

"Bo was always a little different than the rest of us. Smart, but in an off-kilter way. Some things he says don't make a lot of sense, except to Bo."

"*Some things?*" Jane said with great disdain. "*Juice Box Jake? Trash Bag Jordan?* Nah, that's not weird. Sorry, boss, but your friend is a creaking relic. My mother had a term to describe people like Bo...*Crusty.*" She shook her head in confusion. "I have a real hard time picturing you and Bo as rookie partners. Putting the two of you together is like a Hollywood pitch for a bad situation comedy."

Weyler smiled. "I didn't come out of the Academy looking and behaving the way I do today. I had plenty of cocky, youthful gusto to spare."

Jane tried to picture Weyler with *youthful gusto.* "Boss, I don't give a damn how much youthful gusto you had. You and Bo? There's just no...connection."

"You're wrong, Jane." Weyler's voice became serious. "There *is* a connection."

Jane waited. "And...?"

"And hopefully you and Bo will be able to form a connection as well. If he doesn't kill you first." Weyler started up the driveway.

Jane didn't follow. She was blocked once again in her quest to understand the reason why Weyler "owed" Bo and, in turn, dragged her tired ass up to Midas. "I'm sure he had a few choice words to say about me after I left."

Weyler stopped and turned to Jane. "He did."

She was used to being talked about behind her back. Her often-aggressive nature didn't earn her a lot of friends. "What'd he call me? A bitch?" Jane asked with a smirk.

"No. He asked me if you were a lesbian."

Jane looked at Weyler, stunned. "What the fuck? He actually said that?"

"Not exactly. He asked me, 'Does she pitch for the other team?'"

"Because I speak my opinion? Because I don't take shit from people?"

"That played a part I'm sure. But Bo has always been visually driven." Jane already surmised this but was tentative in how it would play out with her personally. Weyler was suddenly uncomfortable. "His perception was based on how you dress."

Jane looked down at her plain dark blue poplin shirt with the powdery stain of orange rust from the bridge, jeans with splattered mud from the adventure, scuffed cowboy boots and beaten leather jacket. "This is not *gay*. This is *comfortable!*"

"Let it go, Jane. We've got a job to do. And now that job is a little more complicated with the media interest." He started to move when Jane grabbed his coat sleeve again.

"Look, boss," Jane felt the world closing in around her. "I didn't know Betty was gonna blast this story on the wire. I just called her to put forth the possibility that..."

"You called her in hopes of getting out of this assignment... *period*. Don't attempt to bullshit me, Jane. I'm too old to buy it and you're too proud to sell it." Weyler started up the driveway.

Jane aborted her improvised regret and followed him. "10-4, Beanie."

Weyler cast a cautionary glance back at Jane. "Jane?"

"Boss, I gotta know. It won't go further than the two of us. Why *Beanie?*"

"We're late, Jane. Come on!" Weyler started up the steep driveway.

"Okay, fine." She followed him. "But what about the *E* on your luggage? *M.E.W.*? What's the *E* stand for?"

"Eloquent," Weyler stated without missing a beat.

"Come on!" Jane cajoled.

"Educated," Weyler affirmed.

Jane shook her head. "*Evasive*," she countered. They crested the long driveway and stood aghast at the massive two-story log monstrosity that the Van Gordens called home. Four gigantic wooden pillars supported the entrance to the overwhelming structure that some might call a "show place" but most would term an over-the-top obscenity. The two pillars closest to the pathway were carved in the shape of owls and gave the appearance of ominous sentries. Jane counted no less than twenty-two perfectly pruned spruce trees that towered twenty-five feet and, she reckoned, cost a good three grand each to truck in full-size and plant in the most appropriate place to generate the greatest visual impact. At least thirty lofty aspen trees were scattered around the side of the house. *Overkill,* she thought to herself. The wide concrete walkway and stairs that led to the front door was tinted in shades of black and grey to simulate the look of marble. As Jane and Weyler approached the front entrance, they felt their size quickly dwarf under the dual-arched doorway, complete with stained-glass panels on each side of the door and above the archway.

Pretentious. That was the next word rattling through Jane's head as she pressed the lighted doorbell. A melodic *ding-ding-DING-ding-diiiing* rang out, followed by silence.

Jane turned to Weyler. "You know, if they're in the back of the house, it might take them a few days to get here."

"Try to control the sarcasm, Jane. They don't know we're coming."

"Why?"

Weyler shrugged. "Why not?"

CHAPTER 8

The heavy, ornate front door opened just as the sound of a ringing telephone was heard. "Could you get the phone, Bailey?" Carol Van Gorden stood apprehensively in the doorway, assessing Jane and Weyler. The telephone rang again and then stopped. "Can I help you?"

Weyler flashed his badge. "My name's Sergeant Morgan Weyler and this is Sergeant Jane Perry. We're from Denver. Do you and your husband have a moment to talk with us?"

Carol looked exhausted as she nervously studied the ground. She was in her early forties, but the stress had clearly taken its toll. Her black wool slacks, black-and-white striped tunic with the cloisonné butterfly brooch and blond bobbed hair looked well put together though. "Uh, you know, it's just that… we've already talked at length with Bo…"

"I'm heading out!" Bailey yelled from an upstairs area.

"Bailey, wait!" Carol yelled back. After Carol let him know that two sergeants from *Denver* were at the door, Jane heard a hard pause followed by determined footsteps toward the door.

Bailey graced them with his appearance. His look did not disappoint Jane, given her earlier derisive generalization of Colorado estate dwellers. He was about six feet tall and his forty-eight-year-old body was obviously acquainted with a gym. Bailey had the chiseled chin and jutting jaw of someone who always looks as if they're about to speak but whose words were usually a bore. His tanned skin—acquired surely from a tanning bed this time of year—appeared more dramatic against his crisp white shirt that was tucked into a pair of pressed, stonewashed jeans. Jane figured the denim cost more than her monthly grocery bill. Around his thirty-three-inch waist was an alligator belt, which perfectly matched his…*yes*…two-thousand-dollar Lucchese alligator cowboy boots. Bailey observed Jane and Weyler like a lab worker regards a specimen in a petri dish. It was obvious to Jane that Bailey instantly labeled them as *amoebas* and he just didn't sink that low. "I'm sorry," Bailey stated, clearly not sorry one bit, "I'm on my way out. You'll need to come back another time."

Jane was floored by his arrogance. "We're here about your son...Jake?"

"We've already talked to Bo in great detail," Bailey stated, his self-importance rising. "I don't understand what you can offer us."

"Sir," Weyler interjected in his warm, congenial tone that never failed to ingratiate, "Police Chief Lowry requested our help from Denver to speed the safe recovery of your only child. We'll only stay a short while."

Maybe it was Weyler's 6' 4" stature or maybe it was his amenable manipulation of a quickly deteriorating situation, but Bailey let out a low sigh and showed them inside the house.

"Who called?" Carol asked her husband as Jane and Weyler closed the massive door behind them.

"Nobody. Probably wrong number," Bailey said, preoccupied. "It rang twice and then nothing."

"You're not getting calls from the media, I hope?" Jane asked.

"Of course, not," Bailey responded in the most dismissive tone he could muster. "Our number is unlisted."

"Right," Jane said with a half-smile. "That usually stops them."

"We've had no calls from the media," Carol offered in a weak, wispy voice. "Just the occasional call from a friend checking in."

The domed entry of their palatial house could fit a medium-sized fishing boat and small truck. Jane looked up at the glass dome above her head that splayed diffused light across the eggshell walls and dual polished stairways that led to the second floor. *How in the hell do you clean that?* she wondered. To her left was another arched doorway that was closed. Straight ahead, across the black-and-white checkerboard floor, stood a massive archway in the center of the double staircases that appeared to lead to an obscenely large family room and kitchen. On either side of the front door were two marble-topped tables, both holding large ivory pillar candles. Jane noted that the wicks were clean, having never been burned.

"Let's sit in the living room," Carol suggested, pointing to the right of the front door.

Jane and Weyler followed Carol and an obviously irritated Bailey into a room that ate up 1,200 frivolous square feet of real estate. The centerpiece for the room was the obligatory stone fireplace that was large enough and deep enough to cremate several human bodies simultaneously. As Jane noted the floor-to-ceiling cathedral window that overlooked the mountain ranges to the north behind the *de rigueur* dark leather couch with thick brass inlay buttons, she privately ticked off another requisite overdone feature of these styles of homes. Jane took a seat next to Weyler on the couch while Bailey and Carol sat across from them in matching leather wing chairs. A highly lacquered, burl slab coffee table created the necessary, weighted distance between them. Sitting atop the table was a graduated candleholder that cradled five medium-sized ivory pillar candles. Again, Jane noted, none of them had ever been lit. The place was starting to feel more like one of those model homes than an actual place where people kicked off their shoes and relaxed.

"Quite a little place you got here," Jane said, doing her best to remain professional.

Carol smiled. "Bailey designed everything."

"You an architect?" Weyler asked.

"No," Bailey answered, again with the indifferent tenor. "I dabble in high-end real estate." He crossed his legs and smoothed his already unwrinkled jeans. "I do have an artistic touch, but I designed this place to show others what could be done if they were serious about crafting the lifestyle of the Rockies."

Jane had only known Bailey Van Gorden for less than five minutes and she hated him. Who in the hell "dabbles" in high-end real estate? And the crack about "crafting the lifestyle of the

Rockies" just about sent her looking for a place to puke. What did this East Coast snob know about the Rocky Mountains? As far as Jane was concerned, "crafting the lifestyle of the Rockies" had more to do with ripping open a bag of greasy corn chips, pouring a jar of salsa into a bowl and watching a Broncos game.

Weyler saw that Jane was getting ready to cast a wisecrack. He quickly spoke up. "You should have your home featured in a Colorado magazine or television show."

"Bailey has a great video he made of the place," Carol offered with pride. "He put it up on YouTube and has gotten over three thousand hits…"

Bailey waved off his wife's comment. "Carol, it's not important."

For a guy who seemed so into showing others how to craft that ol' Colorado lifestyle, Jane was perplexed by Bailey's throwaway remark. "Three thousand hits is impressive. I'll have to check it out," Jane insisted. "What's it listed under?"

Bailey eyed Jane with a guarded glare. "Bailey Van Gorden," he said in a rushed manner. "Listen, I thought you were here to talk about Jake."

"Yes, sir," Weyler stated and proceeded to fill in the Van Gordens on everything that Bo knew about the case, excluding specifics on the clues that came directly to Lowry.

"*Copeland* is who you should be talking to!" Bailey stressed. "It's obvious that fucking nutcase is involved! Little shit!"

Jane detected a slight smirk creasing into Bailey's mouth when he said "Copeland." While she couldn't be certain, her attention to body language and the *tells* it generates, gave her the impression that Bailey was either not believing what he was saying or smugly disapproving of Jordan with an errant facial sign. However, when he uttered, "Little shit," the tenor was completely different. Her heightened auditory sense heard a shift in his thoughts; as if Jordan Copeland was completely separate from the "little shit." It was also accompanied by a defined sneer that Jane always read as a sign of superiority mixed with profound contempt. "Little shit" was an odd tag, Jane surmised. Jordan Copeland was a big man—to refer to him as "little" made no sense to her. The uneasy thought crossed her mind that Bailey was, in fact, referencing his own son in a less than benevolent manner. Jane's eyes drifted to Bailey's left foot that was crossed over his leg. He was twirling it back and forth in an aggravated gyratory motion. She also couldn't help but note his sudden flushed face and clogged sinuses. "You got a cold?" Jane asked.

"Excuse me?"

"You're stuffed up. Look feverish." Jane said, offhandedly.

Carol turned to her husband. "Are you getting sick?"

Bailey looked somewhat trapped by the question. "I don't know. It's probably allergies. You know…springtime?" He jutted his tanned jaw toward Jane. "You fall off a roof?" His tone was insolent and purposely meant to shift the conversation.

Jane glanced down at her rust-stained shirt and mud-splattered jeans. She wanted to reply, "*No, asshole. It was a bridge. The same fucking bridge your son tried to hang himself from because he couldn't stand listening to your arrogant pie hole any longer.*" But she didn't. "No, sir," she replied with teeth clenched. "What was your son wearing when he disappeared?" Jane decided it was time for *her* to purposely shift the conversation to suit her objectives.

Bailey glanced at Weyler and then back to Jane as if he suddenly didn't understand English. "How the fuck should I know?"

Jane looked at Carol. "Any ideas?"

Carol seemed equally baffled. "He might have been wearing one of his vintage shirts," she carefully said in measured beats.

Jane noted how Bailey turned away, seemingly disgusted. "Vintage?" Jane asked.

Carol looked at Bailey who was still turned away. "Uh, yes." Carol looked apprehensive. "He's been favoring these retro shirts lately…"

Bailey quickly popped back into control. "You know, he was probably wearing his normal outfit…black jeans, a dark T-shirt and black jacket."

"Was Jake into the Goth scene?" Jane asked.

"No." Carol looked at Bailey as if to double-check her feelings. "I don't think so."

"He wasn't into Goth. But I'm sure he had one of those *fuck you* t-shirts on," Bailey offered with a roll of his eyes.

"What's a *fuck you* T-shirt?" Jane inquired.

Bailey let out a long, tired breath. "You know? *What the fuck you lookin' at? What part of shut the fuck up don't you understand? Dude, you're fuckin' with my mellow!*" Bailey raised his eyebrow. "Fabulous, articulate statements such as those."

"So, Jake is a pissed-off fifteen-year-old," Jane offered.

"Isn't that a redundant observation?" Bailey replied with a narrowing of his eyes.

"So, *you* were a pissed-off fifteen-year-old." Jane stated unequivocally.

Bailey shifted his steely eyes to Weyler. "*Excuse me?*"

Weyler gently raised his hand. "Sergeant Perry is trying to discern what might have precipitated Jake's disappearance. If he was depressed or angry, there's a chance he might have gone online and attracted a predator…"

"Predator, yes!" Bailey exclaimed. "But not online. The predator is one mile away and his name is Jordan Copeland!"

"There wasn't enough to hold Mr. Copeland," Weyler offered.

"For Christ's sake…" Bailey touched his gelled hair. "Bo Lowry couldn't find enough evidence to hold Hitler!" He leaned forward, both feet planted on the floor and posturing a show of aggression. "Look, Jake has been gone now for five days. First, I had to wrap my mind around the idea that he attempted suicide. *Then*, I start getting these goddamn crazy clues in my mailbox from the fucker who grabbed him off the bridge. So now I have to wrap my head around a kidnapping scenario. It's been nonstop around here!" Bailey rubbed his forehead. "The walls are closing in on me. The last time I was out of this house was six fucking days ago when I went to the gym at lunch…"

"Is that where you were headed when we showed up?" Jane interrupted.

Bailey was taken aback. "Ah, yeah. Exactly. I'm just… *fuck*…." He ran his fingers through his hair, but Jane noticed that he had so much gel in his locks that he could only move his hand halfway. "The fucking walls are caving in on me! So, if I appear anxious to you, I think I have a goddamn right to be that way!"

"Of course, you're anxious," Jane interjected. "That's to be expected." She felt it was time to drop some pabulum, if only to make Bailey feel like she had compassion. The truth was that Jane had no compassion for the man. It was the way he interminably kept referring to how this family crisis was affecting *him*. He could have easily used "we" instead of "I" to at least create the appearance of desperation for himself and Carol. But Bailey's arrogance was so deeply ingrained, that he wasn't able to emerge from it—even briefly—to give the impression that he gave a shit about his wife or his son. Jane factored that living with this son-of-a-bitch was like living with a two-year-old on steroids.

His Stepford wife suddenly spoke up. "It's not just our son's disappearance. Bailey's mother, Louise, is terminally ill with liver cancer. She lives back east where Bailey grew up and it's tough being so far away…"

"Carol, they don't need to know about mom." Bailey's tone bordered on rude.

"Where'd you grow up?" Jane asked.

"Why does it matter?" Bailey snapped, defensively.

"Just…curious…"

Bailey paused. "I'm sure you wouldn't know the town."

Jane turned to Weyler with a smile. "Yeah, we don't get out of Denver much. Farthest we travel is the stock show every

January." Weyler shot Jane a look of censure. She turned back to Bailey. "But try me."

Bailey regarded Jane with an uneasy stare. "Wentworth, New Jersey."

Jane noted that Carol's eyes seem to freeze momentarily. "Never heard of it," Jane declared.

Now it was Bailey's turn to smile mockingly. "As expected." He shifted in his chair. "It's a small town. *Prosperous*, though."

It was obvious to Jane that Bailey wanted to make sure that "small town" didn't mean he grew up in the hillbilly hills. Money and stature ruled this guy. Jane was about to ask another question when Weyler took the words out of her mouth.

"Were you and your son having any problems?" Weyler asked.

"He's fifteen. What do you think?" Bailey's voice was brimming with anger.

"Was Jake depressed lately?" Jane quickly asked.

"Jesus! We already answered these questions…"

"Good. Answer them again," Jane demanded, her patience wearing thin.

Bailey regarded Jane with complete disdain. "Hey, Sergeant, I don't like your attitude! My world is completely imploding right now. *Do you understand that*?"

Jane was tired of Bailey's me-centered rhetoric. "I *understand* that your son was so despondent about something that he took a rope to a bridge and was planning on hanging himself! I'd like to know what drove him to that desperation…"

Bailey's already flushed face glowed an even darker shade of crimson. "I don't have a fucking clue!" he said, pounding his tanned fist on the burl table.

Weyler leaned forward. "Mr. Van Gorden, Sergeant Perry is direct with you because time is of the essence."

Carol brought a shaky hand to her mouth, stifling her grief as tears rolled down her face. "What are the odds after five days of our son's safe return?"

"There are no hard and fast rules, ma'am," Weyler offered. "The fact that the kidnapper is still engaged in sending clues, however abstract they are, is a good sign."

Bailey seemed to perk up. "Bo got another clue since that, ah, that goddamn drawing we got with the tied up kid?"

"Yes," Weyler affirmed. "Two more."

Bailey looked at his wife briefly, a look of angst clouding his countenance. "What...what are the clues? What are they saying?" His voice was rushed.

"We can't divulge the content of the clues being sent to Lowry," Jane said.

"But *you know*," Bailey replied, his tone searing.

"I know what the clues say, but as Sergeant Weyler informed you, they are as abstract in nature as the rest. I mean, we've got a book that you received that features George Webber and his adventures..."

"Excuse me?" Bailey interrupted, his eyes narrowing.

"The first clue you got in your mailbox? *You Can't Go Home Again* by Thomas Wolfe? The main character is George Webber."

Bailey's breathing became shallow. "Really?"

"Does that mean something, Mr. Van Gorden?" Weyler asked.

Bailey looked off to the side, lost in a moment, licking his lips. "No...I never read the book." He shook himself out of his daze. "Jesus! This whole goddamn thing is so fucking out of left field. So...vengeful."

"Yes, sir. Vengeful." Jane said, studying Bailey carefully. "Well, you know what we do with any crime is tick off the possible motives. And, believe it or not, it really just boils down to three: money, sex, and gettin' even. Like you said, vengeance. Revenge."

"We can eliminate money," Weyler interjected, "because there's never been a request for ransom, especially given your obvious financial acumen. If money was the motive, it would have been the first thing mentioned."

"So, that leaves sex and getting even," Jane declared in an offhand manner.

Bailey seemed strangled by the choices. "There's got to be other motives!"

"No, they basically all fall under those big umbrellas," Jane insisted.

Bailey sat back in his chair. His face was still flushed and his nose clogged but he had a grey aura around him. "Well… I…I just…don't know what to make of it…" He shook his head. "There *have* to be other motives!"

Jane thought for a second. "Okay, maybe there are."

"What?" Bailey quickly asked, grasping at straws.

"Control," Jane stated.

"Control?" Carol repeated, meekly. She snuck a guarded look toward her husband.

"Yeah," Jane was still building the premise in her head. "It's kind of connected to revenge but it has its own flavor. The criminal does whatever he does in an effort to control the victim or the family of the victim." Jane wasn't sure how she was channeling this presumptive theory, but she let it flow. "The criminal has lost his ability to feel validated and so his action, whatever that might be, seeks to control a situation that he feels he is powerless to contain." She stared at Bailey. He swallowed hard and turned away. Jane had witnessed this reaction many times in the interrogation room. It was always a sign that the individual was responding with a deep, almost visceral validation of what they were hearing. It was the proverbial *bingo* of body language; a signal that an individual is connecting in an emotional way to whatever is being said. The turning away was an attempt to run or escape because of fear. Jane replayed in her head what she had just said. *The criminal does whatever he does in an effort to control the victim or the family of the victim.* Why was this striking a chord with Bailey?

"Control." Bailey thought about it. "That little shit," he

whispered to himself. Jane heard the sudden shift in Bailey's voice before he even spoke. "Focus on Jordan Copeland!" he exclaimed.

Jane looked at Weyler. "Well, yeah, of course, we'll look into him. But are you saying your son has a connection to him?"

"Who knows? Jake's in his own world! He's either up in his room with the door closed or wandering around town. But the point I'm making is that Jordan Copeland is a known child predator. And the bridge? The bridge is right there on the edge of that asshole's property! If Jake frequented the bridge, then this pervert Copeland had to have seen him and...and...what's going through the asshole's head? You tell me..."

"Do we know for a fact that Jake spent a lot of time at that bridge?" Weyler calmly asked.

"How the fuck should I know?!" Bailey exclaimed. "The point is the connections make sense here! I'm telling you, Copeland is involved in this in some way!" He turned to Jane. "Using your control theory, Jordan is *out* of control, right? So, he *seeks* control in whatever perverted ways he can. I mean, he's convicted for shooting a boy and then, in trying to control an out-of-control situation that *he* created, he hides the boy's body under his bed. So, yes! *Control!* Absolutely!" He jabbed his finger in the air toward Jane and Weyler. "This...this...is a valid path to investigate!" Bailey almost looked as if he were about to jump out of his Lucchese boots.

"You know," Jane interrupted, "just to cover all the bases, it might be prudent to put an officer on your phone so we can trace calls in case the perp decides to call, or if Jake decides to call..."

"We already went through this!" Bailey declared. "It was pointless. Didn't Bo fill you in? I told him I couldn't handle it anymore." Again, it was all about Bailey.

"If your son calls," Weyler said, "and stays on the phone long enough, we can possibly triangulate the signal..."

"We did this already!" Bailey interrupted. "Four fucking

days of people in this house waiting for the phone to ring! I finally convinced them to leave yesterday. There's a limit, you know? A limit to what a person is supposed to be able to deal with!"

Jane noticed that Carol was nervously biting her lower lip. "Mrs. Van Gorden…"

"Call me Carol," she said weakly.

"Carol," Jane continued, "would you show me Jake's room?"

Carol looked to her husband for help.

"Bo already checked his room," Bailey said with an edge.

"I'm sure he did. But like you said, Mr. Van Gorden, Bo couldn't find enough to nail Hitler's ass." She leaned a little closer to Bailey. "I'm not Bo. I can see a lot of things in a room that others never see." Jane wanted to add that she could look behind a person's eyes and hear things, especially since she quit smoking. But judging from the way the guy was squirming, she figured she'd said enough.

"Fine," Bailey said, his gaze turned from Jane. "Whatever." He turned to his wife, seemingly sending her an unspoken message.

Carol tentatively led Jane out of the living room and into the spacious entryway that led to the dual staircases. Jane followed Carol up the closest staircase observing the woman's movement. It was as though she was trying to hold her skin as close to her body as humanly possible. She gave the word *retraction* a whole new definition. It was almost as if Carol was desperately trying to think as quickly as possible, but she didn't have the equipment installed to make that happen. They walked in stony silence up the stairs. Stopping on the landing, Jane couldn't miss another marble table with yet another arrangement of large ivory pillars that had never been lit.

Jane couldn't hold back. "You like candles, huh?"

Carol turned back to Jane, her countenance still detached. "Excuse me?"

Jane motioned to the arrangement on the table. "You

know, if you lit all of them in this house, you'd probably be able to navigate around here in the dark."

Carol actually contemplated Jane's somewhat sarcastic comment. "Well, yes, but then they would be..." She struggled to find the right word.

"Imperfect?" Jane suggested.

A tiny light seemed to flicker briefly in Carol's head. "Yes... exactly!"

Jane looked around the pristine area. "That would screw up the veneer, wouldn't it?" She locked eyes with Carol. There was a split second where Carol looked like she was going to emerge from her self-imposed trance but it was quickly squashed.

"Jake's bedroom is this way," Carol said, turning around.

"What's that room down there?" Jane pointed to the closed room with the arched doorway just off the entry.

Carol turned. She hesitated. "Bailey's office." She quickly turned back. "This way." Carol led Jane down a wide, sconce-lined hallway interrupted by several rooms.

Jane noted a guest room with a neatly made king bed, another guest room with an untouched king bed and finally a third guest room with a turned down twin bed. Jane stopped and took in that room. *Finally*, a room that had a somewhat lived in feel to it. Carol continued walking down the hall, not noticing Jane's observation. "Is this the maid's room?"

Carol turned and took in a quick breath. She quickly walked to the room and closed the door. "That's a mess!"

"Maid?" Jane asked again.

"We have a maid but she's not a live-in." She put her hand on Jane's shoulder and directed her down the hall. "Jake's room is this way."

Jane followed Carol but factored that subterfuge wasn't the woman's forte. If the maid didn't live in there and the Van Gorden's didn't have a houseguest, Jane figured it had to be in use by either Bailey or Carol. From the faint scent of perfume that Jane noted when she stuck her head in the room, she figured that Bailey wasn't the occupant.

The hallway ended at a T with the middle of the intersection appearing to be the master bedroom suite with the over-the-top closed manor house doors. Carol motioned Jane around the corner and down a shorter hallway where the lighting dimmed and dead-ended at a closed grey door. A stolen street sign hung on the door that read: *No Trespassing*. Carol opened the door and took a step over the threshold.

Jane's first impression reminded her of the scene in *The Wizard of Oz* when the black-and-white film turned to brilliant color. It wasn't that the room that lay in front of Jane was dramatic or engaged the senses in all colors of the spectrum. Rather, it was the distinct, possibly deliberate, visual shock that separated this three-hundred-square-foot room from the rest of the ostentatious interior design. Finally, Jane felt as if she were standing in a room in which a human being with real feelings and fears and dreams resided. While the rest of the house smacked of a façade, this room was imbued with honesty.

It was in these moments that Jane always thrived. When the dead bodies were removed from a crime scene, she'd step into the location and allow the vibrations from the walls, the furniture and even the knickknacks to resonate around her. Each sung their own song. All the angst, terror, tears and unspoken words vied for Jane's attention. For her, it was akin to a psychic symphony where the notes were actually feelings and when strung together, played a story of whatever transpired in that space. Sometimes, Jane would close her eyes and feel the slain victims around her, desperately shouting their pain into the ether.

But at *this* moment, there wasn't a dead body—not yet, at least. Standing in Jake Van Gorden's bedroom, Jane inhaled his spirit.

"I'm not allowed in here," Carol meekly offered. "Nobody is…except maybe…Mollie."

Jane recalled the drawings of Mollie in Jake's notebook that

Bo showed them in his office. "Right. Daughter of the Methodist preacher. They broke up two weeks ago. Jake took it hard,"
Jane rattled off, essentially repeating what Bo told her.

Carol's face fell. "They broke up? I didn't know! He didn't
say a word."

It was truly amazing how a buffoon of a police chief like Bo
Lowry could know this information and the kid's own mother
was blindsided. But Jane had a feeling that there were lots of
things that Carol didn't know about her only child. Jane needed
to be alone in the room. "Do you mind if I..." Jane let her inten-
tions hang.

"Oh...sure...uh...I'll be downstairs if you need anything." Carol retreated down the darkened hallway.

There were some advantages, Jane decided, to working
with a woman who was hobbled and acquiesced too much. She
closed the door and took in the room visually.

Three vertical windows stood across from her on the wall
that overlooked the stand of aspen trees and the edge of the
next estate on the cul-de-sac. In the far left corner, a single glass
door led out to a five-foot-square redwood deck. Jake's desk sat
against the right side wall with a closet wedged in the corner.
His single bed with the navy blue comforter was to her left and
situated so that when he sat up in bed, he faced the bank of windows. The walls, painted soft blue, were plastered with posters.
Posters of sleek black Lamborghinis, eye-popping red Porsches,
high-altitude extreme skiing and a snowboarding Shaun White
plastered the walls. But there were two posters that stood out
from all of those. One was above his computer. It was all white
with one word written vertically in fat, black lettering. The word
was: TRUTH. The other poster that stood out was taped above
Jake's bed. It was a photograph of a buxom model in a yellow
bikini blowing a kiss with her highly red-glossed lips.

Jane meandered to Jake's closet and opened it. On the inside of the door, four brass hooks held four different fedoras.
She removed one of the hats and looked at the label. It was from

a vintage clothing store. Studying the hat, Jane remembered seeing personalities such as Frank Sinatra, Joey Bishop and other
notables from the 1960s wearing the same hat. But she'd also
seen resurgence in the hat's popularity with actors such as Brad
Pitt, Colin Farrell and Johnny Depp.

She sifted through Jake's closet. Several shirts reminded
her of what guys who lived in Palm Beach wore in the mid-
60s. These must have been the "vintage" shirts Carol referred to
earlier. Mixed in with those dated styles, Jane found the obligatory "Fuck you" T-shirt Bailey had mentioned downstairs. They
were all black with one stating: *You're One FUCK YOU Away
From My Fist!* Jane hung one of the 1960s Palm Beach shirts
next to the "Fuck You" T-shirt, facing her. She took a step back
and stared at them. They couldn't be more contrary to the un-
knowing eye. But to Jane, they both had statements written
across them. The "Fuck You" was obvious. Jake was small and
undeveloped for his age so he was probably overly sensitive
about that fact. Wearing a ballsy, in your face T-shirt possibly
made him feel a little more powerful. Nothing says "I'm building a wall so you don't hurt me" like wearing a T-shirt that bla-
tantly tells the world to "Fuck off." But the dated offering from
the mid-60s also screamed a statement as well. Yet, no matter
how Jane strained to hear the declaration, the message became
suffocated before she could interpret it.

After replacing the clothes and closing the closet door, she
scanned Jake's desk. A stack of schoolbooks sat to one side of his
computer—behind that, two framed photos of Jake and Mollie.
In one photo, Jake was wearing a fedora and one of the Palm
Beach-style shirts. He was facing Mollie, a cherubic brunette
with piercing eyes, and holding her close to his body. In the
other photo, Jake was dressed in one of his "Fuck You's" with
his arm around Mollie's shoulder and sticking his tongue out
toward the camera.

Jane glanced between the photos, focused only on Jake.
This is when the victim often started telling their story to Jane.

This is when the unspoken became revealed. "You like to rock the boat, don't you Jake?" The words fell from her mouth without formulating them first in her head. Her eyes traveled to the poster with the word: *TRUTH*. Why not *FUCK YOU*? After all, that was the statement he wore on his chest for the world to see. Of all the posters with single words, why *TRUTH*? What resonated in that word for Jake Van Gorden? In a town known, off the record, as a place where you go to hide your dark secrets, wasn't *truth* a dangerous proposition? Were people who chose to plaster that word on their bedroom wall at risk?

She spotted a spiral notebook under the stack of schoolbooks and pulled it out. Inside were pages of notes he'd taken in various classes, with precise doodles edging most of the pages. There was a spate of blank pages followed by one page that held a collection of website addresses. From what Jane could deduce from a few of the names, Jake was checking out a few soft porn sites. Unless, of course, the *pussy* reference had to do with cats and the *big boobs* site had to do with idiots. It was typical fare for the horny mind of a fifteen-year-old boy. But one website address was separate from the others and didn't seem to involve tits or vaginas. It was *mysecretrevelations.com* and it had a bold red checkmark next to it. Jane made a mental note of the website, tucked the notebook back under the school books and was about to turn when she spied a small notepad wedged in between one of the books. She slid the notepad from the book and found an elegant linen pad that had *From the Desk of Bailey Van Gorden* etched in gold at the top of each page. *What in the hell was he doing with his dad's pretentious notepad?* she wondered. The pages were blank, but Jane saw a distinct pen impression on the top page that had been left from whatever was written on the page before it. Jane found a soft pencil and lightly ran the lead over the impression. The only notation she could make out was *01 Imper.* Jane tore off the top page, folded it and put it in her pocket before replacing the pad where she found it.

Jane turned and faced the bed. "Where'd you go Jake Van

Gorden?" she asked out loud, as if the walls were ready to spill their secrets. "What did you do before you left this room with that rope?" Jane felt into the moment. "Did you sit at your desk, or did you lie on your bed and think about what you were planning to do?" She waited for the answer and was drawn to his bed. Jane lay down and stared up at the ceiling. The model in the poster wearing the yellow bikini and propping up the fake tits stared back at her. Jane smiled when she understood the precise placement of the poster above her. The girl's face was exactly over Jane's head, giving the impression that the sex hungry goddess was on top of her. It was slightly unusual to *feel* her way into a fifteen-year-old boy's sexually excited body, but she gave it a shot. Her right hand drifted across the blue comforter, skimmed the side of the mattress and reached under the bed. There, waiting for her in the exact spot Jake left it, was a well-enjoyed, erotic magazine full of nude women with shiny asses propped in the air and enough saline implants to make them bleed seawater. Some of the pages were stuck together—just another sign that Jake benefited from his time perusing the arousing pictorials.

Jane swung her head over the mattress and lifted the comforter to see what else was underneath Jake's bed. Amazingly, there was only one other item. Jane slid the magazine back underneath and removed an 8 x 10 inch artist's spiral-bound sketchpad. Sitting up, she read the front. *The Truth Shall Set You Free* was handwritten in a diagonal sweep. She opened the pad and found a disturbing black-and-white pencil drawing. It depicted what appeared to be portly man, possibly in his late forties, locked in a room with a steel door and small barred window. The tiny window cast an ominous shadow of light onto the man who was hanging by his neck above an overturned chair. What made the drawing even more disturbing was that the man was wearing an exact replica of the 1960s Palm Beach shirt found in Jake's closet along with a plaid fedora on his head.

Jane turned the page and found a drawing almost exactly

like the one before. Turning the next page, the drawing, again, was slightly similar, except the juxtaposition of the man's body was just a hair off. Jane turned to the last page of the fifty-page sketchpad and found a drawing of the same scene. But *this* drawing showed the man alive and posed with one leg on the seat of the chair as if he was about to climb up on it. The page prior to that showed the same scene but the man was farther along in his movement up on the chair. Jane suddenly realized what this was and, starting with the last page, she slowly flipped the pages, creating a deftly drawn animation of a man in a room with bars standing up on a chair, placing a belt around his neck, kicking the chair aside and hanging himself.

Jane flipped through the pages again and again, replaying the disturbing charcoal-penciled suicide scene. The man's face lacked clarity. That is, except for his jutting jaw—a jaw that reminded Jane of Jake's father. At that realization, an electrical shock shot down Jane's spine. She suddenly felt sick and needed air. Securing the sketchpad under her leather jacket, she crossed to the door that led out on the deck and walked outside. The wave of nausea quickly passed. She was about to go back inside when a gust of wind blew the door shut. She tried it and realized it was either stuck or locked. "Shit," she muttered, factoring her next move. She could wait until Carol came up to retrieve her or…with that, Jane glanced to a long black tube that was screwed down to the floor of the deck. A bright, highly reflective, neon-yellow, three-inch tip peeked out from the outside of the tube that faced the edge of the deck. Jane leaned down and gently pulled the yellow tip away and kept pulling and pulling and pulling until she withdrew a heavy-duty rope that easily retracted back into the tube. Lifting the rope up she immediately saw a clear rope indentation burned into the redwood beam that formed the railing. Jane's first fleeting thought was that Jake had fashioned an odd retractable mode of hanging himself. But then, that notion gave way to a more practical use for the invention: a secret mode of escape. Perhaps the kid did it out of necessity after getting locked out late at night and needing a creative way to free himself from the predicament. Or maybe, it was just his way of fashioning a way out of the house without having to journey through the house. Jane leaned over the railing and realized that instead of it being a risky freefall, the aspen tree that grew against the deck served as a kind of stepping stone to the ground with its graduated sturdy branches that safely led to the dirt thirty feet below.

Withdrawing the rope, Jane gingerly rotated her body over the railing and quickly secured the heel of her cowboy boot in the inside cut of a large aspen branch. She continued her careful rappel until she reached a point where she could easily jump to the ground. Before retracting the rope, she wondered how the wily fifteen-year-old retained it on the ground for later use to covertly climb back up to his room. She found the answer in a well-worn scar against the aspen trunk where he had obviously tied off the rope, keeping the neon yellow reflective end detectable. The high visibility yellow told Jane that Jake's sojourns down the rope were most likely at night. She pulled slightly on the rope and then released it, allowing it to slither back into its secret tube.

She secured the sketchpad under her jacket and made her way down the soft dirt path through the wooded area around the house, ending up on the Van Gordens' driveway. To her right, was the ridiculously oversized garage with the doors open. Jane wandered into the first bay where a spotless taupe Lexus sedan was parked. She peered into the vehicle, noting a pair of women's sunglasses and a pink wool scarf. Checking the door, she found it locked. Jane looked across the garage into the other two bays. One held a sporty silver coupe and the other a top-of-the-line coal black Land Cruiser. Nothing like getting ten miles to the gallon and draining your tank as you haul the bucket of steel and leather up and down the mountain passes. Jane noticed how clean the sporty coupe was but the Land Cruiser had what appeared to be freshly caked mud in the tires. She touched the back tire and tried to discern if the mud was wet but the outside temperature made the determination difficult. She checked the driver's side door and found it unlocked. Taking a quick glance around toward the front door of the house and seeing nobody, she opened the car door and sat in the driver's seat. On the dashboard sat a red vinyl pass that read, *Elite Athletic Club Membership* to the local gym. Bailey's name was embossed in gold lettering in the middle. The guy did like his gold lettering. A trio of CDs were scattered on the passenger seat. *Queen's Greatest Hits, Opera's Greatest Moments* and a two-CD compilation of *Elton John's Greatest Hits*. It seemed that Bailey didn't want to suffer through any tune that wasn't certified platinum. Jane's highly acute senses came alive. A rank odor filtered through the interior of the SUV. It smelled sort of like a gymnasium, but…no…that wasn't it. It was sweet mixed with sour and pervasive with the windows rolled up. Odd, she factored, for a car that hadn't been driven in six days, according to Bailey. Jane thought she heard voices approaching and looked in the rearview mirror. But the mirror was flipped to accommodate nighttime driving. "Huh," Jane muttered to herself. The sound of voices became louder. Jane quietly exited the vehicle and closed the door. She was able to walk well past the garage and into the driveway by the time Weyler and the Van Gordens met her.

"We didn't hear you walk out," Carol said, her face looking typically cautious.

Jane saw the same look on both Weyler and Bailey.

"What happened to you?" Bailey asked, jutting his jaw toward Jane's clothes.

She looked down. The white powdery bark from the aspen tree was heavily caked across her jeans, jacket and shirt. Jane thought quickly. "There was a strong gust of wind. I must have been in its path."

Weyler snuck a glance back toward the Van Gordens' house.

Bailey looked at Jane as if she were one taco short of a combo platter. "I'm assuming you found nothing of interest in Jake's
room?"

"No. Nothing." She couldn't resist. "That poster is something, though."

Carol took an embarrassed breath in and put her hand to
her mouth. "Oh, that woman in the yellow bikini..."

"No, not that one. The one by his computer? The one that
just says, *TRUTH*." Jane let the word linger in the high mountain air. She watched as Bailey's jaw clenched and Carol got that
familiar frozen look in her eye. "What's the story on that?" Jane
tried to sound offhand but it came out more probing.

Bailey let out a tense "Heh!" and narrowed his eyes into the
distance. "Jake always likes to push the envelope."

Jane secured her gaze on Bailey. "Push the envelope? Interesting comment."

Bailey's eyes traveled back to Jane. They bled fire. "I do
have to go."

Jane and Weyler walked in silence down the long driveway
back to their respective cars. She didn't speak up until Weyler
unlocked his borrowed patrol car.

"Loved Carol. Usually you have to join the Taliban to see a
woman that subservient to her husband."

"You can fill me in on what you found in Jake's bedroom
when we get to the B&B." He took another look at Jane's disheveled appearance. "You're lucky you didn't fall out of that aspen
tree." He got into the car. "Follow me."

Jane liked the fact that Weyler read through her deceptions—both her impromptu exit as well as the lie regarding Jake's
room. But she hoped he wasn't reading her mind at that exact
moment because she had one stop to make before the B&B. Instead of following Weyler, she lagged a few minutes behind on a
hidden side street until Bailey zoomed by. Then she waited a few
more minutes to give him time. After that, Jane headed toward

Main Street and passed the only gym in Midas. As she fully expected, Bailey's SUV wasn't parked anywhere near the place.

CHAPTER 9

By the time Jane pulled up to the Victorian-inspired, Historic Midas B&B on the main drag, Weyler was already outside the front gate chatting up their hosts. "Shit," she muttered under her breath. There was too much to go over and talk about. The last thing she wanted to do was waste time with the B&B owners chewing the fat. She observed the man, presumably the town's Methodist preacher and Mollie's father. He was a gentle-looking man, around his mid-forties, about thirty pounds overweight with dark curly hair and a well-kept beard and mustache. The woman, around forty, didn't have that *wife of the Christian preacher* vibe. She was less uptight than Jane expected as she leaned her angular body against the wrought-iron fence and let her curly dark locks blow free in the breeze. Her olive complexion was beautifully set off by a jaunty red wool hat, along with an East Indian-inspired top and wide-legged trousers. *Perhaps,* Jane mused, *they head up a more liberal church.*

Just as Jane was bringing the luggage out of the Mustang, she caught sight of the same clean-cut, older guy with the twinkling eyes she'd seen earlier outside the Town Hall during the improvised news conference. He was across the street getting out of the same truck and heading up Main Street. She grabbed her leather satchel and leaned her small duffel bag against the tire, watching the man momentarily. He glanced between the B&B and Jane. *Great,* she thought. Now her little groupie knew where she was staying.

"Jane!" Weyler called over. "I'll get the bags." He waved her over. "This is Aaron and Sara Green," he introduced.

Jane shook their hands and offered a quick hello, excusing her disheveled appearance.

"We were just asking Sergeant Weyler if you guys coming to Midas was a positive sign that there's movement on the case?" Sara pointedly asked.

Obviously, Weyler hadn't let the Greens in on the fact that they were only there because Weyler "owed" their odd police chief some damn favor. She opted for the vague answer cops were well trained in delivering. "We're still sorting out a lot of the details."

Sara offered a weak smile, but it was sharply edged with concern. She fiddled nervously with the gold cross dangling from her necklace. "I know you can't tell us anything. I was hoping if you could just let us know if Jake was alive?" Aaron put a comforting hand on his wife's shoulder.

"We don't know," Jane answered with less of the cop front.

Sara's eyes swelled with tears. "We're all aware of the odds. After five days…"

Aaron pulled Sara closer to him. She tucked her head on his shoulder. "We gotta keep the faith, sweetheart."

Jane observed the two of them. There was true love here, but there was also an overt laidback vibe that most ministers and their wives eschewed. The energy between them flowed beautifully and effortlessly. Their shared, heartbreaking worry for Jake's welfare was honest and sincere—a far cry from the constrained, preoccupied reaction his own parents demonstrated.

Sara wiped away a tear. "I have to figure out how to process this with our daughter."

Process? Jane wondered. That wasn't a word that Christian minister's wives bandied around. Shouldn't she talk about *praying with her*, or *asking God for guidance*? "Does she have any ideas about what happened?" Jane asked, falling back into the detective role.

"Hard to say," Aaron chimed in. "She hasn't said a word. We let her take off this last week from school and next week is

Easter break so she'll have two weeks under her belt. We hoped it would give her the time she needed to deal with everything..."

Jane was floored. "So, nobody's talked to her about this? Not you, not Bo?"

"No," Sara offered. "She needs time to decompress from everything. First the breakup and now this..."

Jane couldn't hold back. "But what if the breakup played a role in Jake..." Aaron's eyes immediately reacted to the word "breakup."

Weyler interrupted. "I think we can get a bead on all of that shortly." He turned to Jane. "You sign us in and I'll get the bags."

Jane hated it when Weyler short-circuited her advancing interview techniques. He always did it when she was getting too aggressive or when the interviewee was getting uncomfortable. It was the standard *good cop/bad cop* routine except this was more *suave cop/bitchy cop*. He captured his flies with honey, while Jane preferred to just slaughter the damn things.

Jane reluctantly followed Sara down the cobblestone pathway, its edges still covered with encrusted snow. Sara did her best to make conversation, telling Jane that she hoped the daffodils popped while she was there and what a quiet town Midas usually was...until recently. The entryway of the bed and breakfast was fittingly done up in keeping with the historic name of the place. Dozens of sepia-toned photos lined the walls, the entry, sitting area and along the wall that led upstairs. Sara suddenly felt a need to play tour guide and told Jane that the B&B used to be a boarding house for young women up until the early 1970s before transforming into an historic hotel. Jane listened with half an ear as she glanced around searching for the source of the familiar aroma that had been following her since the night before.

"Do you have gardenias in the house?" Jane inquired.

"Gardenias? No. I've got some bread in the oven..."

"A potpourri maybe?" Jane forced the issue, almost desperate.

"We steer clear of the usual Victorian *foo-foo* crap. No doilies. No dead roses in saucers."

"That's crazy," Jane whispered to herself.

"What's that?"

Jane thought she'd take a stab in the dark. "You *seriously* don't smell gardenias?"

Sara sniffed the air. "No...just the bread in the oven."

Jane shook her head. "Jesus Christ," she muttered and then realized she was talking to the minister's wife. "Oh, fuck, sorry about that." Jane winced, realizing that her apology was probably worse. Strange thing was, instead of Sara looking aghast or shooting Jane a pursed-lipped show of Christian judgment, Jane could have sworn she saw a little smile creep up before Sara extinguished it.

A downstairs door opened and closed, and out walked Mollie. With iPod in hand and earbuds firmly in place, she effectively locked out the world around her. She looked just like the photo Jane saw in Jake's room, but her eyes were even more beautiful and probing. She was dressed in black jeans, a dark blue T-shirt with a Flower of Life design on the front and a trendy *hoodie* jacket. Her stubby fingernails were painted in black nail polish that had been chewed off around the tips. When Mollie caught sight of Jane, she stopped in her tracks, taking in Jane's dusty and mud-splattered appearance. Mollie released one earbud as if to say that Jane was only worth half of her time.

"Sweetie," Sara said lovingly, "this is Sergeant Detective Jane Perry from Denver. She's here to help find Jake."

Mollie regarded Jane with thick disparagement that reminded Jane of Bob Dylan's advice from the 1960s to not "trust anybody over thirty." The kid took a moment before offering her hand to Jane.

Jane shook Mollie's hand and immediately noticed a thin, woven red string bracelet around her wrist. "Hey," Jane said, trying to not come off too cop-like.

"Hey," Mollie repeated, but her tone was much more sarcastic. It was as if she knew Jane was trying to make her feel comfortable and she was having none of it.

"You goin' for a walk, Mol'?" Sara asked.

Mollie quickly showed ire, removing her remaining earbud. "*Mom!*"

Sara bit her lip. "I'm sorry. *Liora.*"

Jane stood confused.

"I'll be back in an hour." Mollie slid between Jane and her mother toward the front door.

"You have your cell phone, right?" Sara asked, her voice laced with fear.

"Yes, Mom," Mollie tiredly said, replacing her earbuds. "I'll be fine."

Sara watched her daughter leave the house, her face etched with concern. "Until this thing with Jake gets solved," Sara said, still watching Mollie walk down the pathway and onto the sidewalk, "I can't help but worry, you know? What if there's some crazy serial…"

"It's not a serial kidnapper. You don't have to worry about that." Jane's first thought was that for a devout woman, Sara Green was certainly not tasting her faith at the moment. The second thought was, *Liora?* She had to ask.

Sara seemed distressed. "Mollie decided to change her name to Liora about six months ago. It's part of her conversion to becoming a Kabbalist."

Oy vey, Jane said to herself. The red string around the kid's wrist—she was dabbling in the fashionable faith of the rich and famous. Mystic Judaism. Looked like Mollie decided to stick the Almighty cross in her parents' back and twist it. "Why'd she choose Liora?"

Sara shook her head, one eyebrow arched. "It's just so weird…" She seemed lost for a moment.

"Weird?"

"Oh, uh, I shouldn't say *weird*. It's just an…interesting

name to pick out of the blue." Sara let out a hard breath. "It means *my light* and *I see*."

"You checked that out online, huh?"

"No." Sara quickly caught herself. "Well, *yeah*. Yeah. I checked it out. I wouldn't know that offhand."

The woman was becoming increasingly nervous in front of Jane's eyes. It reminded Jane of the same vibe that oozed off guilty suspects across the table in the interrogation room. Her daughter's decision to become a mystic Jew and change her name was having a nerve-wracking effect on Sara.

Jane was at a loss. "I guess it could have been worse. She could have called herself *Delilah*. Explain that name at Sunday service, right?"

Sara managed a smile. "Tell me about it!" she uttered with a wave of her hand. "I'll let you go. I'm sure you want to change."

Jane took a gander at her scruffy appearance and realized that Sara was essentially telling her to put on another shirt and pair of jeans. It was almost like this Christian woman had turned into the Jewish mother who insists she doesn't want to get involved while she's busy getting involved.

After signing the registration and finding out that she and Weyler were the sole guests—thanks to the *off* season timeframe—Jane climbed the paisley-carpeted stairs that led to a crisp white hallway. Lined with more historic photos from Midas and northern Colorado, the hallway led past two cheerful doors, each with a brass plaque and engraved flowery name instead of a number. One was *The Rose Room* and the other, *The Lilac Room*. Sara had told Jane that her room was at the end of the hallway. She had to pause momentarily when she saw the name on the brass plaque. It was *The Gardenia Room.*

Jane crossed the threshold and found a sizeable space in which to spread out. The Gardenia Room featured a generous king-size bed with a gauzy canopy, an ornate writing desk, two overstuffed chairs, a wooden rocker by the window, a dark wooden table and matching dresser along with two sizeable windows that allowed plenty of light into the dreamy setting. The bathroom had a black-and-white tiled floor, a clawfoot bathtub and Victorian-styled sink. A platter of pillar candles sat on a wicker table. Unlike the showy ones at the Van Gorden's monolithic house, these candles had actually seen some activity. As Jane scanned the bathroom and then the main area, she realized this was most likely the *honeymoon suite*. She could almost hear the pillow talk and wet kisses on the conjugal bed and see the longing gazes between past lovers who had occupied the room. The thought crossed her mind that the only action this place was going to see with Jane Perry was late nights spent connecting the distorted dots of a confusing case.

Weyler knocked and Jane opened the door. He carried her duffel bag into the room. "You travel light, Jane."

"I figured three days max."

"And you packed accordingly?" He deposited her small bag on a nearby chair. "We're going to be here longer than three days."

Jane let out a sullen breath. "Yeah, I know that now." Weyler handed her a paper bag with a sandwich inside. It was courtesy of Sara who was apparently concerned that Jane "looked hungry." "You bring copies of the kidnapper's clues?"

Weyler unzipped his briefcase. "No. I brought the originals." He handed Jane the stack of clues, all sealed in their plastic evidence bags. "Vi typed transcriptions of the phone calls."

Jane took them from Weyler. "What'd you have to tell Bo to get the originals?"

"Promise him we'll solve the kidnapping."

Jane carefully laid down the stack on the bureau. "Boss, this whole case has a sick stench. It's got…" Jane tried to wrap her mind around what her gut was feeling.

"Contradictions," Weyler stated.

"Exactly!" This is what Jane liked about Weyler. He was more than a sounding board; he was like having an analytical twin that used careful logic and reasoning to solve crimes. "It's JDLR," Jane stated, realizing she sounded like his good buddy, Bo.

"'Just Doesn't Look Right,'" he said with a smile. "It sure doesn't."

She unbuttoned her leather jacket and brought out the sketchpad she stole from Jake's room. "Check this out!" With that, she flipped the pages to create the disturbing animation of the man hanging himself in a jail cell. Weyler was stunned that she jobbed the pad, but Jane assured him that his parents would never miss it. "Carol's not allowed in his room," she revealed. "And his ol' man? I doubt he's been able to pull himself away from a mirror long enough to remember he's got a missing son." Jane set the pad on the table. "When you go to the gym, do you wear your finest Colorado wannabe duds and pour half a tube of gel in your hair?"

"I don't go to the gym and I don't own a tube of gel," Weyler stated dryly. "But I get your point."

"And that dangling comment he made a couple times? *Little shit?* I don't think he was talking about Jordan. I think he was talking about Jake."

"Let's not jump too fast here, Jane. There are a lot of random emotions going on right now. We can't assume that every one of them creates another dot that we can connect."

Like the fact that Bailey's SUV had an odd, sweet and sour stench to it, Jane thought. Or that she was certain Bailey lied when he said he hadn't been out of the house in six days and that the last time was to go to the gym. And that trip was during the day, according to his own words. Why then was his rearview mirror flipped for driving at night? And the coup de grâce? Bailey wasn't headed to the gym an hour ago. Why lie? Was it that he needed to get away and clear his head? If that was so, why dress up for the occasion? But Jane declined to mention any of these dots to Weyler. Right now, he was right. It was all premature assumptions. But that didn't mean Jane wasn't going to hold them like a grudge in her back pocket and bring them out when the time was ripe.

It took Jane under two minutes to unpack. She removed the cigarette pack that held the single smoke and set it on the table against the wall so it could stand up and be seen from various angles in the room. Sure, it was unnecessary and masochistic, but when you look at life through tortured eyes, it makes sense to create a tapestry where suffering is sewn into the fabric. She changed her clothes, secured her Glock under her leather jacket, gobbled down her sandwich and then decided to attack the first clue sent to the Van Gordens—Thomas Wolfe's, *You Can't Go Home Again.* Jane wanted to take a closer look at the sympathy card and envelope that had accompanied the book. Pulling the card from protective plastic evidence bag, Jane noted the strange *BAWY* scribbled on the envelope in shaky writing. Jane's first thought was that it looked like it was either a child's unsteady hand or done to make it *look* like a child's writing. She opened the saccharin-designed sympathy card and read the two short lines: *So sorry for your loss. JACKson sends his regards.* Jake went by his middle name so why was the kidnapper emphasizing the first four letters of his true first name? Could it be the kidnapper's name? If so, why draw attention to it?

The card had been secured in the book on the dog-eared page of 243. Jane carried the book to the sunny window and scanned the page. The chapter was titled, "A Moment of Decision." The narrative spoke about George Webber attending a social gathering and how uncomfortable it made him feel. Jane searched for anything on the page that could be construed as a clue. Obviously, the kidnapper dog-eared this page for a specific reason. But why? At the top of the page, the narrative read: *He had used the phrases as symbols of something real, something important that he had felt instinctively but had never put into words.* Certainly the bizarre clues were partly symbolic in nature. Jane read further in that paragraph: *There was something else—something impersonal, something much bigger than himself, something that mattered greatly to him and would not be denied.* The sentence seemed to ring loudly for Jane. *Something that mattered greatly to him and would not be denied.* As Jane continued reading, it seemed that every few lines she'd find something that *might* be important. But there were thirty-six lines of type on page 243. Which lines, if any, were noteworthy and could lead her to Jake Van Gorden?

There was an interesting line in the middle of the page that caught her eye. *He watched their faces closely and tried to penetrate behind the social masks they wore, probing, boring, searching as for some clue that might lead him to an answer to his riddle.* Jane set down the book. The term *social masks* reminded her of the disincarnated visage of Carol Van Gorden. What secrets hid so well behind Carol's well-worn mask? And what lurked behind the jutting jaw and perfectly coiffed mien of her husband?

As Jane turned back to the stack of clues, she realized that she needed to create a system in which she could absorb all the material in one fluid motion. She glanced outside and spotted the clothesline across the backyard of the B&B. Yes, this would work. Sneaking downstairs, she quietly exited the house and crept around to the backyard. Checking around to make sure nobody could see her, she untied one end of the clothesline, grabbed a good handful of clothespins and stealthily returned upstairs to her room. Jane secured the line on a window hook and pulled it just in front of the bank of windows in an attempt to create a taut line at eye level. However, she was shy about four feet from where she wanted to hook the other end. Looking down into the backyard again, she factored that another leg of the clothesline would be necessary. She trotted downstairs again, dodging any potential contact with the Greens, and returned to steal the second length of clothesline.

But just as she untied the line and started to twist it into a manageable clump, she smelled a smoky aroma that originated from the stand of trees and bushes that separated the B&B from the next property. Moving guardedly toward the area, the strong smoky odor got stronger. The trail ended with the sullen face of Mollie Green seated against a tree, iPod earbuds in place, smoking a peculiar hand-rolled cigarette.

CHAPTER 10

Mollie's probing dark eyes showed no sign of fear. In fact, the look was more of indignation as Jane approached her. She removed her earbuds. "So, you're a *ganef?*" she stated in a haughty tone. "A *thief!*"

Jane looked down at the clothesline. "I'm using this in the line of duty," she responded, stone-faced. "Like when a cop borrows a car to chase a criminal. Same thing."

Mollie regarded Jane with a curl of her lip. "You're a *meshuggeneh.*"

"*I'm* crazy?" Jane retorted, undaunted. "I'm not the one sitting in a clump of dirt, smoking fake weed and pretending to be a Jew."

"How'd you know it was fake?" Mollie stood up.

"What? The Jew part or the *doobie?*"

Mollie immediately took umbrage. "The Jew part is *not* fake!"

Jane took the bogus blunt out of Mollie's hand and sniffed it. "What is this?"

Mollie spied Jane's Glock under her jacket. "Catnip. If you drink the tea it's supposed to calm you down. Same thing with smoking it."

"Your parents know you smoke catnip?"

"I don't know," Mollie said with a sarcastic flip. "Do *your* parents know *you* smoke cigarettes?"

"I quit smoking."

"Really?" she retorted in a quick snap. "Your jacket reeks."

"I quit yesterday." It wasn't normal for Jane to be so forthcoming, especially with a bratty, self-involved teenager. But it was her attempt at baiting Mollie—make the kid trust her and maybe she'd glean information.

"Yesterday? *Oi!* You're gonna need something to calm your ass down. Here..." Mollie handed the withered-looking catnip joint to Jane.

For a split second, Jane actually entertained the idea. "No. I'll probably get hooked. Then I'd have to join C.A."

"Catnip Anonymous," Mollie chimed, without missing a beat.

"You've got a quick mind."

Mollie eyed Jane carefully, still not sure of her motives. "Jews have quick minds. That's why we run the entertainment business."

"Do you always hide your pain behind sarcasm?"

"Pain?" Mollie tried her best to remain stoic.

"Your black nail polish is half chewed off. You're smoking catnip to calm down. And your breathing is real shallow. I'd say you're freaking out about your boyfriend."

"We broke up. He wasn't my boyfriend when he disappeared."

"Kind of hostile, Mollie."

"*Liora!*"

"*Mollie.*" Jane wasn't going to play her game. "You just turn your love off like that?"

"He tried to kill himself. I have good reason for being *ferklempt!* Suicide is a serious sin."

"According to what? Kabballah?"

"The Jewish Law is clear. Suicide is forbidden. *Life* is what's important. *This* life!"

"I got news for you, kid. You got a red string around your

wrist. It doesn't make you a Jew. Don't act so fucking high and mighty and condemn others about suicide in the name of a religion you don't even own."

Mollie looked at Jane. "I hit a nerve with you. You know someone who committed suicide, don't you?"

The kid crossed the line. Screw the bonding. Jane took her gloves off. "Yeah, paint your hair purple and call it a *revolution*. Why don't you drop the wannabe rebel bullshit. You like to call yourself a Jew because you love to watch your preacher daddy cringe every time you toss out some Yiddish."

"Kabbalah is Jewish mysticism. It's a high order of thought and belief."

"Is that what the website said where you bought the red string for fifteen bucks plus shipping?" Jane asked, pointing to Mollie's bracelet.

"*Kish mir en toches!*" Mollie took a hard drag on her catnip joint.

"What the fuck does that mean?"

"Kiss my ass!"

"Wow, that's a *high-order* attitude."

Mollie moved closer to Jane. "And you're being a *nudje* because I got a little too close to the *truth* with you about suicide. *And* you're jonesin' for a cigarette."

Jane regarded the kid in a different light. "*Truth*, eh? You like to seek the *truth*?"

"You got it!"

"Did you buy Jake his *Truth* poster?"

Mollie pulled back. Jane could tell the kid was surprised that she'd been in Jake's bedroom. "No," she said softly. "That was all him."

Jane was starting to see a puzzle piece fit into place. "Ah, Jake was the one who inspired *you* to seek out the truth."

Mollie's face turned sad. Her eyes drifted to the dirt. "Yes."

Jane leaned down to be on eye level with her. "In a town where secrets rule?"

Mollie looked at Jane. "Yes." There was a steady burn to the kid's dark eyes.

"What's your secret, Mollie?"

There was a tense moment between them. "I don't know," she whispered.

Jane peered closer at Mollie's face. "Is it the eyebrow piercing you're hiding?" Mollie drew her hand to her left eye, brushing her finger against her eyebrow. "That would piss off your good Christian parents, right? Did you just wear the hoop when you were with Jake and take it out before you got back home?" Mollie suddenly looked very meek. "You know, I can't remember. Does the tattoo come before or after the eyebrow piercing?"

Mollie furrowed her brow. "What the fuck? How'd you...?"

"It's called being *predictable*."

The girl stood back. "It comes *before* the eyebrow piercing."

Jane stood up. "A rose on your ass?"

"That's where your *predictable* stops. No rose on my *toches*." Mollie unzipped her jeans and revealed a half-inch blue dragonfly tattoo just below her belly button. "We got them done together. Jake's got the same tat, but it's bigger and it's on his chest, right over his heart."

Jane remembered the hand drawing of a dragonfly on the bridge. "Did you sketch that dragonfly image on the bridge?"

Her eyes saddened. "Yes."

"*Illusions die hard.* That's what you wrote underneath." Jane realized the initials, *L.G.* stood for Liora Green. "What did you mean by that?"

"It was one of the last things Jake said to me before he left."

"You said Jake has the same tattoo over his heart. Why over his heart?"

She zipped up her jeans. "That's Jake."

"That's Jake?"

Mollie looked off to the side and let out a long breath of air. "It's hard to explain. Over the last year and a half, something shifted inside him. He wasn't satisfied to live on the surface. He wanted to dig deeper into his life. He wanted to seek the answers that would explain all the shit he was feeling inside but couldn't communicate." She looked at Jane. "That's why he was my *bubbee*. He was *real*, you know? I wanted to be part of that because I have questions too. I have thoughts that come from deep inside my cells and I can't explain any of them..."

"Like calling yourself Liora and the Jewish *shtick*?"

Mollie rolled her eyes. "It's not *shtick*! I swear to *Hashem*, its not." The kid almost sounded desperate. "Jake understood," she said softly. "He just couldn't..."

"Couldn't what?"

"Couldn't be there for me. He had too many *tsuris*. His head was trying to sort through too much chaos. He went through bouts of depression."

"Is that why he liked to dress all in black?"

"Yeah. He said he was in mourning."

"For who?"

"He didn't know. He just knew he was in mourning." Jane was perplexed by that statement but let it go. "He wanted answers. But the more he sought out the truth, the more the nightmares surrounded him."

"What truth?"

"He tried to explain it to me, but he said I wouldn't understand. He said it was complicated. I told him I was no *shlub*... that I could grasp a lot of concepts. But he wouldn't bite."

Jane's head was spinning. A cigarette would have tasted damn good at this moment. It would slow down the whirring sound she kept hearing—the sound of too many ideas banging into each other. She grabbed the first one that flew to the surface. "The dragonfly tattoo? What does that signify?"

"The way Jake told me, dragonflies remind you that you can be the light in the darkness. But before you can do that, you have to bust through the illusions that surround you. Then, and only then, can you let your *true* light shine and know who you really are."

Jane was dumbfounded. *Little Juice Box* Jake sounded like
an esoteric philosopher. But the kid must have busted through
one illusion too many for him to end up on the bridge with
a rope around his neck. *Illusions die hard* suddenly took on a
whole new meaning. "Light in the darkness," Jane said aloud.
"Your mom told me Liora means *my light* and *I see*. Is that why
you chose the name?"

"No. The name just came to me before I got the tat. I swear
I didn't know that's what it meant." Mollie thought for a second.
"It's creepy, huh?" She shook her head. "I never liked the name
Mollie, but *Liora*…it felt right…like I was finally home."

As if oddly on cue, Sara called out to the girl. "Liora!"

"I gotta go back inside," Mollie muttered, extinguishing
the catnip doobie in the dirt. "She's had such *shpilkes* since Jake
went missing."

"Hey," Jane lightly touched Mollie's arm. "There was a retractable rope outside on Jake's deck."

"Yeah. So?"

"When he ditched his folks and went down the rope, was
he coming to see you?"

"Maybe." She started to move but Jane held her back.

"What does that mean?"

"Jake liked to wander around at night. Sometimes he'd
sneak over here and sometimes he wouldn't. He liked the nighttime because he said he could hear his thoughts better. That's
why he worked the late shift at The Rabbit Hole. It's a sports bar
down the street. You wanna learn more about Jake, go talk to his
boss, Hank Ross."

After securing the clothesline upstairs in her room, Jane
grabbed her leather satchel, sans laptop, told Weyler she was
going to check out the town and left the B&B. It was coming
up on 3:30 pm when she rolled to a halt in front of The Rabbit
Hole sports bar on Main Street. A large handwritten sign in the
front window announced that the place would re-open at 5:00

pm. Jane contemplated returning to the B&B, but her anxious foot tapped the accelerator and continued down Main Street. She meandered up and down the side streets trying to soak in the heartbeat of Midas. But watching the people move about on the street was like observing a carefully choreographed ballet of faces that projected a vacant front that belied the stark reality of what was too dangerous to reveal. This town where secrets collided—where all things hidden came to be buried—was going to be a tough nut to crack. She could almost feel the ghosts roaming the streets, hoping to remain as obscured as the ones who had a pulse.

Jane dropped back down onto Main Street as the sky darkened, filtering the weak sunlight through a bank of black clouds. The weather shift made the shadows on the pavement even more ominous. Jane turned at the end of the main drag and headed toward the bridge. It was beginning to feel like a portentous location to her. Bo may have said that it was an old, unused bridge but Jane knew differently. She was almost certain that Jake spent a great deal of time there, perhaps making it his nighttime destination after he got off work. Maybe it took a certain amount of sensitivity, but it seemed patently obvious to Jane that that little slice of real estate held a wealth of emotions and possibly a lot of secrets.

Driving closer to the bridge, the smell of smoke seeped into the Mustang. Jane rolled down her window and sourced the aroma coming from outside. She passed the bridge and kept driving slowly, paralleling Jordan Copeland's ten-acre expanse of property on the left that sat on the other side of the rushing river. Brackets of bushes and evergreens made it difficult to see the area clearly but after about three hundred feet, Jane could easily see a coal black cylinder of smoke lifting into the darkening sky. She turned the Mustang around and headed back to the bridge, parking her car in front of the rickety structure. Getting out of the car, she pulled her leather jacket tighter across her chest, steeling herself against the growing cold that swept around the bridge. On the other side of the bridge, Jane found a rough pathway in the shade, still covered with pads of snow. She followed the path down a gentle slope where a thicket of evergreens and leafless gambel oaks crowded around her. The smell of smoke grew as she moved closer to a barbed wire fence that laced around Jordan's property. Above her, the clouds joined together, stealing the sun and leaving a swath of gray and ashen gloom across the ground. What in the hell was Jordan burning? The smell was acrid and sickly sweet, like when hair singes. The fact that Jane knew what a dead body smelled like when it burned only intensified her resolve into finding out what he was doing. Yes, this was not aboveboard or a by-the-book endeavor and she knew that if Weyler was with her, there's no way he'd authorize it. But Jane reasoned that Weyler told her he brought her along because she "thought outside the box." Her murky plan certainly fit that criterion.

Jane found a large rock and laid it on the bottom rung of the barbed wire, providing a somewhat larger opening for her to crawl through. She'd almost made it under the fence safely when her brown hair hooked on a barb in the line above her head. It was just enough to throw her off balance and send her forward into the damp dirt. "Fuck!" she exclaimed, as the butt of the Glock bit into her ribs. Peeling her body off the ground, she brushed the palms of her hands against her jeans and canvassed the area. She took about ten steps and nearly tripped on a metal rod that poked six inches out of the dirt. It was painted bright red and seemed to have no reason for being there.

The plume of smoke blew toward her, laying a soft cloudy pillow across the dead leaves. Her cowboy boots sucked into the wet earth as Jane crisscrossed the terrain, holding back now and again behind a spruce trunk to make sure she was hidden from Jordan's view. The smoke seemed to seek her out in the woods, winding its hazy fingers around her muddy boots and exploring every crevice of her body. Jane heard a distinct crackle close by. She ducked behind a tree and carefully surveyed the landscape in front of her. Beyond the coppice, there was a small clearing with a four-foot-wide circular stone fire pit. The fire roared, sending amber tentacles into the air and created an optical illusion of waves in midair. Jane cautiously scanned the forest for Jordan but saw nothing. The fire actually felt good against her chilled frame. It lulled her senses momentarily, but then the realization that a body might be baking in the coals brought her back to life.

Satisfied that Jordan was not around, Jane pushed through the sharp, unyielding branches and into the clearing. The fire licked without prejudice from one side of the stones to the other. Jane's face burned hotter as she inched her way closer to the pit in an attempt to decipher what had been thrown into the inferno. She raised her jacket to shield her face from the heat and took another step closer. The fire popped loudly as she heard his gravelly voice.

"Looking for his dead body?"

CHAPTER 11

Jane spun on her heels, instinctively reaching for her Glock.

Jordan Copeland stood ten feet away right in one of her fresh footprints. Had he been right behind her the entire time, stalking her as she stealthily moved on his property? There was a second of indignity on Jane's part followed by a realization that she was, in fact, trespassing and holding no warrant. Now with only ten feet between them, Jane could take in the towering beast in front of her. He stared at her with those penetrating, hypnotic steel-blue eyes, set under his elongated forehead. Flecks of debris nested in his grey beard and mustache, and continued through the wet, salt-and-pepper tangles of unruly curls that draped heavily across his shoulders and midway down the back of his oilcloth olive green duster. His enormous hands— gnarled, dark and thick with hard calluses—were balled into ready fists, waiting for an excuse to pound.

Jane stood her ground, fingers still inside her jacket touching her Glock. She'd stood up to a few monsters in her life and there was no way she was going to be intimidated by this one. She just hoped Jordan couldn't hear her heart nearly beating out of her chest.

"Go on," he said, his voice raspy and low. "Check the fire. See if he's in there. Maybe I didn't tuck his foot in tight enough."

Jane took a step back. "I'm Sergeant Detective Jane Perry from Denver."

"Jesus fucking Christ, aren't you official?" Jordan's fists relaxed. "I know you're a cop. We've already met. On the bridge? Right before your Negro partner came to step 'n' fetch you?"

"Negro?"

"Oh. Sorry." Jordan's face reeked of derision. "*Black*. Or shall we really indulge ourselves and call him African American so we can pretend we're two whites who give a shit?" Jordan moved closer to Jane. She curled her fingers around the butt of her Glock. "You gonna let that gun see some action or are you just gonna keep stroking it...leading it on?" He sauntered to the left of Jane and stood close to the fire. Jane turned to face him. Jordan grabbed a small branch from the ground and poked the coals in the pit. "Sergeant Detective Jane Perry," he mused out loud, flicking a hot coal back into the center of the flames. "You like the way that vibrates in the air, don't you?" Jordan never took his eyes off the fire. Jane stared into the pit, surveying the remnants of charred trash.

"You know," Jordan said, "every time I get a good fire cranking, I smile because I know somewhere out there, I'm really pissing off one of those fuckin' eco-freaks. Yeah, they love the earth. but they hate the people on it! You're not one of the Green Guilters, are you?" Jane shook her head. "I didn't think so. You don't look like a Nature Nazi. The only time I *go green* is when I smoke some bad shit that makes me puke." He lifted his filthy face and stared at Jane.

Jane gradually took her hand off her gun. "There's a shock."

Jordan remained silent as he continued to gaze at her with his mesmerizing orbs. He tilted his head and peered deeper into Jane's eyes as if he were trying to read words only he could see. Jane felt herself being drawn into the vortex, the same way she was on the bridge. She quickly peeled her eyes away from Jordan and sunk them back into the flames. "Do I frighten you, Jane?" His tenor was purposely disturbing.

That familiar wellspring of grit rose up and warmed her core. "That's ironic." She fastened her brown eyes on him. "I was gonna ask you the same question."

A mocking expression crept across Jordan's mug. "Well, ladies and gentlemen, weighing in at one hundred and thirty pounds in the ring tonight we have Sergeant Detective Jane Perry ready and willing to show me she can't be cowed. I wonder how smart she is? Let's start with something simple. How about a children's riddle?" Jordan stood a little taller. "I am the ruler of shovels. I have a double. I am as thin as a knife. I have a wife. What am I?"

Jane remembered the riddle from Jordan's videotaped interview with Bo. She thought for a moment, recalling it from her childhood. "You're the King of Spades."

Jordan raised an eyebrow. "*Very good,* Jane. Let's try another. How much dirt would be in a hole six feet deep and six feet wide that was dug with a square-edged shovel?"

Jane didn't have to think about this one. "There's no dirt. It's a fucking hole."

"Good, good, good. You stay focused and you aren't swayed by meaningless information." He took a couple steps around the fire pit. "Just one more. When does a Mexican become a Hispanic?"

Christ Almighty, she thought. "When he marries your daughter."

Jordan smiled. "I'll give you a grand if you can find *Hispania* on the map!" He continued his slow pace around the fire. "Three for three. Nicely done. You aren't afraid to expose the politically correct culture for what it is. I'm liking you more and more, Jane Perry. So, let's cut the shit. Ask me the million-dollar question."

"What would that be?" Jane asked, never taking her eyes off him.

"What the fuck do you think it is?" Jordan's tone turned suddenly mean. "Do you think I offed the kid?!"

Jane stiffened. "Did you?"

"I asked you first." Jordan ceased his promenade around the fire pit about four feet from Jane.

"I think you've got the criminal vibe honed to perfection. You've also got the rap sheet and hard time against you. There's also the similarities in the two cases…"

"The fact that a boy was involved? That's pretty general, Jane. Daniel was thirteen and he wasn't on a bridge or trying to kill himself. Daniel was also retarded. This kid wasn't." Jane watched Jordan's face for any sign of deception. She could usually discern some kind of body language, whether for innocence or guilt, but this guy seemed impenetrable. "There's also that pesky term of my probation that says I can't be within one hundred feet of a school or in the presence of a child under the age of eighteen. Jesus, do you have *any* idea how difficult it is to bump off a kid from one hundred feet away? I'm not saying it can't be done, mind you." He grinned. "Where there's a will, there's a way, Jane."

Jane was tiring of the sick banter. She decided to interject a few spines of attitude to irritate him and see if that cracked the surface. "You know the kid's name. Why won't you say it? Feeling guilty?"

"Ah…she's a master of the unspoken. She seeks to uncover the truth by the subtleties she hears and sees."

Jane needed to regain control of this extemporized

campfire interview. "Say his name, Jordan."

"*And* she stays on message!" He moved closer to her, his oilcloth duster dragging across the rim of the blackened stones. "Jake Van Gorden." He paused. "Did you hear anything odd in the way I said his name? Did you detect any whisper of artifice in my cadence?" It was now Jane's turn to remain as impenetrable in her body language. "Let me say it again. Jake…Van… Gorden." Jordan stepped within two feet of Jane.

She searched his face, coming up empty. "You get off on mind-fucking people? Did that buy you extra treats in prison?"

"And now we move to the profiling portion of our number-one suspect."

"You see yourself as quite the little road scholar, don't you? That's *road* as in street, by the way."

"Turn of the word…aren't you a clever girl?"

Jane felt trapped by Jordan's looming presence. She calmly moved to her left and walked slowly around the fire pit. "You don't care what people think because fuck 'em, right? Nobody did you any favors, did they?" She noted a slight wince in his eyes. "Oh, did I hit a nerve?"

"I don't have a nerve to hit, sweetheart. Don't be so full of yourself."

"Because you're dead inside." Jordan stared at her across the flames. Perhaps she wormed into his psyche. "You died a long time ago, but nobody gave a shit. The heart may be pumping, but you've left the building." *Yes*, there was something cracking in his façade. She recalled the brief early history of Jordan that Weyler recounted. "You were eight years old and it all came crashing down." Jordan stiffened. Not knowing the monster's M.O., Jane wasn't sure if she should continue. But she was used to pushing that proverbial envelope. "All you had was silence and isolation to occupy your days. You could cry, but why bother? You were in the way."

Jane looked down at Jordan's hands. They were slightly quivering, but within seconds, the shaking intensified. It was the identical thing that she saw when she first came eye-to-eye with him on the bridge. Instead of hiding the physical reaction, Jordan let it happen, almost disconnected from the strange effect. If she were sitting in the interrogation room at Headquarters, this is when she'd go in for the kill. Now with the fire cracking and hissing below her, it seemed an appropriate time. "Are you involved in any shape or form with Jake Van Gorden's disappearance?"

Almost on cue, his hands stopped shaking. His face became emotionless. "You're the cop. You figure it out."

Jane was damned if Jordan was going to get the upper hand. "You know, I could make one phone call and have three police agencies descend on this place and tear it up from the front end to the ass end."

Jordan regarded her for a moment and then smiled. "You're not gonna do that because you know they had no evidence to hold me and nothing substantial to link me to that kid's disappearance. You can't pull a warrant just because you think I'm disturbed. I know it and you know it so don't try to bullshit me." He stabbed a piece of errant trash with the stick and thrust it back into the flames. "The cops aren't coming back here." His gaze quickly intensified, "But *you* will." Jane felt her heart race but she tightened her mask of bravado. "You and I have business together."

Jane met his intensity. "What kind of business?"

"Very important business," he said, pursing his lips. "*You have something I need.*" Jane's blood turned cold. A jarring electrical shock ran down her spine forcing her to slightly jerk. It was the same shockwave that coursed across her nerve endings when she first saw Jordan on the bridge. Jordan moved closer to her, his blue eyes slightly out of focus. "We can help each other, Jane. I can enlighten you about so many critical things…"

"Like where Jake Van Gorden is?" Jane interrupted, standing her ground.

He took in a haughty breath. "Sure. I can tell you everything

I feel as I feel it."

"And in return?"

"You give me..." He searched her face for the answer. "Life." As Jordan said the word, it was as if he realized it at that exact moment.

"Life?" Jane's first thought was a life sentence.

His eyes drifted to the side. "You bring me...life..." With that statement, Jordan's hands began to shake.

"I'm not sure I understand what the hell you're talking about," Jane said, growing tired of the mystifying banter.

His eyes still locked faraway, Jordan spoke but his voice was drifting in another realm. "I'm not sure I do either. But that's the best I can give you right now." He looked at her. "You need to go now. You got a lot of work to do."

Jane wasn't used to being summarily dismissed, especially when she positioned herself in the authority role. The sky darkened above her as a soft pitter-pat of rain fell. Jane turned to head back into the thicket when Jordan spoke up.

"Don't worry, Jane." His acerbic tone was thick with sarcasm. "When all else fails, we always have...*hope*." Jane thought how much she hated that word. It was empty, impotent, passive and useless. The second that thought crossed her mind, Jordan piped up. "I despise the word *hope*. It keeps you waiting at the door long after you've rung the bell."

Jane felt an uneasy quiver. It was as if he read her mind. Or if he didn't, he somehow felt the same way she did about that ineffectual word. She started back toward the wire fence.

"Jake Van Gorden is not dead." She turned back. His words fell like stone around her. Jordan poked his stick between the crevices of the rocks that circled the fire pit. "But he's not safe. His world as he knows it is about to crumble and be shattered forever." He lifted his head and stared at Jane. "But, then again, he asked for it."

By the time Jane got back to her Mustang, the heavens had let go with a torrent of angry rain and wind. Her boots looked as if she'd trudged across the prairie and her jeans were equally mucky. A hard chill infected her body as she slammed the car door and looked at the clock. It was 5:45 pm. That couldn't be right. She'd gotten to Jordan's fence line around 3:45 pm. Factoring the slinking around, their meeting and her hasty return to the car, she figured it was no more than forty minutes tops. Jane checked her cell phone to see the correct time. 5:45 pm. *Crazy*, she thought as she drove back to town.

The Rabbit Hole was buzzing, crowded and deafening when Jane got there just after six o'clock. There were about seventy-five people on the dance floor and the surrounding tables. Almost every barstool was taken. The band, made up of an eclectic mix of middle-aged rogues, played "It's Five O'Clock Somewhere." They all looked half in the bag, except for the drummer who wore jeans, a Hawaiian shirt and a cowboy hat.

Jane crossed to the highly varnished bar, leaned across and tugged on the bartender's shirt. "I'm looking for Hank Ross," she yelled above the earsplitting music.

"The half-birthday boy?!" he yelled back at her.

"Excuse me?"

The guy pointed toward the band where a banner was strung across the ceiling. It read: *Happy Half-Birthday Hank!*

"What the hell?" Jane muttered to herself. Irritated, she pulled out her badge and flashed it at the guy. "I'm a cop! I need to see him."

The fellow stood back observing Jane with a quizzical look. "Goddamnit! Did that son-of-a-bitch hire a stripper dressed like a cop for his own half-birthday?"

"Hey, asshole!" Jane yelled above the din. "I'm a cop. Dressed like a cop."

He put his thumbs up in the air. "Like the attitude! And

you're in character! I get it." He motioned toward Jane's muddy shirt. "Dirty cop! *Love it*! Hank's the guy playing the drums." He winked. "Knock yourself out."

Jane turned to the band. *Great.* She wormed her way through the crowd as the band wound up their song. Hank capped it off with a dizzying riff and piercing crash of the cymbals. Jane looked closer at him. "Shit," she said. It was the same guy with the pickup truck she'd already seen twice that day on the street. Jane waited until the crowd's appreciation died down before leaning on the stage and yelling Hank's name.

Hank squinted through the stage lights, but when he saw Jane, his smile broadened. He put down his sticks and told the band he was sitting out a few songs before he moved to the lip of the stage. "This is one for the record books," he said, his blue eyes twinkling. "I haven't even blown out my half-birthday candles yet and I already got my wish!"

Jane was confounded. "Look, Mr. Ross..."

"Oh, come on! It's Hank," he yelled as the band swelled into a bluegrass number.

"My name's Jane Perry."

"I know who you are. We get the Denver paper up here." He smiled.

"I need to ask you some questions."

Hank jumped off the stage and spied Jane's holstered Glock under her jacket. "I like the way you accessorize!" He nodded toward her muddy shirt. "You look like you've had a hard day. How about a drink?" Hank led Jane to the far end of the bar. "What can I get you? Beer? Whiskey?"

"I don't drink," Jane stated, building a wall of protection around her.

"A cop who doesn't drink? The only cops who don't drink are cops who *used* to drink. Tonic and lime?" Jane nodded halfheartedly. "Two tonic and limes," he told the bartender. "What do you wanna eat?"

This was getting too chummy for Jane. "I don't need to eat."

"You look hungry. How 'bout a hot dog?"

Hank was the second person that day who thought she looked hungry. She looked at him and noticed how relaxed he was with her. She couldn't recall anyone *ever* being this laid back with her. Most men were either afraid of Jane Perry or disliked her intensely. But there was no fear coming from Hank—just a genuine smile with a hint of innocent, mischievous charm behind his eyes. "Sure. Gimme a dog walking and drag it through the garden."

Hank chuckled. "How about if I make that dog sit?" he yelled to a waitress behind the bar. "Can I get a hot dog for here with everything on it?"

Jane was impressed that Hank understood her street-speak, but she wasn't about to let her guard down. The bartender delivered the two tonic and limes. "You don't have to teetotal on my account."

"Who says I am?" He clicked his glass against hers. "Cheers."

Jane took at sip and looked hard at Hank's face. It had a sun-washed, weathered look but there was also an eternal youthfulness present—even though whispers of grey hair mingled happily with the brown. *Charming.* Yes, that's the word Jane bet a lot of women used to describe Hank Ross. He was easy on the eyes, too. He didn't have that threatening vibe that Jane tended to attract. But as she looked closer, there was something else. "You're sober."

"Yes ma'am. Been a friend of Bill's for ten years."

Jane was stunned. "Doesn't owning a bar go against the whole AA credo?"

"Probably." He took a swig of his tonic. "But I never was one for following the rules of the game. *And* I never let sobriety get in the way of a good time!"

Jane took a look around. "What is all this anyway?"

"An insurance policy." Jane looked perplexed once again. "Based on the stats, I should have been dead five years ago. At least that's what they told me."

"Who?"

"My cop buddies."

Jane put down her tonic. "You're an ex-cop?"

"Yep. Back in Michigan. And as you know, the rule is after you retire, you usually last about five years before something goes haywire and you croak. So, I cut out at forty, cashed out my pension, got sober and then tried to figure out what to do with my life. When I hit forty-five, I figured it was all gravy after that, but that nothing was guaranteed. So, for five years, I've been celebrating my half-birthday just in case something happens in the second half of my trip around the sun." He motioned to a large sign over the bar. It read: DON'T BE AFRAID THAT YOUR LIFE WILL END. BE AFRAID THAT IT WILL NEVER BEGIN—GRACE HANSEN. "Why do you think I hung that up there?"

Jane lingered on the sign. It had been almost twenty-four hours since she'd gotten the grim report from her doctor. She was thirty-seven and those fifteen words up there on the wall gripped her heart. For the most part, she'd been holding her breath much of her life, either waiting for the worst or wondering when the other shoe was going to drop. She'd never had the luxury of sustained peace. Then again, if someone handed her a plateful of peace, she wasn't sure she'd even know what to do with it. It'd be like giving a dog a credit card and telling him to splurge. If there were a sign on Jane's wall, it would be her manta: LIFE IS A STRUGGLE AND THEN YOU DIE. Jane looked a little closer at Hank. He sure as hell didn't look or act like a typical fifty-year-old. There was a genuine charisma that she assumed he used to his advantage to lure the ladies to his lair. But to his credit, he did seem to be living up to that sign up on the wall.

"How long have you been sober?" he suddenly asked.

Jane wasn't ready for that question. She came to do a short interview and get back to the B&B. "Fifteen months," she said reluctantly.

"Congratulations," he said with sincerity, clinking his glass against hers. "I know…it's not easy. In college, the only fraternity I joined was Tappa Keg A Day." Jane started to smile but quickly reined it in. "You know when I hit bottom? When I decided it was necessary to put a bottle opener on the keychain for my car keys." Jane looked skeptical. "No, I'm dead serious. That was my come-to-Jesus moment. What about you?"

She turned away. "I don't know. I had a few come to Jesus moments when I saw Him waving to me as I was leaving the gates of Hell." She shifted in her seat.

"Sorry," he said, backing off. "I don't mean to make your jaw clench."

"Excuse me?"

He put his finger to his jaw. "Your jaw. When you said 'the gates of Hell,' your left jaw tightened. And you shifted in your seat. Classic posture of avoidance." Jane wasn't used to being on the receiving end of another body language pro. "Hey, you can't take the cop outta me." The waitress delivered Jane's hot dog. He quickly changed the subject. "So, you're obviously here about Jake." Hank's lighthearted attitude shadowed with a look of disquiet.

"That's right."

"Five days gone," he said. Underneath those words was the tacit awareness that the odds weren't in the kid's favor. Jane nodded and took a bite of food. "He's a good kid…a *real* good kid. You know how in AA they tell you to get real and be honest with yourself? That's what Jake had been doing for about eighteen months." Jane recalled that Mollie commented on the same thing. "It was as if he was on some sort of personal quest."

"You think in that quest he hooked up with the wrong person online?" She took a hearty bite out of the dog.

"I'd say the odds are against that. Jake wasn't a normal kid in the sense that he spent hours online."

"How do you know?"

"Because I talked to the kid. He read books, loved to draw, but mostly he loved to talk and share his ideas. I think he was hungry for someone to listen to him. God knows his parents don't give a shit."

"Why's that?" Jane took another good bite of the hot dog, realizing how good it tasted and how hungry she was. She found herself feeling more comfortable with Hank. Maybe it was the fact that he was an ex-cop and knew the drill. Maybe it was because he served a helluva good hot dog. Maybe it was the ease in which he picked up on what she was talking about. Whatever it was, she was a bit more relaxed. The wall was still up but there were a few cracks in the mortar.

"Haven't a clue. I think his dad's a prick. And his mom... Carol is fine if you like women who can't think for themselves."

Jane asked what kind of work Jake did at the place, realizing that at fifteen, it was dicey to hire the kid at a sport's bar. Hank assured her his responsibilities involved cleaning tables, sweeping up after hours and working in the kitchen helping the prep cook. He admitted that the kid sometimes stuck around until midnight but that was because he didn't want to go home. Jane raised an eyebrow. "Hey," Hank said, holding up his hand, "I wasn't happy about it. He was off the clock at nine o'clock and then he'd just hang out. Usually, he'd go in the back and read. He loved philosophy books...lots of esoteric stuff. I'd offer to drive him home and he'd turn me down every time. He flat out said that he didn't want to go home and sometimes asked if he could crash at my place. I have a small, three-bedroom cottage on the back of this property. But I wasn't about to get myself involved in his drama. I like Jake, but I'm not his daddy. Instead of going home, he'd walk around town at night...said he could think more clearly."

So far, Hank's story was meshing with Mollie's. "Did you ever see any signs?"

"Suicidal signs?" Jane nodded. "You know as well as I do that sometimes the signs aren't that obvious. Or the rest of us don't see them."

Jane's eyes drifted down to the bar. "Yeah." An unexpected

catch caught in her throat. "I hear you."

"He wasn't displaying the usual ones—giving away possessions, physical appearance shifting…"

"He broke up with Mollie. And his grandmother has terminal cancer."

"I've never heard him mention his grandmother. As for his relationship with Mollie, they were a tight couple. But the way I heard it from Jake, Mollie's dad is the one who told her to break up with him."

"What'd the preacher have against him?" she asked, finishing off the dog.

"I don't know. Aaron's pretty progressive. He's not your typical *sunshine Christian*. It actually surprised me when I heard that."

Jane ran her fingers through her hair. She suddenly realized how dead tired she was. "Why hang yourself?" Jane was tempted to reveal the disturbing animated drawing of the old man hanging himself but she held it back. "He could slit his wrists, take some pills. Hell, for that matter, he could have jumped in the river. If the fall didn't kill him, the water temp would have."

Hank put his hand over Jane's. It was a gesture she wasn't prepared for. "I wish I could give you more insight. The more I go over the way Jake was acting over the last couple months…I realize that, yeah, something *was* off."

Jane slid her hand out from under Hank's and took a sip of her drink. "*Off?*"

Hank tried to put his thoughts into words. "About six weeks ago one Friday night, it was just Jake and me here about midnight. I was counting the receipts and he was sweeping the same spot in the floor that he'd been going over for half an hour. He looked up and asked me if I believed in curses. I said, like what…voodoo curses? And he said, no, *family* curses. He wanted to know if I thought it was possible for a family to be infected…that's the word he used, by the way…*infected*, with a curse. He wondered if it was possible that the curse made them do things and even *become* people who they didn't want to be but they had no choice. I think he got the idea from one of his esoteric books." Hank shook his head. "It was pretty wild."

Jane considered the information. She heard the doctor's voice from earlier that morning ring in her head. *You can't ignore your blood.* For a moment, she felt outside herself. "It follows you..."

"How's that?" Hank leaned closer.

Jane came back in her body. "I don't know...so Jake felt infected. With what?"

"No idea. But I do know that you look worn-out."

Jane wondered if Hank was planning to offer her a soft place to fall in his crash pad. She quickly short-circuited the conversation. "Does Jake have a locker here?"

Hank led her to a back room down a short hallway off the restrooms. A comical sign was nailed above the door that read: *Hippies: Use Back Entrance.* Inside the room, a bank of lockers stood on one side, none with locks. He motioned to the one Jake used and she opened it. Inside, Jane found a bag of hairnets for when he worked in the kitchen, three neatly folded aprons and two white cloth hats—all with The Rabbit Hole's name on them. She stared at the contents and ran her hand across the stack of aprons. One of the pockets crinkled when she touched it. Jane pulled a slip of paper from the pocket. It was a folded page from the linen, gold-embossed letterhead pad of Bailey's she'd found in Jake's room earlier that day. On it was written *1401 Imperial* in what Jane had to assume was Bailey Van Gorden's printing. "You know this address?" Jane asked, showing Hank the paper.

"No street named *Imperial* around here."

Jane tucked the piece of paper in her jacket pocket just as a woman's voice yelled out his name. He leaned out the door and called to her. She appeared in the doorway and gave a happy greeting to Jane.

"Annie Mack," Hank introduced, "this is Detective Jane Perry from Denver. She's here about Jake."

Annie shook Jane's hand and said a few words of small talk. She looked to be about twenty-five with brown hair and twinkling brown eyes of innocent youth. "Hank," she said turning to him with an air of excitement, "they're bringing your half-birthday cake out."

"Jane, you gotta have some cake," he insisted.

"I'll pass." She wanted to focus and eating half-birthday cake would compromise her concentration. At least, that's what she told herself as she patched up the cracks of mortar in her invisible wall.

Hank looked a little disappointed. "I'll be back in ten minutes."

He and Annie walked down the hallway, she with her hand around his shoulder the whole way. Jane figured their relationship was more than friends as their connection was comfortable and almost familial in nature. But there was something else she noted coming more from Hank toward Annie. Jane noticed it when Annie walked into the room. Hank's eyes softened and his gestures were tendered. There was something of substance between them. *A twenty-five year age difference doesn't slow him down,* she figured. Jane would have stayed in that room another half hour just to soak up the vibe and see if she'd missed anything important but she wanted to get out of Dodge before Hank returned with cake. She heard the hundred-plus revelers singing, "Happy Half-Birthday" as the door swung shut behind her.

When Jane returned to the B&B, she found Weyler sitting in the parlor with Aaron and Sara. They'd obviously fixed him a meal as he still had a cloth napkin draped across his suit trousers. He excused himself and met Jane at the foot of the stairs.

"I thought maybe you'd skipped town," he said confidentially. "Why'd it take you four hours to check out a town the size of a postage stamp?"

"Just driving, Boss." She started up the stairs when Weyler

held her back.

"How'd you get all that mud on you if you were just driving?"

There was no way she was telling him she met Jordan Copeland face-to-face. It wasn't exactly police protocol to question a possible suspect on his own property without prior knowledge of the police chief in charge. Since she was already walking a thin line with Bo Lowry, she didn't want to complicate her life or embarrass Weyler. So, she lied. "I had to take a piss in the woods and I lost my balance."

The answer seemed to embarrass Weyler and cease further questioning. He nodded and returned to the parlor. Jane started up the stairs again when she heard a door open and close downstairs.

Mollie appeared in the doorway on the way to her bedroom when she spotted Jane. The girl stopped, observed Jane's appearance. She shook her head and whispered just loud enough for Jane to hear. "You look like a *bohmerkeh*," she declared before disappearing behind her bedroom door.

Upstairs in her room, Jane tossed her mud-caked shirt on top of the one from earlier that day in a corner of her bedroom. She slipped into her *Ron Paul for President—2008* nightshirt and proceeded to carefully hang each of the physical clues that Weyler received from Bo on the clothesline. By the time she was done, she had a perfect visual in front of her. The clues were in order of their receipt, including the transcript of the two ominous phone messages. Jane wrote where each clue arrived on a sticky pad and affixed a note on each clue. She recovered the linen note page that she found in Jake's locker and hung it at the far right of the clothesline. Next to that, she placed the bright green page where Bo had Bailey Van Gorden write Jake's full name: *JACKSON JAKOB VAN GORDEN*. She recalled the red starred website in Jake's notebook, *mysecretrevelations.com*, and jotted it down on a piece of paper before pinning that clue on the far right side of the line.

Crawling on top of the large king-size bed with the gossamer canopy, Jane rearranged the pillows so she could sit up straight and view the clues better. Her eyes drifted to the table to the right with the lonely pack that held the waiting cigarette. *God, that would taste incredible right now,* she thought. There was something about the marriage of nicotine and contemplative ruminating that was a powerful union. The nicotine slowed down the mind. The action of drawing the cigarette to her mouth, inhaling the smoke and slowly blowing it out while observing or reading created an almost Zen rhythm that allowed for focus and revelations. Jane repositioned the pillows several times in an attempt to find comfort, but all she could think of was that damn cigarette across the room—teasing her, torturing her and loving every minute of it.

She closed her eyes, desperately grabbing at anything in her consciousness to help. The soft scent of gardenias began to blossom along the edges of her mind. Jane could feel herself drifting outside of her body, but she forced herself back. Without thinking about it, she pressed the first and second finger on her right hand together and brought her hand to her mouth. In it was an invisible cigarette. As her fingers touched her lips, she sucked in the air, held it and then released it. The movement, repeated several times with her eyes closed, seemed to calm Jane as the gardenias drifted into the ether. She opened her eyes and regarded the clues with new vision.

The first was the book, *You Can't Go Home Again* along with the sympathy card and envelope with the odd *BAWY* written on the outside. This was left in the Van Gorden's mailbox.

The second clue was the message on Bo's voicemail. Vi's transcript included all the pauses and sounds on the tape in brackets. Jane moved closer to the end of the bed and read the words. *[Distorted voice] Do you know what it's like to feel as if you're two seconds from your last breath? Do you? It feels just like this…[Scratchy sound on phone, followed by the whining and begging of young male child in the background. Continues for 10 seconds and then stops. Scratchy sound and the distorted voice speaks again.] He pounds on the window and you do nothing. [Abrupt end.]*

Jane viewed the third clue. It was the full-color figure cut out of from a magazine of an eight-or-nine-year-old boy wearing a vintage red baseball cap. Jane peered closer at the figure that was glued to the page to infer the impression that the child was being dragged by his arm. The other arm—artificially extended and highly exaggerated with a pen drawing— looked like the flat of the boy's palm was pressed against a surface. Letters cut out from various magazines spelled the sentence: *THOU SHALT NOT STEAL INNOCENCE!* below the drawing. The accompanying envelope had the same obscure *BAWY* written across it. In the upper right corner was a lone, uncancelled, twenty-five-cent stamp with an old Packard on it.

The fourth clue hanging on the clothesline was another transcript courtesy of Vi of the second phone message from the kidnapper. It read: *[Sound of young boy crying in background. Scratchy sound on phone followed by distorted voice] He cried like a baby and will never be a real man. [Abrupt end.]*

Jane's stared at the word *cried*. She'd brought this up in Bo's office and it still bothered her. Why *cried*? Shouldn't he have said, "He *cries* ..." since the sound of the kid crying was previously active in the background? Was Jane just focusing on picayune details?

She turned her attention to the fifth clue on the clothesline. This was a duo sent to the Van Gordens: a blank sheet of crinkled paper and the twisted drawing of a child that implied sodomy. Jane's heightened sense of smell detected something malodorous emitting from the crinkled sheet of paper ensconced in the protective plastic cover. It was sickly sweet and pervasive. She snapped that clue off the line and opened the plastic bag. Immediately, the aroma knocked her back on the bed. She knew the smell all too well. It was urine. *But why piss on a blank sheet of paper?* she wondered. *Unless...* Jane jumped off the bed and scrambled to find the lighter in her leather satchel. Taking the crinkled page to the light, she held the flame under the paper, weaving it back and forth until the urine stains turned slightly brownish. Like magic, the words appeared: *Why you piss me off BAWY?* Jane sat back on the bed, somewhat stunned by the sheer creative bent of the kidnapper. She reasoned it could mean a couple things. Either the urine was a symbol of literally being pissed-off or, perhaps, it was a metaphor for being so scared that the kid peed in his pants. Either way, the secretive way in which the words were hidden using urine as the acidic ink certainly instilled a further concealment of the kidnapper's message. The obscurity of the clues bound with the sense that on some level they all made perfect sense frustrated Jane. It was as if it was a secret wrapped in a larger secret and capped within a haunting enigma.

Jane returned the urine-stained page to the plastic evidence sheet, set it aside and turned her attention to the sixth clue that was sent to Bo Lowry's office. It was the riddle that read:

Name this classy car.
Seven letters.
The first four spell what you do before going on a trip.
The first three spelled backward is something you take on that trip and
wear on your head.

Jane sat back and ran through every classy car she could think of. *Mercedes. Rolls Royce. Porsche.* But then her eyes traveled to the twenty-five-cent, uncancelled stamp on the envelope that held the sympathy card. "Packard!" she said aloud. "The first four spell what you do before going on a trip," Jane re-read. "Pack," she muttered. "The first three spelled backward is something you take on that trip and wear on your head." Jane quickly worked it out in her head. "Cap!" she exclaimed. She scanned the clues and locked onto the one with the magazine cutout of the child being dragged by his long arm. The boy in the cutout wore a red vintage baseball cap. Underneath were the words: *THOU*

SHALT NOT STEAL INNOCENCE! There had to be a connection. It was becoming more and more clear that this deviant was not just smart; he was deliberate. Everything in front of Jane had a purpose. She knew it. Each word was carefully chosen, allowing not one spent syllable of verbiage. Even the voicemails were sparse in their words, showing a calculated economy for expressing his message. This led Jane to believe that the kidnapper was unyielding in being heard and understood.

With that in mind, she viewed the final clue sent to Bo Lowry by the kidnapper. It was written in all capital letters:

I BEARED MY SOUL, AND STILL YOU IGNORE ME???

Jane now had a much better feel for the person behind the clues. He was smart and he was purposeful. And when you're smart and purposeful you don't use the wrong spelling for a word. Instead of the correct *bared,* he wrote *beared.* He absolutely meant to write it that way.

She pulled herself back into the crush of pillows and stared at that single sentence for twenty minutes. She felt into the desperation behind every word. There was a sense of being neglected…ignored. Why ignored?

She spent another half hour reading the clues from left to right until she had them memorized.

And then she saw it. Not one, but two startling discoveries.

CHAPTER 12

Jane heard Weyler trod down the hallway. She bolted from her bed and opened the door. "Boss," she whispered with punctuation.

Weyler stood there in his suit and tie and stared at Jane,

wearing nothing but her faded long nightshirt. "What?" he asked, almost feeling a need to avert his eyes.

"I found something. *Two somethings!*" She said, waving him into her room.

Weyler looked a bit askance when he spotted the odd set-up Jane had erected with the clothesline. "What's with all this…"

"It's outside the box, Boss," Jane motioned him to close the door and then stood in front of the clothesline of clues on the left side. "These are the clues in order of their delivery. But you can't read them as individual pieces. You have to read them as a whole because they tell a story." Weyler shook his head, not sure of where this was going. "Just wait! Hear me out. Each clue builds on the one before it. Like this one…" Jane pointed to the first drawing of the child with the red cap on his head. "In this picture, he's being dragged somewhere, possibly in a car. But this one over here," Jane quickly moved to the second, sexually graphic drawing, "is greater and more threatening than the first drawing. This one…" pointing to the second drawing, "is what happens days or maybe weeks after the first one." She moved to the transcript from the first voicemail. "The kidnapper says, 'He pounds on the window and you do nothing.' Then we have a kid conveniently in the next clue looking like his palm is pressed against a flat surface, like a window."

Weyler moved closer to the clothesline, reading through a couple clues in order. "I don't see how the first clue of the book bleeds into the second clue of the voicemail."

"I think the book, *You Can't Go Home Again*, is establishing the theme."

"Theme?" Weyler almost looked irritated.

"The sympathy card that came with it read, *So sorry for your loss*. It's establishing the situation. I'm still not clear why he wrote *JACKson sends his regards* in the card. But I'm sure it means something along the way. Look, the person who did this is intelligent, motivated and vengeful."

"So, you're saying this is a crime of revenge?"

"Maybe. I don't know yet. But I think there's something in the book that's obviously important. Something that literally states the purpose of everything else."

"What was on the dog-eared page?"

"It talked of *phrases as symbols of something real.* And then there was a line in there regarding the main character George Webber about *something that mattered greatly to him and would not be denied.* Maybe the kidnapper is…pretending to be George Webber."

"An intellectual kidnapper?"

"It's not out of the realm of possibility, Boss!"

"Does an intellectual draw a graphic picture of a young boy being sodomized?"

"Sure. If it's part of the story."

"The story…" Weyler looked dubious. "So you think he's telling us what's going to happen to Jake?"

"Possibly."

"If that's so, then where is the demand to the Van Gordens to keep all of this from happening to their son? Isn't it normal for the kidnapper to threaten this, this and this *unless you* do this, this and this?" He looked at the clues again. "There's no request to the Van Gordens. No ransom demand…"

"He wants attention," Jane interrupted, grasping the idea from the ether.

"Come on, Jane. You don't go through all this and take a child just to get attention."

Jane sat on the edge of the bed and stared at the clues. After a moment of silence, she spoke up. "He needs to be heard, Boss. He's a loner. Nobody's ever paid any attention to him. He was dismissed because he was in the way. So he chose a life of silence and isolation." In that moment, Jane felt the unrelenting pain that poured forth from the pages on the clothesline. It was at once suffocating and shattering.

"You just described Jordan Copeland," Weyler stated.

"I know," she said quietly.

"All the more reason to keep him in our sights." Weyler looked at Jane. "But not too close."

Jane looked up at him. Weyler had a look of warning on his face. "What?"

"I know you pretty well, Jane. You tend to go against protocol. We're here to help Bo but, in the end, this is *his* case and this is *his* town. Copeland is the number-one suspect and he knows it. If he's involved in this case, give him all the space in the world so that he can fall on his own sword. We need to keep an appropriate distance from him so we're not accused later at trial of compromising the case and getting it thrown out on a technicality. If we screw this whole thing up for Bo, I'll never forgive myself."

Jane implicitly understood Weyler and did her best to not show offense at his veiled threats toward her. "Because you owe him, right?" It came out far too petulant but she couldn't help it.

"Because I take a promise as seriously as you do."

"Well, Boss..." Jane stood up. "...what if your ol' buddy isn't being honest with you? Would that alter your promise?" Jane followed through with what she witnessed in Bo's office when Vi went out to get the files on Jake and Jordan—the way she ripped off the top page that was stapled to the outside of the folder and slipped it into her top drawer before heading back into Bo's office. Jane's assault on Bo continued when she questioned his need to keep the whole case quiet. It was a fact that raised too many red flags for a guy who claimed to want to *solve* the case before his retirement. And what about his early retirement, she added. Was it a strange coincidence that he and his trusted ally, Vi, were cutting and leaving the joint simultaneously? In her rant, Jane wanted to include the mysterious bright yellow folder on Bo's desk that he purposely covered up but she could see that Weyler wasn't buying her suspicions.

"I think your nicotine withdrawal is causing you to create conspiracies where there are none."

"Then take the edge off my suspicion and tell me the story

between you two!"

Weyler pulled himself up to his full 6' 4" frame. "Is there anything else you want to show me?"

Shit, Jane thought. Maybe it *was* the nicotine withdrawal. God knows her body was speeding through some crazy sensations. Between smelling gardenias where there were none and her heightened senses, she was clearly rotating more outside her body than in it. She jumped off the bed and handed Weyler the blank sheet of paper with the writing in urine. "It says, *Why you piss me off, BAWY?* Every single clue doesn't waste a word. Why does he write this and suddenly sound like he can't speak proper English?" Jane pointed to the riddle about the Packard. "Is it just a coincidence that the answer matches an old Packard postage stamp that he conveniently affixed to one of the envelopes? Is it a coincidence that one of the answers in the riddle, the word *cap*, just *happens* to be what's drawn on the boy's head in both pictures?"

"Copeland likes riddles. What was that one he mentioned on the interrogation video? 'I am the ruler of shovels. I have a double...'"

"'I am as thin as a knife. I have a wife. What am I?' Yeah. King of Spades," Jane acknowledged off-handedly.

"Very good."

"Look, Boss. This guy doesn't make mistakes. That's what brings me to my second discovery. We always say to look for patterns, right? We all have them and we act and react to them unconsciously. Watch this..." Jane moved to the book, *You Can't Go Home Again*. "First clue shows up at the Van Gordens." He nodded. "Second clue is the first voicemail message. That one comes into Bo's office." Jane touched the third clue, "Back to the Van Gordens and then," she touched the fourth clue, "second voicemail to Bo's office. And then, we're back to the Van Gordens for clue number five. Clue number six, the Packard riddle, shows up under Bo's front mat. Clue number seven, *I BEARED MY SOUL*, also suddenly shows up under Bo's front mat." Jane took a hard breath. "It's out of sequence. Somewhere between clues six and seven, the Van Gordens should have gotten something. This makes sense because if I'm right that this a linear story, the clue that says *I BEARED MY SOUL,* relates to whatever came before it."

"I understand patterns, Jane, but..."

"Boss, there's zero connection between the riddle about the Packard and *I BEARED MY SOUL AND YOU STILL IGNORE ME???* I mean, he's saying it right there! *YOU STILL IGNORE ME???*"

"Jane, he's not being acknowledged for any of them!"

"Bo told us that the Van Gordens are only aware of the clues that they received themselves. That's the book and sympathy card and the two drawings. I'm telling you, Boss, there are *really* eight clues and the Van Gordens have number seven and didn't give it up to Bo."

"Why in the hell would they intentionally hold back a clue that could potentially save their son's life?"

Jane said the first thing that popped into her head. "Disgust? I mean, the last clue they supposedly got was that picture." She pointed to the sexually graphic drawing. "Maybe the next clue was even worse. Remember, this family is all about honing that surface impression. If the missing clue was embarrassing to them, I can understand how they'd want to ignore it so save face. And, you know, it's not like they haven't already lied to us."

"Who lied?"

"Bailey. I checked inside his SUV..."

"You went inside his car?" Weyler was stunned.

"Yeah. He likes a lot of Greatest Hits CDs. And the car smelled funky. But he lied to us, Boss. He said the last time he was out was six days prior to go to the gym during the day. But his rear view mirror was flipped for nighttime driving and the vehicle looked freshly caked with mud. And today? Same story about going to the gym. Yeah, right. All dressed up with a half tube of gel in his hair to go to the gym? I think not. The reason I hung back after you left was to check out his story…"

"Jane…" Weyler's cadence was warning.

"His SUV was nowhere near the damn gym!"

"These are the *victims*, not the suspects! He's free to go wherever he wants. Maybe he wanted to go on a drive and clear his head…"

"*Dressed up*?!" Jane wasn't backing down.

"Jane, you're scattered! You're not focusing!"

"I am focusing!" She was falling apart, but she didn't want Weyler to know it. Her head was exhausted from juggling all the unknowns in her own life, as well as the life of a missing boy she was starting to really care about. She wondered if *she* cared about him more than his own parents did. A thought crossed her mind. "Why aren't the Van Gordens offering a reward for Jake's return?"

"I asked Bo that question. He said they were planning on it, but withdrew the plan last night."

"What happened last night?"

"I don't know. Bo said they just decided that they wanted to keep this thing low-key."

"What the fuck?" Jane was disgusted. "They've got *beau-coup* bucks! They could afford to plunk one hundred grand out there. Hell, in this economy, they could get someone to squeal for twenty-five!"

"Jane, we're both bone tired. Let's hash it out in the morning when we're fresh. We're meeting Bo for breakfast at the diner…"

"Oh, shit, he's not going to listen to me, Boss! He doesn't even want me here!"

"Let's do this by the book, okay? Get some sleep."

Weyler wearily left her room, quietly closing the door behind him.

"Fuck!" Jane half-whispered in frustration. Sure, this wasn't technically *her* case, but she was brought in to help solve it and now her *outside the box* considerations were being questioned.

She glanced toward the clothesline of clues. *Who in the fuck lives at 1401 Imperial,* she thought, *and where in the hell is it?* Crossing to the last two clues, she slid her hand between them. She recalled that Bo told them he had received the last one with the *I BEARED MY SOUL...* sentence *that morning* under his front mat. If she was right about patterns and if the Van Gordens actually *did* receive a clue that they didn't disclose, it made sense that that mysterious clue could have been delivered the day before. Perhaps she was right about them feeling disgust at it—so much disgust that they abruptly cancelled the reward. *Jesus Christ,* she thought, you don't withdraw a reward for your only son because you want to keep things low-key.

Jane's head was spinning a million miles a minute. Weyler was right. She *was* scattered. She had to slow down her brain and there was only one way she knew to do that. She spied the single cigarette pack on the table. The torture was too much. She slid the cigarette out of the pack and searched for the lighter she used to decipher the words on the urine-stained page. Suddenly, a wave of pain permeated her lower gut. She grabbed hold of the bedpost to steady herself as she bent over and grabbed her belly. Tossing the cigarette back on the table, she was hit with the strong scent of gardenias once again. She fell to her knees and rolled into a fetal position on the floor. The persistent pain was agonizing. Her pelvis felt as if it was about to break in two. She briefly wondered if this was what it was like to give birth. Then she wondered if something was seriously wrong inside of her.

Jane managed to crawl up onto the bed. She turned off the light and drew the comforter over her aching body. She began to gently brush her fingertips across her forehead, repeating the motion continuously—the same way she did in the doctor's office. The odd, uncharacteristic gesture felt soothing to her, especially as a wave of nausea overwhelmed her. Ribbons of pain engulfed her as the scent of gardenias lingered. She finally fell asleep, the pain abating and the aroma disappearing.

All was silent until she awoke to the sound of creaking in her room. Jane opened her eyes and was met with a mat of blackness and the eerie glow of the bedside clock that showed *3:11*. Somebody was there. She could feel it. And with it, that goddamned sickly sweet floral scent that had dogged her for nearly twenty-four hours. The creaking continued, back and forth, back and forth. It was coming from the corner of the room near the window.

Jane couldn't remember where she'd set her Glock but she was pretty sure it wasn't next to her bed. She could feel her heart beating so hard that she was certain whoever was in the room could hear it too. Sliding her hand out from under the sheet, she contacted the tiny lamp on her bedside table and flicked it on.

She sat up, ready to take on the intruder. But all she saw was the rocking chair in the corner, creaking back and forth, back and forth. *It's the wind*, she told herself, coming from the window not far from the chair. She peered closer at the window but it was closed. With that, the rocker came to a sudden stop.

CHAPTER 13

After a fitful few hours of sleep, Jane awoke with a start at 6:00 am. She'd had a dream but the people in it and the situation were clouded. All she could remember was a sense of something unraveling and of outright chaos. She rubbed her eyes and stared across the room at the rocking chair by the closed window. Was it a dream? It felt like it right then. The whole memory of waking at 3:11 am felt distant and remote.

Jane cupped her palm against her lower belly expecting to feel pain, but she felt surprisingly fine. How could something so profoundly agonizing come and go so quickly? It was as if the pain did not belong to her and that she was shouldering it for someone else. What's that they say about sympathy pains? Perhaps, she pondered, she had gotten herself so wrapped up in the menagerie of clues and her concern for Jake Van Gorden and projected it into her belly? *Sure,* she thought. *That's possible.* It sure as hell was easier to accept than the more likely possibility that her body was turning on her and she was slowly dying.

She heard the purposely soft closing of the back screen door and quickly moved to the window. Aaron Green ambled outside with several stapled pages in his hand and a large red photo album under his arm. He walked to the farthest end of the backyard, sat down on a bench and opened the album. Jane watched as his face gradually lit up with each turn of the page.

Jane threw on the first shirt she could find—which happened to be the mud-caked one from the night before—and pulled on the dirty jeans and her leather jacket. She quietly inched her way down the short hallway to the staircase and gingerly moved downstairs so as not to wake anyone. Figuring it made sense to walk out the backdoor, she stealthily moved toward the kitchen. The speckled linoleum floor, large table and varnished narrow cupboards framed in glass reminded her of a true boardinghouse of yesteryear. Except for the few modern amenities such as the dishwasher and microwave, nothing looked as if it had changed from the years the place served as a home for women. She opened the back door and quietly closed it. Walking around the house, she tried to look as nonchalant as possible as she strolled across the large yard. Out of the corner of her eye, she saw Aaron's reaction to her unexpected presence. He quickly snapped the album shut and purposely slid it under the bench. It was the same gestural extension of shame that she'd witnessed in Bo's office when Bo covertly buried the bright yellow folder.

"Morning, Detective," Aaron chimed.

Jane pretended to take a deep yawn and stretch as if getting up at the crack of dawn to greet the sunrise was a habit. "Call me Jane," she said in the easiest-going tone she could muster. She had to appear as nonthreatening as possible so she could dive in for the kill later and catch him off guard.

He lifted the stapled pages. "I'm going over my sermon for tomorrow morning. You and Sergeant Weyler are welcome to attend."

The idea of sitting in church was about as appealing as being forced to listen to a precocious child sing off-key. "We'll take a rain check. We've got to spend every second on the case."

Aaron's eyes fell to the ground momentarily. "Yes…of course."

Jane saw a look of guilt fall across Aaron's face. God, she wanted to pounce on that moment and ask the question but she knew she had to hold back. She felt a crick in her back. "Shit," she muttered. Aaron looked up at her. "Oh, excuse me. It's just that my back's kinda funky this morning. I fell yesterday."

He glanced at the dried mud on her shirt and jeans. "I noticed. Here…" He moved over on the bench. "Have a seat."

Jane obliged. She couldn't help but peer down at the red photo album. It was obviously old with its cracked cover and faded lettering. "What's that?" she asked, hoping her pitch wasn't too confrontational.

A second of fear gripped his face. But he quickly recovered and turned to the album. "Oh, that's just my inspiration. Whenever I'm feeling a bit of writer's block, I bring it out and it inspires me."

This was intriguing. Jane noted a mischievous glint to Aaron's eyes. "Maybe I should look at it. I could use a little inspiration."

Aaron's mischievous look turned almost embarrassed as he used his heel to shove the album even further back into the grass. "Are you already hitting roadblocks?"

Change of subject. Yes, well done, Aaron, Jane thought. "There's more questions than answers on this case, Aaron."

He slightly winced and shook his head. "I'm sorry."

Jane noted that the *I'm sorry* was more than just a minister's reflective understanding of her trouble. There was also something else mixed in with it—a sense of regret possibly. "I talked to Hank Ross yesterday," Jane offered, her voice more pointed. "He told me what a great kid Jake is."

"Absolutely. Absolutely," Aaron muttered, averting Jane's glance.

"I guess he was a little...how would you put it...unique? Walks to the beat of his own drum?"

"Yes, yes. That he does."

This was starting to sound like pabulum and Jane hated swallowing that crap. "But you liked him, right?"

"We *loved* Jake. He's like the son we never had." Aaron's eyes welled with tears.

"He hangs out here a lot?"

"Oh, yeah," he said smiling. "We aren't his second home. We're his first." Aaron quickly caught himself. "That's not to say that Bailey and Carol don't care. It's just that we're more accessible to Jake."

Aaron had learned the fine art of damning a soul with faint praise. For a guy who considered Jake as the son he never had, Jane found it curious that he would instigate a breakup between Jake and Mollie. It was time for Jane to cast a lie into the water and see what she could catch. "Hank said that Jake broke off his relationship with Mollie."

There was a moment of stunned silence. "Really?"

"Isn't that what happened?"

Aaron uncomfortably shifted on the bench. "Yeah, yeah."

Thank Jesus there wasn't a Bible hanging around the area because Jane could then point out to him that he was breaking one of the Ten Commandments. "It wasn't the other way around?" Jane stressed.

"No...that's the way it went down." Jane's first thought was *went down*? These Methodists certainly did have an easygoing vernacular. She half-expected Aaron to call her *dude* next. He swept up his sermon. "I've really got to focus on this."

Again, she was dismissed. This was getting to be a habit. Jane got up and started across the yard.

"Do you mind if I read this to you?" Aaron asked. "Just the first part. I'm not sure if it flows."

Jane did not want to listen to a Sunday sermon on Saturday morning but she agreed, returning to the bench and sitting down.

Aaron stood up and cleared his throat. "The talk is on fear," he explained to Jane. "I figured with all the unknowns surrounding what's going on with Jake, it was a suitable topic." Jane nodded. Aaron proceeded to read in a commanding yet gentle tone. "'When faced with uncertainty in our lives, I always harken back to something my wife's grandfather told her to say during times of trepidation. It was just ten words but in those words, there was both comfort and courage to continue. Those ten words were: I will be all right and one day I will die.'" Jane felt her gut clench. Aaron continued. "'I can believe the first part and it calms me to the inevitability of the second part. I will be all right…and one day I will die. When we are faced with misfortune or hard luck, we are naturally programmed to revert to that primal essence of fear. And when you break it down—break all the things in life down that make us really fearful—the bottom line is death. When you take away that fear, the rest of the things we fear—whether it be poverty or shame or loss of reputation—the rest is fixable to some extent. Death is inevitable, but to stay in the moment and say *I will be all right* allows us all to keep our faith and not shadow our lives with the castles of fear we often build in the future.'" He stopped reading and looked at Jane. "What do you think?"

She hoped he couldn't see her jaw quivering. "Sara's grandfather sounded like a wise Jedi Master."

Aaron smiled. "I only met him and his wife a couple times. But they were incredible people. They certainly were tested in their lives, but he applied these words during those tests and he came out of everything the better for it. His wife was fond of saying, 'You must be the light you wish to see.'"

Sara opened the kitchen window and softly called to Aaron. "I'm putting coffee on. It'll be ready in a few minutes." Her voice seemed to suddenly catch on and she moved from the window to the back door and joined them. There was a clear nervousness to her gait as she strode between them, her body seemingly blocking the photo album under the bench. She tried to conceal her anxiousness with a forced smile. "How'd you sleep?" she asked Jane.

"Like a baby," Jane lied. She wanted to add "with colic," but opted not to.

It was patently clear Sara was guarding that photo album. Aaron's little red photo album of Sunday sermon inspiration certainly was getting more intriguing to Jane.

Walking into the house, Jane let the back door slam shut which generated a pissed-off yell from Mollie behind her bedroom door. Her angry footsteps stumbled from her bed and she swung open her door. "Mom! It's not even seven!" Out of her drowsy eyes, she saw Jane standing there in the same damn outfit she was wearing when she saw her the night before. "My God, do you even *own* clean clothes?" A look of utter disgust came over the kid as she was about to slam her door. But Jane moved quickly and held the door open with the palm of her hand. "*Ei!*"

"I gotta talk to you!" Jane insisted as she slid into Mollie's bedroom and closed the door behind her.

The room was not your typical teenage girl's room. There was the usual desk and computer but it was absent of rock 'n' roll posters, girly touches and the like. Instead, there was a lone table in the corner that held a copy of the Talmud. A small menorah stood behind that. A votive candle burned in a purple glass holder.

"You burning that for Jake?" The girl was silent. "Is that for his soul or his safe return?"

"Anytime you shed light in the darkness it's a *brocheh*."

"Whatever. Make sure you don't burn down the house." Jane heard the back door open and swing shut. She lowered her voice. "I gotta know why you broke up with Jake."

"It's none of your business, you *yenta!*"

"The hell it isn't!" Jane's tenor was strict. She grabbed Mollie's shoulder. "Your dad forced you, right?" Mollie's eyebrows arched in a look of surprise. Clearly, Hank's information was not meant for general distribution. "*Why?*"

"He said that it wasn't going to work out...that it would never work out and that it was best if I just ended it."

"Why did he say that?"

Her eyes drifted to the side. "How in the hell should I know?" Jane read this as a lie.

"Were you and Jake having sex?"

"*No!*"

"Hey, Jake hung out here a lot. The two of you had plenty of time to be together. Your father being a preacher, there's plenty of reason he wouldn't want his only child bangin' her boyfriend..."

"Good God, woman! What's wrong with you?!" Mollie pulled away from Jane. "We didn't have sex. I'm a *b'suleh*." Jane looked confused. "A *virgin*," Mollie whispered with purpose.

Jane watched Mollie. There was something in the way she said, "We didn't have sex" that sounded uneven. But there was no use pushing the issue. The kid was clearly not going to talk any further. Jane nodded and turned toward the door and then looked back at Mollie. "Hey, I've got a question for you, off topic." Mollie regarded Jane with suspicion. "Has anyone ever asked you if this place is haunted?"

Mollie's gaze was unyielding. "No one has ever asked me that. Is there a problem?"

"I don't know," Jane uttered, feeling ridiculous for asking the girl such an off-the-wall question.

Jane turned to go. "Give my regards to Casper," Mollie

whispered.

Jane quietly crept into the hallway after leaving Mollie's room, but when she turned to ascend the staircase, she couldn't help but see Sara standing on a short ladder in the kitchen and replacing the red photo album in a locked cabinet that was situated above one of the glass cupboards. It was also easy to see where Sara hid the key.

By the time Jane and Weyler arrived at Annie's Place, the local diner, there were wall-to-wall people waiting for tables. A flat screen TV was tuned to the Denver morning news program in the far corner of the diner. Weyler assured her that they had a reserved booth, courtesy of Bo Lowry and his immeasurable pull. Jane had slipped into her last clean shirt, which looked like a carbon copy in color and design of the other two that were sitting in a muddy heap on The Gardenia Room carpet. Her Glock was secured in its shoulder holster. Once situated in the booth next to Weyler, she brought out a stack of notes from her leather satchel, along with the sketchpad with the hanging man she stole from Jake's room.

"I would think twice before I bring that out for show and tell," Weyler warned, eyeing the sketchpad.

"The fact that Jake meticulously takes the time to create an animation of an old man hanging in a cell isn't the least bit disturbing in this case?"

"Baby steps, Jane. You can't come off balls to the wall with Bo. You know that."

"Right. I'm a strident dyke." She stuffed the sketchpad back into her satchel.

"You know what I'm talking about."

"Just don't tell me to sit back and look pretty," she sarcastically added.

Annie arrived at their table with three glasses of ice water. "Hello, Jane," she said cheerfully. Weyler looked somewhat perplexed. "Hank came back to the locker room with half-birthday cake, but you'd already split!" Annie offered in a very familial tone.

Jane had only been orbiting the town for less than twenty-four hours and she was already getting the down-home treatment. "Tell him I had to get back to work," Jane said in an *all business* tenor.

"Tell him yourself. He's in his usual spot at the counter!"

Jane looked up and saw Hank wave at her with those twinkling eyes. *Good God Almighty*, she thought. This was starting to feel like high school. "You got espresso?" Jane asked, desperate to change the subject. Annie nodded. "I'll take six shots in the dark and two in the dark to go."

Weyler ordered a cup of black coffee and Annie left to retrieve the drinks. He handed Jane a menu that was tucked between the napkin holder and a greasy bottle of Frank's Red Hot Sauce. "You've been busy," Weyler surmised, taking a gander at the menu.

Jane explained that she talked to Hank about Jake and checked out his locker. She conveniently left out the whole part about the half-birthday. She did disclose the mysterious notation in Bailey's handwriting of *1401 Imperial*. "You think that's going to come off as too dyke-ish to Bo?" Jane asked curtly, referencing the discovery of the address.

"Jesus Christ, you really are hurting for a cigarette, aren't you? Try sucking on some ice cubes. Heard that takes the edge off."

Jane surveyed the menu. "Even a bag of ice wouldn't work, Boss." She slapped down the menu. "I gotta ask you something before he gets here. Did you notice the boxes in Bo's office? The ones labeled with question marks and exclamation points?"

"I did."

"So…what's up with that?"

"Everyone has their own way of organizing their paperwork. Some people color code. What's your point?"

Jane took a sip of water and slid an ice cube into her mouth.

"I just think it's odd." She sucked on the cube, hoping it would reduce the growing edge that was building around her. "What's with Bo's limp?"

Weyler set down the menu. "It's an old injury that happened in the line of duty."

Jane stared at Weyler as the wheels turned. "Oh, shit. Did you shoot him by mistake when you were rookies? Is that what this whole *I owe you* is about?"

"Suck on another ice cube, Jane. Your imagination is going wild." Weyler motioned to the front door of the diner.

Bo entered, lumbering across the linoleum toward their booth. He dropped into the seat across from Jane and Weyler, with his generous gut arriving shortly thereafter. "Goddamnit! It's colder than a lawyer's heart out there. Sorry I'm late," Bo said, directing his words toward Weyler. "I thought I was dyin' this mornin' when I saw blood in the toilet after I took a dump. Then I remembered I ate beets last night for dinner." He scooped up the menu and gave it a cursory exam. Without looking at Jane, he directed his words toward her. "Beanie tells me you're tryin' to quit smokin.'"

Jane was a little taken back. "Yeah. That's right."

Bo had a strange way of reading a menu, glancing back and forth from side to side as if he were watching a tennis game. "So, is that the excuse for your attitude?"

Jane eyed Weyler. "No excuse. I've got the same mentality whether I'm smoking or not."

Bo regarded Jane over the top of his menu. "Is that right? I quit smoking once." Jane furrowed her brow, realizing Bo was puffing pretty good on his cigar when they first met. "First five days, I'd like to have drawn and quartered every damn person I met. But on day six, everything smoothed out real nice."

"Really?" Jane asked with genuine interest. "How?"

"Because I started smokin' again on day six! Took that damn edge right off!" Bo chuckled, enjoying his joke at Jane's expense. "I sure as hell hope you're quittin' for the right reasons.

I quit because a friend of mine got emphysema. I felt like shit when I heard that. And then, it dawned on me. What in the hell was I thinkin'? *He's* got the disease, not *me*! Why should *I* quit 'cause *he's* dying?!" Jane was dumbfounded. Bo's mind was a seriously odd little place to dwell. Bo slapped down the menu. "Oh, I almost forgot!" Reaching into the inside of his shirt, he pulled out a black-and-white photo. He slid it in front of Jane. "This belongs to you."

Jane looked at the photo. It was a crystal clear shot of her Mustang purposely zooming past the speed camera across from the infamous bridge. The bridge was easy to see, proving the point of her experiment. "Good. It worked. I think you should replace this static camera with a 24/7 video feed for the duration of the investigation…just in case there's activity on the bridge that could prove fruitful."

"Is that right?" Bo snorted in a dismissive tone.

Jane could see this was heading into the same ballpark as the last game they played in his office. "You said on the QT that they're putting up security cameras all over town. Why can't they put one up there temporarily just for this…"

"I'll look into it," Bo said, cutting her off, "but no promises." He pulled a ticket out of his chest pocket and slapped it in front of her. "You can give me a check now for that or pay it at the front desk."

Jane read the amount: *$175.00.* "Is this a joke?"

"No, little lady, this is not a joke. Camera clocked your ol' stallion goin' sixty-five in a forty-five zone."

Jane was dumbfounded. This bloated asshole was doing everything he could to piss her off. She wanted to tear up the ticket and shove it down his throat. Fortunately, Annie arrived with the coffee.

"Hey, Bo!" she said sweetly.

"Hey, sweetheart! This is my good buddy over here, Morgan Weyler." Bo stopped there, effectively omitting Jane. Jane took a hefty gulp of her potent brew.

Annie took their orders, with Bo disregarding the menu and ordering a schizophrenic cornucopia of breakfast items, including sausages, waffles, steak, hash browns, pancakes and three kinds of juice. "Keep the green off my plate!" he reminded Annie. Coffee, he announced, made him sleepy. Jane chalked it up to his backward wiring, possibly dysgenic, bizarre behavior. Once Annie was out of earshot, Bo gave them the rundown on her and this popular diner. It seemed that Annie, all of twenty-five years old, had been a beloved member of the Midas community since she and her late mother moved to town when she was fifteen. Dad was out of the picture, Bo was quick to say, and her last name, Mack, was her mother's maiden name. Jane deduced that the kid was either the product of an ugly divorce or illegitimate. Either way, Jane couldn't care less. She wanted to tackle the Van Gorden case. And yet, they got to hear more about dear Annie.

"All she ever wanted to do was open a restaurant," Bo told Weyler. "It's been her dream since I can remember. This place used to be called *The Crimson Café,* run by a couple of lesbian hippies from Vermont. You should have seen what it looked like before she took it over. God help us. Bathroom was painted in lacquer red. Floor, ceiling, walls, everywhere you looked, shiny red was starin' back at you. God, it was like taking a shit in the middle of a blood clot."

"How does a kid that age afford to buy a place like this?" Weyler asked.

"After her mother died of cancer, she got some life insurance money as a start-up. Then fortune shined on her. An anonymous benefactor sent her a check for $35,000."

"We should all be so lucky," Jane said in a rushed tone as she brought out a stack of pages. "Look, we need to go over some new information I uncovered last night…"

"Don't get your panties in a twist. We'll get to it!"

This was outrageous. "*Excuse me?*"

Weyler intervened. "Bo, Jane's found some new information

that could be pertinent." He nodded to Jane.

She pulled out the plastic-covered blank page impregnated with urine and placed it in front of Bo. When she told him that the funky aroma on the page was piss and that it spelled out a sentence, he was actually speechless for a couple seconds. "He's smart. He knows we can't get DNA off urine. But he's also making a point, I think, with the metaphor." Bo looked baffled. "He's *pissed*-off about something big."

"*Well, obviously,*" Bo responded, dryly. "The guy's deranged!" He pushed the sheet toward Jane with his chubby index finger, not wanting to get too familiar with it. "I don't buy your metaphor idea. See, I think he just wanted to disgust us."

"Have you ever heard of a street named *Imperial*?" Jane asked.

"10-74," Bo stated, using code again for "No." Jane explained how she found the address in Jake's locker at The Rabbit Hole. "What in the hell are you rootin' around in his locker for?"

"For anything, Bo! Anything that might lead us to something!" *This is getting pointless*, Jane deduced. Annie showed up with the food. Bo's multicourses took up over half the table. After rearranging the plates several times, Bo slathered an empty hot plate with butter pads, stirring them around on the dish with his knife until the entire circumference was dripping in the liquid fat. He then piled that buttery plate with food and dove in with the delight of a starving Ethiopian. While he was preoccupied chewing, Jane put forth her idea that the clues were telling a story—a speculation that Bo tossed around with Weyler. She doubted he would care about her next theory, but she laid out the possibility that there was a missing clue that the Van Gordens were holding back. That one didn't go over well.

"Don't serve me a plate of crazy, girl! And don't get all lippy with me either!" Bo said, spitting out bits of egg. "His parents are beside themselves with worry. They've been nothin' but cooperative with us!"

"Bailey said he pulled the officer assigned to trace any calls coming into their house because, after four days, it wasn't convenient for him. That doesn't sound like he's being cooperative!"

"Hey!" Bo leaned across the table with a mean look on his face. "There's a damn limit to what a man can handle. I understand that! So, I didn't see any problem when he asked to pull the cop."

Jane took a bite of her eggs and washed it down with another hearty swallow of coffee. "Well, I *do* see a problem..."

"That's 'cause you're an outsider with an agenda."

"Bo..." Weyler interrupted.

"No, no, let me have my say here! I've dealt with this crap before so I know what I'm talkin' about! We had a group called *Atheists United* a few years back that convinced the county idiots that they were worthy of sponsoring a section of the highway outside of town for cleanup. They posted a sign that proudly displayed ATHEISTS UNITED in big bold letters. Every time I passed that sign, I wanted to blast it to hell along with the heathens that put it up. As the weeks past, that section of the highway was dirtier than it had ever been. I called up the head SOB of the group and said, either you atheists are too damn lazy or you don't *believe* that trash exists. Either way, I said, I want you to give up your contract. Well, he wasn't up for that. He wanted me to be *tolerant* of his sign and his beliefs. His problem was that he had his head up his ass. He had his finger up there too, so it was crowded down there. But I wasn't about to let that God-hating fool tell *me* what was gonna happen! See, within a week, I personally had the wrath of his nonexistent God breathin' down his neck in the form of state agencies, the county and even one of those crazy Eco nuts. You ain't suffered until you've had an Eco nut ridin' your rump from dusk 'til dawn!" Bo sat back. "In short, I made his life a livin' hell and he agreed to give up that section of the highway. I handed it over to a nice little group of blue-haired ladies from the Midas Book Club. It's so clean now, you could do brain surgery on the side of the road."

Outsiders with agendas, Jane thought. *Well, fuck you and the horse you rode in on, Bo Lowry.* After Bo's long-winded story and inference that he could make her life miserable and drive her off the case, she wanted to grab her six shots in the dark, plus her two to go, and drive back to Denver. And she would have done just that if she didn't feel something deeply for the missing kid who everyone else seemed to be using for collateral. She wasn't about to bring up the *mysecretrevelations* website. Nor would she utter a word about the suicidal animated drawing on the sketchpad. Bo was a fucking asshole, she decided. And no matter how tight he and Weyler were or what bullshit happened long ago that caused Weyler to think he "owed" Bo something, she'd work the angles and she'd do it quietly. And she'd make damn sure she kept as much distance between herself and this corn-fed blowhard as possible. Jane crammed one bite of food after another into her mouth and hoped her silence would speak volumes to Weyler.

Bo looked at Weyler. "We gotta focus on the one man who is the most likely contestant in this game...*Trash Bag Jordan.*" Jane happened to glance over to the far corner of the diner. It took her a few moments to realize that it was Jordan Copeland. He sat alone, bent over a plate of food, with his back to her. "I don't have to read his jacket to know what I'm dealing with," Bo continued, referring to Jordan's criminal file. "See, I look at the way people think by picturing a series of nuts in their head. People who think clearly have their nuts all lined up in a neat little row," he said, demonstrating this belief by lining up the salt-and-pepper shaker along with several bottles of condiments. "But then you have people who think up and down and all around." Bo furiously mixed up the bottles. "I call that *uneven nut distribution.* Jordan Copeland has *severe* uneven nut distribution."

Weyler chimed in. "You think he's doing it with some help?"

"Not sure. See, the perv talks to no one. Has no friends. I imagine the only people he would ever talk to for any length of time would be as crazy and nutty as he is!"

Jane's gaze was still focused on Jordan. Now it was her turn to penetrate the back of his neck with her jagged vibe.

"Is this a two-person operation with one person holding little *Juice Box* and the other playing note deliverer?" Bo postulated to Weyler in a hushed tone. "Or did Jordan just kidnap him and kill him, and then confuse us with riddles and notes that mean nothing and go nowhere?"

Bo continued yammering in the background, but Jane tuned him out. She was focused on Jordan's back. There was a slight turn of his head to the right. At first, Jane thought he was reacting to the television that blared above his head. But that wasn't it because the slight turn graduated into a roll that stopped just short of seeing Jane. She'd connected with him. Somehow, he knew she was there staring at him from across the room. She didn't let herself slide back into the booth mentally until she heard Bo mention Jake's name.

"What's that?" she asked, still slightly out of it.

Bo looked frustrated. "I said that the problem with *Juice Box Jakey* was that he thought too damn much! That's when you get yourself in trouble."

"Thinking?" Jane asked.

"10-4. Questionin' everything! See, he never could take a breath because he was too busy rehashin' crap and then re-questionin' all the crap! God, it would make a man weary just watchin' it." Bo let out a long, tired breath. "Now the irony is he's got all of us doin' the same damn shit, tryin' to figure out where his sorry ass is right now. While he's 10-72'n he gets 10-65'd," he moaned, using code for *committing suicide* and *kidnapped* respectively. "I guess at the end of the day all we do is hope."

Jane felt her back stiffen. There was that empty word again. She shook her head, and took another gulp of her dark brew and a bite of food. "Hope lays there waiting for something to happen or for someone else to improve your circumstance. Hope teases you into believing that around that next corner everything will magically change."

Bo regarded Jane with a baneful eye. "Well, pardon me if I disagree with you. Hope, for a lot of us, keeps you alive."

Jane met his mean glare. "It keeps you in prison."

"Well, what in the hell do you suggest we do if we don't have hope for Jake?"

Jane considered his question carefully. "Belief and action. We believe we can save him and we take action to make that happen." She finished the last bite on her plate, grabbed her *to go* coffee and pried herself off the vinyl cushion. "I'll be outside," she told Weyler, throwing a $10.00 bill on the table.

She started down the aisle when she saw the talking head of a Denver news reporter on the flat screen diner TV mentioning the kidnapping of Jake Van Gorden. Jake's face was splashed across the large screen, his ponytail draped around the neck of his black T-shirt. All eyes in the diner turned to the TV and a hush fell over the crowd. The next shot on the television was an establishing shot of Midas' Main Street, taken the day before the film crew visited the town. Jane winced, knowing what was coming next. As expected, there was the scene outside the Town Hall with Bo at the microphone and Weyler and her in the background. But instead of the camera focusing completely on Bo, Jane was easy to see in the frame. She thought she'd hid her discomfort when she was standing up there, but her angst was painted across her face for the world to see.

She wanted to dissolve out of that diner, and she was on her way out when she noticed Jordan Copeland, still seated in his booth. He was staring at the TV with his right arm dangling by his side, shaking uncontrollably.

Outside, the cold bit at her skin. She pulled her jacket tighter around her body. *God, a cigarette would taste damn good right about now.* Every nerve ending was raw; every emotion like a scab pulled off a wound that wasn't healed. The frigid wind whipped around Jane's body. It felt like a storm was moving in and preparing to dump a foot of spring snow in the high country. That was the thing about Colorado—March and April were often the snowiest months of the year. But, in keeping with Colorado's erratic late winter patterns, you could see a foot of snow on Monday and have eighty-five degrees on Tuesday. At that moment though, the cold was unforgiving. She started down Main Street toward the B&B but she only got about thirty feet when she heard Weyler calling her name.

She turned and saw a somewhat uneasy look on his face. Walking toward him, the look of concern grew. Her gut twisted. "What is it?" she asked.

"The receptionist at Town Hall just got a call from the kidnapper. The voice was distorted. All he said is 'I'm waiting' and left the line open. They triangulated the signal and found the scene. There's a black car there. And Jake's body may be in the trunk."

CHAPTER 14

Jane followed in her Mustang while Weyler rode with Bo in a patrol car. It was the same damn, two-lane road with the red rock on the right side; the same road that led to the bridge and Jordan Copeland's hideaway. But now, they drove past the infamous bridge, past the speed cameras and past Jordan's ten-acre fenced property. They continued for another two miles as the sky darkened and thick flakes of snow fell indiscriminately across the landscape. The whole time, Jane felt sick. Weyler quietly told her that the deputy smelled decomposition coming from the trunk of the vehicle—the vehicle that matched the color description of the car seen on the bridge. Was the kid who sought the truth and declared it on a poster in his bedroom lying dead in the trunk of a car, abandoned on the side of the road? Had the *truth* become this dangerous?

By the time Jane and Bo pulled up to the scene, the sky had given way to diagonal waves of snow. As Jane got out of her Mustang and walked along the road to the site, the flakes quickly covered the hoods of the three police vehicles that had already shown up. Weyler brought an umbrella and sheltered Jane as they made the solemn journey past the police vehicles and up a short, dirt incline that led twenty feet further to a two-door, black beater of a car that looked to be a thirty-five-year-old Chevy Vega. No plates. Busted tail pipe. Smashed in passenger side with primer covering the door. A small rock cairn sat in the center of the car's closed trunk, seemingly marking the spot. It wasn't easy in these mountains to successfully triangulate a cell phone ping. Jane asked a cop standing nearby how the deputy discovered the car since it was pretty much off the road and out of sight. The cop pointed to another larger rock cairn positioned neatly on the side of the highway. The kidnapper was doing everything now to make sure his handiwork was seen.

Jane didn't need the cairn to locate the black vehicle. The smell of decomp was overwhelming, starting from the moment the three of them walked up the hill to the scene. Several cops near the vehicle covered their mouths with cloths to repel the nauseating stench. Jane, Weyler and Bo stood waiting while the police photographer took shots of the rock cairn on the hood. The snow subsided as quickly as it started, with only a few errant flakes falling on the ground. Weyler discarded the umbrella as the photographer finished the last shot. Bo gave the order to "Open 'er up." Another cop stepped forward with a tire iron and jimmied the trunk. Jane's heart raced as it popped a couple inches and stuck, releasing the ungodly stink of death. A nearby cop quickly turned, vomiting. One more good thrust and the trunk lifted.

"Good Christ Almighty!" Bo exclaimed. "That bastard!"

Jane and Weyler had to step back. Staring back at them was a heap of animal carcasses, most likely road kill, in various stages of putrefaction. The rotting stench was like getting hit in the head by a two-by-four. What looked like a raccoon had almost dissolved to liquid goo that intermingled with the bloated carcass of a deer. Thousands of maggots feasted on the trunk's contents, moving freely through the empty orbs and out the well-devoured nostrils. While it was difficult to judge—given the fact that the animals were already flattened and disintegrating prior to being tossed in the trunk—Jane wild-guessed that the sickening soup of death had been cooking in the Vega's trunk for at least five days. That was important to her because it meant that this clue had been planned from almost the moment Jake was kidnapped. If her theory that the kidnapper was telling a story was correct, what in the hell did this mean? Where was the symmetry that gave this clue significance?

Looking closer at the putrid pile of death, Jane saw a black cell phone sitting upright in the chewed out ear of the deer. It was on and still connected to Town Hall's main line. Bo's cell phone rang. Jane called out for gloves and an officer handed her a pair. She snapped them on, held her breath and wrestled the phone from the grip of maggots. "I'm sure it's a prepaid disposable," she commented in Bo's direction.

"That was Vi," Bo stated, snapping his cell phone shut. "She said we got a phone number on the Caller ID that doesn't match the first two numbers that came in. This one has an area code from back east. She's gonna track it down."

Moving away from the car, Jane slid the back panel of the phone off and saw exactly what she expected. "No SIM card." An officer handed her a plastic evidence bag into which she deposited the phone. She pulled off the gloves and tossed them in a trash bag.

After the police cameraman finished documenting the frigid scene, Jane drew her leather jacket tight against her chest, walked around to the driver's side door and peered inside the vehicle. The seats were shredded. Springs popped through the upholstery in the backseat. Piles of rodent droppings littered both the front and back seats. After learning that the door handles had been dusted for prints and were absent of anything fresh, she tried the handle on the driver's side door. It was locked shut. The same thing proved true for the passenger door.

"Nobody's driven this car since Nixon was in office," she stated to Weyler who scanned the car interior from the passenger side. She looked at the set of tire tracks that led up to the car. "If Bo takes molds of those tracks, they'll probably match the SUV, van or truck that dragged this piece of junk here. I'd rule out a van, personally."

Weyler revealed that Bo was familiar with the black beater Chevy Vega. It had been sitting at the dump for twenty years, which was located five miles down the road.

"Any chance of security cameras at the dump?" Weyler shook his head. "You said Jordan doesn't own a car, right? So, if he's involved, how'd he get this thing here?"

"He's got to have a partner."

"An outcast and a loner decides to partner up? Does that sound plausible to you?"

"Anything's possible at this point, Jane."

Jane turned around, leaning on the hood of the car. She stared into the thicket of trees and brush in front of her. At first she didn't see it, even though it was fairly obvious. But once she spotted it, she froze. It was another cairn, tucked away behind a stand of trees. It was even bigger than the one located on the highway that alerted the patrol cop.

"See something?" Weyler asked.

Jane spoke before she thought. "No." The minute the word fell from her lips, she regretted the lie. She'd only lied to Weyler a few times in her career and that was when she was either drunk or not thinking clearly. Right now, she figured the latter was applicable, but she didn't correct herself. Instead she told Weyler that she was going to walk around the perimeter of the area to check out things. Once he moved away from the area and she was certain the surrounding cops couldn't see her, she calmly strolled to the cairn behind the trees. When she stood over it, it was easy to see the line of smaller rocks that extended out from the stacked rocks and into the woods, forming an obvious path. *Perhaps it isn't the car with the dead animals in the trunk or the cell phone that's the next dot in the story,* she thought. That might have been just the kidnapper's loud announcement that led to something else…something that had more value.

She stared at the rock path and then back at the cairn. What she did next was called "interfering with an ongoing investigation." She preferred to call it "taking the bull by the horns and ramrodding the investigation." With one good kick, she toppled the cairn. She used the toe of her cowboy boot to toss the long pathway of stones to the side. Checking back at the scene, she was satisfied that nobody was watching her. She turned and followed the well-placed rock path that wound around a stand of spruce trees and graduated up an incline toward a shaded rocky area. She made sure to kick the small rocks in the path as far away as possible to make the clue indistinguishable to anyone else. Jane stopped right before the outcropping of large rocks. The wet snow lay heavy on the spruce branches around her, dipping their tips of new growth toward the earth. But the rocky outcropping had been protected from the snowy blast by the large evergreens, exposing the next clue in the story.

A single cigarette was positioned on a large rock in front of Jane, its tip pointed slightly to the left. Without hesitating, she withdrew her Glock, holding it at her side as she moved closer. She stood over it and easily noted the black mark of a pen encircling the cigarette about one millimeter from the tip. The other end clearly showed the insignia of the brand, *Chesterfield.* Noting the direction the cigarette was pointing, she picked it up and continued on that path. Ten feet farther, up another slight incline, she easily found the next cigarette. It was the same brand and had the same curious mark near its tip in black ink. This cigarette pointed straight ahead and so she collected it and kept walking. Like a game of hopscotch, she followed the cigarette pathway, collecting each identical one before moving onto the next, taking care to move judiciously just in case the kidnapper was watching, gorging on the attention as much as the maggots were still enjoying their juicy banquet in the trunk. After recovering the tenth cigarette, she emerged into a small clearing, smattered with snow. Artfully placed on the bed of dried spruce needles was a heavy glass and leather ashtray with four grooves that each held a cigarette. The remaining six cigarettes formed an arrow that pointed to an empty, crushed Chesterfield burgandy pack. On the front, it read: CHESTERFIELD 101.

It was the sort of scene that needed to be photographed and documented. Whatever it meant, Jane knew it was a vital link in the story that the kidnapper was telling. But, goddamnit, she was tired of being called everything from "lippy" to a dyke by Bo Lowry simply because her out-of-the-box opinions and theories were off-center. Jane stood over the scene for several minutes, wrestling with her next move. Finally, she pulled out her cell phone, selected the camera feature and took four photos of the mysterious set-up before picking up the evidence—including the ashtray—and burying them in the pockets of her jacket.

When she returned to the Vega, Weyler crossed toward her. "Anything?" he asked.

Jane made a point to look away so the he wouldn't read. "Nothing." She turned back to Weyler. "Is Bo going to tell the Van Gordens about this?"

"No."

"If I'm correct about the guy's signature pattern, he's most likely given up now on back and forth clues between the Van Gordens and Bo. If the pattern were still in effect, the Chevy Vega with the dead meat in the trunk would have shown up outside the Van Gordens' house. But he's changed it up because the family refuses to talk publicly."

Weyler turned to Jane in a confidential manner. "You're basing that on the assumption that the Van Gordens are holding back a clue."

"Yeah. I am. But I also know this guy is getting bolder. You watch. The clues will get bolder too. He's tired of playing it safe. This guy is basically saying 'Fuck you. I want the world to *hear* me and understand me.'"

"Understand what? Dead animals in a trunk?"

She felt the corner of the heavy leather and glass ashtray pressing against her side. "Sure. Why not?" Jane moved closer to Weyler. "Listen, I think it would be prudent to put some eyes on Jordan's property. Nothing obvious. Just watch him."

"Meaning you?" Weyler asked, his tone uneasy.

"Yes. The more I can steer clear of your buddy Bo, the healthier we'll all be. Don't you agree?"

Jane made her way back to the Mustang, happy to be clear of both the rotting stench and trail of lies she left at the scene. Carefully removing the ashtray and cigarettes from her jacket pocket, she secured them in the pocket of her leather satchel. She headed back to Jordan's property two miles back up the highway. Parking on the river side of the highway with the car turned so that the driver's side was closest to the river, Jane sheltered the Mustang amidst an opportunistic stand of trees that shrouded the car from view. From this vantage point, she could easily view Jordan's property, including most of his log cabin that sat on stilts. She rolled down the windows to push the stagnant air from the car and popped open her glove compartment, unearthing a small pair of well-worn binoculars. She noted the time as 10:10 am. As she surveyed the river's edge and surrounding acreage, she saw no sign of life. All was eerily quiet until a voice broke through the stillness.

"Whatcha lookin' for, Jane?"

Jane quickly turned toward the passenger window. There, leaning on the partially open window, was Jordan Copeland. How he was able to perambulate there without Jane hearing him was anybody's guess.

He reached inside the car, unlocked the door and opened it. Jane touched the Glock inside her jacket.

Jordan wedged his filthy body with his trademark oil-cloth coat in the passenger seat and slammed the door shut. He turned to her with impunity, his iridescent eyes glimmering. "I knew you'd come back to see me." He winked. "Take your hand off your gun. You're not gonna shoot me. But you *are* going to drive."

CHAPTER 15

Jane regarded Jordan with contempt. His foul body odor filled the Mustang, permeating every inch of the car. Chunks of mud laced with fresh snow fell off his boots and onto the floor mat. His grey beard, coated with stems of dried mud and frosty fingers of snow, matched his scruffy, uncombed and unmanageable curled mane.

"Go on, Jane. There's another small bridge about a hundred feet ahead. Drive across it and onto my property before your merry band of black-and-whites come barreling down the road and see us." Jane remained motionless. "*Jane?*" Jordan said, like a scolding schoolteacher. "What are you waiting for? *Drive!*"

Even though she was the one with the loaded Glock under her jacket, she felt oddly vulnerable. But she still wanted to cross that small bridge. Maybe it was that damned curiosity of hers that never seemed to be satisfied or maybe it was the fact that she always tended to do whatever she was told *not* to do. She fired up the Mustang and followed his directions. As she drove over the rickety bridge, for a fleeting moment she wondered if this was actually a kidnapping. Was this how Jordan lured Jake off the bridge? Did he make the boy feel safe and secure and then do something wicked when he had his back turned? Maybe. But there was no way Jane would ever let her guard down with him. *Never.*

Once across the bridge, Jordan instructed her to drive to a spot behind his cabin where her ice blue Mustang would be shrouded from view. She waited for him to get out of the car before she followed.

"This way," he directed, pointing to an even more densely forested part of the property. Jane stopped. "You don't want them to see you, do you?" He smiled. "Ladies first," he said with that queasy timbre.

"After you," Jane insisted.

"Aren't you a lady?"

"Yeah. A smart one." She motioned forward with her chin. "After you, Jordan."

Jordan smiled and began to chuckle, walking ahead of Jane and leading her deeper into the wooded area. She cautiously pulled her Glock from its holster and held it at her side. "Is that really necessary, Jane?" he asked, still with his back to her.

She was always good at covertly removing her gun, but this guy seemed to have the same heightened sense of hearing that she'd developed over the last two days. "I'll keep it out for now, Jordan."

He sniggered. "Suit yourself." He led her farther into the property. The ground was sloppy from the recent blast of snow. "I have another riddle for you," he said without turning his back. "There is one word in the English language that is always pronounced incorrectly. What is it?"

Jane kept five feet of distance behind him. She considered the riddle. "The answer is *incorrectly*."

"Very good, Jane! You *listen*! *You pay attention*! Well done!"

His response wasn't lost on Jane's suspicious mind. "You need people to listen to you and pay attention, don't you?"

There was another snort of condescension. "You've determined that your cunning kidnapper is doing the same thing, eh?" He stopped and turned. Jane halted, never taking her eyes off him. "One more riddle. Why don't Mormons drink coffee?"

Jane didn't have a clue but she was sure he was winding up

to sling another politically incorrect salvo. "No clue."

"Because if they did, they'd wake up and realize how really fucked up their lives were." He let out a quick laugh.

"You're an equal opportunity hater. I get it." She started to take a step back when her boot slipped in the slick mud. Before she could get her balance, she hit the ground hard, splattering mud over her jeans and shirt. Jane quickly raised the Glock toward Jordan, unsure of how he might take advantage of this opportunity.

"You certainly have a difficult time keeping clean, don't you?" he said, completely unruffled by the loaded firearm pointed at his chest. He reached out to Jane, offering his hand. She waved him off and gingerly stood up, training the gun on him the entire time. He leaned his large body against a spruce tree, unaffected by Jane's aggressive stance. "You got that tough girl vibe on overdrive, don't you? You're not exactly reeking of the pure feminine archetype. More like Betty Butch." Now Jane was really pissed. This was the second asshole in two days who referenced a dyke vibe coming from her. Her first thought was to beat his head into the spruce tree but then she realized that would probably validate his observation. Jordan reached up toward the new growth on the tree, snapped off a few of the pale green needles and popped them in his mouth. "Did you know that spruce needles can prevent scurvy?" he asked, chewing the needles into a mush. "It's true. Natural vitamin C. All those pioneers dropping dead on the Oregon Trail from scurvy and they were surrounded by their cure. Don't you just love irony, Jane?"

"How about if we walk back to your house?"

"No chance. That's sacred territory in there. Nobody's allowed in my dwelling."

"Really? Cops went through it after Jake went missing."

"True. I had to air it out for days to get rid of the *blue* stink. Nah, I like it out here. You spend thirty-four years in a six-by-eight box and you'd be partial to the outdoors too."

"Is that why you roam around your property at night?"

"Who told you that?" A devious smile crept across his face. "Bo Lowry."

"Christ. What a bloated chatter-fuck. Nothing worse than a little man who thinks he has big power. Bo Lowry is a *farce* to be reckoned with! You hear that sucking sound? That's Lowry's career circling the drain."

"But you *do* roam this place at night?" Jane said, moving back on message. "What's curious is that Jake Van Gorden also liked to ramble around when it was dark. It's not outside the scope that the two of you might have made contact, especially with nighttime to cloak the communication."

"I already covered this with you. I'm not allowed within one hundred feet of a school or in the presence of a child under the age of eighteen..."

"You're wily. You'd figure out a way."

"*Wily*. Interesting choice of word." He grabbed another few needles off the tree and ate them. "We talking about me or you?"

"Don't change the subject."

"You're wily as hell, Jane. Must I remind you how you gained entrance to my property the second time we met?" Jordan seemed to know more about her personality than she would have liked. "Yes..."

"Yes, what?"

"I roam my territory at night. But you don't know much about a man, do you? If you did, you'd know that a man's territory is wherever he's standing. A man learns to own that."

"When you're out of your safe zone, you don't own the land you stand over. I saw you at the diner. I bet you sit in the same booth every time you go there." Jordan furrowed his brow, an indication to Jane that she was right. "You don't tread far from your safety zone because that's unchartered water for you. Swim too far and you might drown."

He regarded her with a sharpened stare. After a few heavy seconds, Jordan straightened his spine. "I could swim out there if I chose...if I was unhampered by the unwashed masses. But there's too many sharks waiting to pull me down."

She immediately spotted a vulnerability in him. This monster with the acid tongue had been beaten by a life unlived; a life spent mostly confined in a cell with a small window on a world that felt too treacherous to navigate. "You certainly have a flair for the English language."

"Would it be more conventional for me to be stupid? I wasn't staring at the fucking wall for thirty-four years."

She recalled what Bo told her about Jordan's jailhouse education. "Right. You got two degrees. Philosophy and esoteric psychology, whatever the hell that is."

"Whatever the hell that is," he repeated in a monotone, "I can outthink most people, Jane, with my left brain tied behind my back."

There was no doubt in her mind that he was highly intelligent. Superior intelligence and criminal degeneracy were not mutually exclusive. It was another facet of Jordan's personality that red-flagged him as a suspect in Jake's disappearance. "You own a television?"

"No. I don't need to watch TV so I can be fed all the news they feel I need to know."

"How about a phone?"

"No."

"Really?"

"*Really.*" Jordan looked a Jane more closely. "Your kidnapper is calling and leaving messages?"

"Strange you wouldn't have a phone…"

"I know I'm the number-one suspect…"

"No, actually, you're a *person of interest.* It means the same thing as *suspect.* We just use that gentler term now because we don't want to sound like we're violating your good name until we decide it's time to violate you." Jane moved toward a spruce tree opposite Jordan and leaned her back against it. She kept the Glock close at her side. "You on meds?"

"They wanted to give me drugs to amend my anti-social

behavior. I told them socializing was overrated. I don't do well amidst the groaning clog of humanity. When I left prison, the docs wanted to give me pills that would *quiet me*," Jordan said with a greasy tenor. "I feel too much and they think that a drug is going to help that. *Typical.* Choke the underbelly of emotion even though it has the right to exist in a person." He pulled another few needles of new growth off the spruce tree and ate it, spitting out several needles that disagreed with him. "I think, therefore, I'm dangerous. I observe, therefore, I'm worthy of suspicion. Odd, isn't it, that *thinking* has become a liability in our society. Better I should follow the mediocre sheeple to slaughter than dare entertain ideas that provoke and frustrate the drones. And nobody understands the art of observation anymore. All the zombies wait around for the Big Boys who run the joint to spoon feed them their commentary on what we're seeing because critical thinking died a quick, painful death. Original thinkers are as common as a rotary phone. Those who choose to ruminate outside the box are either condemned or destroyed."

Jane had to check herself. There were too many similarities between the way she and Jordan looked at life. Even though they were standing in a circle of evergreens, she would continue this interview as if they were seated in the green-walled interrogation room back at DH. "You smoke, Jordan?"

"No. Nasty habit. Why? You cravin' a ciggie?"

"I don't smoke."

He observed her the same way she scrutinized liars and smiled. "*Riiight.*"

Obviously, the aroma of tobacco still lingered on her clothing. "I quit."

"Of course you did." His eyes dove into hers. "But they didn't quit you. You haven't smoked your last cigarette, Jane. *Mark my words.* You smoke to smother all those feelings. You suffocate your sensitivity because somebody made you believe that feeling is dangerous." His translucent blue eyes fixated on her. "But you *do* feel, don't you? You feel and see what others can't. Ah, you have the gift! *Yes!*"

Jane ignored him. Her thoughts turned back to the classic Chesterfield cigarettes and ashtray. "You collect antiques?"

Jordan seemed pissed that she changed the subject. "Oh, yeah. *Love* antiquing. Next to romantic walks on the beach at sunset, it really jerks my chain." He gave a sarcastic wink.

"You could go online and buy archaic crap…"

"No phone, no TV, no computer."

"The library has free computers."

"Don't own a credit card. I'm taken care of once a year by a long time friend of my father's. Edward Butterworth. *Eddie.* He *hates* it when I call him *Eddie.* He's a real East Coast, stuffed shirt, cocksucker. Ass so fucking tight he squeaks when he walks. He always stands back at least five feet from me when he slides that big ol' ugly trust fund check in my direction. Doesn't want to get too close to the family's little mistake." He took a step toward Jane. "*Da blackest of da black sheep, dats me!*" Jordan made a point to be as mordant as possible. "Yes, sir, Eddie's been takin' care of business for our family since heck was a pup. He's the cleanup man, you know? Makes sure the status quo is kept up and running. Makes sure everything that has to be buried stays dead."

It was important for Jane to toss out more questions, quickly changing the subject to try and throw off Jordan. "You a religious man?"

"That's hard to say. I don't believe in atheists." He waited for Jane to absorb that retort. "If God resides in every one of us, then isn't an atheist just someone who doesn't believe in himself?"

Jane figured these were the types of philosophical contemplations a person comes up with after spending way too much time wandering the woods at night. "So, you're not religious?"

"Life has enough challenges. I don't need to walk a dogma around and make it more complicated. Ah, religious folk! Why have one limiting belief when two or more makes your life that much more insular?" He stiffened his back. "I don't trust any faith that uses fear to keep me compliant. And I certainly can't be part of a religion that requires the suspension of thoughtful debate. I don't question the belief in God. I question the humanity of those who believe in Him." Jordan's stance relaxed and his facetious posture re-emerged. "I made Jesus a deal. I don't hide behind His name and he doesn't use my name to get into clubs. I've kept up my end of the deal. He's kept up his…as far as I know. It's hard to trust those Jewtians."

Jane was afraid where this was headed. "Jewtians?"

"Jews who go Christian. Slippery lot. They retain their drive for absolute power but now they're doin' it for J.C.!" Jordan winked and smiled. "You can take the Jew out of the synagogue but you can't take his edge off."

"Isn't Copeland a Jewish name?"

"Could be, I guess. But I'm not Jewish. I was raised Episcopalian. Just a wine glass and wafer away from being Catholic and playing *hide the weenie* with a homo priest. I could be a Buddhist, being that I enjoy the solitude and live like a fucking monk. But I couldn't stand having to worry about reincarnating as an inbred lap dog. I could never be a Muslim because I have bad knees and I can't kneel down to tie my shoes let alone hittin' the rug and facing Mecca five times a day. Although, it would be pretty damn cool to pop the cherries of seventy-two nubile virgins when I croak." His expression soured. "Does that answer your question?" He picked up a branch off the wet ground and proceeded to drag it through the dirt. "What are we gonna yak about next, Jane? How 'bout my childhood? That's always good for a few shits and grins. We know I was an outcast, right? I'm sure you've read all the yellowed newspaper clippings on my sordid life. I imagine the psych reports also enlightened you."

This was the perfect opportunity Jane had been waiting for. "Mom and dad were kind of long in the tooth when they had you."

He smiled a Cheshire cat grin. "You *noticed*? *Good for you*, Jane. Your attention to detail is cheering. Yes, Mrs. Copeland was a veritable treat. She kept her girlish figure twenty pounds underweight by drinking her lunch and never staying awake long enough to eat a complete meal. She was the single-handed reason that Valium was such a hot seller in the '60s. She was as soft and sweet natured as a full-blooded German. My dad, on the other hand, was an ascot-wearing, Bentley-driving rambler with polished fingernails and palms so soft because they never saw an honest day's work. When he had his fill of late night cigars, brandy snifters and pâté orgies at the Short Hills Country Club, he lowered himself from his high perch to socialize with my mother and I. He and I had everything to talk about from A to B. The ice clinking against the Scotch glass was the soundtrack of my childhood. That and the suffocating silence and disgust the Copelands showed toward me. It was a grand childhood, Jane. Just like a war without the poignant moments. A young boy's fantasy. Lots of money. Lots of *stuff*. Money buys happiness, you know."

Jane observed Jordan's defensive posture. "Who took care of you?"

Jordan's face slightly froze. It was very slight but Jane caught the pause of expression. "A lovely Negro woman, I suppose I should say African American or I can be PC. But she was from the Carribean. St. Lucia."

"What was her name?"

"Why? You gonna look her up? Don't bother. She's dead. She died a *long* time ago."

Jane caught Jordan's lower lip quivering. "How long ago?"

"When I was eight." Jordan's visage turned cold.

A piece fell into place for Jane. The traumatic event that created the schism, the moment when his world crashed around him came into view. Suddenly, Jane's thoughts turned to the two clues that featured drawings of a child wearing a red cap. The kid in the drawing looked to be around eight or nine.

Jane steadied herself against the tree, holding the Glock tighter. "How'd she die, Jordan?"

He sneered at her. "You think I killed her."

Jane attempted to remain stone-faced. "Did you?"

Insult covered his face. "No. She was asked to leave by my father and died shortly thereafter in a hospital at the age of thirty."

"What did she die of?"

"The inability to be," he said without hesitation.

"To be what?"

"*To be.*"

Jane watched as Jordan's mind sunk deeper into the past. "So, she was an outcast, just like you?"

"Yes. We were two of a kind. She qualified to be the house Negro due to the fact that her shade of skin wasn't as offensive as the other house Negroes that proliferated our neighborhood." His eyes drifted to the left, recalling the woman. "Soft beige. *Lots* of cream in her coffee. Still, Mrs. Copeland liked to call her my 'darky nanny.' And I was her little ivory problem."

"Why were you a problem?"

Jordan glanced at the ground. He abruptly thrust the branch into the wet soil. "Life is more difficult when it becomes unpredictable."

"I'm not following you. Were *you* unpredictable?"

"I was unexpected, and thus, *life* became unpredictable." His eyes were a mix of extreme anguish and unforgiving rage. "The Copelands didn't like hiccups in their schedule. And I was one goddamn hiccup. Mrs. Copeland would communicate with me with the disdain usually set aside for thieves and gardeners." His tenor dripped with odium and scorn.

"Why do you keep referring to your mother as 'Mrs. Copeland?'"

"Because that was the bitch's name."

"So, the nanny's out of the picture at age eight. Your dad is hardly there. And you're left with a mother who despises you.

You ramble around all alone in your big house with no one? Weren't there other kids in the neighborhood?"

"Sure. But I didn't exactly have the skills to relate. The only kid who wanted to hang with me was a thirteen-year-old retard."

"Who you killed…" Jane added, purposely wanting to see how the statement affected Jordan.

He tipped his head to the side. "Oh, *Jane*. What are you looking for?" Jane was intrigued by his seeming ability to read her mind. "Remorse? Anger? Unbridled regret? I can fake all those faces but why bother?"

She pushed back on track. "You chose not to have friends because it was safer to be alone. Nobody can leave you. Nobody can hurt you."

He brushed his oilcloth duster against the bark of the tree, attempting to get to an itch he couldn't scratch. "Is that why *you're* single, Jane? To avoid the pain?"

Jane's body tightened. "No ring on my finger. Brilliant deduction."

Jordan picked at a few errant specs of debris in his long beard. "Ring's got nothing to do with it, honey. You're hard. Your palette hasn't been softened by the brush of the right guy. Your steel cannot bend to the forge of a man because to melt your fear you have to become vulnerable." He leaned forward. "And *that*, my dear, scares the living shit out of you because once you go there, there's no turning back. You'll be toast!"

This was hitting too many nerves for Jane. "Do you…"

"Vulnerability for you equals weakness," Jordan stated, boring into Jane's soft spot. "Your daddy did a number on you, didn't he?"

That was the stinger for Jane. She stood taller in her boots in an attempt to get the upper hand. "Do you know where Jake Van Gorden is?"

"Back on message!" Jordan clapped his hands together and moved closer to her. "Good girl! Can't let a perfect stranger worm their way into your formidable psyche…especially when that stranger may have done something *so vile. So vile, indeed!* You seek the truth about Jakie's disappearance but you don't seek the truth within *yourself.*"

Now it was her turn to get her back up. "I'm here to do a job, not be psychoanalyzed."

He moved another step closer. Jane slightly raised the Glock against her thigh. "You will never be free until you seek the truth *within*! When you have the guts to follow the secrets that defined you and rule you even though you're not aware of them! You want to know whether I'm capable of unspeakable crimes? *Yes!* I am capable of the worst crime on earth. And that is *telling the truth.* As the Arabic proverb goes, *'If you're going to tell the truth, have one foot in the stirrup!' Truth*, my dear, is dangerous, so *I* am dangerous!" he yelled, his voice booming across the property. "In this kingdom of secrets, the man who tells the truth must be destroyed!"

Jane couldn't help but think of the enigmatic TRUTH poster on Jake's wall. She took an equally hostile step toward Jordan. "Read my mind, old man. I've never destroyed anyone for telling the truth. But I *will* destroy you if you took that boy and harmed him in any way."

Jordan stood still. He stared at Jane in a somewhat fractured gaze that lasted half a minute. "God, I can't get you out of my mind, Jane Perry." His voice was laced with an eerie calm. "*You haunt me.* You haunt my dreams at night." His voice became distant. "You and that damn boy."

Jane's gut clenched. He was only a few feet from her. Was this when he would try and take her down? She lifted the Glock a few inches higher. "Jake?"

Jordan peeled out of his semi-trance. "Christ, you're a one-trick pony. No, not *Jake.* The *other* one."

Jane's head spun. "Who in the fuck are you talking about? Daniel?"

Jordan's eyes looked off to the side. "No. *The other one.* I never knew his name."

Jane moved back a step. "There was a boy before Daniel?"

"Yeah. It was about six months before Daniel. He used to hover around the back gate on our property. We had a lot of trees back there and beyond the fence was a half acre of ground that separated us from the house and street on the other side. I'd hear the neighborhood kids building forts in there and playing cowboys and Indians. This kid...I called him 'Red' because he had a shock of curly red hair that fell at odd angles across his freckled forehead. He was seven, maybe eight. He never said a word to me, but I heard him say so much just by looking at him. See, if you haven't noticed it yet, I can do that. I can look at a person and I can feel what they feel. I've been able to do it since I was a child. The gift of clear sight is in my blood. I can hear people's stories just by looking at them. Once I make that connection with a person, no matter if it's a few minutes or a few decades, they're in my brain locked away. And any time I want, I can access that person and download what they're feeling." He looked at Jane. "Sometimes, I can even tell what's about to happen to them with the most frightening precision."

Jane felt cornered against the tree. She was starting to wonder if this extemporized meeting was in the best interest of her long-term health. She decided the best choice was to play along. "Okay. You have second sight. You looked at this kid on the other side of the fence. This eight-year-old you call 'Red' and what did he tell you with is mind?"

"He was very confused and angry..."

"Why?"

"I don't know." Jordan closed his eyes and forced himself back in time. "Nobody helped him. He cried like a baby. He screamed and no one cared." The words *"He cried like a baby"* were an exact match to the voicemail left on Bo's phone. Jordan opened his eyes. "And now, for some fucking reason, he haunts my dreams at night, *every night* for almost one week. He stands at that fucking gate and stares at me and tells me how much pain he feels. 'Listen to me!' he keeps screaming. 'Why won't anyone listen to me?!'"

Jane felt her heart pounding. "Did you kill this kid, Jordan?"

He snapped out of his daze. "Kill him? Jesus Christ, Jane! No! I didn't kill him!"

"You said this all went down six months before Daniel's death!"

"So what?"

"You were eighteen years old! What were you doing hanging around an eight-year-old boy?!"

"Shit! You think I used 'Red' for practice? Which one of us here is the sick fuck?"

"Then what happened to 'Red?'"

"How should I know? One day, he just stopped coming around the back gate and then six months later, my life got really fucked up."

Jane figured she needed to inject some logic into the conversation. "If you can talk to people without saying a word, if you can hear their thoughts, then why don't you know where 'Red' came from, or know his real name or what happened to him or..."

"Jesus Christ, Jane. I don't do parlor tricks. I just sense things when I'm connected to somebody. Just like I know all about you!"

"You've read about me on the Internet."

Jordan rolled his eyes. "Didn't you hear me before? I don't own a computer."

"You read about me in the newspaper."

"I just read the local town rag to check the weather forecast. Look, I'm not gonna debate with you on how I do what I do. Either you believe me or you don't. But don't fucking patronize me." His posture became more aggressive. "You've come into my world for a reason, Jane Perry." He was so close to Jane that she could smell the acrid stain on his breath. "You haunt my dreams at night, alongside 'Red.' I don't know why but I don't question it! All I know, *all I feel,* is that you have something I *desperately* need! *That's* why I shake! I have no control over it. I've done it since I was a kid. People figured I had a nervous condition, but I started to realize that I only shook when I was around a person or a thought that had a profound future potential. It's my barometer of confirmation that what I'm feeling or thinking is momentous. When I saw you yesterday on the bridge, even though we never spoke, I felt it like an electric bolt that shook my etheric body. You felt it, too. *Don't deny it.*" Jane couldn't refute his words, but she fortified that unseen wall between the two of them. "And don't try to build that fucking wall!" Jane was speechless. "You build too many walls thinking they'll keep you safe when all they do is keep you a prisoner. You filter your feelings with restrained joy." He leaned even closer. Jane found it difficult to pull away from Jordan's intense gaze. It was like a drug she would regret taking. "You need fear to feel alive! You're terrified of being happy and feeling contentment because there's nowhere to go from there. Happiness is fatal, whereas struggle and sadness and frustration are familiar and safe, even though they make your life unbearable. Where is the safety in happiness, you wonder? When one is happy, the only thing that can occur is death because the struggle is over." Tears welled in Jane's eyes. "I'm right. I can see it! It bleeds from your eyes. You don't have relationships, Jane! *You take hostages!* And you think you can strategize your way through life. That's why you were a drunk."

Jane used every bit of strength to pull away from Jordan and stagger to the side. She quickly wiped the tears from her face. In the distance, she heard the sound of several vehicles moving fast along the highway. Peering through the dense cluster of trees toward the road on the other side of the river, she saw three patrol cars heading back toward Midas. Her gut told her that Weyler was in one of the cars. She knew he would silently look for Jane's Mustang as he passed Jordan's property and not spot it. *Jesus,* she thought, *this could get complicated with Weyler when I return to town.* The sooner she beat feet to Midas, the better. Jane holstered her Glock and moved several steps away from the stand of trees.

"Wait," Jordan said, his voice modulated and calm. Jane turned. "I want to ask you something." His mood was exceptionally serious. "What if everything you ever believed was false? What if you've lived a lie your whole life because you were carrying that lie for someone you might not even know existed? What if your pain and suffering wasn't all your own? If you found out the truth, would your world crumble or would you emerge transformed?"

"I don't understand."

"You're only as sick as your secrets. Isn't that what they say in AA?" Jane nodded. "Our ancestors have laid a twisted road for all of us. Consider for one second who staked their claim in this great country: conquerors, explorers and Puritans. When they all started screwing each other, confusion ensued. When your nation is born from a Puritan fornicating with a conqueror, you're guaranteed to have deep issues." He leaned toward Jane. "Family secrets, Jane. Of all the secrets we hide, *family secrets* are the most dangerous. They breed like mice. None of us are immune. Turn over any rock in any family and you will find the dark corners and the stories that are only repeated in the *minds* of those who suffered the indignity that lead to the shadows. The happiest-looking family, the sweetest-looking couple, the purest-looking kid all share the DNA of a secret that could never be revealed. Every one of us bears the pain and dishonor of buried secrets that our families refuse to acknowledge.

"Those secrets fester throughout the generations, unspoken and never dared whispered. In our sanctimonious need for concealment, we falsely believe that within our silence is honor. But what they *never* told you…is that the secret you keep and bury takes on a life of its own. The secret becomes flesh and blood and it chases the family from one generation to another, contaminating the bloodline as it goes. It hovers around you and within you…" He pointed his mud-caked finger at Jane. "…and operates quite unconsciously through your ancestry. But here's the crazy thing, Jane. When that secret is not acknowledged, it is doomed to be repeated by the sons and daughters that follow in the shadow of their family tree. You see, buried secrets bubble under the skin of the generations yet to be born. And like little soldiers, we unwillingly support the secret by recreating it in our lives." Jordan began to count them off on his fingers. "Murder, incest, rape, suicide, clandestine adoptions, marital violence, homosexuality, alcoholism, drug abuse. Sounds fucking insane, right? But it's true! If you don't believe me, check it out for yourself. I've seen it play out dozens of times! It's all done on such a *deep*, unconscious level that it seems unbelievable and so, of course, it's easy for the ignorant to disregard this idea. But mark my words, *every single person* on this earth is carrying the heartbeat of another in their bloodline. Whatever was buried long ago, will repeat and repeat and repeat. And you will continue to be the victim of what your ancestors could never say out loud. The *only way* out of this eternal cycle is to listen and then wake up and acknowledge the truth that your ancestors— those discarnate souls—are now begging to reveal to you."

Jordan took a step back, allowing his words to sink in. "But, hey, we all know the way mankind leans. Illusions die hard and the status quo dies even harder." Jane instantly remembered the words, "Illusions die hard," that Mollie inscribed on the bridge under her dragonfly drawing. She said it was one of the last things Jake said to her. "Who wants to face their shadowed truth when it's so much easier to keep the ball rolling that feeds the machine and makes one's life a false existence? How many people have the courage to seek the truth within themselves and within their own bloodline? How many people are willing to live a life of transparency? How many family members would disown you because you have exposed their secret? How many friends would leave you because they see you as a loose cannon? Is it safer to live your life manipulated by a family secret, or is there more freedom in the revelations... no matter how bitter or sick the discovery? *Is the trade-off of loneliness and shunning that comes with that discovery worth the freedom of living without any illusions?* For most people, the answer is a resounding '*No.*'" Jordan ran his dirty fingers through his coarse beard. "Do you have *any* idea the kind of energy it takes to fight the system? I'm talking about the *family system*, Jane? You serve the system for decades and you never serve yourself. Hell, you don't even know what's good for you anymore because that system is so much bigger than you. It's like this unconscious ploy to keep you rotating in the same sludge your ancestors waded through. But let's just say for shits and grins that you said, 'Fuck it!' After years of absorbing and accepting all that pain as your own, you finally realize that it never belonged to you. So you say, 'I'm breaking out!'" He smiled sarcastically. "My God, do you *truly* understand what it takes for a person to do that? Do you have any idea how many levels of people, situations and patterns work to prevent it? It's a choice that ultimately frees your soul but destroys the world you've come to know. Don't think for one moment that altering that energy is easy. Most people would rather live in denial and their comfortable illusions than risk it all on the truth and be set free. Most people are willing to give up their right to see the truth that made them because they don't want to be alone or exiled to a life of what they believe is sheer existence. And that, my dear, *is what the secret is counting on.* The secret wants you to be a mushroom: kept in the dark and fed shit all day long. And even when you wake up briefly and say, 'This doesn't feel right to me' or 'What I see isn't jiving with what I'm being told,' the secret is there to feed you more shit and satiate your psyche with lies. For those of us who are brave enough to seek the truth and renounce the secrets that stalk us, it can be crazy making! But I tell you, sister, what doesn't kill you makes you wiser."

Jordan relaxed a bit, exhausted but somewhat brightened by being able to express himself to Jane. She considered every word of what he said, percolating the abstruse discourse in her mind. As anomalous as it sounded, somewhere deep down, it made frightening sense. Jane couldn't believe she was concurring with this lunatic; this monster who brutally took the life of a helpless boy decades earlier and was possibly involved in the disappearance of another boy. Her heart was at odds with her troubled head. But there at the back of her heart was the feeling that Jake Van Gorden was one of those brave souls who stepped outside the mushroom pit of lies and rejected the damp darkness for the light of truth. By taking that step, did he sign his own death warrant? How could the man standing before her— the man who declared that truth was dangerous—destroy a boy for seeking the one thing that he admitted was so valuable?

But it was the coincidental comments that were identical to what the kidnapper wrote or spoke that still concerned her. And more than ever, the tale of an eight-year-old red-haired boy standing at a back gate and talking to Jordan—not with his words, but *through his mind*—rankled Jane to the core. There were too many odd coincidences competing for her attention. While Jordan's narrative felt prophetic, she couldn't allow herself to accept it as fact or have the luxury of taking down her guard in his presence.

"So, tell me, Jordan. What family secret stalks you?"

He dropped his head for a moment before looking back at Jane. "There are no secrets left buried for me. I've dredged all of them up and laid them bare. Why do you think I live a solitary existence? Why do you think I'm still the outcast? When you live in Midas you are bound by the secrets you share. I can't explain it, but everyone here is inexplicably drawn together by the knowledge that each of them harbors something so unforgivable…so deep and life altering….that they are like *magnets*, sucked together by what they choose to keep hidden. In Midas, we are all born from the same wound and die from the same heartache." He cocked his head. "Turn over a stone in Midas and you'll find five boulders."

"Do the citizens protect one another?"

Jordan seriously considered her question. "They don't know the great mystery that could destroy their neighbor. They may suspect certain possibilities, but the only connections they make with each other are in the ether. The only way they protect each other is with their silence. Silence is worth more than all the money this town possesses. So you *must* appreciate it, Jane, that Midas is a precarious place to live when you have a penchant for seeking the *truth*." He flung his arms into the air. "Is it any wonder that I'm their scapegoat? They've tried to shut me up my entire life!" He moved his large frame close to Jane, hovering over her like a human monolith. "When you go back out into that town today, I want you to ask yourself, what are they willing to sacrifice to keep their secrets? *Who* are they willing to sacrifice for that secret?"

Jane stared at Jordan, showing no hint of fear. "You talking about them sacrificing you?"

He looked off to the side. "That's a given, Jane. I've been sacrificed before to serve my family's secret. Thirty-four fucking years, Jane."

"You served time because you killed a child and hid his body under your bed. How can you say you were sacrificed?" Her tenor was pointed and driven.

"Because every story is only half told. It's what's not revealed that carries the meat." He walked away from her, leaning his battered body against the trunk of a tree. Plucking another few needles off the spruce, he wadded them into a fragrant ball. "Home is where the heartache is. Home is where the secrets hide." He popped the aromatic gob of needles into his mouth. "You know what they say, Jane? *You can't go home again*?" Jane's ears perked up. Of all the statements he could have said, he used those exact words. "But until you unleash your family's secrets, you're a prisoner to that home."

Jane turned and headed back to her car.

"I can hear you, Jane!" Jordan yelled after her, in a singsong manner. "You think I took that kid! You gonna send me up the river, Jane?" He took several steps outside the stand of trees. "Well, good fucking luck! You'll get stalled when you look for a jury of my peers. You will not find twelve people who are as smart as I am!"

Jane continued to trudge toward the Mustang, never turning back to Jordan.

"You'll be back again, Jane!" he yelled loudly toward her. "But the circumstances are gonna be out of your control next time!"

Jane wasted no time speeding like hell out of Jordan's property. She was so preoccupied that she didn't notice the time on the dashboard clock until she hit the pavement on the highway. It was nearly 11:45 am. She'd pulled up alongside the river at 10:10 am and figured she landed on his property around 10:15 am. But there was no way in hell she'd been there for ninety minutes. *What kind of time warp operates on those grounds?* she wondered, as she sped closer to Midas.

She rounded a curve right before the bridge just as a coal black Land Cruiser roared past her on the left. It wasn't hard to spot the driver—Bailey Van Gorden. From her quick observation, it looked like he was alone in the car. Jane pulled out her cell phone and dialed Weyler's number but the tight canyon walls prevented the call from going through. She tried calling again as she neared the turnoff. After four attempts and no signal, she figured she would tell him that she tried to call to let him know what she was doing. Tossing the phone onto the passenger seat, Jane turned the Mustang sharply and crested the hill toward Blackfeather Estates.

CHAPTER 16

Carol Van Gorden stood in the front doorway, looking as apprehensive at Jane as she did the first time they met. "Is something wrong?" she meekly asked, her voice filled with fear.

"No, ma'am," Jane said in as comforting a tone as she could manage.

"Oh, I wasn't expecting you. I'm not really presentable."

Jane wasn't sure what in the hell the woman was talking about. It was closing in on noon and she was dressed in a neatly pressed pair of black slacks, a white cashmere turtleneck and a bold string of black pearls surrounding her narrow neck. Her blond bob looked to be freshly coiffed with nary a hair out of place. If this wasn't *presentable,* Jane wondered what was. She looked down at her own shirt, caked with mud from her fall on Jordan's property and her jeans, splattered in various spots with dirt and affixed with the occasional dried leaf and pine pitch. "Well, I won't tell anybody if you don't," Jane retorted, figuring it was an apropos statement to someone who lived in the town of secrets.

Carol waved her inside, her body tightening. "Bailey's not here," she quickly put forth.

"Oh, really?" Jane responded, trying to sound as surprised as she could. "I thought he said he was trapped in the house."

Carol's face froze. It was the same look of terror she displayed during their first tête-a-tête. Jane desperately wanted to do something, *anything,* to calm the woman down. "Oh, uh, well, he...he, *is* trapped here. Yes, that's quite true. But he got an unexpected call last night from Louise, his mother. She's flying in today from back east. He just left to pick her up in Denver."

"Wentworth, New Jersey. Wasn't that the name of the town where Bailey grew up?"

Carol moistened her lips. "Yes. Right. Wentworth."

"And your mother-in-law still lives there?" Jane made sure her tone was as offhand as possible, yet Carol was acting as if

Jane had a loaded gun to her blond head.

"Yes." The word fell more like an odd question than an answer.

It was clear to Jane that this woman was not equipped to manage a conversation by herself without the annoying presence of her husband to direct the dialogue. "Isn't Louise battling terminal liver cancer?"

"Yes." This response sounded genuine to Jane. "She's in bad shape. Her doctors were not in favor of her taking the trip out here. But she needed to come."

"She's close to Jake?"

"No," Carol said, without thinking, before she caught herself. "I mean, uh, *sure* she's close to him. She's his grandmother. Jake's her only grandchild." The excuses were stacking up higher than a Sunday morning pancake special. "It's just that she lives so far away..."

"In Wentworth," Jane added.

"Yes." There was that same, damn sound in Carol's voice again—hesitation mixed with fear.

Jane's eyes traveled to the side. The left, arched door to Bailey's office was half open. "Ah, I didn't get to see that room before," she said, moving several steps toward the office.

"Oh, it's filthy in there," Carol stammered, her bony fingers clutched at her black pearls.

Jane put a soothing hand on Carol's arm. "Well, that's good. If any mud falls off my shirt, it'll blend right in." She gently pushed the door to the office open and walked inside.

The room wasn't large, compared to the rest of the garish house. Jane figured it took up a measly two hundred square feet. It was trimmed with white-framed arched windows on one side that framed a grove of aspens outside. The other walls held three- and four-foot paintings displaying Colorado mountain landscapes, framed in faux gold and each lit with its own museum light. Bailey's desk sat to the left. As expected, it was a huge, chunk of wood—the kind of desk you feel lost behind and that puts as much distance as possible between you and anyone seated across from you. Jane could easily picture Bailey sitting in the antique highback, weathered, leather chair behind the desk, his feet propped up on the glass top displaying his alligator cowboy boots. The desktop was nearly immaculate, as was most of the room, save for a far corner behind the desk that looked to shelter an empty box and packing materials.

"Bailey won't be back for several hours." Jane noted how Carol's pitch was higher and tenser than it was in the entry hall. She moved her slender body around the desk and positioned herself next to his antique leather desk chair.

The way she moved seemed odd to Jane. "Bailey's an only child?" Jane asked, trying to inflect more calm into the conversation.

"Yes," Carol replied, but her cadence was even more anxious.

Jane noticed that the leather desk chair looked out of place in the room. Instead of "crafting that Colorado lifestyle" that Bailey droned on about in their first meeting, the chair looked like an out-of-place relic that had occupied a less refined setting. "I'm the oldest in my family," Jane said matter-of-factly, running her fingers along the smooth edge of the glass desktop. "I have a younger brother, Mike." Jane heard herself talking and wondered if she'd been possessed by a dim-witted spirit. It seemed that the more she tried to pacify Carol, the more uncomfortable the woman became. Then Jane realized that Carol's heightened sense of panic set in the minute they entered Bailey's office. "Is Bailey one of those guys who hates people coming into his private space without an invitation?"

"Yes." This time, the answer was pronounced and almost defiant for someone as mealy-mouthed as Carol Van Gorden.

"I can't blame him. I'm the same way, Carol. I don't like surprises," Jane mused as she ran her fingers across a ten-inch-long silver cigarette case. Again, the case seemed out of place to Jane in this Colorado-inspired home design. On top of the silver case, was a wildly engraved *V* with enough flourishes and twirls that it barely resembled the letter.

Carol saw Jane looking at the cigarette case. She reached across the desk and moved it closer to her. "Oh, that's embarrassing!" Carol declared. "Cigarette smoking is so disgusting! I never thought he should keep it out like this. He doesn't smoke. Nor do I." She swept up the case, holding it tightly to her body. "It gives the wrong impression, you know, a cigarette case on display. Nasty, *nasty* habit."

Jane couldn't care less what anybody had on display in their private home, so long as it wasn't a meth lab or child porn. And she sure as hell didn't care if anybody smoked. In fact, the idea of a cigarette was sounding pretty damn good right now. But the way Carol held that case against her body bothered Jane. Was this woman so worried about appearances that she thought it was necessary to make such a fanfare? Or was there something in the case she didn't want Jane to see? "My dad had a silver cigarette case just like that on his desk," Jane said, lying through her teeth. Her father wouldn't have been caught dead with something that showy. "But he kept photos of my brother and I in it." That was one helluva of another lie. Jane's dad never cared a bit to carry or display a single photo of his kids. "What does your husband keep in the case?"

Carol looked faint. She wet her lips several times and rested one hand on the leather chair for support. "Odds and ends," she said, her voice barely breaching the level of a whisper.

"Can I see what's inside, Carol?" Jane asked, matching Carol's soft tone.

Apoplectic. That's how Carol appeared as she set the case on the glass top and pushed it toward Jane. Jane leaned forward, picked it up and opened the top. Inside, there were a multicolored variety of paperclips and thumbtacks. Jane moved her fingernail underneath the wooden bottom piece of the box, in search of anything that might be hidden there. But it was sealed tightly. She looked at Carol, who had a nervous smile across her face.

"Silly, isn't it?" Carol offered. "To keep office supplies in something like that."

Jane closed the lid and brushed her fingers across the engraving on top of the *V*. "Shouldn't this be *V.G.*?"

"I'm sorry?" Carol asked, seemingly not hearing the question.

"Van Gorden?"

Carol shrugged her shoulders. Her face froze in a forced grin that made her look like something between a lunatic and a prisoner facing a firing squad. "I don't know. It's from Bailey's side of the family."

"Well," Jane said, carefully setting it back on the desktop, "it's a beauty!" Jane looked at Carol. "Just like that chair."

Carol looked down at the desk chair. A look came over her face that Jane couldn't identify. It was as though the woman was slipping out of her body momentarily. "It belonged to Bailey's father," she said in a distant voice.

"His dad wasn't a doctor, was he?"

"Excuse me?" Carol looked at Jane with distant eyes.

"It's not a doctor's chair. The sides and the armrest are pretty beat up. It wasn't a chair he cared about showing off."

Carol looked back at the chair, totally dazed. "Yes. You're right. You really do have a knack for detail, don't you? That must come in handy with your line of work." She looked off to the side, utterly lost. The sound of the phone ringing broke the awkward silence. Carol jumped, bringing herself back into her delicate body. It rang a second time before she picked it up. "Hello." She waited a few seconds. "Hello?" She hung up. "Wrong number I guess."

Jane recalled that when they first visited the Van Gordens, the phone was ringing when Carol opened the door. Later, when Bailey arrived at the door and Carol asked about the phone call, he said it 'rang twice' and was a wrong number. "I know I already asked you this, but you're not being bugged by media calls, are you?"

"No, thank goodness."

"Does the phone ring two times a lot and then nobody's there?"

"It's happened before."

"Just recently?"

"Recent in what way?"

"Since Jake's disappearance," Jane stressed.

"No, it was happening before that." Jane started around the desk. Carol stiffened. "What is it?!" she exclaimed, backing up a few steps toward the corner of the room.

Jane put a reassuring hand on her arm. The woman was completely overreacting to Jane's movement. "It's okay, Carol. I just want to check the caller ID, if you don't mind."

"That's fine," she said, but she shook her head.

It was one of the most common *tells* in body language; answering a question in the affirmative but letting your body demonstrate your real feelings. Jane had nailed countless perps by noting that giveaway. "You're sure it's okay if I check?" Jane asked again, wanting to see if she produced the same reaction.

"Yes, of course," Carol uttered, repeating the same damn shake of the head.

Jane hit the backward arrow on the Caller ID box, displaying the last number called "Unavailable," she said out loud. "That's convenient." She turned to Carol. "Ever notice when this has happened before if it always comes up as *unavailable*…or is there a number?"

"I honestly have never checked it out."

Well, finally, Jane thought. *A completely honest statement in one full breath from Carol. Somebody send up a flag.*

"Why are you here, Detective?"

Jane realized that for Carol to even utter such an inquiry, it took all the courage she could muster. This was not a woman who wanted to appear rude or presumptuous. And, after all, the only reason Jane was there was because she knew Bailey wasn't.

"Well…"

"Is there something new regarding Jake's case?" Carol fiddled with the hem of her cashmere turtleneck. "I don't mean to sound like a gossip, but I got a call a few hours ago from a friend in town who said she saw several police cars heading down the highway, past where Jordan Copeland lives." Tears welled in her eyes. "I just wondered if you found…" She choked on her words.

Jane put a hand on Carol's arm. "You would have been called."

Carol nodded, tears streaming down her face. "I'm sorry."

"Don't apologize." Carol kept her head down but touched Jane's arm with her shaking hand. *It's the perfect time to jump,* Jane thought. "Carol, if you know something that might help us in *any* way…"

Carol took an even more defined step back toward the corner of the room where the empty box and packing materials lay in a heap. "I don't know anything!" She avoided Jane's gaze and turned her head to the side, toward the corner of the room.

Jane stared at the empty box. It was about eighteen inches long and twelve inches wide. The perfect size for a pair of expensive cowboy boots, Jane surmised. But the way Carol seemed to point her head toward the box even when she said, *I don't know anything,* troubled Jane. "Every second counts right now, Carol."

Carol looked Jane straight in the eye. "I said *I don't know anything*! Now, I really do need to get on with my day. If there's nothing else I can help you with…"

Jane was getting tired of being abruptly asked to leave people's homes and property. She let out a tired breath and walked out into the entry, followed by Carol. But before she got to the door, she turned. "One more question. Bo Lowry told Sergeant Weyler that you and your husband withdrew a reward fund two nights ago. Why did you do that?"

Carol took a hard swallow. "My husband didn't want every crackpot in the world calling up Chief Lowry and offering false clues just to get money." The words fell like stone from her lips.

"Yeah, but, people with genuine information *will* talk for the right amount of money. It's worth sorting through the wing-nuts to get to the cream…"

"No! My husband has made the decision and we are sticking with it," Carol stammered as she moved Jane to the door and opened it.

Carol was the victim personified. Victims, Jane thought, were the bottom feeders of bad luck. The more they stewed in their suffering, the more they attracted a world that validated their misfortune. Jane did her best to make eye contact with the woman but it was useless. Even trained thieves and seasoned liars learned to look a cop in the eye occasionally. It was the ones who were new to the game who kept their heads hung.

Jane didn't cross the threshold at Town Hall until a little past 12:30 pm. The receptionist buzzed her in with a wave and a questionable glance at her mud-encrusted shirt. Right before she rounded the corner of Bo's office, she nearly ran straight into Vi who was carrying a file folder and heading to her desk. Jane quickly realized that she had an impromptu opportunity. She asked if she could see Jordan's file, for no other reason but to find out what mysterious page Vi had torn off the front of the file. When Vi handed her the file, there was only a staple on the front with a torn fragment of paper at the top.

"What's missing here?" Jane asked, pointing to the staple.

"An internal cover page." Vi's answer was polished and succinct.

"What's that?"

"You don't do that at Denver Headquarters? I thought that was protocol."

Jane had never heard of any "protocol" at DH that required a facing page on the outside of all files. And if it did exist, there'd be no reason to rip it off and hide it away in a top desk drawer—unless it had seriously confidential information in it. *If* that was the case here, it didn't make sense that Vi ripped the front page off of both Jake and Jordan's file. And furthermore, if Bo brought them into solve this case in a timely fashion, shouldn't any and all confidential information be brought out into the open? Jane assured Vi that they didn't follow that practice. "Can I ask what's on the page?"

"Sure," Vi replied graciously. "It's the date the file was opened, the contents inside the file, initials of who has read the file and the date they read it and how many photos are in the file."

For a small-time police department, this place sure felt a need to be as thorough and anal as possible with their filing system. Funny thing was, Jane realized, for a town that basically had no crime, it seemed ridiculous that they would go to the trouble of creating such a front page on each file. And furthermore, as far as Jane could tell, the only two people reading said files were Vi and Bo. Was it really necessary for them to "sign off" on it each time they read it? Vi's story was as phony as they come but Jane gave the woman credit for the way she delivered the lie. She talked quickly, with authority and didn't smile too much while she was doing it, so it didn't come off as disingenuous. She was well trained, Jane decided, and this wasn't her first horse in the deception race. "You know, I would love for Sergeant Weyler to get a copy of that front page so we could incorporate it in our filing system back at Headquarters. Could I see one of them?"

"Of course. I've got to make a quick phone call, but I'll bring it in shortly." Vi smiled pleasantly, turned and sat back at her desk.

Yeah, Jane deduced, Vi was a pro. Jane waited. *Now pick up the phone to make it look real,* she said to herself. As if the woman heard Jane's thoughts, she lifted the receiver and dialed a number. *Damn, she's good.*

Jane knocked on Bo's door and walked inside. Weyler was seated across from Bo who was standing at his desk, his belly resting comfortably on the cluttered desktop. He was smoking a cigar.

"Glad you could make it!" Bo said with the usual contempt he saved for interchanges with Jane. "You take part in a hog tying contest?" He motioned with his cigar to her muddy shirt.

Jane glanced at Weyler who shot her a look of silent reproach.

"We got the phone number of the cell phone we found in the trunk. Area code 201." Bo held the paper up with the phone number. "It's in New Jersey. Just like where Jordan Copeland is from. We checked his file and it's real similar to the phone number his parents had when they lived back there. Starts with the same three numbers...379."

"The Van Gordens are also from New Jersey. Wentworth."

"What in the hell has that got to do with anything?" Bo grumbled.

"Well, your number-one suspect *and* the family of the kid he's allegedly kidnapped, hearken from the same state."

"So what's the connection?" Bo asked.

"I don't know. But it's just a little too coincidental. So, let's call the number."

"Call it?" Bo exclaimed. "Why? To hear his cell phone ring?"

Jane maneuvered around the boxes scattered on Bo's floor and sat in the chair next to Weyler. "You said the first two phone calls that came in when the kidnapper left voicemail messages didn't display any number on your Caller ID, right?" Bo nodded, puffing nervously on his cigar. "Now, suddenly, there's a phone number? He's not stupid. If he wanted to block it, he'd block it. He's obviously hip to some kind of technology."

"So what are you suggesting?" Weyler put forth.

"It's too ironic that a disposable cell phone has a New Jersey area code and the two people involved in this case are both from New Jersey."

"Maybe the kidnapper's from New Jersey, too?" Bo offered.

"And he's workin' with Jordan. Maybe they knew each other at some time? Maybe from his stint in prison?"

Bo's presumptions actually sounded reasonable to Jane—everything except the guy was working with Jordan. Then again, there were a few statements Jordan made to Jane regarding the clues that there was no way he'd have any knowledge of unless he was involved in some way. That closing comment of Jordan's, "You can't go home again," was still ringing loudly in Jane's ear. "Call the number," Jane instructed.

"*Why*?"

"I think it's another clue. I think the guy *spoofed* the number. And I think he did it for a reason." Jane had to explain the art of "spoofing" to Bo and Weyler. It was becoming a relatively well-known practice by both pranksters and those with more nefarious motives. Spoofing was the practice of allowing the telephone network to display a specific phone number on the Caller ID, which was not the actual number from where the call was originating. By signing up with one of the many Internet spoof providers, all a person had to do was pay in advance for a PIN number, which allowed them to make a call for a certain amount of minutes. When they entered the PIN number, they were asked to enter the number they wanted to call and the number they wished to appear on the Caller ID. Some of the spoof providers even had options for altering one's voice once the connection was made, allowing for a man to sound like a woman and vice versa. "This guy knows what he's doing. The phone is likely a Wal-Mart throwaway. Just like a drop phone that drug dealers use. He paid cash for it, so no records. Good for one number only. *That number!*" Jane pointed to the New Jersey number in Bo's hand. "Call the number and see who answers. And put the phone on speaker so we can all hear."

Bo looked a little suspicious. He grumbled about not knowing how to use the speaker feature on his phone and promptly called in Vi who effortlessly dialed the number, increased the volume and hit the SPEAKER button. "This is your idea," Bo said to Jane. "You talk to whoever answers."

"Hello?" The man's voice sounded both elderly and ill.

Jane leaned over Bo's desk, speaking into the phone. "Hello, sir. My name is Detective Jane Perry. I'm calling from Denver, Colorado." Bo looked quizzical at her but she held up her hand.

"Where?" The man sounded irritated.

"*Denver, Colorado*," Jane repeated with increased volume and enunciation.

"Don't know anyone in Denver."

"I'm a detective, sir. I'm calling on police business."

"What kind of business?"

Jane asked the usual establishing questions. His name was David Sackett. He was eighty-one. Sackett volunteered that he wasn't well and suffered from emphysema *and* lung cancer. *Christ*, she wondered, is *anybody not dying from cancer these days?*

"How long have you had this number, sir?" Jane asked.

"How long? Oh, well, since we moved into the place. It's been over forty years with the same phone number. We inherited the number from the last family who lived here. Moved here in February of 1968...back when it was quiet."

"I just want to confirm this number, sir." Jane took the phone number from Bo and rattled it off, along with the area code.

"Everything's right except for the area code," he said with a marked wheeze. "They changed from *201* to *973* awhile back." The prospect of spoofing was becoming much more probable in Jane's opinion.

"May I ask what town you live in, sir?"

"Sure. Short Hills."

Bo looked at Weyler with heightened interest. Jane whispered to Vi to retrieve Jordan's file. Vi quickly left the office.

"But when you got the phone number back in 1968," Jane continued, "it was area code 201, right?"

"Yeah. What's this all about?" His breathing was labored.

"We're working on a case, sir. I can't divulge the details right now. But it would be extremely helpful if you could tell me your address."

Vi returned with Jordan's file.

"Sure. It's 43 Warwick Road, Short Hills, New Jersey."

Jane wrote the address down on a piece of paper. Vi scanned the page that held old information on Jordan, including his parents' address. "It's not the same address," Vi whispered to Jane.

Jane whispered back, asking for Jordan's parents' first names. Vi found the information and pointed to it on the page. "Sir, this might be an odd question, but did you ever know Richard and Joanna Copeland. They had a son, Jordan Copeland?"

"Jordan Copeland? The child killer?"

Obviously, forty-one-year-old murder cases die hard in Short Hills. "Yes, sir."

"Why in the hell would I fraternize with that family?"

This was getting tricky for Jane—especially since she had an audience watching her every move. "Well, sir, you say you bought the house in February of '68." Jane checked Jordan's file. "Jordan Copeland was arrested in early July of the same year. I just wondered if Short Hills was small enough back then that you might have run into the family at some time."

Sackett let out a painful cough. "We were new in the neighborhood. We didn't make a point of getting to know our neighbors. We didn't even realize how close the Copelands lived until we heard the sirens and saw the police cars all around their house."

Jane leaned closer to the phone. "How close did they live to you?"

"One block over, directly behind our property as the crow flies." Sackett coughed again, this time longer and louder. "Listen, I gotta go. If you need anything else, you call. Goodbye."

The blare of the dial tone rang out in Bo's office until Vi depressed the SPEAKER button and hung up the phone. She excused herself and returned to her desk. Jane collected Sackett's phone number and address, and stashed it in her pocket.

"Goddamnit!" Bo exclaimed. "Jordan Copeland is involved in this mess!"

"We don't know that for sure," Jane warned.

"I don't have to go to Mars to know it's colder there than a well digger's ass!" He put down his cigar and leaned across the desk. "You talk about coincidences? Here we got a guy who lives one block away from where Copeland lived…"

"Yeah, over forty years ago…" Jane reminded him.

"Who cares?! What are the odds? If you're right and the person who has Jake spiffed, spocked, spoofed this Sackett guy's phone number, there's got to be an obvious reason for it!"

"Yeah, he's setting up Jordan!"

"*Settin' him up*?! Christ Almighty, woman! Which side are you butterin' your bread on? Have you read what Copeland did to that poor little retard forty-one years ago? He shot him point blank in the head in his backyard! And then he dragged his dead body to his bedroom and hid it under his bed!" Bo leaned over the desk. "*Are you hearing me*?"

"Yes! Loud and clear!"

"I tell you, stupidity hangs around longer than a bad cold." Bo settled back in his chair.

Jane regarded him with a hostile eye. "Excuse me? If that was directed at me, then I guess I'm just stupid enough to figure out the whole phone spoof!"

Weyler held up his hand. "Enough!" He looked at Jane with the glare of an unhappy father.

Bo stared at Jane, pointing his chubby finger in her direction. "Look, if you want to water more dead trees, you do it on your own time! We work this case with the clear understanding that Jordan Copeland is most likely involved in this, either alone or with a partner."

"That's an assumption," Jane said quietly. "Just because the light turned red, doesn't mean the traffic stopped." It was a comment meant to mirror Bo's love of corny sayings but it fell on deaf ears.

"Until we have enough hardcore evidence to show differ-ent," Bo ordered, "Jordan Copeland is in my damn scope and I will not hesitate to pull the trigger on his guilty head!"

Vi popped her head into the door. "Bailey Van Gorden is on line one, Bo."

Bo ran his fat fingers through his comb over. "Aw, shit." Bo picked up the phone.

Fuck, Jane thought. This was going to hurt. She leaned over toward Weyler. "I tried to call you, Boss, but I didn't have any cell coverage."

Weyler leaned closer and whispered. "Was that before or after you fell into that mud hole inside your Mustang?" His eyes were tense and unnerved.

Jane figured it was time to get out of there. She stood up, moving around the boxes.

"Hold on there!" Bo bellowed toward Jane. "Hang on," he said to Bailey. Bo motioned Vi toward the phone to put him on SPEAKER. Jane felt the walls closing in on her. "Go on with what you were saying…"

"I'm driving back with my mother who I just picked up from DIA and I get a call from my wife that your Denver detec-tive was nosing around my private office *in my home!* What in the hell is going on over there?!"

Weyler regarded Jane with a look that was between anger and shock. Jane stayed mum while all eyes in the room focused on her.

"Are you there?!" Bailey screamed into his phone.

"Yes, sir!" Bo answered.

"I wasn't being nosy, for God's sake," Jane whispered, in a weak attempt to defend herself.

"I don't know where that bitch got the idea that she has a right to show up unannounced at my home!" Bailey screamed.

"Yes, sir!" Bo affirmed, shooting Jane daggers.

The sound of a woman's voice could be heard in the

background. "It's inappropriate…" the woman said.

"It's *inappropriate!*" Bailey yelled. The woman spoke again in the background saying something about "this case." Bailey quickly spoke up. "She should be taken off this case immediately!"

Jane didn't care what Bailey was saying; she was more interested in the fact that this blowhard, egotist was allowing his mother to feed him verbal cues of righteous indignation. In Jane's opinion, the whole thing was coming off as a bit peculiar, given that Bailey Van Gorden seemed to regard women with indifference and disfavor. What kind of perverse control did this woman have over her only son?

"Yes, sir. I see what you're sayin'! I'll take care of it!" He hung up and pointed his fat finger at Jane. "I don't know how Beanie trained you, but I sure as hell wasn't taught to cross the lines that you do on the job! You show up here with your Denver attitude…"

"My Denver attitude?" Jane questioned.

"You got a mile-high chip on your little shoulder! How you ever got the accolades you got is beyond me! I'd have sent your ass packin' years ago!"

"Hey, I never asked for accolades! I just did my job and went home at night!"

"And then drank yourself under the goddamn table!"

Jane looked at Weyler in shock. It took a lot to sting Jane, but that one hurt. She spun on her heels and bolted out of the building. Weyler followed close behind.

"Jane!" he yelled at her as she headed across the street.

She stopped and turned back to him. "You tell him I was a drunk?"

"Of course not!" Jane walked back to the curb. "He's just looking at you and making assumptions."

"Like the assumption that I'm *stupid?*"

"Good God, Jane. You had no business going to the Van Gordens' house and you know it!"

"I tried to call you…"

"I don't care!" He lowered his voice. "And don't lie to me about how you got your shirt muddy…*again*." Weyler looked around to make sure nobody was listening. "Do you have any idea how you going on Copeland's property and observing him could seriously compromise this investigation?"

Jane struggled with how much she should divulge to Weyler. Between the path of Chesterfield cigarettes that ended with the antique ashtray and her two up-close-and-personal visits with Jordan, it almost seemed like too much to divulge in one setting. He obviously assumed all she'd done was *observe* Jordan. "Boss, whoever is responsible for this is begging to be heard. *Begging*. I think he wants to be caught so he can tell his story. I don't know what the story is, but I bet it's one helluva tale."

"You are basing that on a theory that the clues have a linear explanation. I still don't know if that's correct."

Jane started knocking off the reasons on her fingers. "There's no ransom request. We have a book with a dog-eared page that has references to *social masks, phrases as symbols*, and a main character named Webber who has something that matters to him greatly and *will not be denied!* Then we have explicit drawings of a child, *not* a teenager. A riddle about a Packard that just *happens* to be on an old out-of-print stamp that's stuck on an envelope. The rest are still cloudy but I know they somehow connect. If we don't at least show some agreement with the kidnapper…a reward fund, a news conference, a fucking candlelight vigil that's the top story on the Denver news networks, *something* that says 'We hear you and we want to resolve this,' then he is going to think we don't give a shit and he will have no other option but to kill Jake!" Weyler looked off to the side, his frustration evident. "Boss, if you allow a half-ass police chief to run this case…a guy who only has his eyes on his fucking calendar and the day he gets to shake loose of this town…the last clue we get is gonna be Jake's dead body splayed out in the middle of Main Street. That's the kidnapper saying, 'Do you hear me now, motherfuckers?' And then nobody wins! The Van Gordens lose their only child. Bo walks out of here with his head hung low. We, the big-ass *Denver contingent*, leave saying 'mea culpa' as we drive down Main Street. And you? Whatever deal you brokered with Bo a long time ago...whatever friendship you think you have, is fucking gone!"

"Jane, I hear you. But this is not our normal hunting ground. Even *I* can't strong-arm Bo into doing something he simply won't do. And we can't muscle the Van Gordens into reinstating their reward and then question their intent when we have nothing except a *gut feeling* that they're holding something back!"

"Don't *ever* question my gut! My gut has solved a lot of fucking cases! When I *don't* listen to my gut, that's when people get hurt. That's when people get killed. Goddamnit, I don't need another dead kid!" Jane turned away. Her heart slammed into her chest.

"Since when is this all about you?" Weyler calmly asked.

Jane retreated. He was right. As usual, she was too entwined in the case. "I just want to find out the truth, that's all."

Weyler waited, trying to sort out the options. "How do we acknowledge Jordan when our hands are tied?"

Jane considered her conversations with Jordan. *If he was involved in some* way, perhaps her connection with him might help. "What if I reach out to Jordan? Face-to-face on his property?"

"And compromise this case? No chance! If he's involved with this and you cozy up to him and then something happens to Jake, we're screwed! The DA would say we baited him, entrapped him or twisted his words and any court case would be in jeopardy. *Then* we'd have the Van Gordens handing us a lawsuit, and rightfully so!"

"But what if he's *not* involved, but he can help us?"

"Help us?"

"Maybe he saw something..."

"Saw something?"

Jane caught herself. She didn't actually mean "see" as in witness. She couldn't believe she was entertaining the notion that Jordan Copeland had a psychic eye and could possibly see where Jake was. It was ludicrous and she had to quickly check herself to make sure her rage wasn't compelling her to throw out insane possibilities to Weyler. She had to maintain logic or any argument she waged would be rooted in a bed of water. "He doesn't leave his property very often. He wanders all day and night. That's what Bo told us. Jake wandered around at night, too. Maybe their paths crossed? Not in a nefarious way but a pure, decent way." Her words sounded ridiculous. "Pure" and "decent" weren't exactly the first adjectives she'd choose to describe Jordan or any relationship he might have. Selling this idea to Weyler was like selling symphony tickets to the deaf.

"Jane, you can't reach out to a viable suspect like Copeland on his turf and risk everything." Weyler thought for a moment. "You want to go knee-to-knee with Copeland? We do it above board. We bring him in and question him…"

"That's not gonna work! You saw that video between Jordan and Bo. Jordan doesn't respect him. He thinks he's stupid and Jordan won't lower himself to talk to people who he perceives are beneath him."

"Then *you* question him."

There was a veritable landmine. Jane was caught in between that proverbial rock and a hard place. "With you and Bo on the other side of the two-way mirror? He'll know you're listening and he still won't talk. He'll play one of his games. Start asking me riddles and blabber about cryptic philosophic theories…"

"What are you talking about?"

Jane quickly realized she misspoke. "Didn't Bo say he got a couple degrees in prison? Esoteric psychology, right?"

"Yes. But why would you think he talks about it, unless you…"

"If *I* got a degree in esoteric psychology," Jane said in an attempt to lead the conversation away from her mistake, "I sure as hell would be taking any opportunity to show it off. Wouldn't you?" Jane purposely changed the subject. "Look, Boss, the bottom line is Jordan is no good to us unless he's standing on his own land, on his own territory, where he's safe and where he's not being monitored."

"Who's to say he wouldn't just string you along because he enjoyed the attention? We have a finite amount of time here that is better spent pounding some pavement and trying to decode those clues." Weyler started back inside.

"There will be more clues, Boss."

"How do you know?"

"Because my gut doesn't lie."

Weyler crossed back to her. "You can observe Copeland all you want from a distance. You can track his comings and goings. But you need to give me your word that you're not going face-to-face with Copeland on his property."

Jane struggled a bit with the statement. She looked him straight in the eye. "You got my word." Her gut never lied but, at that moment, *Jane* certainly did.

CHAPTER 17

Jane's gut didn't lie but it sure was rumbling with hunger. After Weyler went back inside Town Hall, she spun on her boots and walked across the street and down the main drag to The Rabbit Hole. The place wasn't jumping like it had been the night before, but it was still feeling the groove of the Saturday lunch crowd. Underneath the din, Lee Ann Womack sang "Solitary Thinkin.'" Jane slid onto a barstool and ordered a sparkling water and hot dog with everything on it to go.

"How come you always want that dog walking?" Jane

turned to the right, just as Hank sat in the stool next to her. "You can't sit in one spot for ten minutes?" He smiled and patted her back lightly.

"I'm on the clock. And it's a good thing I don't drink anymore because this would be day one of a four-day bender!"

Hank took a gander at her muddy shirt. "Isn't that the same shirt you were wearing yesterday?"

"Similar."

"Do they all come with the muddy imprint or do you pay extra for that?"

Jane could have said any number of smart-ass retorts, but for some reason, the way Hank said it to her was sweetly sly and good-natured. She couldn't help but smile.

"I'm glad you stopped in," he said, standing up on the rail of the bar and leaning over as he searched for paperwork in the bay of the bar. Jane's eyes drifted to his backside. She lingered there until she realized that it'd been a long time since she'd gazed at a guy's ass. A flash of embarrassment flushed her face, and she quickly turned away just as Hank plopped back onto the barstool. He placed a short stack of pages on the bar and turned to her, "I checked out…" He stopped and smiled at her.

"What?"

"You're blushing."

Damn. You really can't take the cop out of someone. They notice every detail. "Why would I be blushing?" The waitress delivered the sparkling water, which gave Jane a reason to turn away. "It's hot in here."

Hank grinned. "Okay." He unclipped the pages. "I did some snooping for you. I hope you don't mind."

"That depends," Jane said warily.

"You know the address you found in Jake's locker? 1401 Imperial?" Jane nodded. "I did a MapFind search on the Internet and there is no street named Imperial for the entire thirty-mile radius I checked, using Midas as the starting point. I only mapped it out thirty-miles because basically when you get around here and here…" Hank pointed to the north and eastern quadrants. "…it's just lots of BLM and ranches. Now, that's not to say 1401 Imperial doesn't exist because when you drive up Highway 7…" Hank pointed to a strip of highway on one of the pages. "…it's desolate in spots. There's a lot of little side roads, usually just numbered, but some have names. If the MapFind isn't updated, they could have missed it. But I'm sure you know that already." He shuffled through the pages. "So I did a search of any business using the word *Imperial* in its title, also for a thirty-mile radius." He found the page he wanted. "And what I found was Imperial Cleaners, Imperial Liquors, Imperial Savings and Loan and Imperial Cemetery." Hank gave the page to Jane. "I copied the addresses for all of those in case you want to check them out, along with a map to show you how to get to each one."

Jane was duly impressed and a bit overwhelmed. The interest he took in helping her was reminiscent of what all guys do, no matter their age, when they are trying to impress a woman. Whether it's a thirteen-year-old boy offering to carry schoolbooks, a thirty-year-old man offering to mend a broken pipe or a fifty-year-old ex-cop volunteering to do some gumshoe research, they all had the same intent behind the offer—the inevitable conquest of said female. "Thank you."

"Hey, it was fun. I felt like I was back on the job."

Jane scanned the maps. "What kind of cop were you?"

"Fraud investigation. I couldn't handle the gritty stuff that you do."

Jane looked at the names of the businesses. "Where does the number *1401* play into this?"

"If it's not a street address, it could be anything from a ticket number at the cleaners, a safety-deposit box number at the bank or a headstone number at the Imperial Cemetery."

Jane could see she had her work cut out for her. She half-wished she could put Hank on the payroll so he could do some footwork for her. The waitress delivered Jane's hot dog. She took a hearty bite and couldn't believe how good it was. "Damn, Hank. What do you make these hot dogs with? Crack?"

"Naw. Just a lot of heart," he replied, gathering the pages together and clipping them into a neat pile.

The front door opened and in walked Annie Mack. She still had her apron on from the diner, covered with various sauce stains.

"Hey ya, Hank!" she said in an offhand manner as she strolled up to him.

"Hey, sweetie," he said. Jane noted that same softening of the eyes when he looked at her. He put his arm around her waist tenderly when he greeted her.

Annie asked if Hank had any one-dollar bills she could have for a twenty. He hopped off the barstool, walked to the cash register and doled out the singles to her. "There you go, kiddo," he said with a warm smile.

Annie nodded to him and acknowledged Jane before leaving the place. Hank wound around the bar and came back to rest next to Jane. She must have had a discernable look of judgment on her face because Hank analyzed it for several seconds before speaking up. "What?" he asked, with a cockeyed grin.

Jane took a large bite of the hot dog. "Hey," she said, hiding her mouth full of food, "it's none of my business."

Hank continued to scrutinize Jane's face, something she wasn't used to other others doing. "You think Annie and I..."

"Look, if you can keep her happy with a twenty-five-year age difference, then you ought to ferment and bottle whatever you got and sell it to everyone over twenty-one."

Hank broke into a fit of laughter. "Oh, Jesus, you just made my day. But she's not my girlfriend."

Jane finished off the hot dog and regarded Hank with a doubtful eye. There was no denying the loving look he cast toward Annie—not once but twice, in her presence. If Annie wasn't his girlfriend, Jane deduced that he was working the angles to make it happen. "Everyone lives in Midas for one reason, right?" Jane wiped mustard off her mouth and slid the plate away from her. "You're all hiding something. I get it. I'll keep your secret."

Hank smiled and shook his head, "You like to hover around people, don't you? Like a helicopter? Not too close, but just hover. Try to figure out what's what and who's who? And I bet you wonder why they don't take your advice more often."

Without a doubt, that's exactly what Jane was doing when she ambushed Carol Van Gorden. She certainly wasn't comfortable being around someone who could read her that well. It was one thing to have a telepathic loony like Jordan Copeland worming his way into her head. But to have a fifty-year-old ex-cop with a cute ass understanding how Jane's mind worked was more than she could handle at the moment. Besides, she needed to get back to work. "Look, I gotta go pound some pavement. What do I owe you?"

"Another visit. And if you need me to research something for you, let me know."

Jane considered her words carefully before she spoke. "What do you know about Chesterfield cigarettes?"

"God, that's an old brand. When I think of Chesterfield cigarettes, I think of how they used to sponsor radio and TV shows back in the 50s and 60s. You know, the face of Chesterfield that I remember the most was Jack Webb from *Dragnet*. Didn't Jack used to come on at the end of the show and tell you to buy a carton or two?"

"That was before my time. I'm a child of the 70s." Jane stood up.

"I won't hold that against you. What's a thirteen-year-or-so age difference, anyway?"

"Less than twenty-five," she said with a knowing smile.

"See you later, Chopper."

"Chopper?"

He held his palm over the bar. "You hover like a helicopter. I think it fits."

The familiar aroma of catnip doobie wafted across the backyard of the B&B. Jane's heightened aromatic sensors started detecting it when she was outside the front gate. She walked through the backyard and followed the sweet smoky smell to the strip of land shaded with trees and bushes. Seated on the ground with her back against the tree and listening to her iPod, Mollie didn't see Jane as she moved toward her. Jane lightly tapped the girl on her shoulder, causing Mollie to jump.

"*Oi!*" she yelped, quickly removing the earbuds. "You shouldn't sneak up on people like that!" She dropped the catnip joint on the wet earth.

Jane recovered it and snuffed an errant ember with the toe of her cowboy boot. "I see you're still self-medicating," she said and handed the catnip back to Mollie.

"And I see you're still mud wrestling on the side," Mollie motioned toward Jane's shirt. "How does all this *shmuts* find you?"

She looked down at her shirt and realized that she had two identical ones upstairs in a pile. "Your parents have a washing machine?"

"It's broken. Should be fixed Monday or Tuesday."

"Is there a cleaners nearby?"

"Twenty miles south. And they're only open half a day on Saturday and closed on Sunday."

Jane figured she'd be using her bathtub that night to wash clothes. "How well do you know the Van Gordens?"

"Wow. That was an abrupt shift. You should try *schmoozing* with me before you yank me under the third-degree light." Mollie took a quick puff on the herbal cigarette.

"Just answer the question."

"I know them well enough to know I don't want to know them."

"Because of what Jake told you or because of what you experienced?"

She took another hit of the catnip. "Mostly what Jake told me. But I wasn't too impressed by what I saw of them. Carol's a drone..."

"She didn't know you and Jake split up."

"No shock there. She's not very connected to the earthly plane. She's a white-bread *shikseh*. She wasn't rude or anything. She just wasn't..."

"Aware?"

Mollie looked at Jane. The kid was warming up to her. "Yeah. Exactly. As for Jake's dad...he's a *schmuck*. A *shmendrik*. A tool. I don't trust him." Mollie sat back down on the ground.

Jane followed her lead, if only to mirror the kid's actions and make her feel more comfortable so she would possibly divulge more info. It was a classic manipulative move and it usually worked. "Why don't you trust him?"

"The few times I'd go over to Jake's house and bump into his dad, he was too involved in his own little world to even say 'hi.' When he wasn't checking to see how many people were admiring his YouTube clip of their house and returning emails from prospective clients, he was either checking himself out in the mirror or driving off to meet a customer."

"I got the impression he wasn't interested in generating tons of work for himself. Kinda like if it happened, it happened, but he wasn't going to break a sweat."

"Yeah. They have tons of family *gelt*."

Jane didn't understand. "Is that like family *guilt*?"

"Family *money*."

"Who's side has the *gelt*?"

"Jake's dad."

"Where'd the money come from?"

"Not sure. I think it was like architecture or design. The artistic gene is in Jake's blood...just like his dad." Jane wouldn't call Bailey "artistic." Maybe gaudy and garish, but not much artistry there. "But even though he didn't have to work, his dad was always acting like he had some big deal that he had to follow up on."

"You ever see Bailey working on any of those deals?"

"I wasn't there that much."

"What did Jake tell you?"

"Why are you asking me all this?"

"Because I have to work every angle there is." There was no way Jane was going to tip her hand to the kid, not knowing how well she could keep her trap shut.

"All Jake ever told me was that his dad was too busy for him. And anyway, I'm not sure his dad liked me that much. There was a *broygis* between his dad and me." Jane needed a translation. "We weren't on speaking terms."

"Why?"

"'Cause I stood up for Jake when his dad put him down. You know how Jake liked to dress? The vintage shirts and fedoras? I thought it looked cool. It's why I liked him. He wasn't afraid to look different. But his dad *hated* Jake's style. Jake would put on one of those shirts or a fedora and his dad would get this disgusted look on his face and just *freak out* on him."

"Freak out how?"

"Just totally go postal on him! It's like it triggered something deep down. He'd tell Jake he looked stupid and how the shirts made his small stature appear more obvious. His dad was *always* on him because he was shorter and not as developed as other fifteen-year-olds…told him he should lift weights like he did."

"So when did you stick up for him?"

Mollie took another hit on the dying catnip joint. "One day, his dad was on his case again and said, 'I used to be small like you but look at me now!' And I just couldn't stand it any longer. I said, 'Maybe Jake doesn't want to look like you! Maybe he prefers to dress and think for himself!'" Mollie let out a sigh. "That didn't go over well. Jake thought the comment was great. He thought I had *chutzpah*. But his dad, big *putz* that he is, totally acted like a damn woman. Got all uptight and stomped out like he was on the rag. After that, he wouldn't so much as say 'hi' to me again." Mollie squashed out the catnip doobie into the dirt. "*Then,* the two-faced *drek* suddenly starts initiating conversations with my dad on the street...always just the two of them."

"How do you know they were talking?"

"It's a small down, Jane. Word gets around."

"And then your dad tells you to break up with Jake?"

"Yeah," Mollie hung her head.

"Because you were rude to Bailey?"

"Guess so."

"You're not buying that?" Mollie shook her head. "What do you suspect?"

"I think Mr. Van Gorden is threatened by me. I don't get the sense that he respects women that much. I think he tolerates us...the same way he tolerates his mindless wife. I think he decided to punish Jake by taking me away from him. I think he told my dad that I wasn't welcome in his home anymore and that it was best if we just broke up. And so my dad did what Mr. Van Gorden asked. But I know that when my dad sat me down to give me the news, he seemed kinda disturbed by the whole thing. When he said, 'It would never work out between Jake and me,' I knew he wanted to tell me more but he didn't."

"But you're fifteen. You're just friends. It's not like you're engaged."

"*Exactly.* The whole thing seemed kinda blown outta proportion. I think it really sent Jake off the deep end. You can't have someone controlling your life like that who you don't even like and not feel like your life is fucked six ways to Sunday!"

"You think Jake wanted to hang himself because of you?"

"That would make me sound pretty arrogant, wouldn't it? That a boy would want to kill himself because of me? Sorry. I don't think I have that kind of power over boys. I mean, come on, look at me, eh? I think it was...something about his life he just couldn't face."

Jane thought of the sketchpad with the animated drawing

of the man in the prison cell hanging himself. Was Jake drawing a picture of himself in the process of killing himself to maybe see what it would look like before he did the deed? If so, why on earth would he draw himself as a middle-aged man with a somewhat jutting jaw wearing one of those vintage shirts? God, Jane wanted to show Mollie that damn sketchpad and see what she thought. But that was off the table for now. "What couldn't Jake face?" Mollie licked her lips and turned away. Her jaw clenched. "What is it, Mollie?"

"How in the fuck should I know?!" Mollie yelled, her voice choked with sadness.

It was a classic reaction, especially for a kid—exercise a healthy, stressful pause and then snap back with an emotive response. It was the way a kid who knows something and feels the world on her shoulders reacts when she doesn't feel she can expose all the cards on the table. "What do you know, Mollie?"

"I don't know anything!" She looked Jane hard in the eye. "I only know what I feel." She started off but Jane held her back.

"So tell me what you feel."

She hung her head. "It doesn't matter now," she said sadly. Mollie shook off Jane's soft grip and trod back to the house.

It was strange, Jane thought. In less than a few hours, two people closely linked to Jake told her they didn't "know anything." Jane figured that if they didn't know for sure, they sure as hell suspected something big.

CHAPTER 18

The clothesline in Jane's bedroom was starting to get crowded with the new clues she'd gathered. Directly after the mysterious *I BEARED MY SOUL AND STILL YOU IGNORE ME???* clue, Jane clipped one of the Chesterfield cigarettes to the clothesline. Next to the notepaper with *1401 Imperial* written on it, she attached the short stack of info that Hank copied for her.

Jane stood back and read the clothesline like a book from left to right. Until somebody proved it to her otherwise, she was convinced that this was a story—albeit a complex one—and all she had to do to figure it out was to be as smart as the kidnapper and get into his skin. *Into,* not under. That's the way Jane always worked. She could stare at a photo or a bloody crime scene and eventually, there would be that intuitive nexus that bonded her with either the perp or the victims. She'd feel things that didn't belong to her. When she worked the tragic Stover and Lawrence cases nearly two years prior, the numinous nudges of the dead haunted her and drove her to dive into a bottle of Jack Daniels every night. The booze numbed the pain and darkness that enveloped those two cases. But now she was over fifteen months sober and she had to allow the heartbeat of the person behind the clues to resonate within her. She had to open her eyes and hear what he was desperately trying to tell her.

Desperate. That was the word that Jane kept coming back to again and again. The desperation permeated each clue. She focused on one clue and then the next, and felt herself going deeper within herself. The world around her fell away as the tips of her fingers prickled. Yes, she was moving toward him. She didn't budge an inch, not wanting to jar the connection. Without warning, a wellspring of grief engulfed her and tears fell from her eyes without any concrete emotion to support them. It was unmitigated sadness, fear and abandonment. Jane gasped and shot out of the moment.

She sat down on her bed, trying to sort out what just happened. From the way it felt, she wondered if she was sensing what Jake was going through. But the more she pondered that prospect, the less it felt true. That profound anguish belonged to the kidnapper exclusively. The idea was repellant at first because she was taught the black-and-white dogma of perp and victim.

But she'd learned through working the case with Kit Clark the year before that the perp can become the victim and vice versa within the same lifetime. It was an acknowledgment that Jane fought but had to accept, even though the comfort of black-and-white realities was easier to allow.

She stared at the Chesterfield cigarette on the clothesline and opened the desk drawer to reveal the rest of the cigarettes she found in the forest that day along with the vintage-style ashtray and crushed burgundy *Chesterfield 101* pack. Chesterfield cigarettes weren't exactly her generation, and she was grateful that Hank gave her the hat tip about the celebrity history of the brand. Turning to her computer, she entered CHESTERFIELD JACK WEBB DRAGNET in the search engine and came up with a list of choices. It seemed that the actor was tightly affiliated with the cigarette brand when *Dragnet* was a radio show. While other TV and film stars such as Ronald Reagan and James Dean pimped the cigarette in ads and commercials, Jack Webb seemed to have a longer connection with the product. Jane easily found a vintage newspaper ad of Jack Webb promoting Chesterfield. She hooked up her portable printer that she'd thrown into her duffel bag and printed off the page that showed Webb in a grey tweed jacket, black tie and plastered trademark black hair holding a lit Chesterfield cigarette and smiling.

She clipped the page on the clothesline next to the cigarette and stared at the latest entry on the *clue line*. It was as if Webb was teasing Jane as he comfortably held the cigarette in his left hand. "Look at me," she felt he was saying. "I can smoke, but you can't." Her eyes drifted momentarily to the lone American Spirit cigarette she brought with her. *The temptation.* The face of her struggle. Then she looked at the drawer, full of Chesterfield cigarettes. It was suddenly cigarette heaven. But the idea of smoking the evidence brought her back to reality. She picked up one of the Chesterfields and noted the clear black mark of a pen encircling each cigarette about one millimeter from the tip. Obviously, whoever took the time to draw on each of the twenty cylinders wanted to make sure that whoever found the clues would clearly see this and do some research. Jane started entering everything she could think of that related to the black mark in the Internet search engine. But none of the websites proved fruitful. By chance, she entered, MILLIMETER CHESTER-FIELD CIGARETTE and a cascade of results greeted her.

It seemed that Chesterfield launched a new product in their line in late 1967 called, *Chesterfield 101s*. The product was in response to other brands putting out cigarettes that were longer in length and they wanted to go that extra mile—that extra millimeter—to set themselves apart. Jane found an old advertisement from early 1968 promoting the 101s with the slogan, *A silly millimeter longer than the 100s. It isn't much. But wait 'til you taste it. It's one better.* She found herself grimacing at the idiotic ad, silently wondering how many fools took up the habit just to get an extra millimeter on their smoke. Then she realized she was already sounding like one of those bitchy ex-smokers who rail against cigarette companies.

Doing more research on the Web, Jane tried to find a pack of Chesterfield 101s that matched the same crumpled burgundy pack she found at the staged scene in the forest. Many websites, mostly in Europe, sold the brand but not with the same burgundy packaging found in the ad from early 1968. It seemed that that particular packet had long been replaced by a more modern version. After more than half an hour, she finally found the burgundy packet on a British auction website which was dedicated to selling *vintage shtick* from the 50s and 60s. However, upon reading closer, she discovered that the hard-to-find pack had already been sold several months before and that there were no more available from that seller. She could contact the British seller and ask for records of that sale, once she had a warrant. But that would mean she'd have to confess to Weyler and Bo that she recovered a massive clue and didn't tell them. *God*, the trail of lies was long in pursuit of the truth.

She closed out the web page and realized that 1968 was

a popular year in relationship to this case. Jordan was arrested in July of 1968, David Sackett, the old man who owned the
phone number spoofed on the kidnapper's cell phone, told her
he moved into that house on Warwick road in Short Hills, New
Jersey, in February of 1968. And now, this particularly vintage
pack of Chesterfield 101s, *just happened* to be launched in late
1967 and ramped up their advertising in early 1968. Jane examined the black marker line on each cigarette. Just like the advertisement made a *silly* point of drawing attention to the extra
millimeter, it seemed that the kidnapper was doing the same
thing. Was it some kind of *date stamp* to create context within
the complex story? If so, the year 1968 wasn't boding well for
Jordan Copeland.

Jane turned her attention to the note on the far right of
the clothesline—the one with the mysterious website she found
with a bold red check mark in Jake's notebook when she was
snooping in his bedroom. Typing *www.mysecretrevelations.com*
into the browser, Jane entered a strange, bold world. Against
a black and red backdrop, people from all over the world and
from all walks of life posted their deepest secret revelations,
completely anonymously. Pages and pages were filled with secrets from children, wives, husbands, grandmothers, lovers and
more. Some were poignant such as the 42-year-old woman who
wrote, *I keep my dad's driver's license in my wallet even though
he died ten years ago just so I can see his face.* And the one from
a lovelorn eighteen-year-old boy, *I sit behind you in math class
and wonder what it would be like to press my head against your
chest and hear your heartbeat.* A handful were frivolous such as,
*I broke up with my last boyfriend because he liked classical music
but I told him it was because I met someone new. Now I really
miss him.* A lot were downright disturbing on different levels.
There was the one from the sixteen-year-old boy who wrote,
*Dear Mom and Dad, the brownies tasted funny because I put pot
in them!* Or this one: *I have five children but I only love the first
two.* The one-sentence secret from a supposed twelve-year-old

girl really alarmed Jane. *My cousin raped me and I liked it.*

On and on it went, pages of revelations—thousands of confessions from people who found comfort in writing down their secrets anonymously with only a date, an alleged age and notation of whether they were male or female next to their revelation. Jane wondered if this cathartic regurgitation in cyberspace helped them by releasing the burden of the secret from their shoulders. On the other hand, did those who bookmarked the website and read the newest offerings each day do so with a sense of compassion or a sense of sleazy voyeurism?

Jane scrolled through the pages, looking for the secret revelations posted before March 22nd, the day of Jake's disappearance. Primarily, she was searching for anything written by a fifteen-year-old boy. She had to assume—and it was a big assumption—that Jake Van Gorden, seeker of "Truth," would use his real age and sex when and *if* he added a secret to the website. All the entries for seventeen days prior to March 22nd were identified as adults, but there were two in February and two in March—one of those just sixteen days prior to March 22nd, all from a fifteen-year-old boy—that Jane thought might be connected to Jake. They were startling, to say the least.

The first one from February 10th read: "*I fear that my blood is infected with the sins of my family*". Infected. That was the identical word Hank said Jake used during their conversation when Jake asked Hank if he felt a family could be *infected with a curse.* If memory served her, she was pretty sure Hank mentioned that he had that conversation with Jake about six weeks prior to his disappearance, which would almost coincide with the February 10th entry.

The second entry from the fifteen-year-old poster was from February 22nd. "*How many secrets does it take to curse a family? How many revelations does it take to set them free?*" There was that mention of *a curse* again. But in this post, it appeared that the boy was searching for the possible solution, citing the freedom in uncovering the revelations.

When Jane read the March 1st entry, a shiver bolted down her spine. It echoed too closely to words she'd already heard from someone else. *"The dead are following me. I'm terrified that the secret has become flesh and blood and is chasing my family from generation to generation, contaminating my bloodline."* The second line was almost exactly the same verbiage used by Jordan when he and Jane were discussing his theory of family secrets.

Finally, there was the last chilling entry from the anonymous fifteen-year-old on March 6th. *"I saw you but you didn't see me, YOU FUCKING PERVERT! Which one of us will hang in hell???"*

Jane sat back in her chair. *Pervert* was a word used more than once to describe Jordan, specifically by Bailey and Bo. *Hang in hell? Again, with the visual of hanging.* This was getting to be a sickening, familiar pattern. Sixteen days after those words were written, Jake attempted suicide by hanging. To give it even more impact, the March 6th entry was around the same time when Bailey Van Gorden talked to Aaron privately and Mollie was told to break off her friendship with Jake. Yes, Jane surmised, these posts had to be written by Jake Van Gorden. For Jane, they were akin to another four valuable clues that further confounded and complicated an already mystifying case.

Jane pasted and copied the four comments on a separate page, printed them out and then bookmarked the secret revelations website. She was about to close up her computer when she remembered the remarks that Mollie made about Bailey's YouTube video. As she recalled, Bailey had at least three thousand hits on his download of their over-the-top, Colorado log monstrosity of a house. Jane also remembered that Bailey said it could be found by simply putting his name into the search engine on the website.

Yep. There it was in all its glory. He'd amassed an additional 333 hits on the video, giving him a whopping 3,333, and received a five-star rating as well. Jane clicked on the *play* button, waiting for Bailey's *splendor of the crass* to grab hold of her. As the video cued up, she figured Bailey would have a sweeping shot of the house exterior with pounding music in the backdrop to ratchet up the sales pitch for his architectural services. After all, he *was* a screaming narcissist who needed to make everything big, bold and annoying. But when the video started, Jane's prediction was way off. There was Bailey standing in the kitchen, behind the granite countertop, dressed in a tight-fitting black T-shirt that showed off his muscular physique and speaking directly to the camera. Since the camera didn't move an inch, Jane assumed he had it set on a tripod and was most likely, alone in the room. His voice was surprisingly low-key. He introduced himself, talked about where he lived and how he designed and oversaw the building of his home, which he said was "nestled in the Colorado Rockies." Jane's bogus-meter went off on that one since Midas was more realistically sitting in the proverbial *thumb* of the Rockies *if* the mountain range was lying on its back *and* spread-eagled. But he wasn't the first architect to use hyperbole to make a sales pitch.

Bailey then went on for about two minutes, blabbering about how he loved to create "magic and passion" in whatever he did, how it was important that clients "came to the table with that same passion" and that while they may only "collaborate on one project together" he knew that it would be memorable. The scene cut to Bailey doing a handheld shot of the front and rear exterior of the house, showing the expansiveness of the property. He then walked to various areas of the house, bragging about his "vision" or "intention" when he created this or that gaudy touch. There was the imported, five-tiered, Italian fountain on the back terrace. And then viewers got to hear about the mahogany chair Bailey scored from an estate sale in Africa. The most ludicrous and somewhat embarrassing part for Jane came when Bailey showed off his deluxe Weber outdoor grill with "all the bells and whistles." Only problem was, Bailey didn't have a clue how to operate the grill and even admitted he'd never "fired it up." The whole video was one badly conceived, bombastic bore. The more Jane listened to the eight-minute pitch, the more she felt Bailey should have hired a professional to produce the video. Instead of maximizing the house to show it off, Bailey seemed to spend more time droning on about himself and all the facile appurtenances of his success, using convoluted phrases such as "I have such enthusiasm for the lifestyle and making a creative connection with clients." "Who gives a shit about you, asshole?" Jane exclaimed. "Show me the damn house!"

The video ended with Bailey seated on a large rock outside his house, his left leg bent with his hands encircling his knee, which made his bulging muscles even more apparent. "Thank you for taking the time to watch my presentation," Bailey said to the camera with a stiff smile. "I hope you liked what you saw and that I can be part of bringing the good life to you. Together, we can create something wonderful."

Jane shook her head in disgust. She wouldn't hire Bailey to redecorate her broom closet, let alone her house. What a pompous asshole. It was absolutely shocking to Jane that he had a five-star video rating as well as fabulous comments posted below the video. People wrote everything from, *I love your style!* to *I'll be setting up an appointment soon!* What was wrong with people? Couldn't they see that Bailey was all flash and no substance? Who in their right mind would want to linger longer than five minutes in this egotist's presence? It would certainly drive Jane back to the bottle. What's more, Bailey must have been so self-absorbed when he listed the search engine tags for the video, that he spelled *Italian fountain* as *"Italain"* and misspelled the Weber Grill as *Webber* Grill. Obviously, Jane deduced, all that money didn't buy the pretentious prick an education.

Still, she couldn't allow her distaste for Bailey to compromise his son's case. Jane needed to smooth things over with him if only to make access to their home easier in the future for her. But she needed a valid reason to warrant another visit, especially after causing such an uproar earlier in the day. The idea hit her. She called Weyler and after Jane explained that she needed to check Jake's computer history for possible entries on a suspicious blog—a blog she described as vaguely as possible. He smoothed the way with Bo for her second visit of the day, provided she made the visit "as short as possible."

Before Jane left, she glanced once more at the four obtuse posts she copied from *mysecretrevelations.com*. Her eyes caught the words: *The dead are following me...* Jane furtively looked at the rocking chair in the corner of her room by the window. She did everything possible to keep the insane possibilities at bay.

The blue Colorado sky finally appeared, allowing the sun to steal a few minutes of freedom from the clutch of clouds and to warm Jane's tired body. Had it only been two days in Midas? It felt like years. And now, as she parked her Mustang in the cul-de-sac and started the long walk up the Van Gordens' driveway, she found herself conflicted by what the evidence was showing her and what she didn't want to believe. The last thing any cop wanted to consider was that a child's family was linked some-how to his or her disappearance. And yet, the sad reality was that too often there was a close family member or friend that had a nefarious connection to the crime. The excuses from the perps ranged from "accidental" to "insanity." As Jane crested the Van Gordens' driveway and walked up the path to the front door, she felt that *if* this family was involved, it was full of twists and turns that even she wasn't sure she could traverse.

Jane walked between the two pillars carved in the shape of owls and rang the doorbell. She looked down at her filthy shirt and quickly buttoned her leather jacket all the way up to hide the dirt. After what seemed like a long wait, Carol answered. She was still dressed in her same black-and-white outfit and still looked ever so smart and pulled together. However, the look on her face when she answered the door was one of great stress. Jane immediately assumed she was the reason for the woman's strain and launched quickly into her apologies, using the excuse that her impatience to solve her son's case clouded her better judgment. As Jane spoke the words, she really meant them, but she also made sure to throw in a few well-positioned facial gestures that implied regret and guilt. She hung her head, sighed at appropriate moments and even went so far as to put her hand over her heart in a show of contrition. Instead of getting the response the wanted, Carol stood at the doorway and seemed more preoccupied with matters taking place in Bailey's office. She ushered Jane inside and directed her toward the living room. As they crossed to the right, Jane glanced over her shoulder at the closed arched doors that protected the players behind them—players whose vocal tones reverberated ever so slightly off the walls but failed to reveal the words they were speaking.

Sitting prominently on the large burl wood coffee table was Jake's computer. Obviously, *somebody* got the message that Jane told Weyler and *somebody* decided it was best to bring the computer to Jane rather than allow Jane back into Jake's bedroom. *Somebody* had also plugged in the computer and turned it on to make Jane's time at the Van Gordens' both efficient and speedy. That *somebody*, Jane surmised, was *not* standing in front of her at that moment, rubbing the heel of each palm against the other and focusing vacantly on a spot in the wood floor. Jane thanked Carol for the swift cooperation but the woman didn't seem to hear a word.

"Coffee?" Carol asked Jane, still half in her abstracted world.

"No, thank you."

"Tea?"

"No, thanks. But please, make yourself a cup," Jane suggested, more to shake loose of Carol for a few moments.

Like a dutiful Stepford wife, Carol nodded and walked out of the living room, turned right and clip-clopped into the kitchen.

Jane quickly opened up Jake's Internet web browser and selected the *History* menu and the dates previous to his March

22nd disappearance. Nothing. Zip. *Nada*. She opened each available day in the *history* file prior to that and found the same empty result. Selecting Jake's email box, Jane was stunned. It was empty. Not even spam occupied the lonely box. The likelihood of there being no mail, even junk mail, up to the present date in Jake's mailbox, was ridiculous. There was always the option of taking the computer and scanning the hard drive and hopefully recovering the lost data. But Jane realized that even if she was able to get the Van Gordens to agree to such a thing, the chance of finding a techie in that town who would agree to breach the trust of a fellow secret holder was slim. Her only chance was to talk to Mollie again and ask her if she might have any correspondence with Jake. Before Jane closed out of the windows, she pulled up the browser again and clicked on *Favorites*, hoping to find the *secret revelations* website listed. But she was zero for three. That folder was also empty.

Jane crossed into the entry hall just as Carol returned with a cup of tea balanced on a fine china saucer. Suddenly, the voices got louder in Bailey's office. Carol turned to the closed doors, a look of apprehension carved on her countenance. The door handle turned with an angry twist and Bailey walked out into the entry hall. His face was flushed and irritated. He was dressed in another stiffly starched white shirt, a tight pair of stonewashed jeans and an intricate leather belt with a large turquoise buckle. Bailey was in his own world momentarily until he saw Jane.

"You got what you wanted?" he gruffly asked her, his nose clearly congested.

"Yes, thank you. Unfortunately, I couldn't find anything on his computer."

Bailey stared at her with his steely eyes. "Right," he nodded, sniffing a bit of mucus up his nose.

"You're still stuffed up," Jane offered.

"Excuse me?"

"When I was here and met you the first time, you were

stuffed up and looked feverish."

Bailey regarded Jane with a look that surfaced somewhere between quizzical and aggravated. "Allergies," he said succinctly.

Jane nodded. From what she could see outside, there weren't many trees or flowers blooming yet in the high country. And there weren't any pets scrambling around the ol' log homestead. Jane started to leave when she turned back to Carol. "Oh, did you get anymore of those two-ring, hang-up calls after I left?"

"No," she said with honesty.

"What's that?" Bailey said, moving closer to Jane.

"Your phone rings twice and then when you answer it, there's no one there. And the Caller ID reads *Unavailable*."

Bailey locked eyes with Jane in what appeared to be a death grip. His tanned, flushed face tensed up ever so slightly. "Is this pertinent to my son's case or is this just more chatter?" Before Jane could answer, the sound of a woman clearing her throat with purpose could be heard coming from behind the half-opened office door. Jane watched Bailey pull back and slightly turn his head toward the office. "If this is relevant information, please tell us," he said, his tone more refined.

Whoever was behind the door seemed to have tangible control over Bailey. Jane wanted to look for the invisible cord that was connected between Bailey and the operator on the other side of the door. Jane leaned over as the office door creaked open. There was another cough, but this time, it was generated from deep within the lungs. The door moved further and the wheel of a chair revealed itself. Finally, the door swung open wide and a tiny, gaunt woman, no more than ninety-five pounds, appeared, seated in a chrome wheelchair. She wore white wool slacks, a black button-front shirt and a cream-colored cardigan. Her grey hair was styled in an abrupt coif, with sharp edges that framed her chin. For a moment, Jane thought the woman had to be Carol's mother. Their dress and style seemed to match in an eerie, unsettling manner. The only variance in their look was

Louise's skin color. It was a yellowish tint, an outward expression of her cancerous liver.

"Hello," the woman said, obviously having trouble breathing. Bailey turned to face her. "Wheel me out there," she instructed. Bailey quickly obliged. She held out her hand to Jane. A well-used linen hankie was wedged in the arm of the cream cardigan. "I'm Louise Van Gorden. Bailey's mother. You must be Detective Perry."

Jane gently shook her hand. "Yes, ma'am."

Louise may have been on death's door, but there was a hard resistance in her eyes that gave Jane the impression that this ol' lady wasn't going down without a fight. "You need to excuse my son, detective," she said in a tone that was dry and flinty. "He's forgotten what he was taught. Do you need to leave immediately?"

"No, ma'am."

"Good," Louise declared with an officious tenor. "We've finally got some goddamned sun outside. Wheel me out onto the terrace so we can visit."

Jane wasted no time pushing Louise through the kitchen and out onto the spacious tree-lined terrace that Jane was already intimately familiar with—thanks to Bailey's YouTube video. To her left was the three tiered Italian fountain that Bailey misspelled on his video tag, and to her right was the covered and probably still unused Webber grill.

Carol handed Jane a heavy blanket to drape across Louise's lap before closing the French doors and giving them privacy. Jane took a seat on the stone edge of a large planter box, replete with frozen offerings from last fall's final growth. Louise held her wrinkled face to the sun, squinting but seemingly finding some relief in the late afternoon rays.

"Tiring flight?" Jane asked.

"Everything's tiring these days."

"Which airport did you fly out of?" Louise turned away from the sun and looked at Jane. "Bailey said he grew up in

Wentworth, New Jersey. I've never heard of Wentworth. Is that where you still live?"

"I flew out of Newark. I live in Princeton. I moved there years ago." She reached into her cardigan pocket and brought out a pack of Parliament cigarettes and matches. Jane watched in stunned silence as the woman lit a cigarette with her thin bony fingers, let out a gagging hack and inhaled a hard drag with her thin, cracked lips. "You smoke?" Louise asked, handing the pack to Jane.

"No. I just quit."

Louise smiled and turned to the side. "Yeah, sure. I quit too." She took another hearty puff. "I understand Carol told you about my predicament." Jane nodded. "So, you must be wondering why I'm smoking?"

"That's your business," Jane said matter-of-factly.

"Yes. That's right. It *is* my business." There was a harsh, unforgiving quality in Louise's voice. "I suppose others in my condition would be searching the world for cures or maybe securing their relationship with God. But I'm more the type who just accepts my lot in life. *What's cooked at home is eaten at home.* That's an old saying but it fits. You take what you get and you deal with it." Louise inhaled another drag. "So, Jordan Copeland…" The shift in the conversation was purposeful. "It seems we have the likely suspect in our midst." She titled her head toward the sun again. "Copeland? Isn't that a Jewish name? Do you find a lot of child killers who are Jews or do Jews steer clear of that particular twisted desire?"

Jane felt her back stiffen. "Copeland's not Jewish."

"Are you certain?" Louise returned her gaze to Jane.

"Yes."

"Hmmm. Aaron Copland was a Jew, right?"

"It's spelled differently."

"Really? Well, well, well…" Louise seemed to drift for a second. "How unfortunate to have a last name that has such an undesirable association."

"You have your prejudice?" Jane asked as gently as humanly possible.

Louise smiled. "Only in the morning. By the evening,
I've worked it completely out of my system." She shifted in the
wheelchair, having a difficult time finding a comfortable position. "I think it's obvious that Jordan Copeland is involved with
Jake's disappearance."

"What makes it obvious?"

"His record, for God's sake!" Louise snapped. "His
personality…"

"How do you know his personality?"

"My son has informed me." Louise started to take another
drag on the cigarette but began coughing so violently that Jane
wondered if she was going to pop a lung.

"Wasn't it precarious for you to travel, given your illness?"

Louise wiped her mouth with the linen hankie tucked under her cardigan. "You can say it…terminal liver cancer. Yes.
But I told my doctors in Newark to fuck off." She chuckled a low
laugh. "Forty years ago, I'd never have said such a thing. I might
have thought it, but I sure as hell wouldn't have said it. But ever
since the cancer took hold of my liver, I find myself more impul-
sive, more direct, more *bile*. Cancer seems to extract the bitch in
me that's been buried for years." Her tired eyes, lids heavy, gazed
off to the side. "You know what cancer has taught me, detective?
It's taught me that life is a shit hole into which you sink deeper
and deeper until the excrement smothers you and chokes the
life from your throat."

"That's visual."

"That's *real*, sweetheart! You come into this world and you
have such fantasies that life is fair and you'll marry the man of
your dreams and you'll have the house and the kids and holi-
days on the coast. And then you find out that life is about duty
and obligations to those around you who you can't stand but
you put up with. Pretty soon, you've forgotten who you are and
what you wanted because you're drowning in other's people's

nightmares. But who gives a shit, right? You do what you have to do to keep up…"

"The status quo," Jane interjected.

Louise's weary face studied Jane. "Yes. You understand, don't you?"

"I understand that people do it. But I don't understand why."

She chuckled again but it was edged with scorn. "How lucky you are, dear. You have the luxury of integrity."

"Kind of goes with my job description."

"Oh, Christ, give me a break. As if there aren't dirty cops out there. You still believe in honesty because you still believe that people are good. Once you learn that people are inherently evil and that goodness is just an illusion to draw others into one's scheme, then you'll release the shackles of your integrity and join the rest of us."

Jane considered what Louise said. Wasn't she already there in many ways? Wasn't she knee deep in that shit hole and waiting for more crap to get dumped on her? *Good God,* she thought, was she staring at that moment into the bleak eyes of her near future? A future rife with bitterness and misery where every breath and thought revolves around how fucking miserable life is as you wait to die? The more Jane looked at Louise, the more she hated her. She hated her because she was looking at part of herself—the part that was old before her time and resentful that any happiness in her life had been subjugated to serve a greater need. Here was a woman who had willingly given up her opinions, her options and her voice in favor of whatever she was told to do. And now, with the specter of death enveloping her, she was finally speaking up with the hard carpet of anger underneath each word.

What's to say that all those years of suffocating her feelings didn't invite the cancer into her body that was chewing on her liver? What's to say that if Louise had had the guts to speak up years ago that she wouldn't be destroyed right now, waiting for the death rattle? Jane couldn't help but wonder if the simple act of speaking up and seeking one's truth was the liberating factor in this equation? She'd never had a problem speaking her mind, but facing the truth of her life and her past was still difficult to process. It required forgiveness and vulnerability—two attributes that felt so damn dangerous to her. Forgiveness required releasing the engine of hate; vulnerability could leave her wide open for an attack. It was easier to continue in the way she'd always operated. It was safer. "*Illusions die hard and the status quo dies even harder,*" she remembered Jordan telling her. "*Who wants to face their shadowed truth when it's so much easier to keep the ball rolling that feeds the machine and makes one's life a false existence?*" he'd stressed.

Jane scrutinized Louise seated in her wheelchair, the fading ember of her cigarette pointed toward the cold concrete. The woman seemed to be growing tired quickly. Her body appeared crumpled under her crisp, starched shirt. Her advice to Jane to "release the shackles" of her integrity and "join the rest of us" carried the echo of every malevolent proposition ever uttered on this earth. It held the same oily tenor of the pornographer when he lures an ignorant girl into his trap; it seized the same devious intention of the meth dealer who promises a sweet escape to those who want to disappear. Without even realizing it, Jane was already on the highway, going full throttle, unconsciously "joining the rest of us," and she felt sick. This was not a club she had any conscious intention of joining. For a moment, she forgot the reason she came to the Van Gorden's house. She forgot that Jake was somewhere out there at the mercy of God knows who. This case had suddenly become personal and the players in it had become nauseating reflections of her own inadequacies. A fire of indignation erupted in Jane's belly. "You know, I kind of like the illusion of integrity, Louise. It tends to create an environment where the reality of subversion can be revealed."

Louise's thin lips pursed into an indiscernible line. Clearly, she wasn't amused that Jane had the nerve to think for herself. This withered woman, who looked twenty years older than she was, had played the game her entire life, and she was damned if some bitch with a badge and a brain was going to jump the invisible barriers and not play along. "Aren't you a silly child," Louise muttered with an elitist rise of her brow.

Jane leaned forward. "Is that how you'd describe Jake?"

Louise thought about it. "No," she said offhandedly after a few seconds. "He was ignorant of the way the world works."

"Was?" Jane asked.

"Isn't it a foregone conclusion, detective?"

"That he's dead?" Jane's tone was a blend of incredulity and rage.

"Yes."

"No, it's not." Jane's ire was spiking. "I was brought in from Denver to bring him back alive."

"No, you weren't. You were brought in to investigate and arrest the most likely suspect who is clearly unbalanced, has a disgusting criminal record and is guilty."

"What if all trails don't lead to Jordan Copeland's door?"

"Then he's working with someone. The sooner we get him back into a prison cell, the sooner we can put this to bed."

Put this to bed, Jane thought. For fuck's sake, what in the hell was going on in that bony head of hers? "So, we collar Jordan and we throw him in the box. But what if he doesn't cop to your grandson's kidnapping? What if he doesn't admit that he's aligned with anyone else who might have Jake? What if it's a dead end? Where does that leave Jake?"

"How many mysteries don't get solved, detective? How many bodies are never found? I'm afraid that resignation has become a familiar bedfellow for me...especially now." Her voice was off in the distance, dangling far away from her body.

Jane stood up. She wasn't going to be dismissed this time. *This time* she was walking out on her own volition. "Well, Mrs. Van Gorden, I haven't rolled over yet on this case. And I'm sure as hell not planning to do so in the near future. You see, I actually feel that whoever took Jake *wants* to be found." Jane detected a stiffening of Louise's gaunt face. "And it's my intention to give him exactly what he wants." She nodded toward Louise who returned the gesture with a stern glare of disapproval. But before Jane opened the French doors, she turned around. "I would think you'd want some resolution regarding your grandson before you die."

Louise fiddled with the hem of her sweater sleeve. "Resolution is a myth. The book is never closed. We just play out the same scene in different clothes and different settings."

"That's absolutely true. *Until* someone speaks up and blows the fucking lid off the lies." Jane would never have couched a statement that way to the grandmother of any missing child. But *this* grandmother seemed to be seriously lacking both grief and compassion.

Instead of the statement eliciting fury, Louise simply smiled and shook her head. "Since no one has the balls or sufficient gunpowder to blow a feather in the air, it's highly unlikely we'll ever find out what happened to Jake." She gazed out into the yard. "And then all we'll be left to say is…so sad…too bad."

CHAPTER 19

Jane felt like she needed a shower as she descended the Van Gorden's driveway and returned to her Mustang. She left Louise in the back courtyard where she asked to be left alone. Carol solemnly walked Jane to the door while Bailey, ever the gentleman, stayed behind his office doors talking on the phone.

Popping the Mustang into gear, Jane maneuvered slowly down the winding road and left Blackfeather Estates. As she drove, she recalled the haunting admission that her friend Kit

Clark told her the previous year. Dying of lung cancer, Kit was convinced that she'd given herself the disease as a result of unresolved anger and grief over the death of her beloved granddaughter. When the subject of liver cancer surfaced, Jane remembered Kit referencing "unresolved anger and guilt." During one episode when Jane fell off the wagon, Kit was relentless, warning Jane that her vengeance would "swell up and eat away" at her body one day if she didn't find the middle ground and a more peaceful approach.

In the fifteen months since that fateful encounter, Jane read numerous books that Kit left her, all featuring mystical, philosophic and mind/body themes. The central thesis throughout was that whatever the mind believes, the body responds to in kind. If you think the world is an evil, hateful place, you will attract that reality along with the people who mirror that belief. Eventually, your body will shut down because hatred grows in the soil of discontent and then a myriad of ailments can surface—some aggravating, others deadly.

Suppression, Jane learned, was the first nail in the coffin—suppression of a dream, a love, an emotion…a secret. Whatever is suppressed or hidden, she learned, ironically becomes the eight-hundred-pound gorilla inside the body screaming to be acknowledged. The more it's ignored, the more it growls and tears at the fabric of the body. Keep ignoring it and as one's anger grows—built on a foundation of guilt, resentment and sense of being trapped—the disease takes hold. Once that happens, the gorilla cannot be ignored any longer because the damage he's done is made manifest in a way one can physically see.

But, from what Jane was able to fathom from the pages of Kit's books, if you understand this cycle and release yourself from the choke hold of suppression, anger and all the other emotions that pull you down into the pit of hell instead of lift you up, you can find that elusive freedom everybody talks about. The point was *to feel*; to experience life with an open heart and mind; to shed the fear that feeling was dangerous.

The point was also to speak up and not deny what you've seen or what you've felt and shun the lies when they are sold erroneously as the truth. If a person could do this, they could move through life with greater ease and a sense of purpose, unlocking the manacles with the key they've held all along.

It all sounded so ridiculously simple on the page. But putting it into practice and remembering it when life served another bitter plate, was quite another. Jane's thoughts turned to Louise Van Gorden and she pondered what secrets the old, bitter woman had suppressed. There was that callous *What's the use?* mentality Louise favored, as if it was a foregone conclusion that Jake was dead or would be killed. And that statement that "What's cooked at home is eaten at home"? That spoke volumes to Jane—keep everything under the roof and don't expose it while you continue *life as normal*. What a twisted, fucked-up attitude. If this was the world that Jake inhabited, it's no wonder he didn't fit and rankled against his surroundings. It's no wonder the boy may have been drawn into the disreputable grasp of someone else who he might have thought was a friend but who turned out to be his doom.

Jane continued driving down the two-lane highway but she couldn't get Louise's sickly vibe off her. It was like watching death personified. The dark shadows perched around the old lady were palpable, like vultures waiting to feast on her corpse. Fear rose up in Jane's throat as she drove down the highway; fear that all the changes she consciously made over the last fifteen months were falling short and that she was speeding toward the same end as Louise. She'd always gone through life with a sense of duty, first to her younger brother and then to every victim she encountered. When Louise grumbled that "you find out that life is about duty and obligations to those around you who you can't stand but you put up with" and then "you forgot who you are and what you wanted because you're drowning in other's people's nightmares," Jane related to every word. As cold-hearted as the ol' broad was, Jane understood her. At the age of thirty-seven, was it already too late to turn it around? Had the die been cast and was her fate to have the word *terminal* stamped on her medical sheet and *cancer* cited as the cause of her premature death?

Jane pulled quickly to the side of the two-lane highway and turned right into a secluded stand of trees. Overwhelmed, she fell across the steering wheel, sobbing. Every bit of control she'd fine tuned over the years was gone. Every judgment she'd professed was coming back to kick her in the teeth. She was at the mercy of an invisible hand that she couldn't see but that seemed bent on destroying her. For ten minutes, she cried like she'd never cried before. She cried harder than after any of the beatings she'd been dealt as a child. Within the sobs, the misery and pain were more profound than when she lay bloodied and battered on her father's workshop floor at the age of fourteen. And she felt more alone than any of the countless times she drank herself unconscious, begging God to take her.

After ten minutes, she sat back in the seat exhausted. Where once there was fullness, there now was an empty hole. Everything she thought she knew, now she wasn't so certain. The rawness engulfed Jane, causing her to doubt herself. As she sat in her car, she felt suspended over her body, like an observer with no memory of who she was staring down on. The scab had been ripped off the flesh and underneath was the tender, exposed pulp yet to take shape and transform. To stay in this intangible suspension was impossible. But it seemed difficult to render her body back inside the shell. Just as another wave of fear began, Jane sensed that peripatetic aroma of gardenias. This time, it was strong and nearly overpowering. A gentle, comforting warmth embraced her. But there was also a sense of being pushed to rise up from the pit of despair—a blend of love mixed with firmness. Jane held her hand out toward the passenger seat as tears welled in her eyes again. The aroma nearly choked her and her hand burned with a seeming connection to another world. Was it the one she loved from so long ago who took his life? Or another? There were too many dead souls to choose from and who might want to haunt her now. She couldn't help remembering the sentient words that Jake wrote: *The dead are following me.* At that heart-pounding moment, Jane knew that the dead were closing in on her as well.

As much as she wanted to fall into the void, something bade her to turn to the left. Within seconds, a black SUV sped down the highway, heading out of town. It belonged to only one person—Bailey Van Gorden. There was that sense within Jane that his destination was tainted. The shield of gardenias evaporated and she was back into her body once again and gunning the Mustang onto the highway. Bailey never saw her vehicle so he wouldn't know it was Jane tailing him as long as she kept sufficient distance. Once she was in cell phone range, she dialed Weyler and told him that she was heading up toward Highway 7 to search for the elusive "Imperial" address she found in Jake's locker. Fortunately, he didn't argue and even wished her luck.

It was easy to keep both a bead on Bailey and stay far behind him once they emerged onto a wider section of the highway where other cars helped protect the blue Mustang from view. As Hank told her, the landscape on Highway 7 was fairly remote, dotted with a few campgrounds, vacation cabins, ranch houses and a lone Catholic chapel, built on a rocky outcropping, all separated by several miles. Mount Meeker rose up in front of Jane as she clocked nearly thirty-miles. About half a mile up, she saw Bailey turn left, along with two other cars. She followed him another five miles until he entered a small mountain town the size of a breadbox. There wasn't any name for the town; no welcome sign at the entry point. It appeared that the economic downturn had certainly hit this place hard and fast. Buildings were boarded up and two of the three gas stations were abandoned. The only thriving businesses Jane noted were a video/convenience store, a handful of fast-food drive-thrus and a small market. She continued to carefully follow Bailey down the town's only street, wondering where in the hell he was headed. At this rate, it would soon only be the two of them on the road and then she'd be easy to spot.

But once Bailey turned right and drove half a block, any concern that they were alone was quashed. On the right side of the road, surrounded only by a large parking lot and miles of grassland, was a strip club called The Cat House Lounge. It was 4:00 pm and the Saturday night crowd was converging with gusto at this isolated islet of lascivious satisfaction. Jane drove past Bailey's black SUV and parked the Mustang in the far opposite corner of the jam-packed lot. Not knowing what she might encounter inside, she opted to keep the Glock in her shoulder holster, hiding the gun by buttoning her jacket around it. From the looks of the crowd heading inside, she was probably going to be the only woman in the place who wasn't buck-naked.

The Cat House Lounge was one of those seedy joints that spared no expense on stage lighting but kept the audience pretty much in the dark. It lent a lewd sense of privacy that most men sought from joints like this. They could sit in the shadows in a public place and still be anonymous to the guy seated two feet away in the darkness. Just in case the men forgot where they were, the sleazy club had a red neon sign in script that glowed *The Cat House Lounge* behind the stage. Appropriately, the last three letters in *House* had blown out turning it into the *The Cat Ho Lounge*. Jane doubted any of the men in the large audience observed the obvious irony of the neon faux pas since they were far too busy staring at the three girls prancing through the glittering silver curtains at the back of the stage and taking their place at their respective pole.

Overhead, the speakers blasted Aerosmith's potent tune, "The Other Side," heavy with so much bass that Jane wondered if her inner ear was going to split. Two of the girls on stage gave new meaning to "rode hard and put away wet." But the third girl stood out to Jane. She was a vibrant dancer with shoulder-length blond hair, porcelain flesh and breasts that were still young enough to be the personification of "perky." While the other two strippers performed their routine in a trance-like stupor, this young wild child worked the room, posing, primping and teasing the men with astonishing ease. She owned her corner of the stage. When she stripped down to only her bra and thong and crawled along the perimeter of the stage like a hungry cat, men nervously slipped dollar bills into what material was left on her body. She made each and every one of them feel as if they were her favorite and the poor, lonely men believed her. Using the music to her advantage, she waited for the most climactic moment before stripping off her bra, unhooking her thong and working the pole upside down with only her four-inch Lycra heels to keep her attached. The other two strippers didn't seem to care or notice that this kid owned the show and was getting the bulk of the tips as well as a few business cards tossed in for good measure. Jane had to hand it to the girl. She may have been young, but she was already corrupted and savvy to the disparity between the erotic dancer and the male voyeur. On some level, she knew how much sexual power she had up there. No matter what sordid life lay behind her, no matter who abused and abandoned her, when she danced on that stage and stood nude in the flashing stage lights, she was in charge and the helpless men were just cash beacons to fire up and manipulate. And the girl took advantage of every lonesome, desperate heart because deep down, she despised men. With every dollar they tucked into the buckle of her shoe, the hatred within her grew but the men would never believe that. To them, she was the animalistic ideal of sexual perfection. To her, they were the epitome of all the people who had molested her and left her with no choice but to dance naked in a desolate, dodgy, roadhouse club.

Jane shifted her focus to the crowd of men. Between the cigarette smoke and darkness, it was almost impossible to make out faces. Jane moved to a column and masked herself partially behind it. She peered closer at the row of booths against the far wall of the club. *Bingo!* There was Bailey seated across from a man and engrossed in conversation. There were no drinks on the table and they didn't seem to give a damn about the nude dancers cavorting on stage. From what Jane could make out, the other guy was about late-thirties, conservatively dressed and clean-shaven. His posture showed a certain amount of apprehension, as if he were carefully sizing up Bailey's words.

The music finally faded as the dancers swept up their tips and left the stage. Bailey and the man never once glanced away. From Jane's point of view, Bailey's body language was vastly different than when she talked to him. There was tension in his face but he seemed more accessible. This couldn't be one of Bailey's clients; his own YouTube video seemed to infer that he dealt in only a high-end milieu and *The Cat Ho Lounge* was shooting way below the curb. Jane knew that the only reason someone set up a meeting at a remote strip club was to convene in a brassy public place where the nature of your business was possibly suspect.

Jane squinted to get a better view of Bailey. She wished she could move closer, but there was no way she could do that without standing out. Bailey reached into his chest shirt pocket and pulled out a small piece of paper. He slid it across the table toward the man as he momentarily took a clandestine glance to the side. It was a gesture of guilt to Jane, but as guilty as he may have been, his body language demonstrated a willingness to continue with the deal. The other guy picked up what Jane thought was a piece of paper, looked at it and then slid it into his pocket with the same furtive approach Bailey used. "Drugs?" Jane whispered to herself. Was this a goddamn drug deal? A million possibilities blew through Jane's head. Was the *paper* blotter acid that Bailey was selling to the guy? Or was the paper a card with directions to a drop point? Meth was certainly a feasible drug probability as it had literally sucked in both ends of the financial spectrum. Was that the reason for Bailey's stuffed up nose and flushed face? If he was a meth user, Jane figured he was new to the game because he certainly didn't have the haggard and ravaged physique of a meth freak. Furthermore, meth addicts weren't into working out the way Bailey obviously was. So, what in the hell was Bailey trying to sell him?

Just as that thought crossed her mind, she watched Bailey shift his weight to his left hip and remove something from his back pocket with his right hand. The other man watched Bailey with stone-cold eyes. Bailey took another cautious look around the immediate area and carefully slid an envelope toward the man. The man pulled the envelope off the table and let it drop into his lap. Jane could barely make out his movements but it was clear that the guy was counting a wad of cash. Jane noted discernable tension in Bailey's body and almost a sense of vulnerability that she'd never seen before from him. "Shit," she muttered to herself. Was he conducting his own private ransom deal for Jake? *Fucking idiot.* Was he trying to be a hero or was he trying to cover up something deeper out of fear? Jane considered her options. She could wait until they walked out and then follow them outside where she would hold them at gunpoint until she phoned for backup. But not knowing what kind of possibly complex back end deal Bailey had made, that approach could backfire and put Jake's safety in jeopardy. Following the guy with the cash was the only solution she could come up with at that confusing point.

Jane leaned against the column, her heart racing hard. She was satisfied that she was well-hidden in the darkness until she felt two perky breasts press into her back, followed by hot breath against her ear.

"What's your pleasure?"

A porcelain hand reached around in an attempt to grab Jane's right breast. Jane reached up and touched the girl's hand before she made contact.

"Playing hard to get, huh?" the girl whispered in Jane's other ear.

Jane slowly turned to find the blond dancer with the bewitching eyes standing inches from her face. The girl was barely covered in a creamy satin robe that was loosely tied at her waist. Her nipples punctuated the satin, obviously excited about a possible conquest. Jane was trapped against the column and momentarily speechless as the girl licked her fat, cherry red lips.

"What brings you here?" the girl asked, her youthful tenor bleeding through her attempt at adult sensuality.

Jane attempted a calm response. "Curiosity."

The girl smiled. "You know what curiosity did to the cat, don't you?" Jane wondered how many times the girl used that old saw. "My name's Candy." She tilted her head in a coquettish pose. "Candy is dandy...and so am I!"

Jane regained her cop demeanor. "Let me guess. Your last name's Cane?"

Candy stepped back. "Wow! Are you psychic?"

"No. It's a common street name. I used it myself years ago when I went undercover as a hooker."

First there was a look of confusion. That melted into fear and transformed quickly into anger. "*You're a cop?*"

Jane quickly pulled Candy away from the column and toward the front door. "Keep your goddamn voice down!"

"I didn't think you were a cop," Candy said, shaking off Jane's grip. "I thought you were gay!"

"*Gay?*"

"Yeah! You know..." Candy motioned toward Jane's torso.

Jane looked down at her clothes. "The jacket?"

"No. The jacket's cool. It's the shirt. It's kinda manly."

"Fuck," Jane muttered. This roadhouse stripper was the third person in two days to intimate that she was doing the lesbian limbo. She walked back to the protective column and checked the status between Bailey and his unknown acquaintance. They were still engrossed in conversation. Just as Jane took a step to move a little closer, Candy crossed in front of her.

"Is that your husband?"

"No! Get outta the way."

The girl was used to getting what she wanted and forced a pout before ambling behind Jane. "I just wondered. Since, ya know, he's been here a few times before."

Jane turned to Candy. "The guy in the white shirt?" Candy nodded. "Like, *how* many times?"

"I don't know," she said, her well-honed manipulation fully engaged again.

"Hey, Candy. It's illegal for girls under *the age of eighteen* to dance in strip clubs. I can make one fucking call and have this *Ho Lounge* shut down…all because of *you*." The kid's eyes got as big as saucers. "And that's not going to look good on the ol' resume when you try to score a job in another classy club like this. I think they call that being blackballed." Jane turned around, keeping her gaze on Bailey.

"Please don't call anybody." The bravado was gone and sheer desperation took its place. "I can't go home and this is the only way I can make big bucks."

"Yeah? What are you saving up for?" Jane asked, never taking her eyes off the two men.

"Bigger tits."

"Jesus Christ, why?"

"The bigger the tit, the bigger the tip."

Jane let out a weary sigh. "So this is your life's ambition?"

Candy looked down at the carpet. "Well, no. My mom would die if she found out what I was doing. But I can't go back home."

Jane wasn't about to ask her the reason. She knew it probably had to do with either her mother's boyfriend or a stepfather who had stolen her innocence years before and forced her on the run. "So, you're gonna answer my questions, right?"

"Right."

"The guy with the white shirt?" Jane nodded toward Bailey. "You're *sure* you've seen him in here before?"

"Yeah. He kinda stands out, you know?"

"How many times and when did he start coming in?"

Candy clearly struggled with the question. "I'm not really good at time…"

"Yeah, that's one of the first signs that the drugs are starting to fuck up your brain." Jane gave her a warning eye.

"I know. I know." Candy tried to piece her memory together. "Um, I'd say he's been here like two or three times. Maybe more."

Jane turned and focused on Candy. "For how long?"

"A week? Two weeks?"

"How long have you worked here, Candy?"

"Two weeks…I think. Time kinda warps for me."

Jane shook her head. *What a waste.* The kid was beautiful, had a great body and was a terrific dancer. With the right education and training, the legit world would be her oyster. But instead, she was already brain addled. "What about the other guy? You seen him before?"

"I'm not sure. I just remember the guy with the white shirt 'cause I walked over to his table once and asked if he wanted a private dance and he said, 'Fuck off, cunt!' So, I took that as a *No.*"

Bailey was earning more daggers in Jane's little black book of bad karma. "That's all you can give me? By chance, you didn't hear the name *Jake* when they were talking?"

"I…uh…I don't know…" Candy stared at the floor, frustrated.

"It's okay, kid." Jane patted her on the shoulder and turned back to the men. The booth was empty. "Shit! Did you see where they went?"

"No. Maybe they went out the back door…"

Jane sprung toward the front door and headed toward where she saw Bailey's SUV. It was gone. She peered into the distance, attempting to see his vehicle, but the setting sun forced a hard glare that prevented any clear view. "*Fuck!*" she screamed. Jane paced for about a minute, debating her next move. She went back inside the strip club and spotted Candy by the bar. The kid was just about to down a shot of whiskey when Jane placed her hand over the shot glass. "You're too young to drink."

"You also think I'm too young to strip." Candy moved Jane's hand off the glass and downed the shot like a hardcore pro.

Jane wrapped her arm around the girl's shoulder and directed her to a more private area of the club. "Look, if I give you my business card with my cell phone number, will you promise to call me the minute you see that guy with the white shirt back in here?" Jane handed Candy her card.

The kid took it but lacked enthusiasm for the job. Jane opened her wallet. "Would a hundie make you remember to call me?" She folded a hundred-dollar bill in Candy's eager hand.

Her eyes lit up. This was the only exchange she understood. "You betcha!"

Jane pulled another hundred out of her wallet. "Here. Buy yourself a sweater."

Candy took the money and, for a moment, the kid who she *really* was under all the makeup, shone forth. "Wow. Thanks. I will…and I'll call you."

The sun set fast over the high mountains, draping Highway 7 in soft shadows. Jane sped down the road back to Midas, another day wasted in the pursuit of the elusive truth. She half-wondered what she'd do if she spotted Bailey's black SUV on the road, but the closer she got to Midas, the more she realized that he'd either turned off another road or drove in the opposite direction. Jane surmised that it fit Bailey's arrogant demeanor to take matters into his own hands and work some sort of deal behind the backs of law enforcement. But why? Had the people involved in Jake's disappearance scared him so deeply that he chose to keep the cops out of it? He wouldn't be the first parent to play that card. The problem with that scenario was that it usually ended up badly—the kidnappers got their cash and the kid ended up dead.

She debated about calling Weyler and filling him in on what had just transpired. The only reason she hesitated was her concern that he'd accuse her of stalking Bailey. For the next ten miles Jane weighed the pros and cons of alerting him. Finally,

she worked up her courage and dialed his number as she headed into the narrow canyon. But the call kept dropping each time
she dialed. Darkness was falling fast, especially now that she
was locked inside the red rock fold of the canyon. The rushing river rose and fell violently on the right side. For five long
miles, with each new curve of the road, Jane redialed but kept
losing the signal. She flicked on her headlights and approached
another bend. For a moment, she looked down to press the RE-
DIAL key on her phone. When she looked up, the only thing she
saw was the fixated eyes of a deer standing in the center of the
lane. Jane turned the wheel sharply to the left, but the Mustang
skidded toward the rocky wall. She overcorrected, forcing her
right front and rear tires onto the uneven gravel shoulder that
banked down to the roaring river. She slammed on the brakes,
but the rear tire dug into the gravel. Within seconds, Jane was
spinning uncontrollably.

The sound of the river moved closer as she heard the tires
squealing like a pig headed to slaughter. The rear view mirror
shattered and the scent of gardenias infused the spinning car.
As the Mustang slid toward the river, Jane felt a numinous hand
cover her own. Suddenly, the car spun in the opposite direction
as icy splinters of glass stabbed her scalp. Just when she thought
the Mustang would never stop moving, the high-pitched squeal
of burning rubber came to an abrupt halt. Jane's head slammed
hard against the broken window, driving the shards deeper. She
floated between worlds, as a warm trickle of blood traveled to
the crease of her lips and forced its way onto her tongue. The
ghostly hand that had guided her gradually dissipated and was
replaced by another. But instead of the sweet scent of gardenias,
the stench was foul and fetid. Jane tried to fight off the intruder,
but he easily took control of her injured body.

The last thing Jane remembered was the unrelenting sound
of the river beneath her and the fear that she was about to die.

CHAPTER 20

The putrid odor wafted in and out. For a moment, Jane traveled back to when she was ten and sitting at her mother's deathbed in the living room of their house. The cancer was just about to take Anne's life and she sat up, projectile vomiting across the white bed sheets. Bright red blood mixed with bile. There was a gagging aroma that filled that room twenty-seven years ago and, at this moment, as Jane slid between the worlds, the same sickening smell weaved through her senses.

And then there was darkness, clean and silent. There was no fear or apprehension—just black all around her. Was this death? If so, where was that light she'd read about in books that was supposed to be there to greet her? To be conscious of the darkness and waiting for something or someone to come for her was very odd to Jane. She tried to turn her head, but felt a calloused hand gently prevent the movement. Jane attempted to speak, but all she could manage was a low moan. Hell? Was this hell? With that thought, fear gripped her for the first time and she felt herself hyperventilating. Almost simultaneously, a sharp pinprick of pain emanated from her scalp. She let out a scream. The aroma of burning beeswax filled her nostrils. On her tongue, a sweet, pungent taste stung. She swallowed and an other trickle of liquid with the same flavor fell into her mouth. She swallowed again, this time taking more of it into her body. Four more times, she drank the mysterious brew. With each sip, the pain in her scalp subsided and she floated more freely on a wave of consciousness that lived just beneath the only reality she knew.

Heavy footsteps moved away from her, walking across a creaking wooden floor. Moments later, the footsteps approached her and the sound of a man clearing his throat. She opened her eyes. The room was filled with shadows. It was hard to focus, but as the room came into view, the first thing she saw were candles—tall, honey-colored beeswax pillars of different heights and widths—illuminating the darkened room and releasing a warm, comforting light. The taste of sweetness lingered on her tongue accompanied by the feeling she used to get by downing a fifth of Jack Daniels. A large figure sat in a chair near the bed where she lay. The face was hidden in a slice of darkness where the candles didn't touch.

"Where am I?" Jane whispered to the figure.

"Safe," the voice replied.

Her astral body hovered closer to her physical body. She looked around the room. There was a round wooden kitchen table that held stacks of books, four chairs, a kitchen sink and sideboard and windows covered in brown cotton curtains. To her left, there was a small table that held a smaller candle and a bowl of water along with a washcloth. The water was tinged red and thin fragments of glass were next to the bowl. The realization hit her as her physical body received the full impact of her etheric and slammed hard into the host. "Jordan?!"

Jordan drew a beeswax candle toward him from the kitchen table and held it between himself and Jane. "Did you touch the other side, Jane?" Jane felt trapped. She tried to sit up, but Jordan gently held her back. "Don't," Jordan calmly said. "You hit hard. Let yourself come back slowly."

Jane's memory trickled back. "My car?"

"I drove it behind the cabin. You busted the side window, a little front-end damage, but that's all. You're lucky. The tire tracks showed you heading for the river and then you turned and went the other way before you skidded to a stop. I don't know how you managed that."

Jane clearly remembered the sound of squealing tires and the unknown hand that covered her own and turned the wheel. "I didn't."

Jordan leaned closer. "Spirit?" Jane looked at him with guarded eyes. Jordan smiled a knowing grin. "Yes…I knew from the moment I saw you on the bridge that we were two halves of the same whole." Jane felt queasy. She suddenly remembered her gun and started to reach toward her jacket when Jordan quickly spoke up. "Your gun is still in the holster, Jane." She felt the butt of the Glock bite into her side. "I'm not allowed near a firearm. You know that. And don't worry. I didn't look at anything else I shouldn't have…" His eyes showed that he was telling the truth, along with a slightly unnerving mischievous wink.

Jane turned to look outside, hoping to see light, but it was clear from the crease between the brown curtains that night had fallen. "What time is it?"

"Past seven."

"Shit! I've got to get back to Midas." She sat up, but the room spun. "Fuck!" She grabbed her head. "What did you give me? Did you give me alcohol?"

"Of course, not. You're an alcoholic."

"How did you know that?"

"I told you before. I feel and understand things that I can't comprehend, but that I know to be truth. I've done it since I was a boy. I can see a person just once, either in the flesh or in a photograph, and I can know them instantly as if we'd spent decades together. It's in my blood."

Jane was dubious. The peculiar taste on her tongue resurfaced. "So, what did you give me?"

"An herbal tea made from the sacred blue lily. The uneducated call it *blue lotus*." He stood up, crossed to the kitchen windowsill and returned with a fluted glass container a foot tall and eight inches wide. Inside was five inches of dirt saturated and covered in water, which rose to the top of the container. Growing out of the water were three aromatic flowers with vibrant blue petals that were nearly closed and sinking beneath the water. The scent was magnificent and intoxicating. "The ancient texts of Egypt wrote about this powerful flower. Egyptians used it as a bridge between realities. With the blue lily, the veil between the worlds was lifted and they could communicate with the dead, in the same manner that you and I are talking right now. All the dark secrets are answered on the other side of that veil. There's no more need to hide. No more need for absolution."

Jane worried that Jordan seemed preoccupied with the dead. "You talk to the dead, Jordan?"

He softly touched one of the blue lily petals with his ragged finger. "All the time. When you light a candle for the dead, their spirit is present in the light. When the dead have their place, only then are they peaceful and can be experienced by mortals as a pure, loving energy." He leaned closer to Jane. "You talk to the dead, Jane?"

Jane was leery of Jordan's question. "I don't make a habit of it."

He sat back. "Oh, you should. The dead have a lot to offer if you have the balls to listen to them. Their ego is stripped and they can freely speak the truth for the first time."

Jane weighed her next question carefully. "Should I be talking to Jake?"

There was a heavy pause. Jordan sat forward, his dirty face fully illuminated in the honeyed light. "I told you. He's not dead…yet."

"How would you know that?"

"All I have to do is see someone in person or in a photograph once and I understand everything about them, then and now. I saw Jake's photograph in the newspaper. The local rag and *The Denver Post*. That's all I needed to make that assessment." Jordan held the flowers closer to Jane. "Did you really look at the flowers, Jane? The Egyptians saw the blue lily as the symbol of the sun and of creation and rebirth. The system of death and rebirth are consecrated in this flower. When you make a tea from these sacred leaves, you are offered that same chance to move from the darkness and into the light of transformation."

"You gave me an hallucinogenic?"

"*No,*" he said emphatically. "It's also used for pain and to calm the mind. You had shards of glass in your head." He carefully set the glass container on the kitchen table. "Do you have any idea how long it took me to grow these flowers? They told me it couldn't be done in a container, but no one told the sacred lily that."

Jane recalled Jordan commenting the first time they met that his cabin was "sacred territory." Maybe it was the blue lily that gave it that moniker. Either way, for whatever reason, he must have trusted Jane enough to carry her all the way from the highway back to his cabin. Even though her scalp ached from the accident, she felt surprisingly alert the more she conversed with Jordan. "I wouldn't have labeled you as a plant buff, Jordan."

"I'm not a plant *buff*," he replied, slightly irritated. "Using plants for medicine is in my bloodline, just like my ability to connect with others on a higher plane."

"The Copelands of Short Hills were into picking leaves and flowers and making poultices? Interesting. I didn't catch that vibe from their photos when they were walking down the courthouse steps back in '68."

Jordan sat back, his face half-shadowed in the darkness. "Tell me, Jane. Do you believe in evil because you believe in the Devil or because you've seen evil with your own eyes?"

A cold shiver slid down Jane's back. "Because I've seen evil with my own eyes."

"Are you sure it was evil? Or were you just taught to fear it from someone else? Do you believe in something because you've felt it in your sinews, or do you believe in something because you've been taught to believe it? Think about it, Jane! Do you fear because of what it does to your gut or because someone told you should fear? How much of what you believe and act on is purely an illusion? How many necessary illusions exist in order to keep us all paralyzed?" Jordan eyed Jane with an intense glare.

"I suppose I fall into both categories. But mostly, I feel…"

"So what happens when you are told something by another that contradicts with what you're feeling?"

Jane had experienced that identical situation too many times over the last two days. "It pisses me off."

"But what if they keep telling you that you're imagining it or making it up or any number of manipulations that rape whatever your heart is telling you?" His demeanor became aggressive. "Do you begin to doubt yourself, Jane? Do you decide to deny the truth you feel from within in order to pacify what the masses are selling you?"

"Where is this going, Jordan?"

He let out a hard sigh. There was a long, thoughtful pause that seemed filled with deep angst. It resonated to Jane with the same torment that criminals used right before they confessed their darkest crimes. Jane's gut clenched down, not sure of what she was about to hear. "The Buddha said, 'Three things cannot be long hidden: the sun, the moon and the truth.'" He picked up the beeswax pillar and walked across to a small, three-drawer wooden dresser in a far corner of the room. The candle in his hand shed light on an unmade single bed, along with a small loft and two large bookcases that were jam-packed with books. Jane peered closer and noted that stacks of books littered the floor as well as the steps leading up to the loft. Jordan opened the top drawer of the dresser and reverently removed a small leather book, four by six inches in dimension. He stared at the book before closing the drawer and returning to Jane's side. Sitting down, he opened the book and withdrew a black-and-white photo. He let out another breath, but the tension in his body was evident. He handed the photo to Jane and held the candle closer so she could clearly see the figures in the shot.

Jane saw a beautiful, light-skinned black woman who looked to be in her early twenties holding a two-year-old boy in her arms. They were in a backyard garden, and it was either spring or summer because she wore a short-sleeved dress and sandals. "That's your nanny?"

Jordan's eyes filled with tears. "That's my mother."

Jane stared at Jordan. "What?"

"Her name was Maureen Lafond. She was from St. Lucia. My father and Mrs. Copeland first met her when they spent the fall of 1949 on the island. They rented a private villa where she worked as a cook. Her mother was a cook. Grandmother was a cook. Great-grandmother...so on and so on. They were all herbalists too...healers. Maureen was carrying on in that tradition too. She was twenty-one and beautiful. Eyes so sweet and a heart that dreamed of a better life with more opportunities." Jordan took the photo from Jane and stared at it. "She could only speak a little English, *Patois* being her common tongue. It's derived from French but it has no written history. Sort of a bastard tongue." Jordan smiled at the unintended pun. "The strange thing was that Maureen and my father communicated better than he and Mrs. Copeland ever did. My mother could read his thoughts because she had the gift of sight just like *her* mother and grandmother. So, he would think something and she would respond to it with her actions. He was captivated. He may have worn the hat of the rigid, East Coast country club set when he was in Short Hills, but when he was on the island, I think he cast all worries to the wind and perhaps reveled in who he really was. I'm not sure if she seduced my father or if he seduced her, but they came together in St. Lucia. From what I feel in my mind's heart, he was never as happy as he was that fall."

"You have a pretty good take on their relationship," Jane offered.

"Yeah, well, it's easy to have perspective on relationships between others because when you stand outside of them, there's no need to support illusions."

Jane sat up. "Did Mrs. Copeland know what was going on between your dad and Maureen?"

"Yes...but she preferred to *pretend* away uncomfortable elements in her life. Sort of like, if I don't acknowledge it, it doesn't exist." Jordan shook his head in disgust. "That became a little difficult when Maureen told my father that she was pregnant. But Mrs. Copeland, the cold-hearted, frigid bitch that she was, decided it was certainly worth a try. And so, the pattern of ignoring me before I was even *born* was set in motion. My father and Mrs. Copeland returned to Short Hills before Christmas of '49 but my father was desperately unhappy. Around the New Year, he informed Mrs. Copeland that he wanted to bring Maureen to the States that summer and that she was to live with them and raise their child under their roof."

"She didn't fight him?"

"Sure. The same way Mrs. Copeland fought every battle. She disappeared. Hell, she could disappear in a house or a room. But *this* time, she disappeared to Florida under the ruse that she was not well and needed a better climate to recuperate. Since she always looked frail and ate just enough to fit into a size 0 Chanel suit, nobody argued. Her absence allowed my father free reign to travel back and forth to St. Lucia and spend time with my mother. His friends assumed he was involved in a new business in the Caribbean so everybody was taken care of." Jordan's tone was clearly sarcastic. "Over the next six months, my father and Mrs. Copeland, along with Maureen, built the foundations of the lie that my life would soon rest upon. In late June, my father brought Maureen to the States and hid her away in a New York hospital until she gave birth. My mother returned several weeks later, looking weak and peaked and explained her appearance to stunned friends by telling them that, at the age of forty-three, she had quietly given birth to her only child."

"Nobody questioned that story?"

"I don't know. My parents were very private people. My fraternal grandparents had already died. Mrs. Copeland's father was dead and her mother would pass several years later. I'm not sure if her mother ever knew the truth. I think she probably did and just agreed to keep quiet. *Familial myth* is a potent narcotic. You have to remember...the Copeland side of my bloodline has a pattern of hiding things. Affairs, illegitimate mulatto sons, false pregnancies...we hide things."

"Like you hid Daniel's body under your bed after you shot him?"

Jordan regarded Jane with a reserved manner. "Yes, Jane.

Like I hid Daniel's body...yes...I was just doing what my blood-line taught me to do. When something that deep operates in your blood, it's very hard to not act upon it and play it out... quite unconsciously sometimes...in your own life."

"Were you taught to kill? Is that also in your bloodline?"

Jordan bristled at the question. "No, Jane. Killing is not in my bloodline."

Jane was beginning to feel more centered. "So, killing was something you started on your own?"

Thick silence fell between them. "I don't think we have enough candle power in this room to build a third-degree light, do you?"

For whatever reason, Jordan wasn't interested in discussing the notorious murder of Daniel Marshall. "Do you know all of the stories that came before your birth because of your intuitive gift that you got from your mom?"

"Some of it. The rest I read in this little book." Jordan handed the weathered leather book to Jane. "My mother's diary."

"I thought she couldn't speak English?" Jane opened the book.

"She learned it quickly during the time my father and she spent alone together in St. Lucia. And my mother also had help from her own mother who picked up some English from my maternal grandfather...a white Englishman." Jane looked up at Jordan with a slightly stunned look. "Yes. You see? *Patterns*, Jane. Patterns of deception breed unchecked through the generations."

Jane glanced at the pages, many yellowed and stained by time. There was a sentence written in Patois that repeated throughout the diary, usually written at the end of one of Maureen's entries:

Mwê ní èspwa pou la yonn kílès kí sa fè mwên tjè feb antyè ankò

"What does this mean?" Jane asked, pointing to the *Patois* words.

"I don't know. Whatever it says, I have to assume she wrote

it in *Patois* to keep it a secret. *Patois* was never a written language so when people eventually tried to translate it, the words were written phonetically and not always with the same letters."

"Can't you go on the Internet and find some references?"

"I don't own a computer. Remember? No phone. No TV."

Jane asked Jordan for a piece of paper and she copied the mysterious sentence with the flicker of the candlelight to illuminate the page. "So, when did you find out that Maureen was your mother?" She folded the paper and slipped it into her jeans' pocket.

"I always felt something was off. When you unconsciously live a lie, you live a false life. Even if you don't know you're living a lie, you still feel it. You never feel like you're home. Like you're safe. I always wanted to know the truth, no matter how painful that truth might be. Living a lie is always more painful."

"Not to be rude here, Jordan, but I can't tell your skin color under all the grime. Was that an obvious factor?"

"Oh, Jesus. Drop the bullshit, PC politeness, Jane! My mother's a mulatto and so am I. For all I know, I've got cream in my coffee from way back. Except for the curly hair," he touched his tangled locks, "I can easily pass for whitey. *We sho is good at dat!*" he said in an exaggerated ghetto drawl. He leaned forward. "It wasn't skin color that made me question my truth. You look for patterns in crimes. I've learned to look for patterns in families. Patterns of subterfuge fascinate me...the way a secret festers and develops a heartbeat of its own. When you think you can hide or suffocate something, you're kidding yourself. Because the thing that is hidden will always reach out and demand to be acknowledged. *That* is how I started on my quest." Jordan leaned forward, clasping his dirty hands together. "We learn about ourselves through two ways: the stories we're told and our experiences. But then there's your gut! You know? That middle section that churns when two and two doesn't equal four. When the stories you're told don't resonate with your own experience or your gut, *that's* when you feel like you're going crazy. But you're not crazy at all...even though everyone *else* keeps telling you that you are! The past holds the answers that influence the future. You'll never walk freely into your future if the ghosts from the past are clawing at your heels and begging to be acknowledged."

"It's one thing to suspect something is false. It's quite another to have it proven."

"Yes, yes. The moment of realization." Jordan stood up and walked around the kitchen table. His towering presence seemed larger than life in the tiny cabin. "I was eight and I heard a fight one night downstairs in my father's study. It was between Maureen and my father. Mrs. Copeland was gone that night...some charity event in the city. The voices in the office got louder and so I crept downstairs and listened at the door. I didn't understand most of it, but I sure remember my mother saying that when two are of the same blood, they both have the right to know. My father said that if she was going to insist on making demands on him, no good would come of it. I remember he said he cared for her, which I thought very odd at that moment because my father was such a cold individual. But he said as much as he cared for her, he couldn't risk his reputation." Jordan stopped, the memory still bitter. "As much as he loved her...and he *did* love her...his fucking reputation was more important." Jordan returned to the seat next to Jane. His eyes filled with heavy tears. "I went upstairs and crawled into bed. A couple hours later, my mother came into my room. She was crying and it scared me. She held me for what seemed like forever and then she whispered in my ear the words I will never forget. 'You're my blood and you will forever be in my heart.' I didn't know what that meant when I was eight. I never told a soul what she said so there was no one to explain it to me. But that didn't mean that the truth didn't speak to me in my own heart." He held the leather book tightly to his chest. "She gave me this book before she left. She told me to keep it in a safe place and for me to read it when I was much older. And so I hid it under a floor board that was under my bed..." Jordan looked off into the distance for a moment. "Humph...I guess that was the first time I hid something of value under my bed."

Jane felt slightly uneasy with that revelation. "You told me that she died when you were eight. What happened?"

"She scared my father. Her ability to see the future and have a knowing that defied logic was a liability. *She was dangerous*, Jane. So the son-of-a-bitch called the family clean-up man, Edward Butterworth...*Eddie*...and he drove my mother to an asylum in upstate New York where she was locked away and her secret buried forever." Jordan balled his fist on the kitchen table. He appeared to go into a slightly altered state. "Four years later, when I was twelve, I was alone in the house. I missed my mother desperately, and so I uncovered the diary for the first time since she'd given it to me and started reading. I didn't understand the sexual aspects of it, of course, but I got loud and clear who she really was to me and those words she whispered in my ear before she left suddenly made sense. I was vindicated! All those feelings I'd felt...all the disconnect...all the lies...Suddenly, I wasn't crazy anymore! I had to find her! I went into my father's study and looked through every drawer to find anything I could on where she might be. I found a check stub written out to a hospital in upstate New York and another one to the same place for *expenses*. They were four years old. I got the phone number from Information and I called the place. I was pretty savvy for a twelve-year-old. I asked in the most adult voice I could muster if there was a Maureen Lafond there and they told me that she had lived there for only a short time before she departed." Jordan's voice filled with emotion. "She died and I know why. When you don't allow someone to be who they are...when you take away their heart, they die. I'm sure my father got the call and made arrangements for the burial, thus, the check written for *expenses*. The Copelands have to make sure they tidy up all those nasty loose ends. Once again, *Eddie* Butterworth made sure any whisper of Maureen Lafond was silenced." He leaned forward, rubbing the front of the leather diary with his thumb. "You see, Jane, you can't cage a spirit like my mother. You can't drug it. You can't strap it down in restraints or put it in a strait-jacket. The only way you shut up that kind of person is to *kill them.*" Jordan sat up, awash with bubbling anger. "They must be destroyed! They must be annihilated! They must be sacrificed!" He twisted his foot into the ground. "Squashed like a bug until nothing is left to show they existed! Destroy them!!" With that pronouncement, he violently kicked over the small table next to Jane that held the glass bowl of bloody water and the small candle. The glass shattered, as the crimson water quickly extin-guished the candle's flame. "But you know what? *You never kill their spirit!*" His face flushed with rage. "And when wronged, that spirit will haunt and stalk a family bloodline forever until they are acknowledged and their secret is brought into the light of day." He stood up and screamed, "The only way to stop the pattern of deception is to shout from the rooftops the thing that is considered so vile, so sick, *so humiliating* and let it live in the light! Then, and only then, can the dead be free and you can live your life on your own terms, without carrying the hell of others on your back!"

Jane let Jordan's frenzy subside as her fingers crept closer to the Glock. She watched as he separated from himself and then gradually come back together. Once he was back inside of his body, there was a profound sadness that gripped him; a pain so deep in his bones that she thought he would break in two. "You think any of the asses in this town have the guts to dig their hole and scream their secrets into the ground?" Jordan asked.

"I'm not following you, Jordan."

"Don't you know the story of how Midas got its name?" Jane shook her head. "It's based on the legend of King Midas. You'd think it had to do with gold, with all the money that flows through town. But it's got to do with the Greek legend when Midas had the temerity to declare that Pan's music far outshone Apollo's. Apollo declared that King Midas' ears were depraved and, thus, were transformed into the ears of a jackass, long in length and hairy. But Midas felt he could hide this curse under his turban and so he did and no one knew his secret...except, of course, his barber. But when Midas confronted his barber and asked him, 'Barber, do you see anything odd about me?' the barber, knowing he would be killed if he acknowledged what was so obvious, shook his head at King Midas and said, 'No, sir. I see nothing.' And each time Midas saw his barber and asked the same question, the barber continued to deny the obvious deformity. Until one day, it became too much for the barber to keep silent because the secret was eating away at him. So the barber went out into the meadow, dug a hole in the ground, and kneeling down, whispered the story into the hole before filling the hole with dirt. But then, a thick bed of reeds sprang up from the hole where the secret had been buried. Along came a musician, who fashioned a flute from the reeds. But when the piper played the flute, no music was heard. The only sound was the echoing cry, 'King Midas has donkey's ears!' And that declaration was caught by the wind and carried back to the townspeople, never to be a secret again." Jordan looked at Jane. "But none of *these* dwellers in Midas can even get around to digging their hole! It's quite a town to call home, isn't it?" He seemed to drift away. "Home...you can't go home again, Jane. But if you don't make peace with it, home will always haunt you."

There it was again, that damned literary connection to the Thomas Wolfe novel. She'd heard it twice from his lips. Jane recalled the overpowering way she felt when she was sitting on the bed at the B&B and falling into the written clues that were draped on the clothesline. As she moved into the core of the person who wrote those lines, she recalled the desolate ache of isolation and heartache that reverberated from the pages. There was the graphic horror of desperation and the imploring for someone—*anyone*—to listen. The clue that echoed right now to Jane was the non sequitur: *I BEARED MY SOUL AND STILL YOU IGNORE ME???* Indeed, Jordan had bared his soul to Jane.

Quite possibly, she was the only person he ever shared his family secret with and perhaps, she hoped, he would divulge more soon. As long as she acknowledged him, the door might still be open. If he was involved in any way with Jake Van Gorden's disappearance, she needed to keep that proverbial door ajar.

"Are you able to…connect with your mother on the other side?" Jane asked.

Jordan hung his head. "No. There's a wall that I can't ascend. No matter how much I meditate or drink the blue lily tea, I can't find my mother in the ether. But I dream about her. It's always the same dream." He walked to the window by the front door and pointed outside. "I walk up the path that leads to this house and I stand still. And I feel her close by. The front door opens and my mother walks out onto the porch. She's not thirty anymore. She's in her eighties. But she's still beautiful. She walks over to me and she holds me and I'm whole again. She whispers in my ear, the same way she did the last time we were together on this plane. She says, 'And in the quiet it comes. Not from a shout. But in a whisper.' All that went before is washed away and my heart is finally free. And then I wake up and I'm back here and I curse God for his indiscriminate love." His hand began to shake uncontrollably. Jordan looked down at the hand as if it didn't belong to him. "I've never spoken that dream to anyone." His face etched with apprehension. He turned to Jane. "You… have you had that same dream?"

Jane tried to remain stone-faced even though the question sounded psychotic. "I don't think so," she replied in the kindest way possible.

He moved closer to her, his boots crushing the broken glass from the shattered bowl. "*Are you certain?*"

"Yes. I'm certain."

His hand still shook with an anxious tremor. "This *means* something," he said, regarding his shaking hand. "This *always* means something!" He grabbed Jane's shoulders. "We're connected, don't you see?" His eyes were wild and remote.

Jane wondered how quickly she could get to her Glock. The only way out of this was to change the subject, but she was coming up short on options. She blurted the first thing she could think of. "You mention dreams…what about that other dream you told me about? Remember? The one about the little kid you call *Red*? You know, the one you said came to the back gate of your property in Short Hills and talked to you with his mind? You still dreaming of him?"

Jordan's eyes washed with sadness. She could see that he wanted to pursue the obsessive connection he had regarding the dream of his mother and how it could be tied to Jane. The fact that Jane disarmed him by altering the subject didn't seem to set well with the man. Almost instantly, his hand stopped shaking. He let out a long breath of air. "*Red*…Yeah…Every fucking night he comes to me. Why? Is he coming to you?"

Jane remained stoic under a ball of nerves. "No, Jordan. Why would I dream of *Red*? That's your dream."

He thought about it. "Who said it's a dream?"

Jane felt trapped. In her opinion, the conversation had taken a seriously dark turn. Whoever this *Red* kid was, whether he was real, made up, a projection of Jordan as a troubled child or a twisted version of Jake Van Gorden, she didn't know. But she craved more physical distance from Jordan. Jane stretched, allowing a few more inches of freedom from his glare. "You told me it was a dream." She slowly got up, making sure that her movement was calculated and smooth.

Jordan stood up, engaged by the new shift in conversation. "I know. I know. But what if…what if he's coming to me and trying to tell me something? What if he's trying to send me a message?"

Jane needed to end this fast and get out of his cabin. "Okay, look, you told me that you just started dreaming about this *Red* kid recently…"

"Right!"

"And you don't know his name, and the last contact you

had with him in the real world was a few months before you killed Daniel Marshall..."

"*Six months!*" Jordan corrected. "It was six months. He stopped coming to the gate. But I never knew why!"

"Right. Exactly..." Jane maneuvered her way around the kitchen table.

"So, why am I suddenly dreaming about him now, Jane?" Jordan's voice was becoming distressed.

"It's okay, Jordan. You need to calm down."

"Don't tell me to calm down! I can't stand it when people tell me to calm down!"

"Fine. Stay up all night and obsess on *Red.*"

"I might just do that..." Jordan turned away, buried in his private thoughts.

"I'm going to go now."

"Yes. Right," Jordan's mind was occupied elsewhere. "Goodnight."

Jane observed him. Suddenly all the fear she felt just minutes before dissolved. She walked to the door, crunching the broken glass bowl under her cowboy boots. For whatever reason, she felt a need to reach out to him verbally. "Thank you for helping me tonight," she stammered.

"Yeah...sure..." He was still locked in his thoughts.

They didn't call the guy anti-social for nothing. "Okay," she touched the door handle and he suddenly turned to her.

"Hey, Jane?" She turned to him. He'd quickly lifted out of his quandary and was focused on her with renewed interest.

"Yeah?"

"I got another riddle for you. The strange man who lives in the log cabin promised the detective today that he will tell her a *big* secret on the day before two days from the day after tomorrow. Since today is Saturday, on what day will the strange man who lives in the cabin tell the detective the big secret?"

Jane's mind worked out the numbers in her head. "Monday?"

He smiled. "See you then."

CHAPTER 21

It was closing in on 8:45 pm when Jane rolled back into Midas. All she wanted to do was head to her room at the B&B, soak in a hot bath and go to bed. But after she took a gander at her leather jacket and saw the splatters of blood across it, she knew she had to resolve it before she encountered Weyler. The high country night air carried an icy sting through the shattered driver's side window. *Shit.* That was going to be another complication to explain.

There was only one person she could think of to go to for help.

Jane parked the Mustang around the back of The Rabbit Hole. Checking the menu on the outside of the building, she found the phone number and dialed. The bartender answered. Jane announced who she was and told him to ask Hank to meet her at the back entrance. No sooner did she walk around the building than Hank was waiting for her.

"Hey, Chopper," Hank said gently. "You okay?" Jane walked under the backdoor lamp. Hank could easily detect the blood on her jacket. "Holy shit. What happened?"

"Can we talk somewhere private?"

Hank nodded and led Jane back to his three-bedroom cottage behind The Rabbit Hole. The place was light and airy and fairly immaculate for a guy's bachelor pad. The first thing Jane noticed when she walked in and the lights came on were the bookshelves. There were three, floor-to-ceiling units neatly filled with all types of books. Literature, old police manuals, poetry, modern fiction, crime and suspense and even a few of the esoteric titles she inherited from Kit Clark's library, made up Hank's diverse collection. Whenever she entered a homicide scene in a private home, Jane tended to check out the vibe of the house before she canvassed the dead bodies. When she spotted a large bookcase, it immediately impressed her, if only because it told her that the poor butchered stiffs on the floor covered in blood had been literate. There was a huge difference, in Jane's opinion, between the kind of people who owned a lot of books and the kind who accumulated DVDs. The latter fell short on the intellect meter. Hank's well-read assortment of books earned him a few points in Jane's book of judgment.

The floor plan of Hank's place was wide open, allowing the dining room to flow into the kitchen which then flowed into a small living room. Two bedrooms were located down a short hallway with a third room located off the living room dedicated to Hank's office. A small bathroom sat just off the front door next to a large poster of Pavarotti wearing a costume from Puccini's *Turandot*. Again, she was impressed. For a guy to plaster Pavarotti near his front door, it had to mean something to him. She had to ask.

"He's one of my favorites," Hank told her. "I have *The Three Tenors* on DVD and CD. Bought it on one of those PBS pledge drives."

Jane smiled. Sergeant Weyler and Hank would get along just fine since Weyler was a card-carrying member of PBS and had probably purchased every single CD and DVD that they pimped during their annual begging ritual. While she wasn't a huge opera fan, there certainly was a soft spot in her heart for "Nessun Dorma." The evocative melody from *Turandot* had followed her throughout her life, becoming the emotional background melody for everything from her mother's death to a painfully personal case she'd worked two years prior. It wasn't the only Puccini melody that haunted her though. There was another that she could never listen to; one that ripped at her heart and drew her back to that fateful, shocking scene she would never get out of her head.

"You like Puccini?" Hank asked.

"Yeah. I do."

"I got a compilation of his work somewhere around here." Hank started to search his neatly organized CD holder.

"It's okay," Jane said, her voice full of tension. "I don't need to hear it right now." Jane took off her jacket and crossed to the kitchen sink.

"Here," Hank took her jacket, "I'll take care of it. Sit down, Chopper." He pulled out a chair from the kitchen table. Jane reluctantly took a seat. She wasn't used to having someone else in charge. But at that moment, the shock of the events that occurred earlier was starting to coagulate in her consciousness. And to top it off, she was still feeling the peculiar perspective-shifting effects of the sacred blue lily tea Jordan had given her. Sure, she figured, Hank could clean the blood off her jacket, but that would be the extent of it. She suddenly felt thirsty and was about to ask Hank for some water when he strangely grabbed a glass, filled it with water from the filter on the tap and handed it to her.

"Why did you do that?" Jane asked, suspicion rearing its ugly head.

Hank looked confused. "I figured you might be thirsty and I didn't think a shot of Jack Daniels was appropriate."

Jane took a sip. "Right." There was definitely something otherworldly happening to her. It was as though she had a heightened understanding of her surroundings. It wasn't a high or a buzz but a focused realization that attracted to her what she needed. Her thoughts seemed to project outward and mingled in the unseen field before becoming reality. It was disturbing to a point but Jane noted that there wasn't any of the usual fear attached to it. Instead of blocking the effect, it was as if her body was more willing to accept the experience—devoid of all the second-guessing and scrutinizing—and allow whatever occurred *to just be.*

The more Jane thought about it, the more she realized that it went against her typical M.O. to approach a total stranger like Hank Ross to help her. But for whatever reason, she opted against her usual tough-girl approach. Even the reliable wall that she built with such precision between people wasn't properly established. The crazy thing was that Jane didn't care. The bricks and mortar were still available, but the need to construct the barricade wasn't a paramount concern.

Hank dabbed at the jacket with a wet cloth and some leather cleaner he found beneath the sink. He looked perfectly content standing there in the dim light. "So, you gonna tell me what happened, or am I gonna read it tomorrow in the paper?"

"I danced with a deer on the two-laner out of town." Hank's eyebrows arched. "Don't worry. The deer's just fine." She proceeded to tell him the abbreviated version of her accident, minus the ghostlike hand that grabbed the wheel and swerved the Mustang away from the river. "Jesus, Jane. Maybe I need to take you to the hospital..."

"No, no, no. The glass is out of my head."

"How do you know?" Hank was obviously concerned.

Jane let out a sigh. "If I tell you, you gotta promise you're not gonna spill it to anybody." She was, after all, in the land of secrets.

"Who in the hell would I tell?" He took his attention off her jacket and focused on Jane. "What's going on?"

Jane laid out the story regarding Jordan, doing her best to minimize and eliminate some of the more odd comments he made. She did not disclose the fact that Jordan was a mulatto, figuring that was actually too private to share. Jane also purposely left out Jordan's parting comment, cloaked in a riddle, that he would reveal a "big secret" on Monday to her. Some things, she felt, needed to stay unspoken right now. Hank pulled out a kitchen chair and dragged it next to Jane. He took a seat and, after a thoughtful pause, he spoke.

"Jane, he's a serious suspect in Jake's case. That's general knowledge. He's the first one we all considered being involved when Jake went missing. What if he really is linked with Jake's disappearance? If he tells somebody what happened between the two of you..."

"You see? This is why I like to work alone!" Jane felt her back go up...well, as up as it could travel feeling the way she did.

"Hey, come on," Hank put a hand on her thigh. "You *know* I'm right," he said quietly.

"Fuck," Jane muttered. "Of course, you're right. But I was unconscious at the time it happened. So, you know..."

"Wait a second." Hank stared at Jane as if she was one of his former fraud suspects. She could feel his tentacles of understanding wrap around her unrehearsed story and forcing out the unspoken words that would tell the whole story. "Jordan Copeland is as private as they come. He doesn't just go save somebody's ass and willingly bring them onto his property... *into his cabin*...if he doesn't have some prior relationship with them."

"Relationship?" She shifted in her chair and turned away. "Jesus! You make it sound like Jordan and I are lovers..."

"Hey," Hank gently reached up and touched Jane's chin, turning it back toward him. "You can't bullshit another drunk, Jane."

Maybe it was the smoothing effects of the blue lily tea, but Jane couldn't come up with her usual "*Fuck you*" retort. She touched Hank's hand and pushed it away. After a careful moment, she began talking. She told him about her first outdoor, campfire visit on his property in detail. After Hank digested that confession, he got up and whipped up an impromptu chicken salad with leftovers from his refrigerator, before sitting back down and listening to Jane recount the second visit she shared with Jordan. She included everything she could recall of Jordan's sermons about secrets.

"Remember that comment that Jake made to me?" Hank offered. "The one where he asked me about family curses and if a family could be *infected* with a curse?"

Jane took another bite of the chicken salad. Maybe it was the lingering effects of the blue lily tea but she couldn't remember when she'd had a chicken salad that tasted so damn good. "Yeah. You said it was six weeks before he went missing."

"Right. Where do you think Jake came up with that

philosophic idea? You gotta admit it, Jane. That's a little too coincidental."

"I know." Jane's mood darkened. She was actually starting to feel compassion for Jordan Copeland, especially after hearing about his fractured childhood. There was a part of her that didn't want to believe he was guilty and another part that cried out, *What are you? Crazy? He's guilty!* The fact that she was feeling sorry for a guy who shot a retarded kid and then hid his body under his bed went against the norm for Jane Perry. Up until fifteen months ago, she saw the world in black-and-white. Perps were perps and any excuses they gave for their abhorrent behavior didn't wash in her book. She'd always been fond of telling people who cut perps slack that if one's tortured past gave them carte blanche to destroy another's life, then *she* should be doing hard time.

But after discovering the mind-shifting secret of her own violent father's upbringing, she had to step back and reevaluate her beliefs. She learned that there was a lot of covert, shape-shifting between generations and that, as far as her father was concerned, his abusive actions toward Jane and her brother coalesced because of what had happened to him as a child. As much as she wanted to continue to despise him and carry the hatred to her grave, she had to let it go. It was one of the hardest things she ever did. All Jane had ever known was unrelenting odium toward her father. To regard him like she would another victim took a lot of time and solitary thought. But it was because of that deeply personal experience that Jane began to accept the world with more hazy tones of grey. And now, with Jordan Copeland, the grey was starting to lean toward black— even though there was a part of her that simply did not want to believe he had anything to do with Jake's disappearance.

"That was the only time that Jake mentioned anything about curses in families to me," Hank added. "But it came out of nowhere..."

"You said he read a lot." Hank nodded. "Maybe he read it

somewhere?"

"Okay. Where'd he get the book?"

Jane looked at the bookcases across the room. "You got a lot of books. Maybe he got it from you."

"Well, I know it's only my word, but Jake's never been in here and I've never given him a book."

Jane studied Hank's face. If he was lying, he was a great liar. And there *were* those two walls of bookcases in Jordan's cabin, crammed with books, along with the stacks of literature that cluttered his tiny cabin. "Jordan Copeland is not stupid. He knows that if somebody drove by and saw Jake on his property, he'd be reported. He's not allowed within one hundred feet of a child or school. You know the drill."

"So, he stays a hundred and one feet away."

"Oh, come on! What? He's yelling a hundred and one feet away to have a conversation? And toss Jake a book or two? That's stretching it, don't you think?"

"Hey, the smart ones always figure out a loophole. Some of the fraud criminals I dealt with were ingenious! I used to say that if they used half their brains and energy for legitimate purposes, they'd be millionaires!"

Jane finished the chicken salad and pushed the plate away. She rubbed her head and, forgetting for a moment that it was still tender, winced.

"You okay?"

"Yeah. I just gotta get to bed." The minute Jane said that, she wished she could take it back. It was an obvious entrée for an invite from Hank; something she wasn't interested in.

"I'll take care of your car for you. I know the guy who owns the automotive place in town. He owes me some favors. We'll get the window fixed by tomorrow afternoon." *Wow*, Jane thought. Not only was there no invitation to the sack, Hank was going to call in a favor for a guy to work on her car on a *Sunday*. "If you need a vehicle tomorrow, you can use my truck," he added.

This was getting to be too much. First it was free hot dogs

at The Rabbit Hole, then it was voluntary information on the 1401 Imperial address. After that, he gave her a good tip on Chesterfield cigarettes, which was followed by a clean leather jacket and outrageous chicken salad. What was this guy's motive? There *had* to be a motive, Jane pondered, and it had to be less than noble. That's all she ever experienced with men…well, except from the first one.

She stood up and retrieved her exceptionally clean jacket. "Thanks."

"No big deal," Hank said, shrugging his shoulders.

Jane noticed that his eyes lingered a little longer on her than before. There was a softness there too. It was not the same softness she noted when he looked in Annie Mack's eyes; this was more like a calm, familiarity with a hint of sexuality underneath. Like meeting an old friend for the first time. Yes, that was *exactly* it…Like meeting an old friend for the first time. Jane suddenly felt a similar connection with Hank, but she couldn't attach any logic behind it. The blue lily was really doing a job on her mind, she deduced. She started to turn toward the door when she reconsidered. "Hey, you up for some more detective work?"

Hank smiled broadly. "Hell, yeah."

She dug her hand into her pocket and retrieved the *Patois* sentence she'd copied from Maureen's diary. "If you could translate that for me, I'd appreciate it." She handed it to Hank. "It's in *Patois*…"

"Oh, French Creole," Hank replied offhandedly.

Jane took a step back. "Don't tell me you speak French Creole."

"Nah. But I speak a little French. That should help. *Patois* is mainly spoken in Martinique, Trinidad and some other Caribbean islands, right?"

"And some others…right," Jane said. "You gonna ask me where I got it and who wrote it?"

"No. I figure if you want me to know, you'll tell me."

Well, when in the hell did Jane lose control of this conversation? Now, Jane *wanted* to tell Hank where it came from just to show him that he wasn't so smart, thinking he knew her so well. Then again, maybe that was the whole point of his remark—to manipulate the information out of her. She kept batting the possibilities back and forth as he led Jane to the front door and walked outside with her.

"You want me to walk you to the B&B?" Hank asked with a concerned look on his face.

Do I look that confused? Jane wondered. People weren't usually this invested in her welfare and she wasn't sure how to take it. There *had* to be a motive. "I'm fine." Jane said. But she wasn't fine. She didn't want to go back to the B&B and lay alone in her room waiting for sleep to overtake her. What in the hell was happening? She felt so bloody vulnerable at that moment, standing there in the yellow neon of The Rabbit Hole's roof sign. It wasn't the same vulnerability that hit when she stared at her single cigarette in the American Spirit packet. It wasn't the same vulnerable sensation she felt when Jordan got into her car and told her to drive over the bridge to his house. Both of those had an element of fear attached. This vulnerability felt more like an ancient part of her psyche melting and revealing the skin of who she really was under all the bravado and crustiness. For some strange reason, she heard Jordan's voice and the cutting words he said to her the first time she met him. "*Vulnerability for you equals weakness,*" he said. "*You're hard. Your palette hasn't been softened by the brush of the right guy. Your steel cannot bend to the forge of a man because to melt your fear you have to become vulnerable.*" Jane winced, recalling what Jordan told her after that. "*Once you go there, there's no turning back...*"

Jane looked at Hank. She moved a step closer to him but fear gripped at her heels and she pulled back.

The B&B was less than a block away but it was the longest damn walk of her life.

It was well past 10:00 pm when she crossed the threshold of the B&B. Thankfully, the lights were dim and everyone, including Weyler, had retired to their rooms. She had started up the stairs when she spied a pink note attached to the banister. It was written by Sara and simply said: *Fresh cookies on the kitchen table. Help yourself!* A smiley face followed. The first thing Jane thought was that some people in this world were actually quite sappy. The second thing she thought was, *cookies.*

Jane tiptoed into the kitchen and found the large plate, brimming with an assortment of oatmeal and chocolate chip cookies. She slid one off the plate and took a bite. Turning around, she noticed a collection of framed sepia-toned photos on the kitchen wall. Many had the same theme as the ones that lined the stairway and upstairs hallway, in that they depicted Midas and the surrounding area as it looked throughout the Twentieth Century. In the center of the collection was a photo of five women taken in front of the B&B. The date handwritten on the photo was 1919. The sign behind the women read: *The Garden—A Boarding House for Ladies.* Jane took another bite of the cookie and peered closer at the women in the photo. Instead of the refinement one might expect from the group, there was an uncharacteristic loutish flavor that permeated the gals. Jane could almost hear their uninhibited irreverence and frivolity seep from the aging film. One of the women in the photo had the audacity to turn her heel in what looked like a coquettish stance.

Jane grabbed another cookie and turned her attention to the glass cabinet where she had seen Sara protectively hiding the mysterious red photo album. She inched closer to the cabinet, knowing full well where the key was hidden. After considering the action, she started to open the bottom cabinet when she heard Mollie's bedroom door creak open. Quickly, Jane stood up and grabbed another few cookies just as Mollie appeared in the archway. The kid observed her with an appalled look. Jane stood there, her leather jacket draped over her arm, exposing the encrusted dirt on her last clean shirt. Jane caught her reflection in the glass of one of the picture frames. Her hair had seen better days and she was sure her face looked pretty haggard. To cap it off, she clutched four cookies in her hand and was in the process of chewing and swallowing another. Jane had to admit there was a definite slovenly slant to her nocturnal pit stop. "Hey," Jane muttered, as a piece of oatmeal spewed unexpectedly from her lips.

Mollie curled her lips. "Seriously. You look like a *schlub*."

"Your parents' washer still on the fritz?"

"Uh-huh."

"Shit." Jane was exhausted and didn't look forward to washing her shirts in the bathtub. "Hey, I gotta ask you something. You keep the emails you exchanged with Jake?"

"Why?" Mollie's suspicion was apparent.

"I need to see them."

"Just check his computer…"

"Yeah, funny thing about that, Mollie. They've been erased. *Everything* on Jake's computer is erased."

Mollie's eyes showed fear for the first time. "There's not a lot of them. And they don't say much. He wasn't really into email and texting."

"I need to see them." Mollie's face showed stress. "They're just between you and me, okay? If there's anything about him sneaking out of his house to come see you…" Mollie looked at Jane with a nervous edge. "I won't tell your parents. It'll be our secret. Hey, when in Midas…"

"I'll print them out and give them to you in the morning," Mollie acquiesced.

Mollie turned back to her bedroom. "Did Jake ever mention a website called *mysecretrevelations*?"

Mollie turned around. Her breathing was shallow. "Why? Is something wrong?"

Jane stepped forward in a show of intimidation. "Do you know about the website?"

"Yeah…I'm the one who told him about it. Did he post on it?" The kid's face was etched with trepidation.

"I think so." She asked Mollie to check out the four specific posts in February and March from the anonymous fifteen-year-old boy, giving special note to the one sixteen days prior to Jake's March 22nd disappearance. "Read them carefully," Jane stressed, "then tell me if you think Jake wrote them. But keep it to yourself, okay?"

The kid nodded and returned to her bedroom. Jane looked back at the glass cabinet that held the red photo album. She was too tired to pinch it, figuring her reflexes weren't as sharp as they could be that night.

Upstairs, she walked carefully past Weyler's room and nearly had the knob on her door fully turned when Weyler stepped out into the hall. He was still in his dress shirt and slacks, albeit his power tie was removed and the top two buttons on his shirt were undone.

"Jane," Weyler said. Jane turned. "What happened?"

"I couldn't find the address. But I'm going to try again."

Weyler moved closer to her. "Are you all right?"

"Yeah," Jane said, offering an offhand smile to cover the lie. "Just tired."

He stared at Jane, a serious expression clouding his face. "You eat?"

God, he was relentless. "Yeah. No worries." She opened her door. "See you in the morning."

Once inside her room, Jane let out a long sigh. She was back in her little Victorian cave with the exploitive honeymoon motif. She clicked on one of the small ornate lamps on the table, but the bulb sputtered. Something felt off as she glanced around the room. It was as if she'd entered a zone that was thick and vaporous. Draping her jacket over the chair, she checked every clue on the clothesline but nothing looked like it had been touched. Still, the syrupy mood in the room hung like lead. Turning off the light, she tried another floor lamp in the corner, but that also seemed to have electrical issues. "Shit," she murmured, holding her head. The day had caught up with her. She'd wash her three shirts in the bathtub, wring them out and go to bed. Stripping off her clothes, she donned her nightshirt and found the well-used collection of romantic candles in a large dish in the bathroom. She lit them and was amazed at how much light they produced. Jane turned off the sputtering floor lamp and started the water in the bathtub. One by one, she dumped her identical muddy shirts into the hot water, squeezed in a healthy dollop of lavender scented bath gel to the water and swished them around until the water rose above them. Looking at the shirts drowning in the water, Jane had to admit that they did look "manly," as Candy so succinctly stated. You certainly couldn't look at the shirts and confuse them with anything that remotely resembled femininity. But neutered clothing was what she preferred. It was safe. She would never be accused of flaunting her merchandise to get what she wanted. Besides, lace and soft flimsy material made her feel too vulnerable. You can't build strong walls to keep people out when you're wearing silk. The dark colors she preferred also reflected Jane's need to disappear and hide in the cloak of shadows. As the mud loosened from the material, the water turned a decidedly murky brown. Turning off the faucet, Jane felt a wave of fatigue grip her. The claw-foot bathtub absorbed the heat from the water and felt good against her skin. The pink bathmat beckoned her. She resolved to curl up against the tub and wake up in half an hour or so to finish her laundry.

As soon as her head touched the soft nylon on the thick, cushioned bathmat, she felt herself falling backward. Instead of fighting it, she let it happen. She heard the candles spit wax into the dish. The room vibrated around her as the energy draped its arms around her body. She fell backward further, down an unseen hole that lay within the shadows of her consciousness. The intoxicating scent of the blue lily filtered through her senses, hovering like a guardian above her head. She moved in and out of sleep, aware that she was lying on the bathroom floor but also alert to a sentient reality that was quickly emerging next to her. Jane saw a fleeting glimpse of a diaphanous purple veil waving in a slow breeze. Beyond it, a figure emerged and, with eyes wide shut, the veil ripped, forcing white-hot light against her body. The heady aroma of gardenias replaced the scent of the blue lily. She felt herself begin to hyperventilate but then a calming hand rested on her chest. Jane heard the candles pop and hiss. It only felt like a few mystifying minutes when she opened her eyes.

The enamel tub was cold. A lone flame flickered in a pool of wax. Peering around the corner of the bathroom door at the digital clock by her bedside table, she saw *3:11 am*. What felt like minutes had been more than four hours. In that instant, she felt a presence in the bedroom. It was the same knowing sense she had from the first night. The rocking chair creaked with pressure against the wood floor. Jane swallowed hard and crawled toward the door. She'd left her Glock on the desk in its holster. There was no way she could reach it in the dark.

She sat up and braced her back against the doorjamb that led into the bedroom.

Creak.

Weighing her options, she decided to speak. "Who's there?"

"Turn on the light," a voice whispered in the pitch black room.

Jane began to hyperventilate. She knew the voice, but it was impossible. It had been too many years since that timber had echoed against the walls.

"*Turn on the light, Jane,*" the voice whispered, this time more resolute.

Jane crawled to the bed and lifted herself onto it. She searched for the lamp on the table and found the switch. Facing the rocking chair, she flicked on the light.

CHAPTER 22

Jane stared into the eyes of a woman she didn't recognize. But the voice was unmistakable.

"Hello, Jane."

"Is this a dream?"

"No."

"Am I dead?"

"No." There was a soft smile, followed by a mischievous giggle.

Jane peered closer at the women. Her skin was youthful and her eyes were bright. She looked nineteen or twenty years old. "But *you're* dead..."

"Of course."

Jane gazed at her. She wore a tight-fitting, sexy red satin halter dress that looked like it was painted on her lithe body. The V-neck plunged, exposing her firm mound of plump, young breasts. A fresh gardenia was pinned to the center of the neckline. Her hair fell in soft brown glossy waves, brushing her tanned shoulders. A pair of black dressy sandals with two-inch heels completed the ensemble. "I don't remember you ever looking like this."

She got up from the rocking chair and walked to the end of the bed. It was then that Jane noticed her fire engine red fingernails. "I know," she stared into Jane's eyes. "The flame was extinguished before we ever became acquainted."

Acquainted, Jane thought. What a cold word to use.

"Bad word choice," she said, reading Jane's mind. "Let me rephrase that. Life had done a number on me before I gave life to you." She looked around room with an innocent awe. "Wow. It's real pretty in here."

Jane heard a distant hum that seemed to be holding the realities together. "What do I call you? Anne or Mom?"

Anne leaned down and rested her elbows in the bed's comforter, framing her tanned face with the palms of her hands.

"I guess we could be modern and you could call me Anne. Or keep it traditional and call me mom." She smiled a warm, vibrant grin.

Jane was taken back. "You never smiled like that."

"Yeah, I know. Not much to smile about, was there?" Anne bit her lower lip. Suddenly, she stood up, a restlessness overtaking her. "Oh, this room really is dreamy with the canopy bed and the nice furniture."

Dreamy? Jane wondered why in the hell her mother gave a shit about the décor.

Anne giggled, reading Jane's mind. "I just like it, that's all!" She sounded more like a teenager than the woman who was her mother. Anne strolled around the room, checking out the pictures on the wall.

"Why are you here?" Jane asked cautiously.

"I'm not just here," she said, more interested in the artwork. "I've been a lot of places. I was in the doctor's office when you got the news, then the closet, then your car." Anne turned to Jane, a strand of hair falling seductively across her face. "I saved your ass today, didn't I?" She laughed a knowing chuckle.

"That was you?"

"Who in the hell did you think it was?" Jane unintentionally sent her a message. "Oh," Anne's face grew slightly more serious. "You thought it was *him?*" She returned her tour of the room. "Nope. It was little ol' me."

"You were in the doctor's office? So you know?"

"Know what?" Anne was more intrigued by the floral wallpaper.

"If I'm dying?" Jane's tenor was irritated. And the realization that a ghost was irritating her wasn't lost on Jane.

She looked at Jane. "Oh, hell, we're all dying, Jane." Anne thought about it. "Or *dead!*" A carefree giggle followed.

"I thought maybe you were here to tell me I was jumping over to your side of the fence soon."

Anne stretched and sighed. She pursed her lips. "It

depends."

"Depends on what?"

Anne's blithe spirit diminished a bit. "On whether you're prepared to see things for how they truly are...and were." Anne turned away, a sense of duty enfolding her. "You shouldn't carry it if it doesn't belong to you."

"Carry what?" Anne stared at her for what seemed like an eternity. Suddenly, a wave of excruciating pain hit Jane's pelvis. Anne winced as her daughter doubled over onto the bed. Tears filled Jane's eyes. It felt like an ax had been flung into her groin, splitting her in two. She looked up at her mother who remained motionless. "Help me," Jane whispered, through the tears.

"Can you accept what you've never known?"

Jane was losing consciousness. She tried to speak but the pain was overwhelming. Burying her head in the comforter, she waited to pass out. She felt herself drift away from her body. The soft cushion of the comforter against her forehead could again be felt and the horrific torment in her gut dissolved. She opened her eyes and the room was dark. Reaching out, her hand hit the side of the enamel bathtub. Beneath her was the pink bath mat. Disoriented, she stumbled to her feet and stood in the bathroom doorway. Outside, there was the faintest glimmer of light. She looked at the clock—*6:00 am*. Jane turned on the bedside lamp and stared at the rocking chair.

Nobody. Nothing.

She sat on the bed in stunned silence, the memory of her mother's visit still fresh in her mind's eye. It was insanity, Jane thought, to believe that she had just seen a glimpse of the woman before the storm of life swallowed her. But it was as real as the table or chair in front of her. There was a window into a world Jane never knew her mother dwelt in. Before the lifeless gaze Jane only saw as a child, her mother bubbled with energy and carefree exuberance. Her face wasn't yet mapped with lines of misery and regret; her eyes hadn't been dampened by profound sadness. But who broke her heart? It wasn't just Jane's

father and his violent, booze-fueled rages. The honeymoon photos Jane found in the box in her closet proved that. What happened between age nineteen or twenty and twenty-two when
Anne LeRoy became Anne Perry? Was it an erstwhile lover who
left her heartbroken and bereft? Jane had a hard time picturing
the woman *she* knew cavorting with men. God, it was akin to
watching a nun in a burlesque show. But if it was a man who
gutted her emotionally, what kind of hold could he have that
would essentially destroy her so deeply that she attracted Jane's
father and lived a life of quiet desperation that ended in agony
at age thirty-five? What kind of man had that kind of power?

Jane lay back on the bed in a fetal position, hoping sleep
would overtake her. But she was still awake when she heard
Weyler's footsteps in the hallway and the knock on her door.

"Jane?" Weyler said softly. "You up?"

"Yeah, Boss," Jane said, still slightly in a dissociative state.

"Sara's got breakfast downstairs for us. Then they're heading to church. We need to talk."

Jane felt her heart race. "I'll be down."

Jane heard Weyler's footsteps walk downstairs. She willed
her body back together and sat up. Out of nowhere, a fountain-
head of resolve suddenly took over. From where it originated,
she didn't know. But it was dynamic and inexorable.

Roused by this newfound determination, she turned to the
clothesline of clues. One by one, she was determined to reveal
every single lie that tainted this case. She would sink her teeth
into the marrow of the guilty parties and not let go until the answers were laid bare. She would be ruthless because, more than
ever, she truly wanted to see everything for what it really was.

Jane's enthusiasm for her plan was somewhat dimmed
when she walked into the bathroom and found her only shirts
still soaking in a tub of cold water. She quickly rinsed the shirts
and wrung them tightly before hanging them in the sunniest
window of her room. It wouldn't halt her progress, she vowed;

she'd wear her Ron Paul nightshirt covered by her leather jacket. Yeah, she'd have to tuck in the generous material, but she'd make it work. Jane showered quickly using the tub's handheld shower adaptation and tossed on her dirty jeans, boots and nightshirt.

Downstairs, the house was quiet, save for Sergeant Weyler seated in the kitchen, quietly turning the pages of the Sunday *Denver Post* and enjoying a cinnamon roll. As usual, the man was dressed in a suit, soft blue shirt and red power tie. His jacket was carefully draped over another chair and a thick cloth napkin covered his shirt and tie.

"Is that what you're wearing today?" Weyler asked, tipping the newspaper to take a gander at Jane's odd appearance.

Jane removed a covered dish from the oven. "Yeah. I got it figured out." She uncovered the lid and found a hearty egg, mushroom and cheese medley dotted with fresh cilantro. "Damn. You gotta love B&B food, right, Boss?"

Weyler was still askance regarding Jane's appearance. "What happened to you last night?"

Jane served herself three generous spoonfuls of the egg dish, thankful to have a physical action to deflect her words. "I tried to call you about five o' clock, but I didn't have service. I had car trouble."

"Car trouble?"

"I think it's the muffler," she said, her actions focused on placing the covered dish back into the oven so the lie wouldn't be detected by Weyler. "I had to wait on the side of the road for two hours before I got someone to stop and help me." Jane continued her intricate fabrication, making sure not to concoct too detailed a story so that it would be difficult to remember. "The tow truck didn't roll in until like…eight…" Jane sat down and took a hearty bite. "Where's the coffee?"

Weyler pointed to the sideboard. Jane popped up and poured herself a cup of strong coffee. "Who helped you?"

Jane returned to the table. She could see that Weyler was suspicious. It was time to inject a modicum of truth. "Hank

Ross. He owns the sports bar in town. Said he knows the guy who owns the automotive joint and that he's going to pull some favors for me so I can get the car back today." She tried to sound as offhand as possible as she drove another spoonful of food into her mouth. "Shit, food really *does* taste better when you quit smoking!"

"Your car's getting fixed on a *Sunday*?" Weyler was now looking more like the doubtful father, questioning his daughter the morning after the night before. "That's highly unusual."

"Yeah, well, you know..." Jane drifted off, taking a good sip of the dark brew.

Weyler set down the paper, sat back and folded his arms across his chest. "Goddamnit, Jane! What in the hell is going on?"

"My car's in the shop. Go check for yourself..."

"*Stop it!*" Weyler leaned forward. "Don't insult me any-more!" Jane's gut clenched. "I've known you too damn long. I know the way your mind works. I know that the more I advise you *not* to do something, the more likely you are to do it." Jane hung her head, studying the food on her plate. "You've reached out to Jordan, one-on-one, face-to-face." Jane looked up at him, her eyes anxious. "I haven't said a word to Bo. Don't worry."

Jane felt like shit. Weyler had always defended her, supported her and lifted her up through the years when she was too drunk or self-destructive to care about her own welfare. He *did* deserve better from her. And Weyler was absolutely right—the more anyone told her not to do something, the more she'd do it...and with salient impunity. "I'm sorry, Boss." She felt a catch in her throat. "I'm not thinking really clear these last few days."

"Why?"

A wave of emotion hit Jane. "I might...I might have can-cer." It was the first time she'd said it out loud and the reality brought the fear front and center. She swallowed hard as her eyes welled with tears. "I don't know for sure. I gotta wait for the test results."

Weyler's face fell. "Oh, dear God." He reached out to Jane. "Why didn't you tell me?"

"I didn't think it was relevant…"

"*Relevant*? Jesus, Jane! Your welfare happens to be extremely relevant to me!"

"I've always had that *carry on* mentality. You know that. This isn't the first time."

"You should have told me."

"So you could do what? Worry about me?"

"I always worry about you."

"Oh, Boss—"

"Stop calling me *Boss*, would you? I'm your equal."

Jane played with her food. "Oh, fuck. You're my better half. You're the eloquent me. You're certainly the better-dressed me." Jane took a deep breath and told Weyler everything about her encounters with Jordan—from his philosophical dissertations on the perils of keeping a family secret to the truth about his parentage. She mentioned his obscure dreams involving the mysterious "Red," his frightening insight into Jane's life and the conflicting issues she had with Jordan's inexplicable references to *You Can't Go Home Again*. She wrapped it up with car accident and Jordan's rescue. The only part of the long story she left out was the unresolved issue of her dead mother's reappearance. *That* freakish aspect was too bizarre for even her to process.

Weyler took it all in, gravely weighing every word. She couldn't read his face as to what he was thinking until he spoke. "You did what you had to do, Jane." Jane was stunned. She obviously hadn't given him enough credit. "I would have done the same damn thing. You've always been brash. That's why I relate to you in a lot of ways. You remind me of the way I used to be. Only problem was, that brashness got me into trouble a long time ago."

Jane leaned forward. "Is that where your favor to Bo fits into this thing?"

"Yes." He took a sip of coffee and looked off to the side,

bringing up the memory. "I may appear to be the epitome of calmness and thoughtful repose today, but when I was a rookie, I was an unmitigated show-off. I wanted to prove myself, no matter the cost." He got up and dished himself several large spoonfuls of the egg combo. "Bo was about two years ahead of me in the Department and we got assigned together on patrol. He was an affable guy. People liked him and felt comfortable around him. One day at a coffee shop, this Caucasian guy came over to us and asked to talk Bo alone. I watched the guy as he discussed something obviously important with Bo and then scribbled some words down on a scrap of paper. Bo looked at the paper and stuffed it in his wallet. When he came back to the table, Bo said the guy was worried about his sister who lived with a crazy boyfriend. The guy asked us to drive by their house occasionally and check it out.

"A few weeks later, Bo ran across the scrap of paper in his wallet. He said it was 714 South Myrtle..."

"Wait. You remember the address after all these years?"

Weyler sat down, secured his napkin over his shirt and took a bite of food. "Oh, yes. You'll see why in a second. I thought to myself, *714 South Myrtle? That's a bad part of town...gangs, drugs, bad scene.* But at the same time, I was eager to cut my teeth on something more than traffic stops. I didn't tell Bo, but I was secretly looking forward to it. I wanted to break down a door and save a woman from her abusive boyfriend." He rolled his eyes at his youthful ignorance and took another bite of food. "I told Bo we needed to check it out, and so we get to the house and everything looks okay. But I insist that we get out of the car and check closer. So we do. The house is a ramshackle dump. We stand on the porch and then Bo tells me he's got a feeling like we shouldn't be there. But I'm all piss and vinegar and ready to rumble.

"That's when we heard it. It was a bloodcurdling scream and it was coming from a child. Bo wanted to call for back-up, but I'd already made my asinine rookie decision. Before he could stop me, I kicked in the front door."

"With nothing to go on but a kid screaming?"

"I figured justifiable entry, right? I call out 'Police!' and suddenly there's *no* sound. We pulled our guns and Bo motioned for us to go in the back of the house. We made our way down this dark hallway that led to a backroom. And what do we see?" Jane was transfixed, like a kid listening to a malevolent bedtime story. "Fifty kilos of Columbian cocaine. Bo and I looked at each other with the understanding that this was way bigger than we could handle. Then we heard this guy yelling, 'Shut up! Shut up, bitch!' coming from the bathroom. We shout, 'Police!' and bust in, guns out. But there wasn't any girlfriend and the guy wasn't white. What we saw was a strung-out Mexican guy, drowning his six-year-old girl in the bathtub. Bo screamed at him to let her go, but the guy reaches in his boot and, before either of us could react, he's got a pistol out and he shoots Bo in the hip. Bo returned fire, nailing the son-of-a-bitch in the side. It all happened in a split second and I didn't know what to do. Bo's down, Mexican guy is down and the little girl is floating face down in the bathwater. I froze. Bo's voice brought me out of it. He screamed at me to cuff the guy and grab the kid and lay her on the floor. I do it but she's turning blue and not breathing. I panicked, but Bo dragged his bleeding body over to her and breathed the life back into her." Weyler shook his head and took a sip of coffee.

"Jesus…" Jane mused.

"Of course, by the time we radio for backup and the Chief of Police gets on scene, we look like heroes! I mean, nailing a stash of coke that big and saving a little girl's life? That's golden. It makes a rookie look good. He tells us the D.A. will look at the collar as a 'good-faith mistake.'"

"I'm sensing a catch here."

"We get to the hospital and Bo goes into surgery. The Chief takes me aside, shakes my hand and asked me 'What made you go in that house?' I told him we got a tip from a citizen who wanted us to check out the house and make sure his sister was okay. Chief said he needed some proof for the paperwork. So, later that day, I go collect Bo's personal effects and root through his wallet and find the scrap of paper. And that's when I know we have a problem. The address wasn't 714 South Myrtle. It was 714 *North Maple*. Which made sense, in retrospect, since the whites lived on Maple and the Mexicans lived on Myrtle."

"So you busted down a door and made entry without probable cause?"

"Yes, ma'am. And by doing so, I nearly got my partner killed."

"But then you also found the large stash of coke and saved a girl's life."

"You got it."

"Quite a quandary."

"Not at all. It's called covering your ass. I tore up the scrap of paper in Bo's wallet and manufactured another scrap of paper to look just like it. With the oddest handwriting I could fashion, I wrote *714 South Myrtle* and crumpled it up to make it look like it'd been folded in a wallet. I handed it to the Chief and everyone was happy."

"Everyone? As in you and Bo?"

"It was our secret. The shooting left him with a bad hip. Never got the bullet out of him. That's why he limps and still has pain. He stayed on desk duty in Denver before he was hired here in Midas."

"So that whole fiasco is what brought him here?"

Weyler nodded. "I guess it all worked out in the end. He slowly moved up in the ranks and became a big fish in a little pond. I did okay too. But I always told him I owed him. I owed him for keeping his mouth shut about a rookie who should have thought first before he kicked in a door and nearly got his partner killed in the mêlée. But being the kind of guy Bo is, he said it was no big deal and that he should have memorized the address better. I think he actually was happy to get out of the city and be part of a smaller venue. But no matter, I never forgot the promise. That's why when he asked me to come up here, I didn't hesitate or ask a lot of questions."

Jane thought about the story. "I'm just curious. The Chief just took the piece of paper that you forged as proof of this anonymous *Caucasian guy*? Didn't they want to track him down to confirm everything?"

"Well, fortunately the case never went to trial because the Mexican guy copped to the drugs and attempted drowning. But, yes, we figured an angle to float our story. We said that Bo got approached by lots of citizens and they all just used first names. So we told the Chief that a guy named *Gomez* gave Bo the tip."

"Gomez?"

"Certainly a popular Mexican surname."

Jane gave it a moment of thought and the light bulb came on. "Ah! Bo used that term in his office the other day. He said we couldn't '*Gomez*' this case away.'"

"It means there's no anonymous fall guy to link the case to."

Jane took a bite of eggs. "But there *is* a *Gomez* in this case. It's Jordan Copeland."

"You really believe that?"

Jane thought hard before she answered. "I'm ninety percent there." Weyler questioned her with his eyes. "Okay. Eighty percent. There's still something he's not telling me…but he's going to."

"How do you know?"

"He told me he would reveal a 'big secret' to me tomorrow." Weyler looked worried. "You want me to go with you?"

"No! He won't talk if you're there. He's a wing-nut paranoid. It's just gotta be the two of us."

"What if he tries something?"

"He won't." Jane realized her own odds gave Jordan a twenty percent chance of turning on her, but she was willing to take that chance.

Mollie popped out of her room and appeared in the

doorway. She was still in her pajamas. She took one look at Jane's appearance and shook her head before returning to her bedroom.

Jane leaned closer to Weyler and whispered. "I'm working on her. Don't worry."

Weyler stood up and crossed to the sink, rinsing the dish and setting it to the side. Jane heard him sigh, something he wasn't known to do a lot.

Jane turned around. "What is it?"

"You know the odds, Jane." Weyler stared out the kitchen window in the backyard.

Jane understood what he meant. The odds of a kidnapped child found after three days was slim. Now, nearly eight days later, the chances got slimmer with each passing hour. "Yeah. But you know what, Boss? This case is stacked with long-shot odds, starting with the odds of a fifteen-year-old *boy* being kidnapped. And how about this one:...what are the odds of Jake's computer being completely erased, including his Internet favorites and even his spam, *beyond* the day he was taken?" Weyler turned to Jane, eyebrows arched. "And don't get me started on the odds of a terminally ill grandmother who doesn't really give a rat's ass about her missing grandson, *suddenly* showing up to do...what? Is liver cancer less deadly in the high altitude? I think not."

Weyler sat back down across from Jane. Concern covered his face. "His computer was *completely* erased?"

Jane leaned forward. "Not even spam from Nigeria." She studied his face as he silently contemplated. "We have to at least consider the fact that Bailey Van Gorden is keeping something useful from us." The vision of Bailey exchanging an envelope of cash with an unknown man in a strip club came into Jane's vision.

"Your theory that he's keeping a missing clue?" Weyler asked.

"Yeah..." Jane struggled with revealing what she saw in the

strip club. Weyler seemed like he was on her side, but she didn't want to assume too much and have him pull the reins in on her. And while she was fairly certain that Bailey was working a back end deal, she didn't have proof. "Why do people keep secrets?" she asked, more as a point of debate.

"Allegiance to another person...embarrassment, humiliation..."

"Covering up...maintaining control..." Jane recalled her improvised discussion with Bailey during their first meeting when she threw out the three most common reasons people commit crimes—sex, money and gettin' even. When Bailey didn't resonate with any of those, Jane proposed another possibility—control. She remembered how Bailey jumped at that postulate and eagerly used it to attach Jordan to his son's disappearance. "Control," Jane repeated. "For some reason, Bailey found it necessary to strong-arm Aaron Green into forcing Mollie to break up with Jake."

"Why?"

"I don't know. But I'd say that's pretty controlling on Bailey's part, wouldn't you? Two weeks later, Jake goes missing. Coincidence?"

"Two weeks later, Jake tries to kill himself and *then* he goes missing."

"If the suicide was real...and I think it was...the only options are that someone happened to be near the bridge and saw Jake with the rope or..."

"Someone was stalking him for awhile and knew his patterns so he was already there...waiting..."

Jane hung her head. "Back to Jordan," she said sadly. She knew that Weyler was right. It had to be a stalker—a stalker with a driven aim and a premeditated plan. She'd already deduced that the clues were well thought-out and far too intricate to come up with *after* Jake was already in his grip. The spoofed Short Hills phone number with the 1968 area code that belonged to the family who lived directly behind the Copelands was an example of something that took some thoughtful time to concoct. But then again, why would Jordan, who didn't own a phone—and might not even know about spoofing—create a phone number that was linked so closely to his childhood home?

If there had been a ransom request, Jane would simply chalk it up to a calculated capture of a rich man's son with the intention of gaining a million-dollar prize. But whoever did this, didn't want money. Again, Jordan's name popped up. He lived on a healthy trust fund, doled out by *Eddie* each year. From what she could tell, Jordan's main expense was books. But he probably had enough cash in the bank to live a more opulent life if he chose. Between the hypothesis that a stalker by the bridge was involved and whoever did this was not interested in financial gain, Jordan was starting to look like a more likely suspect—albeit with conflicting data. "Fuck," Jane murmured, as she ran her fingers through her tangled hair, still wet from her shower. "Okay…I'll start digging on Jordan. I have to piece together those missing pages from his file that you gave me on him. I hope Midas keeps its library open on Sunday." Jane downed her coffee and rinsed off her plate. She glanced at the glass cabinet and, without hesitating, opened the bottom drawer and removed the key, which was located way in the back.

"What are you doing?"

Jane stood on a stepladder and unlocked the high cabinet. "I'm not sure. Collateral? Maybe blackmail." She removed the red photo album and then noted an additional brown box marked, OLD PHOTOS. She grabbed that too, locked the cabinet and replaced the key. "What are your plans today?"

"I brought plenty of paperwork to keep me busy. Then I'll have lunch with Bo."

"You guys are reconnecting, eh? That's good. Once he moves to Florida, you probably won't see him again."

"Probably not. More reason than ever to make this a good case for him."

Jane started out of the kitchen when she turned back to Weyler. "One more thing…why does Bo call you 'Beanie?'"

"I kicked in a door and entered a property with no real cause. What would you technically call that?"

Jane thought. "Breaking and entering?" Weyler nodded. "*B 'n' E*…Beanie."

"That's how Bo's mind tends to work."

Upstairs in her room, Jane hid the red album and box of photos under her bed and then collected the paperwork she would need when she got to the library. She heard a scratch of paper under her doorway and turned. It was the small collection of printed emails between Jake and Mollie.

Jane opened her door and unexpectedly found three T-shirts and a couple dressy shirts on hangers resting on the door handle. She looked up just as Mollie was heading downstairs.

"Mollie!" The kid kept walking. Jane remembered. "Liora!"

Mollie stopped and turned. "What?"

"Come here." Jane took a peek at the youthful assortment of shirts. One of the T-shirts had cap sleeves and pronounced in gold lettering, *I LIKE BOYZ!* Another was a tie-dye T-shirt with the word, *Groovy* across the front. Yet another proclaimed, *I Must Be Trippin' 'Cuz You Look Cute!* The other two were dressy, somewhat vintage-looking, with chiffon fronts, flutter sleeves and delicate lace and embroidery around the collars.

Mollie walked back to Jane. "What is it?"

"I appreciate the offer, but I can't wear these." Jane handed them back to Mollie.

Mollie refused to touch them. "Are they your size?"

"Yeah. Sure. But they're not my style." Jane attempted another transfer.

"Oh, *geh vays*! There's a shock. Don't be a *nudnik* and stop your *kvetching*!" Mollie let out a tired puff of breath. "Are you a dyke?"

Jane was taken back. "For Chrissake…what is it with everybody?! No, I am *not* a dyke!"

"Then I suggest you wear those shirts." Mollie leaned closer. "It wouldn't hurt for you to *girl* it up a bit. Know what I mean? Start with this one…" Mollie removed the T-shirt with *I LIKE BOYZ!* "Just to quiet the rumors, ya know?"

Mollie turned on her heels and left. Jane looked at her three identical, soaking wet poplin shirts still dripping water on the carpet by the window. She glanced down at her unkempt nightshirt. The choice was undesirably clear to her.

CHAPTER 23

A headache-inducing medley of chemicals, silently off-gassing from the hoards of new plastic-encased equipment, computers, furniture and recently installed carpeting, hit Jane square between the eyes. Her heightened senses were getting to be a pain in the ass.

Instead of your typical small-town, musty and dank library, the Midas branch was one of the most modernized small-town ones she'd ever seen. It *was* true. Money *did* buy a lot of stuff and in this case, it bought state-of-the art workstations and an incredible amount of printed resources for the townspeople.

The only inhabitants were Jane and the beleaguered librarian. The poor woman, who Jane guessed was in her late fifties, wore a pair of glasses on her head and another on her face, attached with a black cord that had a ceramic book dangling from the neckpiece. She was busy opening boxes and reading through technical manuals for the newly installed computer system. The stress was evident on her face as Jane approached the counter and laid down her satchel.

"Oh, you know, we're not supposed to be open today." The woman removed her glasses and secured them on top of her head, next to the other pair. "This is one of my last days to go over all the new systems before we get rid of the old ones."

Jane knew a gentle but pointed approach was needed. She casually unbuttoned her jacket to reveal the Glock in her holster. "I was hoping you'd have microfiche files available? I'll stay out of your hair. I promise."

The librarian sized up Jane. "You're one of the Denver cops up here about Jake?"

"You got it." The woman silently observed Jane once more. God, it was like she was asking to see the Dead Sea Scrolls and this woman had the golden key. "Look, I'll just tell Bo you were too busy." Jane grabbed her satchel to leave.

"No! No!" The woman walked around the counter. "This way."

Obviously, the townspeople knew that when Bo Lowry needed something, they jumped. They walked to a windowless backroom where Jane found stacks of boxes, all marked *Microfiche* with the corresponding years noted. A lone microfiche viewer and printer sat unplugged in the corner. The librarian explained that everything had been packed up and would soon be shipped to a lab for digital transfer—just another example of Bo Lowry's town jumping feet first into the Twenty-First Century.

The librarian left Jane alone in the room and she went about the arduous task of locating the box that held microfiche for the *New York Times* for July through October of 1968. After an hour, Jane finally found what she was looking for. She brought out the printed material from her satchel, quickly reviewing the exact dates. Plugging in the microfiche viewer and printer, she slipped the film sheet under the glass viewer, slid the glass under the machine and sharpened the image using the *focus* button. The microfiche screen was scratched and stained with ink in places, but it magnified the forty-one-year-old publication with fairly good clarity. Jane spent another ten minutes painstakingly going from page to page in the August 10th edition that corresponded to the article that was in Jordan's information file. She located the large photo above the story that showed a cleaned-up eighteen-year-old Jordan moving through a crowd of reporters on the courthouse steps, accompanied by his horribly harried parents. When she looked at this same photo four days prior, Jordan Copeland was just another convicted killer doing the perp walk in court. Now that Jane knew more about his splintered family life, the boy in the photo appeared more lost. He had a vacant, dissociative look in his eyes. Jane wasn't sure if it was shock or post-traumatic stress. Whatever it was, it pervaded his young body.

Jane scanned to the next page of the story, which had been missing from the file. She skimmed the text.

> Mr. Copeland's son sat quietly in the courtroom, looking up only to address the judge with short 'yes' and 'no' answers…The teenager appeared thinner than his first court appearance last month and seemed to be exceptionally withdrawn from his counsel…

Jane skipped further down in the article.

> When Jordan Copeland entered a plea of 'Guilty,' the judge asked him to speak louder. After repeating the words, the teenager sat down and buried his head on the table in front of him, clearly distraught. Defense attorney, Ira Cornett, told reporters outside the courthouse, "It's clear that Jordan Copeland is wracked with guilt over what he has done. It would serve the best interest of everyone concerned if we could bring this case to a speedy conclusion and allow the Copeland family to retreat from the spotlight and let the family of Daniel Marshall grieve in peace…"

Jane checked the index listings for articles pertaining to Jordan Copeland in the large book near the microfiche viewer. One titled, "Scene of the Crime in Millburn Township" from *Time* magazine piqued her interest. It took her half an hour to locate that microfiche file but it was well worth it. The first line of the article was chilling: *Murder has never come this close to Millburn Township.* It featured an aerial illustration of the Copeland's neighborhood in unincorporated Short Hills, indicating with a circle where Daniel Marshall's body was purportedly shot on the Copeland's property. From what Jane could determine, it looked like it was just inside the back fence at the rear of the property—near the half-acre stretch of wooded ground that Jordan described to her. It was also the same spot, Jane surmised, from where Jordan stood and had his *mind-reading* conversations with the mysterious child named *Red* six or more months previous to Daniel's murder.

Jane peered closer at the page. She wasn't certain how accurate the artist's illustration was, but it looked like the Copelands' back fence was linked in a straight line through the forested area with the back fence of the house located directly on the other side. This had to be the house where David Sackett lived and whose number was spoofed by the kidnapper. Jane dug into her jean pocket and brought out the crumpled piece of paper that held Sackett's phone number and Warwick Road address. Warwick Road was indeed directly behind the Copelands' house. The illustration inferred that the only way into this forested spot was either through the private fences of the two homes or by jumping the fence that lined the streets where the wooded area extended in the other directions. Jordan mentioned that he'd hear kids playing inside the area, building forts and running around.

Jane connected the printer and attempted to print out the illustration. Unfortunately, the clarity of the copy was streaked and blurred, but it gave her something to hold and analyze. For whatever reason, Jane kept being drawn to the house on the opposite side of Copelands' property. It had to have value or the kidnapper wouldn't have taken the time to spoof the number that belonged to that house. Jane knew Daniel Marshall didn't live in the house since it had been stated before that the child resided next door to Jordan. Sackett lived in that house since February of 1968, five months before Jordan killed Daniel. Jane stared at the printed page and circled the house on Warwick Road with her pen. If her theory that the kidnapper was telling a story with his clues, then perhaps the house attached to the spoofed phone number was also part of the story. She dialed Sacket's phone number and he picked up on the second ring. Jane introduced herself again and he remembered her through fitful coughing spells. It was obvious the elderly gentleman couldn't linger on the phone, so Jane cut to the chase.

"Mr. Sackett, I need to know who you bought the house from in February of '68."

"It was a couple in their late forties. I forget their name."

"Did they have children?"

"I can't remember…Let me think…My wife and I were only at the house when the family was there a couple times." Sackett thought about it. "Yeah, they had a daughter. She was in her late teens."

"Did they ever mention why they were moving?"

"Oh, hell, I don't know. We're talking forty-one years ago!"

"I know, sir. But anything you can remember could be really helpful to us."

Sackett hung on the phone in silence, trying to bring up a useful memory. "I can tell you it was a quick sale. We were the first people to see the place and make an offer and they took it right away. They wanted a thirty-day escrow and they were packed up and gone in three weeks."

Jane figured that even high-priced executives who get transferred suddenly and have to move don't usually vacate a house that quickly. "Do you think their behavior had anything to do with Jordan Copeland?"

"Jordan? Oh, I doubt it. I didn't know Jordan existed until he shot that little retarded boy that summer. Besides, Jordan was into *boys*, not girls. And, like I said, this family had one child and it was a teenage girl."

Jane stared at the circle she drew around Sackett's house. It *had* to have significance. "Mr. Sackett, are you absolutely certain there were no other children living at that house? We understand that young boys played in the wooded area behind your house…"

"Yeah, yeah. You're right. I forgot about that. Hang on, now. Wait a second…" Sackett coughed hard and then returned to the phone. "Christ, I hope this cancer kills me soon." Jane winced at his comment. "Yeah…there was a boy… He lived in the back house with his mother. She was a Russian immigrant. Single mother, I suppose. I think she was the family's live-in maid."

Jane felt her heart race. "Did he have a shock of curly red hair?"

"Yes! Yes, he did. Short kid. Little red-haired kid. About eight years old… I only saw him once though. They were packed up and gone by our second visit to the house."

Jane thanked Sackett for his help and hung up. A quick sale of a house and the speedy disappearance of the live-in maid and her eight-year-old red-haired son—Jane knew that child killers don't usually start with murder. They work up to it slowly. And those who target children, typically start with stalking or seemingly innocuous chatting in order to gain the child's trust. Once the kid feels comfortable and even safe, the criminal has a better chance of luring them into the net. Perhaps this *Red* who lingered by the Copeland's back gate was Jordan's first conquest? Jane recalled Jordan's disturbing description of the boy he called "Red." "He was very confused and angry…" Jordan told her. At least, that's what Jordan claimed the boy told him *telepathically*. "Nobody helped him. He cried like a baby. He screamed and no one cared… He stands at that fucking gate and stares at me and tells me how much pain he feels. 'Listen to me!' he keeps screaming. 'Why won't anyone listen to me?!'"

"Shit," Jane said out loud as Jordan's voice echoed in her head. Something happened to that kid. The boy's Russian immigrant mother felt victimized and fled with her son. In turn, the family decided it wasn't the safest neighborhood for their own daughter. But you don't leave your comfortable house because of simple harassment. You get the cops involved first and only when a criminal act is committed do people often make the decision to leave the area. Looking through the file on Jordan that Jane carried in her satchel, it was clear that he had no prior criminal history or complaints against him. "So what scared you people?" Jane asked the illustration in front of her.

Jane checked the clock. It was past ten o'clock and she had another stop to make. But before she left the library, she sauntered over to the librarian. A sign above her head beckoned everyone to *Read the 20th Century Classics.*

"Do you have a list of classics you recommend?" Jane asked with another intention forefront in her mind.

The poor, overwhelmed woman looked at Jane through her thick glasses. "Huh?"

Jane motioned to the poster. "The classics?"

The woman stood up and shuffled through a stack of paper. "Here."

Jane took the page—a list of Top 100 titles. She hoped it would be on there and it was. "Ah, Thomas Wolfe's, *You Can't Go Home Again.* Great book. Is it available?"

"We're really not open today..."

"This is about police business," Jane said with a serious tone.

The woman nodded and checked the computer. "It's available." She looked at Jane. "I suppose you would like to get a list of people who checked it out."

"That's private information, last time I checked. And I don't have the required subpoena."

"Right. You do need that. Unless, of course, it's a matter of Homeland Security…" The woman arched an eyebrow.

As much as Jane wanted to see the list, she was damned if she was going to play the Homeland Security card or trot out the ever-popular Patriot Act to muscle information from someone. Jane shook her head. "No, thanks. I'm not going there."

The librarian appeared to have newfound respect for Jane. "Well, I need to visit the ladies room…*way* over there…and I'll be gone for about five minutes." She smiled and walked away.

Jane caught the not-so-subtle message. Moving around the counter, she scrolled down on the computer screen to view the history of names and dates when Wolfe's book was checked out. Not once, but twice on the long list, Jordan Copeland's name appeared. The earliest date was one year before with the latest date just three months ago—another nail in his coffin.

The second service was still underway at the Methodist Church when Jane snuck in the door and quietly sat in an empty pew. Aaron stood in the center of the altar in a cream-colored frock and, without notes, was in the final minutes of his heartfelt sermon to the rapt congregation.

"And so, my friends, we can't escape from the things we fear…especially our greatest fear of death. But we can build a bridge between fear and faith. Whether it is our faith in Jesus Christ or the faith in each other that gives us the strength to carry on, in the end it is always faith that will persevere against the diabolical manipulation of fear." Aaron paused, reflecting on his words with purpose. "As I said at the beginning, the words of my wife's grandfather who endured great uncertainty… Who…" Aaron paused again, looked at Sara in the front pew and carefully formulated his words. "Who understood fear, but who rose above it and who stated so beautifully an affirmation that we can all repeat whenever we feel lost. 'I will be all right and one day I will die.' Death is inevitable. Loss is inevitable. I can believe the first part and it calms me to the inevitability of the second part. 'I will be all right...and one day I will die.'"

The words hit Jane as hard this time as they did when she first heard them in the backyard. As the music swelled and the congregation streamed out of the church, Jane made her way toward the altar.

"You joined us after all!" Aaron said to Jane with a friendly smile.

"Just for the dramatic finish. Can I talk to you privately?"

The cheerfulness dimmed. "I usually greet the congregation on the way out."

"They'll understand," Jane replied, moving Aaron toward the side door of the church.

He agreed to talk with her in his office. It was a small room with a bank of narrow windows. His desk was cluttered with books, Bibles and handwritten notes. A needlepoint plaque on the wall declared:

What I tell you in the darkness, speak in the light, and what you hear whispered in your ear, proclaim upon the housetops.
(Matthew 10:27)

"In the light," Jane re-read out loud. "Light a candle in the darkness," she murmured. "My light? Isn't that what your wife found out the name Liora means in Hebrew?"

Aaron's face froze momentarily. It was the same look he had in the backyard when Jane asked him about the red photo album. "Yes, that's right," he said, removing his ministerial frock and hanging it in the narrow closet.

Jane glanced around the office. She spotted an old book on the far right of his desk. At first she thought it was an antique Bible, but a closer look showed it was a battered edition of the Talmud. "Wow! You Methodists *are* a liberal bunch."

Aaron swallowed hard. "Oh, that's not because of Mollie's interest in Judaism. I read many tomes of various faiths."

"Really?" Jane took a closer look at the old book. "That

book is well-read."

"Yes, I picked it up in an old bookstore in Denver." Aaron casually moved toward the Talmud and covered it with a few pages on his desk. It was the same unconscious gestural extension of shame he had done with the red photo album when he slid it under the backyard bench.

"I guess that photo album of yours did the trick, eh?"

Again, he froze. "Excuse me?"

"You said the photo album gave you inspiration for your sermons when you were stuck."

He nodded and smiled, nerves still evident. "Ah, yes. It does."

"Well, it worked. You had the audience's full attention with those heartfelt words of Sara's grandfather. He must have been quite an influence on you."

"I only met him and his wife a couple times but…" Aaron appeared momentarily lost. "They were the epitome of courage." He looked at Jane. "But something tells me you're not here to discuss my wife's grandfather."

Jane smiled. "No. I'm here to discuss your daughter's boyfriend's father."

"Bailey?" Aaron licked his lips as his mouth grew dry.

"Yeah." She folded her arms in front of her. "I need to know what he said when he strong-armed you on the street and convinced you to get Mollie to break up with Jake."

Aaron sat down at his desk chair, flustered for a moment. "Ah, I can't… I can't reveal those conversations. They fall under the minister's privilege of privacy…"

"Oh, give me a break, Aaron. It was on the street, not in the church. Not in a confessional…"

"And it was between a minister and a…"

"Is he a member of this church?"

"No…"

"So, did he make a generous contribution to the church?"

"Of course not! It's nothing like that."

"Then it doesn't fall under the ministerial privilege." She leaned closer to him. "Aaron, if you push me, I can legally compel you to speak. We have a missing boy who you care a lot about, and there may be some germ of information in what Bailey said to you that could help us out."

"I cannot allow you to…"

"You know, Aaron, I hate to say it, but you're looking complicit in Jake's disappearance." Jane was lying through her teeth, but she sold a good threat when she had to.

His eyes widened, both in fear and slight anger. "My God! How can you suggest that?! He was like my son! I'd never hurt that boy!"

"Well, you're hurting him now! What in the hell did Bailey say to you?!"

Aaron looked at Jane with shame. "I…I…I can't do this." He got up and started to leave.

Even though his big-boned, tall body towered over Jane, she held him back. "Goddamnit, Aaron! Tell me what you…" Jane's cell phone rang. Checking the number, she saw it was Weyler. She answered quickly. "Yeah?"

"Jane, you need to get over here to Bo's office immediately. We've got another clue on the front door of Town Hall…and it's not good."

Jane hung up. "Fuck," she murmured.

"What is it?" Aaron asked, his voice shaking. "Is it Jake?"

She shook her head at him and headed out the door. "Let me give you some advice, Aaron. Take another read of your little needlepoint Bible saying on the wall over there…the one from Matthew? *What you hear whispered in your ear, proclaim upon the housetops?* I *will* persuade you to tell me what you know. Mark my words, *whatever* you're hiding, I'll uncover it."

CHAPTER 24

By the time Jane ran down the street and crossed to Town Hall, it was evident that whatever was waiting at the front door had attracted a small crowd. Bo and Weyler were doing their best to move the onlookers back from the scene as a deputy took photos of the front door. The crush of bodies made it impossible for Jane to see, but as she slid through the crowd and moved toward the deputy, the sickening display became visible.

A black-handled knife penetrated the door. Wrapped around the handle of the knife was a five-inch, blond ponytail secured with an elastic band. Three items were lodged in the steel point of the knife: a printed note, the Ace of Spades and a single Chesterfield cigarette. Pressed into the playing card was a clean, bloody thumb print.

Jane sidled closer to Weyler and spoke quietly. "Who found it?"

"Bo. He was coming in for a couple hours to pack up some boxes."

Jane saw movement near the window inside Bo's office. "Who's in his office?"

"He called Vi. She's more adept at operating the video playback of the new security system." Weyler nodded to the camera above the front door of the building.

Even from ten feet away, Jane could see that the camera wasn't positioned correctly. She turned to Bo who was holding back the growing crowd. "Who set up that camera?"

Already aggravated, Bo turned around quickly, took a quick look and turned back to the crowd. "One of the techie guys I guess."

The deputy announced to Bo that he was finished and Bo urged the crowd to disassemble. Weyler handed Bo a series of plastic evidence bags. After slipping on a pair of gloves, Bo carefully slid each of the five pieces into separate bags. They went into Bo's office where he immediately closed the blinds on his office window that faced the street. Vi was still checking the technical manual on how to operate the new video system while she fiddled with the buttons on the keyboard.

"Well, that was goddamn awkward!" Bo exclaimed as he lit up a fat cigar. "I haven't had to dodge this much awkwardness since old Miss Hyman named her cat *Buster* and then got him a subscription to *Cat Fancy* that they addressed to the cat: *Buster Hyman.* The postmistress damn near had a stroke." He turned to Vi. "Any luck with the video?"

"I'll have it up in a second," Vi replied.

Bo turned to Weyler. "How long is it gonna take for the Denver lab to match that bloody fingerprint?"

"Depends how backed up CBI is. Rush orders are about a two week turnaround."

"Two weeks?!" Bo yelled. "Jesus Christ, Beanie, I'm hangin' it up in a week!" The walls were clearly caving in around Bo.

"I'll make some calls," Weyler said in an assuring voice, "and see what I can do." He laid out the five plastic bags across Bo's cluttered desk. "We can send the knife too. The guy's been good about wearing gloves, but he could have slipped up."

"He's not slipping up," Jane offered.

"What in the hell are you yappin' about? He's dumb as a box of hair to stand under a goddamned camera and leave a clue!"

"He wants to be found. Every clue is getting more in our faces. He wants to make his mark publicly so that people gather 'round and see it! He wants to shock us. That's why he cut off Jake's ponytail and left the bloody fingerprint." She examined the fingerprint more closely, sizing it up with her own thumb. "Check out the size of this print. That's too big to belong to Jake. And look how clean it is." Jane considered the print a blaring cry for attention. It was if the kidnapper was screaming, "*Look at me! Discover who I am!*" He *had* to be in the system, she deduced, because there was no other reason to leave such a clear imprint of who you were. Perhaps, she wondered, there was something about discovering the owner of that print and what that might lead to. God, it was like one long scavenger hunt with the disturbing prize of a broken or buried boy at the end.

"Vi," Bo interrupted, "when you're done here, get me Trash Bag's file. I want to compare prints."

"Wait," Jane countered, "you can't eyeball a print..."

"The hell I can't! Back in the day, before we had all this bullshit technology, we eyeballed a whole helluva lot of things!"

"And sent innocent people to prison because of it! This is not a fucking good ol' boys' club!"

Bo's eyes flared with white-hot anger as he slammed his fat fist onto the desk. "Well, that ain't my fault!" There was something way too defensive in the way Bo said it. "If I want to eyeball Jordan Copeland's fuckin' fingerprint, I will damn well do it so back off, girl!"

"*Bo!*" Vi spoke up.

He turned to her. There was a meaningful pause from Vi. "What?" Bo asked, his voice tamed.

"I got it synched up."

Vi stood back with the remote control and hit the PLAY button. The full-color playback was crisp and clear. But it was also clear to Jane that whoever set up the camera outside the front door desperately needed direction. A figure of what appeared to be a male, somewhere between five foot eight and six foot three or so, wearing all black, including a hat and long coat, walked up to the front door and stabbed the knife into the door, securing the assortment of clues. The entire movement from start to finish was fast, taking less than six seconds. And his head was down the entire time; which made Jane assume that whoever left the clue knew that there was a camera above him.

Bo instructed Vi to play back the video repeatedly, painstakingly using the slow-motion feature that Vi discovered to try and detect anything that could identify the individual. But there was nothing. All they knew was that, based upon the video's timer, a possible male wearing all black approached Town Hall at 6:29 am that morning and stabbed a public clue into the front door.

Bo dropped into his chair, wincing a bit as his ass hit the cushion. "Shit," he uttered, taking a few nervous puffs on his cigar. "If that don't look exactly like the oilcloth duster Trash Bag wears around town! Goddamnit! Get me Trash Bag's file," he asked Vi in a quiet tone.

Jane furtively watched Vi through the open door as she pulled out Jordan's file, removed the front page, placed it in her top lefthand drawer and retrieved a sheet of paper from the center of her desk. When she returned to Bo's office, she handed him the file and turned to Jane, giving her the single sheet of paper from her desk.

"You asked for a copy of the front page material on our files?" Vi asked.

Bo's mouth dropped open. "What… *What…*"

Vi calmly turned to Bo. "Sergeant Perry asked me to make her a copy of our front page with all the formatted data regarding the contents of the file." Bo looked at her as if she'd lost her mind. "She thought maybe Denver PD might want to incorporate the system." Weyler shot Jane a suspicious glance. Vi turned back to Jane. "If there's anything you need from me, don't hesitate to ask." With that, Vi smiled and walked back to her desk.

The woman was such a wonderful liar, Jane decided she should work for the CIA. She said everything in such a smooth, casual and comfortable delivery that it was obvious to Jane she'd been spouting the same drivel for decades. It was the old adage that if you repeat a lie enough times, it becomes the truth to you and, therefore, it was easier to declare with conviction. Like Bo, she was out of that office in one week. But whatever artifice she and Bo shared would stay hidden forever.

Bo snorted and settled back into his chair, sucking a few more agitated puffs on the cigar. He opened his desk drawer and brought out a magnifying glass. Flipping open Jordan's file, he brought out the page with his prints and dragged the

Ace of Spades card with the bloody fingerprint toward him. Jane watched as he waved the magnifying glass between the two prints in an effort to find commonalities. Without looking up, he waved his cigar at the remaining clues spread out on the desk. "So what in the hell does all this crazy ass shit add up to? What do you make of that note, Beanie?"

Jane glanced at the white paper with black printed words. It read:

Who Ever Believes Bad Eventually Resolves

Weyler repeated it out loud. "Could be a warning of what he has planned for Jake. It almost has the tone of someone who is giving up…"

"*Whoever* is one word, not two," Jane interjected.

Bo tossed down the magnifying glass. "This ain't a goddamn English class!"

Jane was impervious to Bo's snide remark. "And if you're starting a sentence with the word *who*, you'd put a question mark at the end. There's not even a period there."

"Well, how 'bout if we correct it with a red pen and send it back to him?" Bo replied.

"She's got a point, Bo," Weyler gently issued.

"Aw, hell! Let's check the writin' on the Chesterfield cigarette! See if there's any spelling errors there! And what in the hell is he stickin' an ol' timey smoke on the pile?"

"It's certainly a new addition to the line of clues," Weyler said, looking at the imprint of CHESTERFIELD 101 closer on the single smoke.

Now it was Jane's turn to feel the walls caving in around her. Sequestered in her desk drawer back in the The Gardenia Room were twenty matching cousins to keep this deserted cigarette company. The realization that Jane had absconded with that dramatically laid out clue—including the crushed pack *and* antique ashtray—with only a few photos on her cell phone to preserve the moment, was beginning to concern her. The longer she waited to tell Weyler about it, the worse it would be. However, this was certainly not the appropriate venue to confess that particular sin.

"And the Ace of Spades?" Bo asked, directing the question to Weyler.

"I'll do some digging," Jane affirmed. "It could be a symbol or somebody's name for all we know."

"Ace?" Bo asked, somewhat incredulously.

"I don't know, Bo. Let me check it out," Jane said, irritation growing.

Bo shook his head. "What in the hell am I supposed to tell the Van Gordens? I guarantee you this is gonna be all over town before noon!"

"We need to tell them face-to-face before they hear it on the grapevine," Weyler advised Bo. "We should probably show them these clues just in case it triggers a possible connection for them that could help us."

Bo buried his balding head in his fat hand. "Shit. How in the hell do you show a parent their son's sliced off ponytail? *Good God!* This ain't right!" Bo was unexpectedly putting himself in the shoes of a tortured parent—something Jane hadn't seen him do prior to this. It was a rare moment of humanity from a guy who seemed sorely lacking in that department. Bo nailed another layer of toughness against his skin. "This mess has got Jordan Copeland's creepiness writtin' all over it and I'm sittin' back here with my hands tied because I don't have satisfactory evidence to arrest his paroled ass! He's fuckin' with our heads and laughin' the whole way. Well, I say, people like him who live in glass houses, shouldn't."

Jane waited but Bo was finished talking. "Shouldn't what?"

"Live in glass houses!" Bo replied, as if Jane were stupid.

The three arrived at the Van Gordens' house, sharing a single patrol car. Jane sat in the backseat and stayed silent while Weyler and Bo volleyed stories of their days in Denver together.

While the infamous break-in using the wrong address wasn't mentioned, he did use the "*Gomezing*" term a couple times in the discourse. The Van Gordens knew they were coming after Bo called them to say he needed to discuss "a recent development." Jane figured that they'd probably already heard exactly what it was, thanks to the gossip siren that tends to blare in most small towns.

Carol opened the enormous front door before Bo rang the bell. She looked pale and shell-shocked. She was dressed in a three-quarter sleeve faux leopard-skin tunic with black slacks and her hair was styled in the usual manner. But Jane noted something slightly off with the woman. Maybe it was the strands of blond hair that weren't as neatly plastered on her scalp or perhaps it was the ever-so-slight stain of food that remained on her pants. It was as if the burden was becoming too much. Errant cracks were forming along the surface of the mantle.

"Is he..." Carol started to ask just as Bailey swooped in behind her.

"We've gotten four calls already but they all tell us a different story! What in the fuck's going on?" Bailey bluntly asked. In contrast to his wife, Jane didn't note a single crack in Bailey's exterior. In fact, if anything, there was a sturdy reinforcement that buffered his arrogant resolve. Furthermore, his pressed stonewashed jeans and starched white shirt looked impeccable. There was nary a scuff on the heels of his Lucchese boots. This man was certainly not dressed for distress.

In the most respectful good ol' boy manner available, Bo asked to come into the house so he could show them the clues. Bailey impatiently waved the trio inside. It wasn't until Jane was inside the door that she realized Louise Van Gorden had been seated in her chrome wheelchair, just outside of view. She wore the same crisp button-front shirt, this time in black, while a heavy white blanket covered her lower body. Jane nodded toward her, but she got the impression that the old woman was more comfortable in the role of the hawkish observer. Louise studied Bo and Weyler with the same steely glare her son had learned, although Bailey hadn't mastered the precision in which Louise coolly delivered the glower.

Jane started to move toward Bailey's office on the left of the entry, but Louise's strategic positioning of the wheelchair prevented her movement.

"This way," Bailey gruffly instructed Jane and the men.

Jane let the others lead while she lagged behind, moving next to Bailey and closely tailed by his mother who maneuvered her chair slowly behind Jane. There was awkward silence until Jane quietly spoke to Bailey. "You got those allergies under control." He regarded her with a shadow of annoyance. "You're not stuffed up or flushed anymore."

"Right," he sneered as they settled in the spacious living room and Bailey closed the large double doors behind him. He turned to Bo. "Cut to chase, Bo. What in the fuck was on public display this morning at Town Hall?!"

Bo proceeded to lay out the first of four plastic evidence bags on the burl wood table. First came the knife with Jake's severed ponytail. Jane stood back from the group, taking in the scene and casually observing the reactions from each family member. Louise's countenance never changed. Bailey curled his lip. Carol covered her pale face and turned away, clearly distraught. *Jesus,* Jane thought, looking at Bailey and Louise. *It's one of the goddamned identifying aspects that represents Jake,* short of sending his fedora or sending a chunk of skin that displayed the matching dragonfly tattoo he and Mollie shared. Of the three family members, Carol was the only one emotionally affected by the ponytail.

"Carol..." Louise said in a low, controlled gravelly voice that sounded like a warning. Almost robotically, Carol wiped her tears and turned back to the burl table. "Focus..." Louise instructed, almost as if she was the programmer and Carol was her little chip.

Bo laid the evidence bag with the oddly worded note, *Who*

Ever Believes Bad Eventually Resolves, next to the knife and ponytail. Again, Jane watched them. Bailey screwed up his face,
clearly not understanding the words. There was a blank stare
from Carol and the same stoic glance from Louise.

Bo stepped forward and laid down the bag with the cigarette in it. "It says *Chesterfield* on it," Bo advised the family.

Bailey's eyes narrowed. Carol looked blank. Jane caught a
subtle flutter in Louise's eyes.

"Finally this," Bo reluctantly said, "and there's blood on this
one." He set down the bag holding the Ace of Spades with the
bloody fingerprint. "We're sending this to Denver, along with
the knife. We don't think that's Jake's blood. I want you to know
that. We think the kidnapper did it to give us a clear identifying
mark."

Carol looked repulsed by the bloody print but it was the
reaction of both Louise and Bailey that struck Jane the hardest.
Before Bo even mentioned anything about blood, Louise and
Bailey, almost in unison, showed pinpointed wrath in their eyes.
Jane casually turned to Weyler to see if he was picking up any of
this odd behavior, but he was more focused on the clues.

Bailey turned around, his nostrils flaring. He walked a few
feet away from the group, grabbed a heavy crystal vase on a side
table and hurled it across the living room toward the large stone
fireplace. "Fuck him!" The vase smashed into thousands of pieces. Carol winced and moved toward Weyler. "*Fuck him!*" Bailey
screamed again, his voice more high pitched than normal. It
was an audio cue for Jane that often signaled fear mixed with
unbridled rage.

"Bailey!" Louise shouted in a quick command. "Get a hold
of yourself!" Bailey turned to his mother and they exchanged a
meaningful glance. Louise's grey face carried malice, but Jane
determined that it wasn't cast toward her son. Bailey stormed
out of the living room through the double doors and, leaving
them open, walked outside. They could hear his angry screams
of "*Fuck him, fuck him, fuck him!*" Louise wheeled herself closer

to the group. "You'll have to excuse my son," she announced, her thin lips carving out each word with a knife of contained hatred as she stared at the clues on the table. "He hasn't learned to control himself properly."

"It's completely understandable, Mrs. Van Gorden," Bo allowed.

"No, it's not!" Louise spat back. "A man who cannot control his impulses loses everything!" The words echoed like a stern pronouncement to Jane. "Which brings me to Jordan Copeland. Why in the hell has that man not been arrested?! He is clearly involved in some way!"

"It's not clear at all, ma'am," Jane interrupted, her tone edgy. Bo shot her a look of contempt.

"Of course, it is!" Louise yelled back. "Do your fucking job and arrest him!"

Bo moved between Louise and Jane, obviously creating a barrier between them. "Mrs. Van Gorden, you have my word we are working like hell on your grandson's case every damn day of the week. If Trash…" Bo caught himself. "…Jordan Copeland is linked, we *will* arrest him. All of us want nothin' more than to find who did this and get your grandson home safely."

"Jake is dead!" Louise screamed. A black aura enfolded the old lady. Her eyes spit venom toward Bo. "Wake up, you idiot!"

Bo looked as if he was about to coldcock the dying bitch. Instead, he took a hard breath and shut up.

"And you?!" Louise continued, leaning forward and addressing Jane. "You're not doing shit, except to cause problems! Arrest the damn Jew or whatever the hell he is and let's get this over with!" Carol choked on her tears and ran from the room, disappearing into the kitchen. Louise glanced at Carol with disdain. "Goddamnit! What in the fuck is happening to people?!" Her breathing became labored.

Bo kneeled down to placate her as Weyler walked around and sat on the couch to get closer to the woman. She wasn't interested in their pandering, but she also wasn't able to breathe easily so her fight was temporarily diminished.

Jane took the opportunity to covertly sneak out of the room and into the kitchen. There, she found Carol vomiting into the kitchen sink as waves of sobbing heaved her body forward. Jane wasn't known for playing the comforting cop role, but she knew this was no act on Carol's part; the woman was wracked with grief and heartbreak. Jane quietly approached her and gently laid her palm on her back.

Carol jumped, not expecting anyone to be in the room. "Oh, my God!" Carol yelped, quickly wiping her mouth and turning on the faucet, whisking the vomit down the drain. "I'm sorry. I'm sorry!"

"For God's sake, Carol. It's all right."

"No, no! I shouldn't let it affect me like this. She's right! I should have more control." She started to rock back and forth against the rim of the sink. "I need to focus, focus, focus..."

Jane regarded Carol with an apprehensive stare. It seemed the woman was losing her mind in front of Jane. "Carol," Jane said softly, almost in a whisper, "was something delivered here from the kidnapper...something that you didn't give us?"

Tears poured down Carol's face as she continued to rock back and forth. "I've got to focus, focus, focus..."

"Carol?" Jane said, slightly stressed. "You can tell me and I'll keep it a secret." Carol turned to Jane with a frightening daze. "*I'll keep it a secret.*" Carol studied Jane in her stupor. "Is it the engraved silver cigarette case in Bailey's office? The one with the paper clips in it?" Carol swallowed hard, a sign to Jane that something about that silver case triggered fear. "Is that what the kidnapper delivered?" Carol shook her head slightly. "Okay," Jane said, keeping her voice low and modulated. "Then what was it?"

"Carol!" Louise yelled from the living room. "What are you doing?!"

Carol turned toward Louise's voice in fear.

Jane gently touched her tear-stained face, bringing her

focal point back to Jane. "Carol? Tell me what they delivered here..."

"*Carol! Come here! Now!*" Louise screamed.

Carol stared at Jane, almost hypnotized. In an obvious directive, Carol looked off to the side toward the left of the sink where a partially filled, clear trash bag was propped against the cabinet. "Over there?" Jane asked.

Carol nodded almost imperceptibly, but it was enough of an acknowledgment for Jane. Still disconnected, Carol wiped the tears from her cheeks and headed out of the kitchen toward Louise's screaming voice.

Jane dove toward the trash bag, its contents opaquely exposed through the plastic, and picked it up. She quickly relocated herself in the large pantry several feet from the sink, closing the louvered doors behind her and opened the trash bag. She heard heavy footsteps head into the kitchen. Looking through the wooden slats on the door, she saw Bo.

"Jane?" he gruffly said. She held her breath and stayed still. "Goddamnit!" he growled, exiting the kitchen and moving back into the house.

With only the filtered light from the outside windows, Jane opened the bag of trash. There were several discarded soup cans and kitchen scraps, but she recognized the empty box and packing materials immediately. They were identical to what she'd spied in the corner of Bailey's office; the same corner Carol crept backward toward when Jane questioned her. Jane didn't realize it then, but she now knew that Carol was physically backing up into a clue. It was at once covering it up, but also pointing it out to anyone with eyes to see the way we unconsciously reveal our deceptions. Jane ripped the large address label off the box. It simply said *BAWY!*, but this time, with an exclamation point. The same uncancelled Packard stamp was affixed to the label—a single stamp to mail a large box that was hand-delivered. Okay, Jane figured, now the Packard stamp was germane to the other clues and worthy of closer inspection.

Jane secured the address label in her jacket pocket and lifted the box out of the bag, taking care to be as quiet as possible. It seemed heavier than it should for a box that just held packing material. She removed the reams of bubble wrap and paper and touched something soft and pliable. Jane lifted the item closer to the louvered door. It was a well-worn, child's teddy bear, measuring about eight inches tall and wearing a faded blue jumper. The front of the bear's jumper was crusted with an old, brown and white stain. Jane sniffed it. Her highly tuned sensory mechanism detected a sour stench, akin to vomit or urine.

"Jane?" Weyler called out from the entry hall.

Jane quickly wrapped the stuffed bear in a piece of packing paper and wedged it under her leather jacket, buttoning her jacket around it. She crammed the contents back into the trash bag, carefully opened the pantry and placed the bag where she found it. Walking into the entry hall, she found Weyler, Bo, Carol and Louise waiting. "I had to use the bathroom," Jane offered. Carol looked at Jane with abject fear while Louise regarded her with heightened suspicion.

"Mr. Van Gorden had to take a business call, so he won't be seeing us out." Weyler informed Jane.

Jane's antenna immediately perked up. If the cash drop occurred the day before at the remote strip club, was this the call to pick up Jake's body? She nodded and followed Weyler and Bo out to the patrol car. It wasn't until they were almost back to town that Jane recalled the non-sequitur clue that had fueled her suspicion regarding the Van Gordens holding something back from them. Now the ostensibly misspelled clue made sense:

I BEARED MY SOUL AND STILL YOU IGNORE ME???

CHAPTER 25

Jane tried to get Weyler's attention when they returned to town, but Bo was monopolizing his time. She needed to show him the teddy bear and confess her forensic sin of swiping the Chesterfield cigarette evidence from the forested crime scene. But it would have to wait until they could talk privately.

She rushed up the stairs of the B&B, removed her jacket and laid the teddy bear on the table. Examining it, she noted that a portion of stuffing had fallen out of the back seam and been re-sewn several times with an unsightly whipstitch. The bear's face looked old-fashioned; certainly not in the style of teddy bears that had been manufactured in the last twenty years. The size of the bear was curious in that it wasn't the typical larger size that was relegated to being displayed on a bed but, rather, small enough to be carried around as a toy for a youngster. It certainly was well worn and, possibly, well loved. The right ear was half gone and the left arm of the bear was visibly battered, leading Jane to believe that whoever owned this bear carried it by its arm.

The more Jane inspected the stuffed animal, the more she believed it was a source of security for its owner. Jane couldn't ignore the swath of what she now believed to be vomit across the front of the bear's blue jumper. This bear had been everywhere with its owner, through sickness and in health. She also understood that this clue had serious meaning. Otherwise, the Van Gordens wouldn't have kept it from law enforcement. If Jane's memory served, it would have been after the receipt of the bear that they unexplainably retracted their reward offer. The stuffed animal must have caused quite a visceral reaction for them to do such a thing. In keeping with all things clandestine, they opted to cram it into the trash, bury it deeply and will it from their consciousness.

She debated where to hide the missing clue and opted for the most reliable location—under the bed. Jane touched the edge of the photo album as she placed the bear and removed the large book. Sitting on the edge of the bed, she opened it and found a series of heavy black cardboard pages filled with glued family photos of both Sara and Aaron from their respective childhood pictorials. Jane skimmed through the dizzying assortment of both black-and-white and color shots. Someone had written the corresponding years at the top of each page. Jane skipped forward in the book, finding a section someone called *The Good Ol' Days*. The date at the top read *1988*. The first page was a collection of Polaroid prints showing Sara and Aaron in the first blush of love, arms entwined around each other and looking lovingly at each other. Sara was around nineteen and Aaron in his mid-twenties. He looked decidedly like a hippie with his long hair down his back and an unkempt beard and mustache. Sara, in turn, shared the groovy vibe with her long hair parted in the middle and two braids, each secured with a small feather and string. Jane had to smile, realizing that sometimes the most religious people started out as free spirits.

Jane turned the page. At first, it didn't register. But she stared at the series of Polaroids on the page and the next page and the one after that. She looked even closer at the details in the photos and realized that, *yes*, she *was* seeing what she thought she was seeing. Outside, she heard the sound of a car roll into the driveway. She leapt toward the side window and saw Aaron and Sara in his sedan. Jane slid the photo album into her satchel and ran down the stairs and out the front door. Aaron was still retrieving items from the backseat when she met Sara.

"Hey, there," Jane replied.

"Well, that's a coincidence. Mollie's got a T-shirt just like that!" Sara said, staring at the *I LIKE BOYZ* shirt.

Jane looked down, completely forgetting she was wearing the ridiculous outfit. Nevertheless, it wasn't going to thwart her present objective. Sara excused herself and walked inside while Aaron continued to avoid eye contact with Jane. She sauntered around the car to the driver's side where Aaron was still seated.

"You know, even though it's Sunday, I'm still on duty. And the law says that if I see illegal activity, even when I'm technically off the clock, I can make an arrest or issue a ticket." Jane was being honest, however, she hadn't issued a ticket to a citizen since she got off patrol duty as a rookie over fifteen years ago.

Aaron looked at her with uncertainty. "What are you talking about?"

"Where do I start, Aaron? I noticed your front headlight is busted. You also came to a *sushi stop* at the corner..."

"A *sushi stop*?"

"A California Roll? You didn't stop at the stop sign."

"I didn't?"

"Not completely. Then, there's the LTO..."

Aaron grew suspicious. "LTO?"

"Lying To an Officer. Now, as far as the B&B, the fire exits are not clearly marked and the smoke detector doesn't seem to be working in my room. I can come up with a bunch of other code violations in no time."

"This is not going to work." He got out of the car and closed the door. "I told you what Bailey said to me was confidential. I have ministerial privilege."

"And I have your little red book of *inspiration*." Jane withdrew the album from her satchel

Aaron's face turned ashen. His pupils looked like giant black orbs. "Holy shit."

Jane nodded. "Holy shit, indeed, preacher."

He glanced toward the B&B and then out to the street. "Let's walk," he told her, motioning toward the sidewalk.

They turned left outside the gate and walked in silence for fifty feet.

"Give me the album, Detective."

"Give me the information I asked you for."

"Detective..."

Jane stopped. "Or I will tell everyone in your congregation that before you were God-fearing Christians you liked to take

Polaroids of each other, posing provocatively...while naked and roaming through your exceptionally lush garden of marijuana."

Aaron stopped in his tracks and looked at Jane. It was as if he waiting for more. "That's what you got, huh?"

"I think they'll be especially interested in the close-up shots of you covering your penis with a pot leaf and Sara exposing that classic rose tattoo she had inked under her pubic hair." Jane realized at that moment that Mollie just happened to chose a few inches above her pubic bone for her dragonfly tattoo. It was as if the kid instinctively copied the memory of her mother's youthful expression.

Aaron buried his face in his hand. "Good Lord."

"Lord's not gonna get you out of this one, Aaron."

"You don't understand, Detective..." His eyes pleaded. "Please give me the album." With that, Aaron attempted to snatch the album out of Jane's hand. But Jane held onto it firmly. "For God's sake, give it to me!" His sheer size won the battle, but as he recovered the book, three of the older black-and-white prints of Sara's grandfather were dislodged from the album. "No!" he yelled, his eyes panicked.

Jane touched her Glock, never intending to bring it out of the holster. "Stand back, Aaron."

"*Please.* I beg you. Don't do this." He was shaking as his worst fear was coming to fruition.

Jane kneeled down, keeping an eye on him, and picked up the photos. She backed up several feet to gain more distance. He was crumbling emotionally before her. She looked at the photos. One showed Sara's grandfather and his wife wearing bathing suits and posing at the beach. The other two were shots of the old man from the waist up. He was waving at the camera in both shots, his left arm raised. The tattoo on his left forearm was easy to see but it wasn't from the military or his wife's name. It was a series of numbers. Jane looked up at Aaron. "He said 'I will be all right and one day I will die.' You said he had great courage and that he overcame fear." Aaron nodded, tears falling down his face. "How many years was he in the camp?"

"Two," Aaron said softly.

"Is that where he met his wife?"

"No. They met and married in Israel a few months after the end of the war. That's where Sara's mother was born. Shortly afterward, they relocated to the United States."

"So, you married a Jewish woman who converted."

Aaron took a deep breath. "We both converted."

Jane looked at the photo. "Was being Jewish too dangerous?"

"It's hard to explain. We felt greater serenity with the Christian faith. But we weren't afraid of being Jews."

"Then why not acknowledge it? It's your blood."

Aaron dropped his head. "I know. Both of our parents downplayed their Jewish past. You know? The persecution complex? Don't advertise it. Blend in."

"And yet, the more you bury something...the more you suppress who you are...the more it finds a way to the surface..." Jane realized she sounded a little too much like Jordan.

"Yes. I know what you mean."

"Mollie..."

He looked up at Jane. "Exactly. Her sudden interest in the Jewish faith was startling, to say the least. We thought it was just a fad but it's not."

Jane looked at the photo of Sara's grandfather and his wife. "Your last name...Green? Did you change it?"

"Yes. My family name is Greenfeld. I changed it long before I was baptized. My family was okay with it. They understood the stigma."

"Right. They agreed to bury it."

"Yes." Aaron looked off to the side. "Names are a funny thing, though." He shook his head. "No matter how much you run from a name, it comes back to haunt you."

Jane stared at him. "What do you mean by *haunt*?"

"Sara's grandmother? She went by Lee. But her given name was Liora."

Jane wasn't sure she heard him at first. "Mollie must have heard the name mentioned…"

"No, I assure you, she did not. We rarely referred to her great-grandmother by name except to call her *Nana*. She may have heard us call her *Lee*, but it was usually *Nana*. It was as if she heard the name through osmosis. I have no explanation for it."

"Osmosis." Jane quietly pondered the notion. *The dead are following me.* That's what Jake posted on the secret revelations website. To not acknowledge them was to incur their wrath…a wrath that could only be resolved by speaking their name in the light. "You have to tell Mollie the truth."

"That her last name is really Greenfeld and her great-grandmother's name was Liora? That she's a full-blooded Jew by birth? I'm the minister of the Methodist Church, Detective. I have a good following and I have good Christian people who trust me. If we reveal ourselves to Mollie, we will have to reveal ourselves to everyone else in this town because I will not allow my child to carry a secret like that on her shoulders."

"But you and Sara will carry it."

"It's our burden."

"It doesn't have to be. And anyway, on some level, Mollie already knows."

Aaron looked stunned. "Has she said something to you?"

"No. She knows in her heart. And if you keep lying to her, she's not going to be able to rectify what she feels. Talk about a mind-fuck." Now Jane was really starting to channel Jordan Copeland. "Is the burden of the secret equal to the burden of the truth?"

"Think of the ramifications of telling the truth, Detective…"

"Oh, hell, Aaron. Haven't you ever heard of *spin*? You could spin this to your benefit." She assumed the voice of a PR guru. "The man who only accepted the Old Testament embraces the New Testament and, like the book of Revelations, he now discloses to his flock things that were only previously whispered in the dark." She let the idea sink in. "Jesus, Aaron. Don't be a *shmuck*. This could be *gelt*...gold."

Aaron couldn't help but smile at Jane's words. She handed him the photos and he replaced them in the album. "Are you going to spread this around town?"

"What kind of a person do you think I am?"

Aaron regarded Jane with pensive eyes. "I think you're a good woman who just wants to know the truth."

"Thank you. So, are you going to tell me the truth about what Bailey said to you?"

Aaron struggled. "This has to be off the record." Jane reluctantly nodded. "You know I love Jake..."

"Yeah. He's like your son. *What did Bailey say, Aaron?*"

"It was in Mollie's best interest that they break up. There was no future and I didn't want her to get hurt."

"Why would she get hurt?"

"Because Jake is gay."

Jane let the information settle. "This is what Bailey told you?"

Aaron nodded. "He said he...caught him...looking at gay porn on his computer and that, when he confronted Jake about it, the boy didn't deny it. In fact, he said he was already hooking up with other homosexual boys he'd met on the Internet..."

"Hooking up how? He doesn't have a car and only a learner's permit."

"I asked the same question. Bailey said Jake was sneaking out at night. He fashioned some kind of rope apparatus off his bedroom deck. He'd steal one of his dad's cars and meet these guys. Bailey was...how can I say it...*disgusted* doesn't even come close to his reaction. He described in very graphic detail the kind of stuff that he found on these gay porn sites...I just...I just couldn't allow my daughter in good conscience to continue associating with Jake. These boys he's meeting on the Internet... they could be drug addicts or perverts. It's a dangerous world out there, Detective. You know that too damn well. In God's name, why would I put my daughter in harm's way?"

"I understand. You had no choice."

Aaron shook his head in dismay. "I think my fears were validated by what happened to Jake."

"What do you mean?"

"He struggled with being gay and after his dad found out about it, he was humiliated. But the damage had already been done. He went to the bridge to kill himself, but some freak who he attracted from an Internet chat room caught up with him and..." Aaron struggled. "And murdered him."

"That's what you think happened?"

"I do. But I would never say a word of that to Mollie."

Jane realized that when you don't have all the facts, evidence or clues, it's easy to jump to erroneous conclusions. With only the titillating elements to draw upon, it was simple to create what seemed like the most viable and obvious outcome. But Aaron didn't have the benefit of a bevy of clues that told a different story—a story that was told by someone who was highly intelligent and who wanted to be caught. Aaron didn't have the knowledge that the Van Gordens held back a clue. He didn't follow Bailey to a seedy strip club and watch a payoff being made. He didn't suffer through a disturbing one-on-one conversation with Louise Van Gorden and walk away from it feeling filthy. There were too many questions and not enough answers to float a possible conclusion regarding Jake's fate.

They parted, with Jane retreating to her room. She checked her cell phone in hopes of finding a voicemail from Candy at the strip club. It was reasonable to believe that if Bailey was on the phone with his connection when they were leaving his house, he most likely would be at the club by now. Of course, it was Sunday and it could be Miss Cane's day off to rest, wash her thongs and polish her tassels.

Jane hung the teddy bear by its one good ear on the clothesline in its appropriate timeline slot. She turned to the address label with the mysterious *BAWY!* and the reoccurring twenty-five-cent Packard postage stamp. She'd already considered the relevance of the stamp as it was the answer to the cryptic riddle set forth by the kidnapper early on. A quick check on Jane's computer showed that the stamp was issued in 1988 as part of an edition featuring old cars. Either the kidnapper owned the stamp in a collection or he bought it online, much like he probably bought the classic pack of Chesterfield 101 cigarettes. But why the Packard?

Jane found the third clue—the one with the magazine cutout of the young boy with the red cap holding out his arm—and looked at the envelope it came in with the uncancelled Packard stamp. She hadn't noticed it before this, but the lower edge of the stamp on the envelope was slightly separated from the envelope. Wedging her fingernail under the stamp, it easily peeled off the paper. Underneath were the printed words: HELP ME!

"Shit," Jane mumbled as she grabbed the address label she retrieved from the box that held the bear and peeled off that Packard stamp. There were five extremely small words printed under the stamp: TELL HER WHAT YOU SAW! Jane threw the label on the desk as an electric shock coursed up her spine. She heard Weyler's footsteps outside in the hallway and swung the door open, motioning him to come into her room. "Look at this!" she said nervously, showing him the two pleading statements.

"Jesus," Weyler said, examining the writing carefully. "Why would he hide them under the Packard?"

"Maybe he drives a Packard and he's saying these statements inside the Packard?"

"That's a stretch."

"No, I don't think it is. You have to think like this guy. He's under the Packard? In the Packard? I'm not sure. But these words are connected to the Packard."

"So, this black vehicle that the woman saw on the bridge before Jake went missing was a Packard? Don't you think she'd mention something about the car being rather old?"

"If she doesn't know cars, then maybe not," Jane offered.

"Is this Jake's writing? If a guy in a Packard kidnapped him, is he writing *Help me* and *Tell her what you saw!* in hopes that we're going to peel off the stamp? That's a little out there, don't you think?"

"If he's being held captive and at the point of death, why would he risk that?"

"Maybe because he's not being held against his will." Weyler took a seat on the desk chair.

"So the kidnapper wrote it," Jane deduced.

"Why would the kidnapper write *Help me* and *Tell her what you saw!* Jane, this is starting to seem like something Jake's involved with."

It seemed appropriate at that moment to divulge what Aaron told Jane about Jake. She relayed the information to Weyler in a matter-of-fact tone.

"Oh, for Chrissake. Well, that might explain why his dad erased his computer, including all the current emails and website history. If Jake visited gay chat rooms or websites, he'd most likely be getting daily spam from those sites to this day. Maybe his dad didn't want to have his son further humiliated?"

"I don't think Bailey gives a shit about his son. I think whatever Bailey Van Gorden covers up, he does so for Bailey Van Gorden! When he saw the Ace of Spades card with the bloody fingerprint, he screamed 'Fuck him!' Who was he talking about? Jordan or Jake? Do you remember the first time we met the Van Gordens? Bailey was telling us to investigate Jordan but he was also focused on Jake. As an aside, Bailey said, "*Little shit*." I told you then that I thought Bailey was referring to his own son and *not* Jordan. Just the same way that I think he was thinking of Jake when he screamed, 'Fuck him' today! There's no love lost there!"

Weyler nodded in agreement. "If Bailey's disgusted by Jake's homosexuality, he might feel that Jake got whatever he had coming to him if he was hooking up with guys on the Internet…"

Jane cogitated. "But then, what has the Ace of Spades got to do with anything? Bailey and Louise clearly reacted to the card *before* they realized there was a bloody fingerprint on it!"

"Are you positive?"

"I was watching those two like a hawk. I *am* sure!"

"What does the Ace of Spades represent?"

"The number *one* or *eleven*."

"There's got to be a deeper meaning."

"I don't get the sense that Bailey and Louise are deep thinkers."

"Wait a second. Isn't the Ace of Spades known as the Death Card? I recall hearing how the Ace of Spades was laid on the bodies of Vietnamese killed by U.S. soldiers during the war. Soldiers would cover the ground with the Ace of Spades as a calling card of death. It was used as psychological warfare."

Weyler's idea of *psychological warfare* rang true to Jane. In her mind, all the clues—as bizarre and unconnected as they might appear—were all meant to trigger a psychological schism. Still, the revelation that Jake was gay still gnawed on Jane. "If Bailey is personally disgusted by his son's homosexuality, it doesn't compute that he's going to take the time to confront Aaron about his son's gay liaisons without knowing where that information is going to end up. In my opinion, it was done purposely to *humiliate* Jake. Bailey could give a shit about Mollie and her feelings. Mollie said Bailey hardly ever talked to her when she was at their house." Jane contemplated further. "No, this has got massive manipulation written all over it."

"If Jake's gay, this could turn the case in an entirely different direction."

The light bulb came on. "Exactly. I gleaned the information *off the record* from Aaron. If I breech that trust, it's Aaron who gets hurt for being a minister who breeched a confidence. *Then*, Jake is publicly humiliated once the information streams through town. We're sent on a gay trail to who knows where to track down people we have no record of because Bailey conveniently erased the alleged emails and websites. And while that's all going on, the Van Gordens and whatever they're hiding is tossed to the side while we chase our tails. It's *brilliant evil.*"

"But it can't be ignored, Jane."

"Hang on…" Jane suddenly recalled a comment Bailey made during their first meeting. "You know, a guy can't have it both ways. When we first talked to Bailey and I suggested that Jake may have met a predator online, he was adamant that Jake didn't meet anyone online and then he was quick to add that the predator was Jordan Copeland!" She shook her head. "Damn! This is where understanding people is so critical. You can't set the dominos in a clear direction if the first domino is a lie. Supposedly, Bailey told Aaron his son was gay to protect Jake. But the truth is he doesn't give a shit about Jake. So everything else that follows after that lie is corrupted and meant to confuse the real issue."

"Why would a father tell another man that his son is gay if he's not gay?"

"I don't know. But there's a lot of things about Bailey I don't know." She turned to Weyler with a smug look. "Except for one thing…" Jane crossed to the clothesline and carefully removed the stuffed bear. "I told you they were holding something back from us." He sat in stunned silence as Jane detailed her tense encounter with Carol in the kitchen and how Carol slyly directed Jane to the missing clue. "You can't tell Bo about this one," Jane advised, "because he'll want to talk to the family about it and that's going to put Carol in one helluva spot. Please trust me on this one."

Weyler nodded. "I'll say nothing for now. But if things shift, I'll have no choice."

Jane swallowed hard. "There's one more thing I have to show you." Walking to the desk, she slid out the top drawer, removed the ashtray and cigarette pack and dumped the twenty Chesterfield 101 cigarettes on the desk. She gently removed the remaining Chesterfield off the clothesline and tossed into the pile. Jane took a seat on the end of the bed and confessed what she'd done. Just to make sure he didn't think she totally sabotaged the original crime scene, she showed him the photo of the cigarette layout in the woods that she captured on her cell phone camera. After a heartfelt *mea culpa*, she could see that Weyler was not thrilled. "Hey, I was pissed-off at Bo for being an asshole. I shouldn't have done it, but there it is and you can take it to him and tell him what happened."

Weyler scooped the cigarettes into a pile. "That should go over well," he said dryly. "The DNA's completely compromised."

"They were lying in the snow. It was already compromised."

"I'll see if I can sell that excuse," he said with an edge as he got up with the evidence in hand. "Anything else pertinent to this case that I need to know about?"

Jane figured she was already in enough trouble, it was time to give away the farm. She told Weyler how she followed Bailey to a strip club and watched him hand over an envelope of cash to another man and then disappear.

"Good Christ Almighty, Jane!" Weyler said, his voice rising. "When were you planning on telling me Bailey was working a back end deal?!"

"Soon?" Jane tried to ameliorate the news by informing him of her stripper contact, Mo, Candy Cane, and that she promised to call Jane if Bailey returned.

"And you really think she's going to call you?"

"I gave her a hundred bucks to buy a new sweater. She seemed impressed enough to return the favor."

"Jesus, Jane. Have you ever followed any of the rules or gone by the book?"

"I'm sure I have," she replied, having a difficult time coming up with an example.

"You understand that I've got to tell Bo."

"He won't know what to do with the information. He'll either ignore it because it came from me, or he'll confront Bailey in his erratic manner which will likely compromise the entire deal that Bailey's got set up. Either way, the whole thing will blow up."

"I still have to tell him, Jane."

Jane nodded. But inside, she thought, *Not if I can get there first.*

CHAPTER 26

After reading the thin stack of emails Mollie had given her from Jake, Jane grabbed Jake's sketchpad and darted downstairs. Sara and Aaron were sitting in the backyard. Jane knocked on Mollie's bedroom door and tried to open it but it was locked.

"Who is it?!" Mollie yelled with teenage attitude.

"It's Jane! Open up!"

Mollie opened the door. "Nice shirt. Where do you shop?"

"Let me in."

"I'm doing prayers."

"It's Sunday. Friday evening to Saturday evening is *your* Sabbath…unless of course, you're jumping back into the Christian saddle?"

"I can do prayers any day of the week," Mollie said with her back up.

"Are you going to let me in?"

She looked at Jane's Glock. "Are you gonna shoot me if I don't?"

"Not fatally," Jane replied, stone-faced.

When it came to *chutzpah* and banter, the kid had met her Gentile match. "Fine!"

Jane closed the door behind her. "I was reading these emails you printed off. This is really the extent of them?"

"Yeah. Jake didn't spend a lot of time on the computer or the phone. He liked talking to people face-to-face."

Jane had already had this confirmed by Hank. She considered how that information could break either way for Bailey's allegations. If Jake didn't like to spend time on the computer, maybe he wasn't obsessing with gay porn. But on the other hand, if he liked one-on-one encounters and he was desperately lonely at home, maybe he was using the Internet to hook up and attain that up close and personal contact with strangers. "Okay..." Jane located the only email that intrigued her. "What did he mean when he wrote you on March 8th, *I'm sorry about last night. It's my fault, not yours. Please don't think less of me...*"

Mollie snapped the pages out of Jane's hands and threw them on her bed. "Shut up!"

"You saying that to me or Jake?"

"I told you that it's none of your damn business!"

"Hey, Liora?" She started to back the girl toward her bed. "I don't know if you're coming down off a catnip high, but you *are* going to tell me what in the hell he meant by that and you're going to tell me *now!*"

Jane had a way of intimidating some people and Mollie was one of those people. "Okay, okay." She sat on her bed, sliding a large pillow on her lap for security. "I swear to God if you tell my dad..."

"Oh, shit, I'm getting so tired of this. *Tell me what you know!*"

"He was referring in the email to when he snuck out of his bedroom and down the rope—which I'm *sure* you've already discovered—and over to my room." She nodded to a corner window. "He tapped on the glass and he crawled in."

"Okay..."

"We usually just sat up at night and talked until early morning. Sometimes, we'd kiss, but that was it."

"But not that night."

Mollie was clearly not comfortable relaying the information. "He showed up and he was all *ferklempt*...just an emotional mess. I tried to calm him down but he was like crazy, you know? He said he had a huge fight with his dad…I guess it was the absolute worst but he wouldn't tell me what it was about. And then, out of nowhere, he crawls on top of me and I'm like, damn, don't be a *shlemiel*! But then I'm kinda liking it too." She smiled softly, embarrassed. "We start to make out like we never have before and I'm thinking, *Oi*! Where is this leading? That's when he pulls out his *shmeckle*."

"*Shmeckle*?"

Mollie was really embarrassed now. "You know? His… dick. I'd never seen it before. I swear to *Hashem, never*! But I just wasn't ready to do it. I want everything to be perfect for my first time. Rose petals, candles…"

"The age of consent," Jane quickly added, which elicited a roll of the eyes from Mollie. "Hey! You're fifteen, for God's sake. You shouldn't be having sex!"

"*And we didn't*! He couldn't get his *petseleh* up! But it wasn't like he didn't keep trying. *Gloib mir*, he kept trying! But what a *klutz*! No matter how much he wanted to *schtup*, it wasn't happening that night." Mollie looked up at Jane. "He couldn't stop apologizing and I was like, 'It's no big deal.' Geez, all the frenzied groping and this off-the-wall need to prove himself." She shook her head. "But there was no consoling him. He left and I didn't hear from him until I got that email telling me it wasn't my fault, it was *his*."

"What do you think he meant by that?" Mollie started to speak but held back. "What were you going to say?" Jane probed.

"That he's a *faygala*," she said softly as if saying it too loudly would make it true. She realized Jane needed a translation. "Gay."

"Why?"

"I don't know… He's been wearing those old time Palm Beach shirts and fedoras… So, either he's gay or he's secretly Jewish."

Jane glanced at Mollie and thought, *Kid, if you only knew the truth*. "Clothing aside, you're assuming he's gay because he can't get his pecker up?"

She shrugged her shoulders. "Well…yeah…"

"Did you ever think that when a guy is stressed or emotionally distraught, it sometimes affects the rate of ascent down there?"

"I thought guys were always ready to go…even when they're asleep."

"You're fifteen. You don't know everything."

"So, what was he stressed about?"

"The fight he had with his dad." Jane paced the small bedroom. Over the last fifteen months, she'd spent substantial time meditating about life, and she'd come up with a few enlightened observations. One of those involved the root of our primal self and the instinctive reason why we do what we do. Jane broke it down to two causes—survival or salvation. We're either looking to survive on this plane or seeking the promise of salvation on the next one. Some people do both. But in the end, our modus operandi is still centered on the preservation of the *self* now or the *self* after death.

When the *self* is threatened or compromised—usually involving its survival—it acts out in a parallel primitive manner. If a man is threatened by his wife's male admirers, he might physically assault them because his own survival and identity is wrapped up in the relationship and the thought of having that connection destroyed creates a need to act out in a knee-jerk, primal manner. The more enlightened option—salvation—still held the echo of survival, in that the chaste woman who guards her purity and denies any whisper of the flesh is counting on her eventual survival into the Kingdom of Heaven. As Jane tested this theory in her own life and in the lives of the desperate killers and victims around her, she saw it played out repeatedly. However, the need to survive was the dominant M.O. for nearly everyone she encountered, including herself. She couldn't escape the irony that for all the years she felt dead inside and even contemplated suicide, the DNA-driven need to fight for one's own breath and security in this world motivated her primordial impulse.

So what in the hell triggered Jake's survival mechanism? What did his father say or do that night that drove him down that rope and to Mollie's house and then forced him to act out a sexually dominant role? Taking it a step further, what threatened Jake even more two weeks later so much that he abandoned his inborn survival instinct and threw a rope over a bridge support beam with death as his soul's objective? And if the two were somehow connected, why was his death aborted by another who then used Jake like a pawn in a game of chess?

Jane handed Mollie Jake's sketchpad. "Have you seen that before?" She shook her head. Jane instructed her how to flip the pages from the back forward to produce the smooth animation of the older man standing on a chair and hanging himself in a jail cell.

"Oh, my God," Mollie whispered, stunned. "Jake drew this?"

"Do you have any idea who that is?"

"No. But, hey, he's wearing the same type of vintage shirt and fedora like Jake wears."

"I know."

"Why would Jake want to copy the way this guy dresses?"

"I'm more interested in knowing why he wanted to copy how he died."

Mollie handed Jane the sketchpad. "You know, I told you how Jake liked to wear black and that he told me he was in mourning for the dead. What I didn't tell you, is that the last time Jake and I talked, he said the weirdest thing. He said he had an obligation...no, wait...he used a different word..." She thought hard. "...an *allegiance*. That's what he said. He said he had an allegiance to someone he'd never met and that he didn't understand it, but he had no choice."

Jane turned away. When she stood on the bridge and felt into what Jake was feeling at that precipitous place, she distinctly recalled the thought that imprinted on her mind. There was despair and an *allegiance* to death. At the time, she couldn't understand it, but now it had been confirmed. And when she and Weyler were discussing why people keep secrets, one of his theories was an allegiance to another person. But if that loyalty was unconscious, what in the hell kind of warped psychological game was going on in Jake's life?

Jane wasn't waiting until Monday for her big secret tête-à-tête with Jordan. Sprinting across the street to The Rabbit Hole, she located Hank working the bar for the mid-afternoon lunch crowd. He'd promised her the use of his truck while her Mustang was being repaired and he kept his word, tossing her the keys and telling her that he filled it up for her. There was a wink that followed that statement which turned heads in unison at the bar toward Jane.

"Like the shirt, Chopper!" he yelled out to her as she left the bar.

It took some getting used to, but Jane actually enjoyed the feel of the truck underneath her. She'd seen the world out the window of a '66 Mustang for so long that she'd forgotten what it looked like to view everything a few feet higher off the road. The Mustang had become so closely identified with Jane that people who'd only known her for a short time didn't know she'd actually inherited it more than fourteen years ago. It had taken her a good seven of those years to get his smell out of the car. But his memory always lingered around the edges.

Jane pulled into Jordan's property, parking the truck around the back of his cabin. Just in case Bo happened to be cruising down the highway, she didn't want him to think that Hank was hanging with Jordan. Looking around the property, she saw no one, but she didn't yell out Jordan's name. She ascended the four steps that led to the narrow porch of the cabin and gently rapped on the door. When Jordan didn't answer, she peered into a side window. Nobody home. Checking the door, it opened and she crossed inside. "Hello?"

Nothing.

A thousand thoughts crossed her mind—scenarios of where Jordan might be, interlocking with strategies for her opportunistic visit. She was drawn to the overflowing bookshelves across the room, up the two steps near the loft and single unmade bed. The cluttered collection was arranged in an erratic manner with some books facing forward and others set in backward. Jane hopscotched around the various titles that gave new meaning to the word *eclectic*. Modern classics were juxtaposed next to art books which were wedged tightly against history texts that were cloistering Chinese herbal encyclopedias. There was a section of the center shelf that was less dusty and gave Jane the impression that Jordan frequently sourced reading from that area. Each of the titles appeared to be esoteric in nature. One caught her eye, titled, *Sacred Symbols of the 52-Card Deck*. Jane was about to pull it off the shelf when a large hand touched her on the shoulder. She jumped and spun around.

"See something you like?" Jordan asked in a low, eerie voice.

"Jesus!" Jane said.

He smiled and chuckled. "Did I scare you?"

"I didn't hear you come in."

"That's because I was already inside."

"Then why didn't you respond when I called out?"

"I wanted to see what you were up to. I like to observe people…just like you do." He stood back, reading her *I LIKE BOYZ* T-shirt. "Thanks for clarifying your sexual preference. Now I can sleep peacefully at night." Jordan sauntered to the cluttered kitchen table, still laden with stacks of books, and eyed Jane more closely. "You look different, Jane." His eyes bored into her. "You've been awakened by the blue lily, haven't you?" Jane remained stone-faced. "Yes! I'm right. You've had an otherwordly experience." He smiled a knowing grin. "You've been awakened! You'll never be the same again, Jane. *Never!* Awareness is a demanding mistress. Once she wakes you up, she won't let you go back to sleep." He walked around the table. "It's nice to meet a fellow compatriot on the path. There aren't many of us brave souls. There's *too* much ignorance out there. Ignorance is bliss but the ignorant are too stupid to recognize their bliss by virtue of their ignorance. If that ain't irony, I don't know what is!"

Jane tired of Jordan's chatter. "We have to talk."

"Patience, Jane. Patience. I promised I would tell you my big secret on Monday."

"I gotta know now."

Jordan tilted his head, probing Jane's psyche. "Oh, dear. Did he slip up?"

"Who?"

"Your kidnapper. Did he? They always do. Did he reveal something quite by accident? Or…maybe *not* by accident?" Jane remained stoic, but Jordan seemed to read past the exterior. "Yes, of course." Jordan's eyes drifted, appearing suddenly remote. "He really wants attention, Jane. He needs you to listen to him. You're the only one who will listen. As much as we work to hide our secrets, the unconscious mind prods our soul to reveal all. The unconscious mind is *relentless*. We leave a trail of mistakes that can only be deciphered by the truly aware and gifted…like you, Jane."

Jane was never one to succumb to flattery, whether genuine or done to manipulate. Her eyes drifted to the disorderly kitchen table. She saw a deck of cards splayed in an uneven arch hidden between two stacks of books. Her stoic façade evaporated.

"What is it, Jane?"

She felt her heart beating harder. "Where were you the night of March 22nd?"

He slipped out of his altered state. "I already told Bo Lowry that story. He got it on video. Why don't you watch it?"

"I did. Tell me again."

"You want to see if the stories match? Checking for inconsistencies? Smart people like myself can maintain the consistency of lies better than the dumb fucks out there. You know that, Jane."

"Why were you covered in mud? Why were your hands bloody? Why were you wandering on the Highway in a daze?"

Jordan appeared legitimately troubled. "I was outside... walking...I could smell spring in the air, but I also smelled death. Yet, it was more in the ether."

"The *ether?*"

"The world around us! But this was far away."

"How far away?"

"I don't know," Jordan replied, his eyes shifting to that night in his memory. "But I smelled it and then I felt it...right here." He struck his fist into his chest near his heart. "It stabbed at me. I started to run but the more I ran, the more I felt the tentacles of death coming closer. It was the same way I felt that night so long ago." Jordan's chin trembled. "When Daniel died." He shook his head. "But this time...this time, it was stronger... It was closer to me. It was *part* of me!"

"What do you mean, *part of you?*"

He looked at her, his eyes wild yet tortured. "*I don't know!*" he yelled emphatically. "I've never felt anything as profound as this in my entire life."

"Except the night you killed Daniel?"

He dismissed her statement with a toss of his hand. "It was twenty times stronger than that. I tried to fight them off. Honestly, I did!"

"Fight who off?"

"The demons. At least, I think they were demons. The storm was so fierce, I can't be sure. I hid under a scrub oak and saw the blood on my hands. I didn't know where it came from. But it was like a nightmare. And that stabbing pain in my chest was unyielding. I had to run. I had to get away. But I fell down the embankment that leads to the river. That's how I got muddy, I guess." He turned his head, as if he were back in that moment and reliving it. "There was a squeal...or maybe a scream. I'm not sure. From over there..." He pointed outside his cabin and in the direction of the infamous bridge. "That's all I remember until one of the deputies picked me up the next morning on the road. Somehow, I'd walked out there. But I don't remember how." Jordan came out of his daze. "And then they told me a boy named Jake Van Gorden was missing. Last known location was on the bridge where he'd left a noose." He shook his head. "Jesus Christ." For the first time since Jane had known Jordan, there was an indubitable sense of sadness regarding the missing boy. "I knew it was obvious to them."

"Obvious how?" Jane asked carefully.

Jordan looked at her with a knowing stare. "What in the hell do you think, Jane?"

"That you killed another boy, Jordan?! Is this what you're saying?!"

"Fuck, Jane! You're better than that!"

"Jordan, we're pissing away time here! If you took Jake or if you know who did and where he is, you have to tell me now!"

Jordan hung his head. "I know what it feels like to want to die. I recognize what it takes to get to that point. I understand the emptiness...the desperation and the sorrow. Jake felt he didn't have a choice anymore." He looked up at Jane, his pupils screened in a ghostly glaze. "But you know all about suicide, don't you, Jane?" Jane swallowed hard. "You reached that point a couple years ago but you didn't pull the trigger." He shook his head. "Oh, Jane...but *he did*. And you're the one who found his lifeless body." This was impossible. There was no way Jordan could know any of it. "You're just shy of your twenty-second year and on your way to a better life. But there's a man who can't follow you. His conscience is dark and damaged and he turned a corner a long time ago."

Jane shook her head. "Stop it..."

"He sits in a wingback chair and he puts the cold steel under his chin and he hesitates. Yes, you wondered if he ever hesitated...whether he thought about you before he did the deed?

Oh, yes, Jane. He did. But he was too lost down that pit that has no soft surface."

Jane felt trapped. She backed up but the ladder to the loft stopped her progress. "Stop it, Jordan!"

Jordan moved closer to her. "And when you found him, he was there, sitting on the couch watching you and realizing that he'd fucked up. And he was with you later that night in bed, holding you, but you were too drunk to feel his ghostly touch. But he was there and still feeling the pain he thought he killed."

Jane bolted for the door. "Shut up!"

Jordan stood in her way. "It wasn't his time, Jane. He still had life in his veins. It was still pumping and meant to vibrate on this plane for many more years. So, he hung around you... haunted you. He lay between your thoughts." Jordan moved within inches of Jane, his hot breath stinging her face. "He woke you in the middle of a dream with his scent. You felt him inside you and his breath against your skin. You heard his heartbeat in your throat. And you thought you were going crazy but he was tearing at your etheric body, begging to be seen and heard." Jane reached for the door, but Jordan grabbed her arm. "Then one day, he left you for good. He slipped into the silence and dragged his memory with him. But he still hovers on the edge of your consciousness...especially when you think there's a chance of finding him again in another man. The *good* part of him—the part that was true and noble and who loved you desperately no matter your faults. You want that but you're scared that it's impossible to attain. As if love were only for the fortunate."

Tears welled in Jane's eyes. She shook off Jordan's grasp. "You have no right!"

"Jane..."

"Fuck you!" She opened the door and stormed to the truck. Peeling out of his property, she caught Jordan's reflection in the rear view mirror. He was standing in the cabin doorway with a cruel glare.

CHAPTER 27

Jane parked Hank's truck in front of the B&B and walked upstairs to her room. But even after a long shower, she couldn't shake Jordan's incisive dive into her buried past. Nobody was allowed there. *No one.* You talk about sacred territory? Even her brother knew better than to utter his name. And this crazed, wild-eyed child killer had the audacity to not only bring the ragged memory to the surface but to validate all those weird, sentient encounters she'd had after he died. No, it wasn't acceptable to Jane. There were lines you simply didn't cross. There were dark memories that needed to stay buried. But now they were bubbling to the surface again and the pain was as potent as it was fifteen years ago. *He had no right.*

Weyler knocked on her door, but Jane was still wrapped in a towel. "Hank brought your car around front and left your key on the entry table," he said outside the door. "Here's the two clues that weren't dispatched to CBI." Weyler scooted two envelopes under the door. "I'm going to dinner."

Jane acknowledged Weyler and retrieved the two envelopes. Inside the first was the one sentence note and, in the other, the lone Chesterfield cigarette. She hung the duo in their respective spot on the clothesline and grabbed one of the three nearly identical blue poplin shirts. But before she finished buttoning it, she stared at her reflection in the bathroom mirror. The woman staring back at her looked drab in that far too sensible shirt. Jane fingered through the girlish offerings Mollie had loaned her and stared at the long sleeved, plunging necked, cream number that skimmed the hips with its silky fabric and lacey embroidered accents. It was so unlike anything she'd ever wear, but she removed the navy blue poplin number, tossed it on the bed and slipped the feminine frock over her head. Turning back to the mirror, she didn't recognize her reflection. It wasn't that it was unattractive. On the contrary, it was close to stunning. The fabric clung to her breasts and defined a waist she'd hidden for years. But it just wasn't who Jane was. Who *she* was, was lying in a wrinkled, indigo heap on the bed. Her eyes glanced between the two shirts—one embracing the past and the other whispering of where she could go. Jane grabbed the poplin shirt and put it over the new one and headed downstairs. Grabbing the keys to her Mustang off the entry table, she headed outside. As she caught her reflection in the Mustang's side window, she recognized how clearly ridiculous she looked. She removed the poplin shirt, tossed it into the backseat of her car and walked across the street toward The Rabbit Hole.

After knocking several times on Hank's house door, Jane meandered around to the front of the sports bar. The chairs were on top of the tables and the place looked vacant. It seemed odd for an early evening on a Sunday night. The door was unlocked so she walked in and called Hank's name.

"Over here," he replied, standing in the recesses of the far stage.

Jane walked across the dance floor toward him. "Why are you shut down?"

Hank had his back to Jane momentarily. He was dressed in a knock-around denim shirt, with a frayed collar and cuffs, and a pair of jeans that framed his backside perfectly. "We close down for a few days during the off season to clean." He turned around and looked at her. "Well...you sure can't hide your Glock under that, can you?"

Jane felt exposed, a sensation that didn't set well. "Yeah... well...it was the first thing I grabbed off the hanger."

"Really?" Hank wasn't buying a word of it. "Lucky hanger."

She threw him his truck keys. "Thanks for the loan. What do I owe on the Mustang?"

"Nothing. I had some favors coming so it's a wash."

Her back went up against the clingy silk. "Now, wait a second..."

"Jane, he didn't charge me. Don't worry. You don't owe me anything."

This was the most ridiculous thing she'd ever heard. "Can we just cut to the chase?"

"Who's chasing who?"

"It's a term," Jane said with a humorless look.

"I'm aware of that." Hank moved to the rim of the stage. "Maybe I look like a dumb puck, but I'm not."

"I never said you were dumb."

"Are you hungry? You look hungry." Hank jumped off the stage and headed toward the kitchen.

Jane stood flabbergasted. "When did I lose control of this relationship?" she murmured to herself before following Hank into the kitchen.

Hank donned a chef's apron and brought down a fry pan from a hook. "You like shrimp?"

Jane sidled up to the stainless steel center table. "Sure."

"Good. I'm going to make you the best shrimp, tomato, garlic, and basil stir-fry you have ever tasted. Have a seat." He pointed to a wooden stool next to the table.

Jane reluctantly sat down. "You know, I can find food on my own. You don't have to feel the need to feed me all the time."

He heated olive oil in the pan and then plopped what looked like homemade tomato sauce into another saucepan. "I like cooking for you. I like talking to you." He smiled at Jane before walking to the refrigerator and bringing out several cloves of garlic and a handful of fresh basil leaves.

That feeling came back to Jane—the one she'd had when they were standing outside The Rabbit Hole the night before; that comfortable sense that she was meeting an old friend for the first time. She'd never felt anything like it before. *Comfortable* was not in her standard repertoire. But here she was, sitting in a commercial kitchen of a sports bar wearing a silky shirt with a plunging neckline and having a man cook shrimp for her. None of it made any damn sense. And she couldn't blame the effects of the blue lily this time. She wanted to say something to break the sudden silence. "By any chance, did you translate that

Patois sentence I gave you?"

Hank chopped up the garlic with fine precision. "I started looking into it but there's a couple words I can't figure out. I'll get it. Don't worry. Have you read about the *Patois*. They've got a very mystical history."

He got her attention. "Mystical, how?"

"They still use plants for medicine. A lot of them are natural-born healers. Many of them to this day are deeply imbedded in voodoo. But even those who've turned away from that practice, still keep a deep connection to the spirit world. It's a link that's inbred and passed from mother to child."

"From mother to child," Jane said to herself.

"I read a passage on some website that said, *To deny the spirit world, is to deny their own breath. To fight it, is pointless.* They're very connected to the dead, and some of them have an almost innate understanding of the psychic realm."

"So, as an example, they could look at a photo in a newspaper of a person and be able to tell you all about them and what they're feeling?"

Hank set the garlic to the side of the cutting board and starting chopping the basil. "I don't know. But I bet it's not impossible."

"So, you believe in that stuff, huh?" She was testing Hank.

"Yeah." He looked up at her. "And so do you." He brought a bowl of shrimp out from the refrigerator.

"I have a lot of questions..."

"Good! You should. But it doesn't mean that you don't accept the fundamentals that there's more under the sun than heaven and earth."

Jane remembered the few esoteric-themed books in Hank's library. "Do you have an understanding of symbology?"

He stirred the basil and garlic into the tomato sauce and tossed the shrimp into the fry pan. "There's lots of different symbology. Be more specific."

"The Ace of Spades."

"Isn't that the *Death Card*?"

"Yeah. But is that all it means?"

"No. It was an emblem for lots of secret societies in the past." Jane listened spellbound. "You know, the key to the ancient mysteries? The truth that lies behind the veil of illusion?" Jane couldn't believe what she was hearing. "A lot of people and businesses use it in their advertising or letterhead and they don't really understand the meaning…" He tossed the shrimp in the pan. "Or maybe they do on some level."

"Unconsciously?"

"Sure. You're a cop. You know how most deception is usually revealed unconsciously."

Jane immediately recalled Jordan's statement: *The unconscious mind is relentless.*

Hank tasted the sauce. "Carl Jung, one of my favorites, said, 'The unconscious mind of man sees correctly even when conscious reason is blind and impotent.'" He turned to Jane. "And I say… soup's on!"

They ate the meal across from each other, with the steel glare of the table reflected back into the overhead light. And once again, Jane enjoyed every bite of it. They chatted about current events, finding their opinions on everything from politics to the cultural demise on equal footing. But eventually, Jane wound the conversation back to Jake Van Gorden. She prefaced her next question with the understanding that it would go no further than the two of them. "You think Jake is gay?"

Hank nearly coughed up a shrimp. "Gay?" Jane nodded. "If Jake's gay, then *I'm* also looking for a good man."

Jane considered the answer. "So, are *you* gay?"

Hank looked at Jane with the utmost of sincerity. "Would I be sitting here right now if I were gay?"

Jane took another bite of shrimp. "Maybe Jake is good at hiding it?"

"No way. Whoever told you that is nuts."

"The guy I heard it from got it from someone else who

supposedly caught Jake checking out gay porn."

"That is total bullshit. Let me guess. The guy who told the other guy is Jake's dad."

"I can't say," Jane replied.

That crooked grin emerged across Hank's face. "You just did, Jane."

"Hey..."

"It's okay. I won't say a word. But I already told you about Jake's parents. They don't give a shit about him."

"I think Carol cares."

"Maybe. But does she care enough to leave her prick of a husband?" Hank sat back. "Bailey Van Gorden cares about Bailey Van Gorden. If that bastard has to sink so low and make up stories about catching his son with gay porn, you can bet he's got an agenda." Hank carried their empty plates to the sink. "Son-of-a-bitch," he muttered, shaking his head. He removed the apron and hung it on a hook. "Jake deserves a better family than what he got." He reached out for Jane's hand. "Enough of this. Follow me."

Jane reluctantly followed Hank out of the kitchen and onto the empty dance floor. He told her to wait while he went on stage and fiddled with a CD. Dimming the lights, the first strains of Etta James' "At Last" blew across the spacious room. Rejoining Jane, he asked, "May I have this dance?"

"Is this the payment for the car?"

"No." He put his arms around her. "It's just a dance." There was a slight awkward moment. "You don't mind if I lead, do you?"

Jane rolled her eyes and kept up her guard for the first half of the song, but gradually relaxed as Etta's voice melted like warm syrup against the walls of the bar.

"Why don't they play this in elevators more?" Hank asked. "I knew I was getting old the day I heard a Rolling Stones tune in an elevator."

Jane looked at him. "I knew I was old when the Playboy

centerfolds were younger than I."

Hank smiled and held Jane closer. They were still dancing well after the song ended.

Jane got back to the B&B shortly after 9:00 pm. She helped Hank with some of the seasonal cleanup until he called it a night. There was no invitation to stay over, although he seemed to linger with her outside before she walked across the street. As much as returning solo to the honeymoon suite wasn't appealing, she wasn't ready to make another mistake. Putting it mildly, the last relationship she had two years ago ended badly.

After slipping into her cotton nightshirt, Jane propped herself up on the bed and stared at the clothesline of clues. The knife with Jake's ponytail along with the Ace of Spades and bloody fingerprint were probably already in Denver, thanks to the expedient courier service Weyler used for transporting evidence. She retrieved the two envelopes that Weyler slipped under her door earlier and removed the clues, each protected in a sheet of plastic. She clipped the handwritten note and the lone Chesterfield 101 cigarette on the far right of the clothesline, next to the scrap of paper with the scrawled *1401 Imperial* address.

Sliding back onto the bed, Jane read the clothesline from left to right, searching as she always did, for the common thread or for an understanding of what story the kidnapper was trying to tell. The newest note with the statement, *Who Ever Believes Bad Eventually Resolves*, still made no sense to Jane, except that when she said it out loud, it sounded like it was written by an immature author. As Jane ruminated on that discovery, she realized that there were other clues that also sounded as if the writer was either extremely young or mentally challenged. The piss-stained page with the words, *Why you piss me off BAWY?* was another good example. Then there was the second audio recording and the statement, "He *cried like a baby* and will never be a real man…" There seemed to be a discernable flip-flop between a traumatized child and an adroit, if not educated adult. After staring at the clues for another half hour, Jane decided the most logical explanations so far were that this was either one man with a split personality or two people—one mentally challenged and the other pulling the strings. She lay back on the buffet of pillows and realized that, using that logic, Jordan Copeland could fit either assumption.

Jane was weary, but she wasn't tired. With no TV in the room, she had nothing to focus on that wasn't related to Jake's case. The only thing in that room that wasn't attached to the case was the box of photos she'd pinched from the Greens' locked kitchen cabinet. While she wasn't one to pry unnecessarily into other people's private lives, she figured that she needed something to take her mind off the complicated case. She removed the box from under the bed and removed the lid marked, OLD PHOTOS. It was immediately clear that these photos were not connected in any way to the Greens. They looked to be a collection of sepia-toned and black-and-white photos that had been taken by others who owned the B&B when it was a boardinghouse. Many of them had already found themselves into frames and adorned the walls of the B&B.

Jane pulled a stack from the box and chuckled at the dirt Main Street in Midas captured in a 1905 photo. The monied classes obviously hadn't found their way to the town as she viewed a collection from the 1930s. The bawdy broads posing in the 1919 framed photo in the Greens' kitchen seemed to be replicated in the smiling lineup of women who posed in front of the B&B—still known as *The Garden, A Boarding House for Ladies*—in the 1932 and 1934 shots. On the back, someone identified the names of the animated women, using first names only. Names such as "Gracie," "Tulula" and "Roxie" stood out to Jane. It seemed that this place had a history of attracting what they might have called "loose" women back then and what we'd now call "adventurous" or "wild."

The next photo was circa 1960 and it took Jane a second

to realize it was taken outside what was now The Rabbit Hole but was formerly named The Hayloft. Again, a lineup of women—dressed in capris and sleeveless shirts, and sporting beehive hairdos and lots of attitude—waved at the camera. Two men knelt in front of them for the photo, each with a cockeyed grin. They looked like trouble. If Jane had seen the duo on the streets today, she'd make the assumption that they were up to no damn good. More photos of The Hayloft followed with various groups from the 1960s photographed in front of the popular establishment.

She shuffled through the dizzying assortment until she found one dated *Spring, 1967.* There was a bright-eyed girl standing in front of The Hayloft, arms circled around a handsome, 6' 3" guy who wore a striking suit. The girl, about nineteen, Jane figured, pursed her lips toward the man as if she were about to kiss him. Although the shot was in black-and-white, the dress looked like it was red or dark blue and hugged her svelte figure. Jane turned the photo over. When she first read the words, they didn't register. But then she read it again:

Anne LeRóy (one of the girls from The Gardens) and Harry Mills
(1967)

Jane sat up in shock. She peered closer at the photo and realized the dress Anne wore was identical to the one she appeared in when Jane saw her. An even more careful scrutiny exposed the fresh gardenia pinned to her mother's revealing neckline. Jane flipped the photo over again, reading the handwritten words. *One of the girls from The Gardens* flashed at Jane like a neon light. She could easily rationalize how her mother's spirit materialized in front of her, chalking it up to the car accident, the blue lily or fatigue. But *this photo…*this was real and two-dimensional. Jane turned the photo back and started at the man name Harry Mills. "Who in the fuck are you, buddy?" Jane murmured. He looked like a matinee idol with his slicked back hair and jaunty demeanor. Harry was the kind of guy you have fun with but who doesn't settle down. Looking at her mother's blissful countenance, Jane wondered if her mother knew that back then, or if the girl in the photo even cared.

Jane shuffled through the remaining photos but found no more of the woman who put an accent on "LeRóy," even though the traditional spelling never had it. She replaced the pile of photos in the box, leaving the one of Anne and Harry in front of The Hayloft out on the bed. She looked around the room and felt a bit foolish when she asked, "Are you here?" When Jane was met with stony silence, she glanced over to the bathroom and spied a trio of pillar candles tucked next to the sink. She carried one to the side table by the bed, lit the wick and turned off the lights. With the cushion of pillows behind her and the photo in her hand, she noted the time on the digital clock—*10:24 pm.* "Ridiculous," Jane whispered to herself. But still she waited. She beckoned the sweet aroma of gardenias but her sensitive nose detected nothing. She wasn't the least bit tired as she checked the clock again—*10:25 pm.* "Jesus," she muttered. The candle cast an amber glow against the room, its soft light fading at the edges around the bed. Jane stared into the shadows across the room, her mind summoning her mother. Her ears pricked for any sound; her eyes volleyed for any motion. She took a hard breath and waited—but nothing.

Jane peered down at the photo, illuminated by candlelight. Gradually, her vision blurred and she felt her head bob forward. Recovering, she lifted her head and checked the clock—*3:11 am.* How was that possible? The room filled with that same electric buzz as if the world as it is and world beyond were merging in an unsteady union. A heaviness clung close to Jane as the aroma of gardenias swept across the walls. Gradually, the slow crick of the rocker could be heard. Out of the darkness, Jane saw the orange glow of a cigarette illumine and then dissipate, followed by the familiar whiff of unfiltered tobacco. "Who's there?" Jane asked, her voice shaky.

"Who in the hell do you think?" Anne remarked, standing

up from the rocker and moving to the foot of the bed. She was dressed in the same tight-fitting red dress with the fresh gardenia pinned to her chest. Anne took another meaningful puff on her cigarette, her red lacquered fingernails grasping it in a manner that showed Jane it wasn't the first time she lit up.

"I never knew you smoked," Jane said in a stunned voice.

"Oh, honey. There's lots of things you don't know." She motioned toward the photograph. "I see you found my favorite snapshot." Anne arched an eyebrow. "Don't you think the accent over the 'o' makes LeRóy sound French? I sure did!" Anne leaned forward looking at the photo. "He was a cool drink of water, doncha know?"

"Yeah…looks like he was a lot of fun," Jane added, still patiently aware of the strangeness to this ghostly exchange.

"Oh, that he was," Anne replied, picking a speck of tobacco out of her front tooth. She looked around the room. "But he also had those moments where depression would just knock him over. You know what I'm talking about. Your first love had the same damn problem, didn't he? Lots of fun until it wasn't fun anymore." She took a hard drag. "Aw, hell, I don't want to talk about that! This room really *is* divine!"

"This was your room, wasn't it?"

"Yeah. But it sure didn't look like this back then. There were three single beds along that wall. I shared the room with two other girls to save money."

"What were you doing here?"

Anne sauntered to the desk and leaned against the chair. "Living my life. Feeling my oats. I wasn't easy to contain. I didn't care where I lived as long as there were interesting people and a good place to dance." She smiled. "You never knew that you got your dancing chops from me, did you?" Anne chuckled. "I dug my heels into the floor of The Hayloft many a night."

"It's called The Rabbit Hole now."

"Is that right? Down the rabbit hole we go…where we stop, nobody knows."

"Why do you always show up at 3:11?" Jane's tone was probing.

"Three eleven," Anne mused, her demeanor suddenly less lighthearted. "My goodness, I had no idea." She took another hard drag, seemingly desperate to numb her long-departed senses. "Three eleven..."

Jane stared at her mother. "Are you all right?"

Anne's eyes darted back and forth. "You never answered me the last time. Are you prepared to see things for how they truly were?"

"I found the picture of you and Harry." Jane's tone was agitated.

"Right. Baby steps, I guess." She forced an uneasy smile. "I never told anybody, Jane."

Jane looked down at the photo. When you lose your mom at ten years old, the chances of hearing about her first lover during those prepubescent years isn't high. "I understand." She looked back up at her mother. Tears fell down her youthful face.

"I couldn't tell a soul," Anne said, her words choked with emotion. "Not a soul." Anne let the ash of the cigarette fall but it vanished into the darkness. "And when he killed himself, it was all my fault!"

"Killed himself?" Jane asked, stunned. "Why'd he kill himself?"

Anne shook her head, tears flowing freely. "You shouldn't carry it, Jane, if it doesn't belong to you..."

Jane moved closer to her mother. "Carry what?"

"How are you feeling?"

"Feeling?" Jane regarded her mother with a questionable gaze. "I'm feeling fine."

"Is that right?" Her tenor was eerie.

"Yeah. I'm..." Suddenly, that horrific pain bored into Jane's gut. Her pelvic bone felt as if it was being crushed. Jane looked up at her mother with pleading eyes. "Make it stop, please!"

"I wish I could," Anne said, detached from the emotion.

"But it's to be expected."

Jane fell back on the bed, beads of sweat prickling across her forehead. The room spun as she held out her hand to her mother. "Make it stop!"

Anne looked at Jane with eyes suddenly lifeless. "I wish I'd been stronger."

The pain was too much. Jane closed her eyes and screamed into the darkness.

"Jane?!"

She opened her eyes. Morning light streamed into the room. The pain was gone.

"*Jane*?!" It was Weyler's voice.

She wobbled off the bed, still half asleep and opened the door. "What is it?"

He stood there in a blue dress shirt, sans tie and slacks. "I heard you scream."

"I…was having a nightmare."

Weyler looked uncertain. "You need to get dressed and come downstairs immediately. It looks like our kidnapper left something else just for you to scream about on your car."

CHAPTER 28

By the time Jane threw on a pair of jeans and donned her jacket over the nightshirt, a small group of onlookers was already staring at the back of her Mustang. Jane's gut seized as she maneuvered around the vehicle and came to rest next to Weyler at the rear of the car. Scrawled across the hood of the ice blue finish in dried blood were three words: FUCK YOU, JANE!

"What in the hell's going on?" Jane demanded.

"Aaron found it when he came out to get the paper."

"This doesn't make sense!"

He turned to her. "You're becoming the focus and that's not what we need."

"You think this is part of the clues?"

"How many times in your life have you had these three words written in blood on your car?" Jane turned away. "My point exactly. When the Van Gordens hear about this, all hell's going to break loose. I think you should probably get out of here before Bo arrives. I'll do what I can to smooth it over with him. This is a crime scene now so see if you can take Hank's truck..." He moved closer. "Talk to Jordan but *be careful*. We need to ramp this up and fast." Jane pulled her cell phone from her jacket pocket and quickly captured the graffiti with a quick snapshot.

Racing upstairs, she changed into one of Mollie's T-shirts with the word *Groovy* across the chest. She donned her shoulder holster and Glock, leather jacket and grabbed her satchel. Downstairs, she slugged down a cup of java and grabbed a piece of toast and a few sausages that Sara offered her. After making sure that Bo was still AWOL on the scene, Jane slipped out the side door of the B&B and jogged across the street toward The Rabbit Hole. Without questioning Jane, Hank happily tossed her the keys to his truck and she sped out of town.

Jane peeled onto Jordan's property, leaving a trail of dust in her wake. She brought the truck to an uneasy halt behind the cabin and raced to the front door where she found a tacked handwritten note. It read, MEET ME NEAR THE BRIDGE, JANE.

She ripped the note from the tack, stuffed it into her jacket pocket and headed across his property, through the thicket of bushes and spruce trees, toward the bridge. Jane yelled his name, only to hear it echoed back to her. A kaleidoscope of green shoots burst through the spongy soil where patches of snow lay in frozen heaps only days ago. Jane ventured deeper into the stand of spruce, pointed toward the bridge and the fenced area where she trespassed onto Jordan's property the first time she met him face-to-face. She started to call his name again when she stumbled over the same bright red metal rod sticking out of the ground that she'd avoided during her first venture onto Jordan's property. Hitting the dirt hard, Jane released a barrage of four-letter expletives before springing to her feet and screaming into the air, "Goddamnit, Jordan! Where are you?!"

"Here," he said quietly. Jane spun around. Jordan stood twenty feet in front of her, toward the bridge. He looked sedate and exceptionally pensive. She waited, not knowing what to expect. He turned his back to her, gazing at the bridge. "A man has recently escaped from prison and is making his way home on foot. He is walking along a straight rural county highway in bright daylight. He's walked about two miles from the prison, when he sees a police car coming toward him. Despite knowing that all squads were on the lookout for him, he runs towards the car for a short while, and only when he was ten feet away, did he turn and run into the woods to hide." Jordan turned to Jane. "Why did he run towards the police car, Jane?"

Not knowing what was coming, Jane contemplated the riddle. She looked at the bridge. "He was on a bridge when he spots the police car. He's more than halfway across it, so the quickest way off the bridge is to run forward and into the woods."

Jordan smiled and nodded. "Yes." He looked at the bridge. "Two people look at a bridge. One sees a place to jump and the other sees a place to cross over. But when it's all said and done, it's still just a bridge. It's our perception that gives it power." Jordan turned to face her. "People need to have someone to hate. They need their monsters. They create their dragons because it gives them something to slay. That's how they procure their power. And when they're slaying other dragons, they don't have to ponder the beasts that lurk under their own bed, do they? They don't have to face the very real possibility that the monster they need to vanquish is really within *them*! I slay the monster inside me every day, Jane. I face him and I conquer him and each time, I fear him less. But it seems that I've been made the face of evil again. I'm the dragon up for slaughter, aren't I?"

"If you're involved with Jake Van Gorden's disappearance," Jane replied coolly, "then, yes."

"Because I was convicted for killing Daniel Marshall?"

"Of course."

He nodded calmly. "So, it's Monday. Time to tell you my big secret." He paused, the weight of what he was about to say lying heavy on his battered body. "I didn't kill Daniel Marshall."

Jane studied Jordan's face. Against the shade of the conifers, she detected no deception. "Who killed him?"

Jordan took a long breath. "He killed himself. It was an accident. He was always far too interested in my father's gun case that stood in our entry hall. My father had a nasty habit of failing to secure the cabinet, and I had a habit of double-checking that lock every day and making sure it was secured, especially after Daniel became obsessed with the guns." Jordan's demeanor remained calm but edged with sadness. "I was born from a dirty little secret and, thus, I was an outcast from my first breath. I was shunned and ignored and never able to make a connection with anyone except my true mother. When my father took her away from me, my world became so utterly lonely. I was alone whether I was by myself or standing in a crowded room. But I could feel things they couldn't even begin to understand and I had no one but the walls or my dead mother to talk to." Tears welled in his eyes. "Jane, can you even begin to understand what that does to one's heart? To feel nothing from anyone, except the knowledge that you're an unaccustomed burden? To be treated like a maid who doesn't know her place? You can fire that maid but you can't fire your blood son. You can only pray that the stars align in such a way that he's forced to go far away and be forgotten. So, was it fate or destiny that I was doomed to create a situation where I was forced to leave?"

"Why in God's name would you cop to a murder you didn't commit? You could have explained what happened, why you got scared and hid his body..."

"Nobody would have listened to me, Jane, because no one

ever listened to me. And even if they did, I would have been asked to leave for good. But I could hardly navigate my own home let alone have the social skills to figure out how to live in the world with nothing but my shattered wits. No one made me feel as if I was worth knowing. How in the hell was I supposed to strike out on my own with no money, no connections and no sense of self?"

"Tell me what happened on the day Daniel killed himself."

Jordan's eyes traced the ground. "The natural desire to want to belong and not be a pariah is a powerful opiate. Here I was, my only friend being a thirteen-year-old retarded boy. *That* was who would lower himself to be my companion. I hung around with Daniel, but I was always embarrassed by his presence. As much as I hated it, my youthful ego still wanted to belong to something or someone who was normal. And Daniel wasn't helping in my flagging pursuit of normalcy. One day, it all caught up with me. My ego overrode my integrity and I purposely didn't double-check the lock on my father's gun cabinet."

Jordan disappeared into the past. "It was pouring rain—that kind of late afternoon summer rain where the air is thick and foreboding. My parents were gone. Daniel had visited and was babbling about being a cowboy and riding a horse. I was sick of it. I told him to leave and I went back up to my room. About ten minutes later, I hear this ridiculous hooting out in the backyard by the far gate. I looked out the window and there was Daniel standing in the pouring rain with my father's hunting rifle between his legs and he was riding it like a fucking bronco. I could have opened that window and yelled down to him and told him to put down the gun, but I didn't. I could have raced down the stairs and out into the rain and grabbed the gun from him. But I didn't. I just stood there watching that poor son-of-a-bitch ride that fucking gun and wave his hand in the air like he was a rodeo cowboy. He was looking right up at me when he accidentally pulled the trigger. I watched his face disintegrate in an instant. He fell back onto the wet grass and I just stood there, motionless, as the rain beat down on his flesh and washed the blood away. I must have stood in that damn window for half an hour before I came back into myself and went downstairs. I picked him up, brought him to my room, wrapped him in a sheet and rolled him under my bed. I put the rifle back in the cabinet and locked it. But then the world just started to close in around me. I couldn't stand my weakness and I was ashamed that I allowed the one person who had given me his friendship to die. I was no better than the bourgeois couple I lived with who looked down on me and treated me like yesterday's trash." Jordan's face etched with profound misery. "I don't remember much after that. I was in shock. The next memory I have is hearing Mrs. Copeland scream and being pelted with her bony fists after she found his body under my bed. She kept screaming, 'You bastard! Look what you've done to us! We're ruined now, you little freak!' After that, it's just a blur of jail cells, courtrooms and my final sentencing. I didn't really wake up and become aware of my own breath until about four years later. Up to that point, I was as good as dead. But when I woke up, all I felt was anger toward the conventions that gave me no choice but to hide my family secret…to bury that which was evident. I was taught to hide mistakes because *I* was a mistake. Hide a family secret, hide a person…the point is *hide it*. Bury it. If you can't see it, maybe it will disappear. They hid my mother away in an asylum until she conveniently disappeared by dying.

"But after a few years of being awakened to my own psychological torture, I was determined to learn why a secret becomes flesh and has a heartbeat just like you and I. I read every book I could find on sociology, psychology and family systems of dysfunction. The more I read, the more fascinated I became and the more I was determined to understand the way a buried secret can infect a bloodline and cause generations of pain."

Jane's ears pricked. "Where did you read that a secret can *infect* a bloodline?"

"That's my term for it."

"Yours?"

"Yes. What's your point, Jane?"

"Jake Van Gorden used that same word, both in conversation and in writing in regard to *the sins of his family*. It's an odd word and even stranger when a missing boy you're accused of taking also used it."

Jordan's back went up. "I won't be a martyr for their cause, Jane! No one loves a martyr except the Church. To everyone else, they're just dusty bores."

"Why don't you ever give me a straight answer?!" Jane yelled.

"Because I would hope that you'd trust me by now to know the answer!" His manner hardened. "There are two things people can't handle—death and the truth. Ask yourself some questions, Jane." Jordan took several steps toward her. "What are people willing to sacrifice to keep a secret? *Who* are they willing to sacrifice for that secret?! *I* was sacrificed to serve the secret of my father's affair! People are sacrificed every fucking day, Jane, in the name of a *secret*. And the darker that secret, the more it must be kept at all costs!"

"The cost of a life?"

"*Especially* at the cost of a life! Wasn't my life sacrificed? You *can* sacrifice someone without killing them physically. You take away their honor, their right to be heard, their right to exist. You can bury a man without putting him in a box." He moved closer to her. "I *exist*, Jane. I exist in this town like I've existed in every other town. I exist under a *modus vivendi*—a practical arrangement that allows conflicting people to coexist until a final settlement is reached. The final agreement is usually my removal from the town. Take away a man's sense of safety and he never feels as if he can exhale. It's psychological warfare at its finest. You never have to do anything else to him. Just keep him on the slenderest of edges so he feels a bit unsteady and you'll own him because the tension within him will prevent him from fighting back." He raised his hand. "But I'll be damned if they're going to lead me toward desperation because I don't believe in desperation. It always leads to compliance!" Jordan stood within an uncomfortable foot of Jane. "I know how the game is played, honey. I may be half black, but I won't be their nigger."

Jane had enough. She turned and moved through the thicket of trees back toward the truck. Jordan followed closely on her heels. "You know what it feels like to be alone, *don't you, Jane?*" he yelled. "Staring at the ceiling when you're in bed and wondering if there will ever be another warm body next to you that won't end up *destroying you!*"

She stopped and stared daggers at Jordan. "You've crossed the line one too many times with me. I *can* make your life a living hell if I choose to!"

"But you know the truth, Jane." He held her arm, more in desperation. "Most women who leave a man to *find themselves*, end up finding themselves in the arms of another man because truly *finding yourself* is a lonely and terrifying proposition. You have an understanding of what abject loneliness feels like. You understand my life more than anyone!"

Jane shook him off. "Stop dragging me into your fucking nightmare!" She turned around and moved quickly toward the truck.

Jordan remained relentless, hugging her shadow as she walked. "We're all magnets in this town, Jane! I've told you that before! We're drawn to each other in the electric haze and with a synchronistic aim, we shoot into each other's lives. Because the more we try to run from our secrets and hide our past, the more we encounter it and are forced to reconcile our sins." Jordan grabbed Jane's arm and turned her around. "How else could you explain you and I coming together? *You,* the one who holds the thing I so desperately need but don't yet understand. *You,* the one who can bring me my life." His left hand started to shake. "You see?! It's *confirmation!*"

"Let go of me!" Jane seethed. He released her arm and she

stormed toward the truck.

Jordan stood still. "Don't abandon me, Jane! You're the only one who can bring me my life!" Jane's gait increased. "Just because you don't believe in something doesn't prevent it from still operating in your life." She moved into a slow run but she could still hear his screaming voice. "If things don't work out here, I'm heading to south Florida and opening up a hair salon called, *Mien Coif.* Think it'll fly, Jane?" She flung open the door to the truck but the narrow canyon caught the echo of Jordan's voice and carried it back to her. "Don't believe their lies, Jane!"

She backed the truck away from the cabin and took a hard spin, spraying gravel across the dirt. Barreling out of Jordan's property, she turned right to head back to Midas. Her face was flushed with anger and indignation. *Goddamn him,* she thought. This was the second time in less than twenty-four hours that the bastard hit tender nerves that no one dared inflame. She craved revenge; to shut him up so she wouldn't have to hear him remind her of the awful truth. Who in the hell wanted to hear the truth, even when it was callously staring one in the face? To have her private thoughts laid bare and screamed into the wind made Jane feel far too exposed. She could make him suffer. A cascade of devious police tactics lobbed for attention. There were loopholes Jane could exploit; meddlesome search warrants she could execute. Even though she knew she had nothing but her bruised ego to blame, Jane didn't care. The gaping private wound needed to be covered. It would quash any popularity she had with Jordan. But then again, Jane never suffered the burden of popularity in her life. Why start now?

Jane was so deeply entrenched in her desire for retribution, that she didn't see the speeding patrol car buzz by her truck on the opposite side of the highway. It wasn't until she looked in the rear view mirror, that she saw the car skid to a stop before making a hairpin U-turn and race up the road toward her. Jane kept the truck at an easy 45 mph as she hit a straightaway section of the road. The patrol car raced within inches of her bumper. Checking the side mirror, she saw it was Bo and he looked enraged. He suddenly jerked the patrol car into the oncoming lane next to her and forced Jane off the highway and onto the shoulder in a blizzard of rage. She skidded to a wobbly stop as he tucked his patrol car behind the truck and exited well before the car came to a standstill. Jane didn't make it out of the truck more than two feet before Bo's angry frame loomed closer and launched a stinging attack.

"So, you're all balls to the wall, is that it?!" Bo screamed, his nostrils flaring and pupils narrowing in for the attack. "I see you got your big-girl panties on and you're gonna show me how it's done!" He proceeded to tell Jane how Weyler handed over the twenty Chesterfield cigarettes, along with the pack and ashtray that she absconded. Fortunately, Weyler left out the fact that Jane followed Bailey to the strip club because the pointed message on her Mustang that morning clearly sent Bo over the edge. He figured he knew who wrote it. "You've been talking to that child killer behind my back! Don't you lie to me no more! Beanie laid it out for me! You got him riled! And now *you* are the one at the center of all this mess! *You!*"

Jane felt slightly intimidated by Bo's hulking figure. She spoke in a calm voice; the kind of tone she reserved for talking jumpers off the ledge. "I screwed up, Bo. I admit it. I thought if I drew him into my confidence, he'd open up about Jake..."

"But he didn't, *did he*?! He just talked in circles with lots of riddles that don't mean nothin'! Don't you think I know the way that son-of-a-bitch acts?! See, I've kept him safe ever since he dragged his guilty ass into this town. I did it because that's my job. For three goddamn decades, I've protected every person who came here to live and leave their past behind. And in four goddamn days, you have done nothin' but take a wreckin' ball to everything I've built!"

Jane took a step back. "Now hang on. I admit I should have told you about the cigarettes. But you can't lay the blame on me for all the chaos Jake's kidnapper has set forth!"

"Let's call the kidnapper by name, Perry! *Jordan Copeland.* And you obviously must have said somethin' that pissed him off for him to leave his four-letter calling card on your car in deer blood!"

"Deer?"

"The first thing I did was test it. Good God...there's people standin' around your car thinkin' that it's Jake's blood! I had to put their minds at ease. But now all they want to know is when this hell is gonna stop. 'When are we gettin' our town back, Bo?' And I can't give 'em that answer because I don't know how much you've compromised the case by chattin' up the Trash Bag!"

"What about the Van Gordens? Did you ever consider that they're not opening up to you and that they could be putting their own son's life in jeopardy?"

"Jesus Christ! Jake is *never* comin' home. You know it and I know it! And if he ain't dead, he's ruined for life."

Jane stared at Bo in silence. There was something intensely jarring in the way Bo's face filled with sadness. "So keep him lost? Is that what you're saying?"

He swallowed hard. "Sometimes a man has to accept when his son ain't ever gonna be right and when he's never comin' home." Bo's chin trembled. "See, the damage is done!" he said, recovering quickly. Bo shifted his stance closer to Jane. "Let me tell you somethin', Perry. When you take away everything, a man is left with two things—his integrity and his reputation. I've worked my ass off my entire life for both of those. I may not be the smartest man on this planet, but I'll be damned if I'm leavin' this town without both of them intact." Bo stared at Jane, in one breath fearful and in the next, obdurate.

"If you keep turning away from what you refuse to see or don't want to hear, it doesn't speak much for your integrity and it sure as hell tarnishes your reputation."

Bo's eyes narrowed. "You think you know me, Perry? Don't be so goddamn sure! I've heard and seen too damn much in this life." He turned and lumbered back to his patrol car, wincing in pain as his large frame hit the driver's seat.

By the time Jane rolled back in front of the B&B, there were only a few people gathered around her ice blue crime scene. The spring sun warmed the pavement, taking the edge off what had been a cool morning. A lone deputy finished taking photos while another dusted for prints. Weyler stood on the sidewalk, calmly answering questions from a concerned citizen. When he saw Jane, he excused himself and met her as she exited the truck.

"I tried to stop him, Jane…"

"I'm sure you did. He thinks Jordan did this," she said, motioning to the Mustang.

"Any other likely suspects?"

Jane considered the possibilities as she removed her jacket. "Bo?"

"You serious?"

"I've pissed him off plenty. Maybe he's trying to scare me."

"That isn't his style, Jane. *If* this is the work of the kidnapper, and if it's not Jordan, then he's suddenly making it very personal. Somehow, he knows you're working the case."

"I've never been connected to this case in the media."

"There was that impromptu news conference the day we showed up. You and I were included in the frame during Bo's sound bite."

Jane thought it through. "So, if it's not Jordan, whoever did it was watching TV that one day and caught a twenty-second glimpse of me in the background. But my car wasn't featured in the shot so how would they know what I drove based on that TV clip?"

"The only people who know what car you drive are people in this town."

"And Jordan…"

"Did he offer anything of value this morning?"

"He told me he didn't kill Daniel Marshall. He said the boy shot himself by accident."

Weyler's eyes widened. "That was his *big secret?*" Jane nodded. "Fascinating timing, don't you think? Just when the heat's bearing down on him, he throws out that bone to make us question everything."

"I don't think he was lying," Jane said, hating to admit it.

"But you're also not sure he's innocent either."

Jane moved to the rear of her car. "I just want to get as much distance from him as possible..." The deputy took the last shot and headed back down the street toward Town Hall. The other continued dusting for prints. "Any idea when we'll hear back on that bloody thumb print you sent to CBI?"

"I said to rush it because we've got a pending case up here, but we'll get it back when we get it back."

Jane stared at the graphic assault on her trunk. "You know, this doesn't compute. All along, I've said that the M.O. of our guy is that he wants to be heard. He's tired of being ignored. I've actually made quite a point of exposing whatever I can. If I'm right that this individual wants attention, he wouldn't write, *Fuck You, Jane!* He'd write *Thank You, Jane!*"

"It could have also been a knee-jerk response to an exchange that tripped off his anger. When you left Jordan's yesterday, did you leave on a good note?"

Jane easily pulled up her parting words to Jordan. "I said, 'Fuck you!' And I meant it." Weyler furrowed his brow. "Hey, he crossed the line with me." She turned away. "He's got a bad habit of doing that. And frankly, I'm sick of it!" The desire for retribution swelled up again. "I'm ramping this up, like you said. I'm tired of playing games with Jordan."

"What did he say to you that made you change your opinion?"

The first words that came to her mind were—*the truth*. But Jane wasn't about to admit it. "I'm just tired. I want this to end. I've got my own health issues I have to deal with." Jane started inside the gate. "Hey, you said Bo lost his wife to cancer last year? Did they ever have any kids? Maybe a son?"

"I never heard of any kids. Why?"

"Out there on the highway, he said something about how a man has to accept when his son isn't right and when he's never coming back. The way he said it…it was a little too close to home."

A deluxe dark blue sedan slowed to a crawl in front of the B&B. The male driver, the only occupant in the car, squinted toward the B&B sign and then parked several spaces away from Jane's Mustang. Jane noted the yellow rental stickers on the front window of the sedan. A wiry gentleman in his mid-eighties got out of the car and retrieved his small suitcase from the back seat. He was attired in a three-piece, striped suit and was impeccably put together, down to the watch fob and polished dress shoes. His black wool overcoat set off his carefully coiffed grey hair. Stern eyes peered from his narrow-rimmed spectacles as he read the *Fuck You, Jane!* message.

"Good God," he muttered, turning away from the profanity. He quickly sized up both Weyler and Jane in an elitist manner. When he saw the butt of Jane's Glock in her shoulder holster fastened across her *Groovy* T-shirt, his left eyebrow arched ever so slightly. "I assume this is *still* the only bed and breakfast in town?" When he spoke, he regarded them over the top gold rim of his eyeglasses, as if he were at a cheese-tasting mixer and was examining the placards on two rounds of Brie.

"Yes, sir," Weyler replied. "The Greens are inside. If you catch Sara, you could probably talk her into a late breakfast."

He scowled. "Yes. Well, I've already eaten. And I'm only enduring this place one night."

Weyler extended his hand. "I'm Morgan Weyler and this is Jane Perry."

The elderly gentleman shook Weyler's hand with little enthusiasm. There was a constant sense that he was so above them. He refrained from shaking Jane's hand. "Jane?" He turned to her Mustang and the three-word bloody graphic. "So you're the recipient of this declaration?"

Jane shifted uncomfortably in her cowboy boots. "Yes. That would be me."

He glanced up and down her body, looking askance when he read her T-shirt. Jane suddenly felt like she was on the auction block, and this old guy wasn't going to make an opening bid. "Is it a prank?"

"No, sir," Jane replied. "It's actually a crime scene."

He put down his suitcase. "Is this part of the Copeland mess?" His thin tenor meant business.

"I'm sorry, sir," Jane said, now her turn to judge his right to take up space on the street. "Why would that interest you?"

"Because I'm in charge of Jordan Copeland's trust fund and I'm here to make an assessment in regard to the recent events that have taken place."

Jane nodded. "Eddie..."

The man prickled. "Excuse me?"

"Edward Butterworth, right?" Jane asked. She realized immediately how much this East coast, stuffed shirt must bristle when Jordan called him "*Eddie.*"

"Yes," Butterworth replied in a careful manner as he slid his thin body next to them and headed toward the B&B. "I really must be going." He disappeared up the steps and into the building.

Jane turned to Weyler. "The Copelands' cleanup man."

CHAPTER 29

Jane grabbed another hot cup of coffee inside the B&B and some leftover bacon from the serving pan before walking down Main Street to the Midas Library. There was a little more action in the joint than on the day before, but it was still empty enough that she could turn any corner and fire her gun without hitting

a soul. She wandered to the section that displayed MODERN LIT-
ERARY GREATS OF THE 20TH CENTURY and scoured the shelves
for anything about author, Thomas Wolfe. She was confident
that Wolfe's book, being the first clue, meant something more to
the kidnapper. Jane uncovered a biography on Wolfe. Scanning
the front pages, she learned that he was considered by some to
be the "most overtly autobiographical novelist," so much so that
his hometown of Asheville, North Carolina, banned his 1929
book, Look Homeward, Angel from the Asheville Public Library
because the depictions of the characters were too "frank and re-
alistic," due to the fact that Wolfe apparently didn't use enough
"artistic license." Flipping forward to the chapter on You Can't
Go Home Again, Jane read how it was published posthumously
in 1940 and followed the life of George Webber, a man who
seemed to mirror Wolfe's own short life. Webber, a novelist,
writes a successful book about his family and southern hometown only to find his life shattered by the voices of outrage that
greet him. Jane found two passages intriguing. The first one
spoke about how in the story, Webber's family and friends, felt
naked and exposed by the truth they read in his book. Jane looked
up momentarily. "The truth..." she whispered. Returning to the
book, she continued reading. This is a story of a man who flees
scandal and leaves the only town he knew to search the world for
his own identity. When Webber returns to his humble hometown
later, there is love for the distant memories but the sad revelation
that...You can't go home again. Her thoughts turned to Jordan
and his pattern of using those five fateful words in her company.
     She considered what he said only hours ago, "I exist in this
town like I've existed in every other town. I exist under a modus
vivendi...a practical arrangement that allows conflicting people
to coexist until a final settlement is reached. The final agreement is usually my removal from the town." Since Jordan never
felt at home anywhere in his life, did it make sense that he created an event that would release him from his fractured existence
and return him to the safety of confinement? He wouldn't be the

first ex-con to play that card. When you've spent more of your life in the slammer than out, freedom was like riding a wave of razors. Just as he claimed to have created a *situation* by hiding Daniel Marshall's body and pleading guilty to his murder simply because living behind bars was more comfortable than his hometown of Short Hills.

Jane returned the book to the shelf and thought about the series of clues pinned on the clothesline in her room. Her belief that the kidnapper was telling a story—albeit one with hidden messages and even hazier motives—made more sense to her now, *if* he was using the platform of *You Can't Go Home Again* to launch his message. George Webber exposed the truth and nakedness of people who wished to remain anonymous. Webber himself then goes on a search for his own identity only to realize that he'll never be the same again. Thinking back on the voicemail messages left by the kidnapper in a disguised voice, it had always bothered Jane that he used the wrong tense when he said, "He cried like a baby and will never be a real man." It should have been "he cries" since they heard the sound of a crying child in the background. Maybe she was nitpicking, Jane wondered, but she'd learned fast that the person behind these clues was a calculating master of the written word and knew how to manipulate it to his benefit. The mere fact that he spoofed the phone number on his throwaway cell phone of the house directly across from the Copelands' home seemed to be jaggedly pointing to some relevant information. The pieces only briefly came together after Jane dialed David Sackett and found out that an eight-year-old, red-haired boy lived in the back house on that property with his Russian immigrant mother and then quickly left for unknown reasons. It was getting frustrating as hell to Jane because whatever story the kidnapper was telling was so confusing to those who were trying to solve this crime, that nobody in charge understood it. They almost needed a program to decode the clues.

But, wait a second, Jane reflected. The Van Gordens were

no Mensa minds, but both Louise and Bailey seemed to jointly react to the Ace of Spades playing card along with the Chesterfield cigarette when Bo laid them out on their living room table. Those two items triggered something within them almost simultaneously. Maybe, possibly, *they* had at least a part of that elusive program needed to decipher what the kidnapper was trying to say? It had to be the reason they held back the teddy bear with the *BAWY* note attached to its front bib. It represented something to them...something about Jake perhaps? And what in the hell did *BAWY* stand for?

Jane scooted over to the library's computers and did a search for *BAWY* but came up with nothing. She tried every acronym tool she could find but nothing made sense. After nearly an hour, she got up and wandered back into the microfiche room, figuring she'd pull up that *Time* magazine article on the Copelands and re-examine the illustration of Jordan's neighborhood. But when she opened the door to the windowless room, less than half the boxes remained. She spent nearly half an hour reading the outside label contents but couldn't find the one that included the *Time* article. Jane tracked down the same harried librarian from the day before and inquired as to where she could find that specific microfiche document. It seemed that it was one of the first boxes shipped to Denver for digital transfer. Jane returned to the room and stared into the disheveled mess. The only copy she had of the illustration was blurred and streaked, and of little use.

Her eyes drifted across the stacks of brown cardboard, her brain picking up one word or so from each outside label. Suddenly, she spotted, *The Millburn Township Register* and quickly zoned in on the box. Millburn Township was the area where Short Hills, New Jersey, resided. Opening the box, Jane brought out a series of plastic boxes with microfiche reels, each holding several years of the weekly local newspaper. She located the reel that covered 1967 through 1969. Setting it into the microfiche viewer, she scanned reams of black-and-white pages, starting in late 1967. It was fairly easy to skim through the slim daily offering since the meat of the paper was found within the first five pages and the rest of it was dedicated to advertisements and classifieds. She wasn't sure what she was looking for, but she figured that there might be some mention of Jordan Copeland in the local rag. By the time she reached the January 1st edition of 1968, her eyes were getting bleary, but she continued the dizzy turn of pages that revolved around holiday events, local awards and town council reports.

Then the headline words, MISSING BOY jumped out at her. Jane quickly spun the reel back to the page and sharpened the focus. It was a short article on page two, but the headline was gripping: SEARCH IS ON FOR MISSING BOY. The date was January 5th, 1968. The child's name was mentioned at the top of the article but the transfer of the old paper to microfiche had compromised the integrity of many of the words on the page, including the kid's name. No matter how much Jane twisted the *focus* button on the reel, the name of the child and many of the words in the short article kept warping so that they were illegible. One thing was clear—the boy was eight years old and was thought to have wandered off three days prior to the story being published. Outbuildings and ditches had been thoroughly searched while his mother prayed for his safe return. Since the paper was a weekly publication, they were a little late in reporting this time-critical event.

Jane quickly jumped to the following week's edition for any update. On page three, she found another five-hundred-word article titled, "Missing Millburn Boy Feared Drowned." This article theorized that police felt the boy, who loved to wander, may have fallen into an icy pond and died. The rest of the story was a virtual repetition of the information from the week before. Just as Jane was moving forward on the reel, the door opened and three guys wearing jumpsuits and carrying hand trucks walked in. They seemed surprised to see Jane.

"Hey, ma'am, we got to stack all this up and put it on the

truck for Denver right away," the larger of the three stated.

"I'm in the middle of something kind of important…"

"So are we," a second man added. "We're already late on picking up the second load."

They started stacking boxes one on top of the other. Jane connected the printer. Even though the quality left a lot to be desired, she wanted to have a hard copy document of what she'd discovered. While the men noisily worked around her, she printed off page after page, starting with the initial January 5th edition. When she had a good handful of pages, she scanned the reel to the following week, in search of any mention of the boy. But one by one, the pages became barely readable. This continued for nearly half of the year's weekly editions.

"*Lady*," one of the guys stated in a loud, impatient voice, "we gotta have that reel you're lookin' at."

"Shit!" Jane exclaimed, sitting up and turning off the microfiche viewer. She removed the reel, put it back in the plastic box and handed it to one of the guys. As she turned around, all the men reacted to her holstered Glock strapped across her *Groovy* T-shirt.

"*Whoa, Nellie!*" the big guy exclaimed. "Is that gun for real?"

Jane kicked the chair under the table and headed out the door. "No. I just wear it to scare the horses and children."

CHAPTER 30

Outside, the sky darkened with rain clouds, seemingly converging solely over Midas. The air had an ominous tang that did little to settle Jane's churning gut. She secured the pages from the *Millburn Township Register* under her T-shirt. Pellets of rain began to fall as she headed back to the B&B. But the wind whipped up suddenly, driving the rain harder and forcing Jane to make a quick detour to Town Hall, where she took refuge under the front awning. She heard a knock on the glass behind her and saw Vi motioning her to come inside. Once inside, Vi handed her a roll of paper towels to absorb the dripping water off Jane's T-shirt. The place looked vacant, with only Vi and two tech guys in the background setting up more equipment. Jane carefully turned to Bo's office.

"Don't worry," Vi assured, "he's not here."

"You heard what happened between us?"

"I knew it would happen before it happened," Vi said with a smile.

That basically said it all. Vi knew what Bo was feeling before Bo even felt it. She really *was* his right arm, left arm, and everything in between, just as Bo told them on their first day in Midas. "I probably shouldn't linger not knowing when he's coming back."

"He'll be gone at least another hour. He's at his house packing boxes."

Jane was never one to pry into people's lives unless it was in regard to a pending case. But since she was standing before the woman who knew everything about anything, she figured she'd pose a question. "Did Bo have a son?"

The rock steadiness that defined Vi cracked ever so slightly. Others would have missed the momentary freezing of her eyes and unconscious twitch at the corner of her lip. But Jane saw it. "A son?" Vi repeated. "No."

"You've been with him since he came to Midas, right?"

"Yes."

"Maybe he had a son before that."

"No. I don't think so." Vi turned back to her desk.

Jane noted a change in Vi's movement. Instead of the confidence that she normally exuded, there was a halted progress in her gait. Jane had observed the same preoccupied behavior from others during an interrogation when something had come up in the course of conversation that made it impossible for them to continue *business as usual.* The fact that Vi turned away only personified her need to turn away from the subject as well.

Since Jane didn't want to ostracize the woman, she changed the subject. "You have that video handy of Jordan's lie detector test?"

Vi turned back to Jane, her confidence resurrected. "Sure."

There was a moment in that tape Jane actually wanted to review. As Vi set it up in Bo's office, the rain continued to pour outside in an unremitting deluge. A crack of thunder broke overhead, jarring Jane. Vi cued the tape and hit the PLAY button.

"Is your name Jordan Richard Copeland?" the man asked Jordan.

"Yes." Jordan answered quietly.

"Do you live in Midas, Colorado?"

"Yes."

"Do you have a beard and mustache?"

Jordan shifted slightly in his chair. "Yes."

Jane leaned forward. "Could you rewind it to that last question?"

Vi rewound the tape and resumed playback.

"Do you have a beard and mustache?"

Jane focused on Jordan's feet as he shifted in his chair.

"Yes," Jordan replied.

"Okay, pause it," Jane quickly instructed. If Jordan was going to *beat the box*, he would do it during the control questions, creating a false baseline response that would make the peak comparison values for later, more important questions, not equate. The two most common ways to alter the stress response was to squeeze one's anus or place a tack in the toe of your shoe and press down on it to cause a moment of pain. The shift Jordan made in his seat concerned Jane. "Is there anyway to highlight his feet?"

"It's a video. Not a computer. Sorry."

Jane asked Vi to replay that five-second section ten more

times, each time with Jane moving closer to the monitor so that she was almost flush with the screen. Jane shook her head. "I don't know. Keep going."

Vi resumed playback.

"Are you the son of Richard and Joanna Copeland?"

Now Jane was really interested and she watched Jordan carefully.

"Yes." Jordan said, staring straight ahead, his voice exceptionally modulated.

"Play that part again," Jane asked, leaning closer to the monitor.

Vi backed up the tape and started the playback.

"Are you the son of Richard and Joanna Copeland?"

Jane focused on Jordan's feet. There was slight movement from his right foot. This was a control question to the man running the test, but in actuality it was a question requiring Jordan to lie. However, the stress factor would also need to be seen on the chart in order to throw off the results. "Play that question again, please," Jane said. The thunder rolled loudly down Main Street, followed by a crack of lightning that sounded as though it was directly overhead. Vi rewound the tape and replayed that part. Jane still wasn't positive and asked to see it again, but just as Vi was hitting the remote control, a deafening bolt of lightning rang out and the power blew. "Shit!" Jane exclaimed.

Vi checked the lights and the phone and found nothing. She went to the door and called out to the tech guys, asking how long it would take to get the backup power running. They needed her to unlock the upstairs room where they had previously installed the equipment. Vi quickly excused herself, unlocked the side drawer in her desk, removed the keys and hustled out the far back area and up the stairs with the techies. Jane leaned back in her chair and noted the opened desk drawer. Without hesitating, she quickly moved to Vi's desk in the semidarkness and slid the drawer open all the way. The first thing she found taped to the inside of the drawer was a worn sheet of paper, frayed at the edges. On it were symbols, each relating to a word. But it was nothing like the usual cop codes she already knew. Jane heard footsteps above her and wasn't sure how much longer she'd be alone. Checking the symbols again, Jane caught a fairly good grasp of their obvious meaning. A single key that looked like it would fit into a file cabinet lay in the front corner of the drawer. Jane grabbed it, turned and used it to open the file cabinet behind Vi's desk. The footsteps moved across the upstairs floor as she found Jake's thin file. She removed it and stared at the front cover sheet. "What in the hell…?" Jane whispered to herself. She quickly stashed it back into the file and removed Jordan's file, only interested in the front cover sheet. She stared at it, taking in what she saw before returning it to the file cabinet. She grabbed two more files, one having to do with Christmas decorations and the other office acquisitions. She saw what she expected on the cover sheets. Opening the file having to do with office acquisitions, the puzzle pieces started to come together. Jane quickly stuffed the files back into the cabinet, locked it and returned the key to Vi's desk drawer. She made sure the drawer was exactly as Vi left it before quickly walking back into Bo's office.

Jane spied the stack of file boxes lined up in his office, each sporting either a *?*, an *!*,a thumbs up and a thumbs down drawing. Darting to his desk, Jane canvassed the cluttered paper strewn across the top. Opening Bo's front desk drawer, she removed an appointment book. She flipped it open and stared at the entries for the first several weeks of the year. "Oh, Bo," Jane murmured.

Her eye caught the bright yellow folder on his desk, still hidden under several sheets of paper. She opened the folder and quickly read the cover letter. The clip-clop of feet could be heard descending the stairway. Jane slid Bo's appointment book back into the front drawer, slipped the yellow folder under the pages on the desk and jumped back into the chair within seconds of Vi returning to her side.

"I figured you'd be gone," Vi said.

"I wasn't sure if the power was going to come back on and we could keep watching the video."

"Doesn't look like it. We'll have some backup power but we have to reserve it for only the essential equipment. Town's probably down for at least a couple hours."

Jane left Town Hall and sprinted through the falling rain back to the B&B. She was soaking wet again by the time she crossed the threshold. Upstairs, she removed the pages she'd copied from the *Millburn Township Register* and laid them on the carpeting one by one to let them dry out. Jane showered in an attempt to warm up and changed into a clean pair of jeans and another one of Mollie's shirts—this one a three-quarter sleeve T-shirt with the proclamation, *I Must Be Trippin' 'Cuz You Look Cute!* in bold letters.

As she towel-dried her hair, she caught sight of the black-and-white photo she'd found of her mother and Harry Mills standing outside The Hayloft. She picked up the photo and looked at the two lovebirds. She'd never seen her mother look so content. "*A cool drink of water.*" That's what her mother said the night before about Mr. Mills. Yes, he was that. But according to Anne, he also suffered from depression, killing himself and leaving her to feel it was all her fault. "*I couldn't tell a soul,*" she told Jane, her voice clearly emotional.

Jane looked out the window at the still pounding rain. What were these unconscious patterns that operated in our lives, she wondered. Up until last night, Jane had no idea that Harry Mills existed. Nor did she know he killed himself. But as uncanny as it seemed, somewhere on the ethereal waves, that buried secret replicated itself in Jane's own life and played out to its tragic conclusion nearly at the same age that her mother experienced her lover's loss. *Patterns.* It was something Jane always looked for in criminal cases. But could patterns within a family emerge and repeat throughout the generations on an unconscious basis simply because the stories remained untold and, thus, the secret needed a physical vehicle for its manifestation? To Jane, it seemed preposterous on one hand and, yet, on the other hand, she couldn't deny this enigmatic mirroring of events that she and her mother unknowingly shared.

There was a knock at the door. Jane tucked the photograph under her laptop and opened the door. It was Sara.

"Thought you might need this," Sara said, handing Jane a flashlight.

"Thanks," Jane tossed it onto her bed. When she turned back to Sara, it was apparent that the woman looked apprehensive. "Is something wrong?"

"Aaron told me about the conversation you had with him," she whispered. Guilt covered her face. "I know you and Mollie..." she caught herself, "*Liora*, are talking..."

"It's crazy about her choosing that name, isn't it?" Jane asked, genuinely intrigued now by the strange whispers of awareness that bleed through the generations.

Sara nodded. "It's beyond crazy." She turned, making sure that nobody else was around. "What's even crazier is that when she starts talking in Yiddish, she has the same tone as my grandmother, Liora. Every time she does it, I can almost hear the ghost of my grandmother begging me to tell Mollie the truth." She held her hand to her face. "God, you must think I'm half-cocked."

"Oh, Sara," Jane said, shaking her head, "that sounds fairly reasonable to me."

"*Seriously?*"

"Yeah. You should tell her. Because if you don't, I think your grandmother's ghost will have a field day with you." Jane turned and retrieved the box of photographs she stole from the kitchen cupboard. "I borrowed these when I took the photo album."

"I wondered what happened to that."

"This place has gone through a lot of incarnations, hasn't it?"

Sara smiled. "Oh, yeah. It's got quite the history."

"It was a boardinghouse for women, you said?"

"Yeah. Single women. Somewhat wild, I'm told."

"Wild in what way?"

"*Spirited.* They weren't forging the paths that were expected of them. This place attracted decades of women who wanted to experience life on their own terms and I guess the town let them do that. It actually served a good purpose in the later years when it was a boardinghouse, especially in the late sixties."

Jane looked at Sara. "What do you mean?"

"It became a secret retreat for unwed, pregnant women."

The floor felt as if it was about to fall away from Jane's feet. She leaned against the doorjamb, not quite sure she heard Sara correctly. Her mouth tasted like cotton. "They weren't *all* unwed and pregnant, right?"

"From '66 on, yeah…every single one of them." Sara saw the sheer shock in Jane's eyes. "Are you okay, Jane?"

"I need to go." Jane closed the door and slid down to the floor. The incessant rain pelted the bedroom windows and swelled into another stormy downpour. That familiar pain in Jane's pelvis started to flare up as the nauseating scent of gardenias permeated the room. Jane pulled her knees to her chest, wrapping her arms around her legs. "Go away!" she murmured with an acid pitch. This wasn't happening. It was insane. She had to be dreaming. "Leave me alone!" she said with more vitriol. The full throttle comprehension of what Sara told her slammed into her heart. The ramifications also became blisteringly apparent.

She had to get out of there. The walls were caving in and her mind was moving toward scenarios that seemed improbable. Jane grabbed her leather jacket and bolted out of the room. She walked outside into the diagonal downpour and kept walking for four blocks. The late afternoon had turned into a queasy nighttime scene as the blackened clouds suffocated any light that should have still existed at that time of day. Coupled with the power outage, the streets took on an eerie quality, which only served to deepen the collision of restless thoughts within Jane's head. The pain subsided in her pelvis, but nothing quelled her mind. She walked up and down the blocks that framed Main Street, oblivious to her surroundings or the ruthless storm overhead. It was moments like this in her past where she'd kill the chaos with a bottle of Jack Daniels and half a pack of cigarettes. But now, with nothing but doubt to comfort her, the rawness of sobriety stung. A surge of debilitating helplessness engulfed her. Thoughts of the warm amber liquid overwhelmed her senses. She could feel herself falling again, like she'd fallen before. Jane turned and ran hard and fast. The thunder rolled, shaking the pavement beneath her soaked boots. That desperation demanded to be served—to anesthetize what she couldn't face. Loneliness and desolation, her two steady companions, entwined her body and urged her to feed her addiction. Soon, the voices would start their cacophony and she would plunge back into the void from which she thought she'd escaped.

Jane raced across Main Street, down the sidewalk and across the gravel until she reached the front door of the tiny house. Like the rest of the town, she could see it was dark inside, save for the candles illumined in the kitchen windowsill. She pounded on the door until he opened it.

"Help me...please help me..." Jane whispered. With that, she fell into Hank's arms.

He closed the door and held her soaked body close to his as she shook from both the cold and the fear.

"It's all right, Jane," he said, moving his hand across the back of her head.

"No, no" she stammered, "it's not...I have to forget..." She held him as if he were a lifeline in the ocean.

"Never forget. No matter how painful it is."

The world around her collapsed. All the walls she'd put up fell; the steel encasing her heart melted. Jane brushed her cheek against Hank's face, searching for his lips. The storm pelted the roof as she softly kissed him. He held her face gently between his hands and tenderly kissed her. It had been so long since she'd been with a man who wasn't rough that she'd forgotten the way it felt to be cherished. She traced his lips with her tongue until the passion could no longer be restrained. Still interlocked, Jane moved with Hank to his bedroom where they fell onto the mattress side by side. They explored each other's bodies, never saying a word but understanding what the other needed. As they shed their clothes, their bodies melded in a fervent connection. Hank kissed Jane's breast, moving slowly toward her neck. She arched her back, drawing Hank closer and entwined her leg around his, urging him inside her. He entered slowly as Jane relaxed and they moved into a gentle rhythm that built with quiet intensity. Kissing him passionately, she couldn't distinguish his heartbeat from hers as the fire within each of them erupted into a powerful crescendo.

Jane shook, pulling Hank tightly toward her. She held him inside, their breath rising and falling in unison. For the first time in too long, she felt as though she was finally home and safe. Then the stark realization came that this was the only time in her entire life that she'd made love sober. *My God.* Hank started to move, but Jane wouldn't let go. "No," she whispered. "Not yet." He held her, stroking her forehead with a soothing motion. "My mother brushed my forehead like that," Jane said softly. She'd forgotten until that moment. But the memory slipped forward and Jane recalled the reassuring hand of her mother brushing her hand across her forehead. Down and up, over and over. It was the same unexplained motion Jane found herself doing in the doctor's office. Hank intuitively seemed to know that it calmed Jane as his hand continued the comforting motion. Tears welled in her eyes. "It was the only way she could calm me down when I lost control."

Hank looked lovingly into Jane's eyes. "That's because you and she had a strong connection."

"I never thought it existed."

"Just because you don't believe in something doesn't prevent it from still operating in your life."

Jane looked at Hank, stunned. "Where'd you hear that?"

"I think I read it in one of my woo-woo books." Jane turned away. "Are you all right?"

"You sure you read it somewhere?"

"Yeah. What is it?" Hank rolled to the side, cupping his palm on Jane's breast.

"Lately, I hear statements repeated back to me that all came from one person."

They lay together until sleep overcame them. Jane awoke hours later to find Hank gone. Checking the large battery clock, it was past seven. The afternoon had succumbed to the gloaming, allowing only a hint of light into the room. Her soaked clothes that she'd flung onto the floor were missing. Even her boots were AWOL. She jumped off the bed and suddenly noticed a man's white terry cloth robe draped across the bed, seemingly waiting for her. She slipped it on and made her way toward the main room. Her acute senses picked up the scent of melted beeswax. As Jane entered the living room, she was met with a well-placed assortment of candles, spread throughout the kitchen and living room so that the area was clearly illumined. She figured the power should go off a lot more often.

Hank stood in the kitchen over the gas stove, preparing dinner. He wore only a T-shirt and white chef's apron around his waist. He seemed completely comfortable and smiled broadly when he saw Jane walk into the room. "Hey, Chopper!"

"I thought you left me," she said.

"Left you?" Hank replied, his brow furrowed. "Why in the hell would I leave you?"

"I don't know." She shrugged. "Isn't that the way it works?"

"Come here," he moved around the counter and pulled out a stool, patting it and urging her to come and sit down. When he turned, she could see his adorable naked backside peeking out from the apron. She crossed to the stool and sat down. Hank kissed her gently on the lips before returning to his specialty of the evening. "Your clothes are almost dry," he said pointing to her jeans, T-shirt and underwear hanging in the living room. "The boots may take a bit longer."

"You didn't need to do that. I could have figured it out..."

"Of course you could figure it out. But I thought I'd give you a hand."

Jane sat bemused. "Okay..."

"Chopper, let me ask you something. Didn't you ever have someone take care of you?"

"No. I was always the one in charge of my younger brother and myself...especially after my mother died."

"I'm sorry."

"Why are you sorry?"

He checked the label on a jar of seasoning with the light of a nearby candle and added a dash of it to the two chicken breasts in the pan. "You didn't deserve that."

"It's all I know."

"Taking care of yourself and being abandoned?"

Jane considered the finality of his statement. "Well, when you put it that way, it sounds pretty depressing."

"That's because it *is*." He set a bowl of *pico de gallo* in front of Jane along with a bowl of chips. "That's your appetizer, Chopper."

She slid a candle closer to the salsa. "Did you make this?"

"Sure," he said offhandedly as he snuck a taste from the steaming pan and added a pinch of salt.

"*Sure?*"

"It's not that complicated. It's tomatoes, jalapenos, onions, cilantro..."

"What are you? Betty Crocker's little brother?" Jane scooped up a large helping of the *pico de gallo* with a chip and gobbled it up. Within seconds, she realized she had a new flavorful addiction. "Maybe I'll call you Crocker."

He chuckled. "Crocker and Chopper? I don't think so. It

sounds too much like a bad 70s TV cop drama." He motioned to the food. "There's nothing to this. I like to cook and I like opera." He quickly turned to her. "And I'm *not* gay."

"And you're a recovering alcoholic, ex-cop who owns a bar. Did you just hear that? That's God laughing at me."

Hank brought out two plates from the cupboard. "No, I don't hear Him laughing. I hear Him saying, 'Thank myself! She finally said *what the hell* and dove into that pool!'" He served the chicken breasts and buttery slivers of zucchini onto the plates. "And *I* say, thank God she did."

He sat next to her at the counter, the flickering candles casting mesmerizing shadows against the walls. They ate in near silence as Hank softly stroked Jane's thigh under her terry robe. After about five minutes, she looked at him. "This is nice."

Hank broke into a wide grin. "Coming from you, that's one helluva compliment!"

She contemplated what he'd asked her not long before. "You asked me if I ever had someone take care of me? It's going to sound crazy, but I just remembered how I had this strange fantasy when I was less than six...I pretended that I had an older sister to watch over me." Jane dropped her fork against the plate.

"Why not a big brother? Wouldn't that make more sense?"

She stared into the flickering flame from the candle on the counter. "Yeah. You're absolutely right. It would have, wouldn't it?" She found herself briefly lost in the recollection. "But I remember it was a sister...an older sister."

They finished the meal and stacked the dishes in the sink before blowing out all but four of the candles and carrying them back into the bedroom. Nestled under the covers, Jane pressed her naked body against Hank. "When do you think we're going to get the power back up?"

"It came back on two hours ago, Chopper," he said, turning over and drifting off to sleep. "I just wanted to make it last a little longer."

Jane shook her head in disbelief as she spooned her body

next to his. She quickly slid into slumber as the world and her worries fell far into the distance. Her dreams were placid and brief and she slept soundly. But then, in the darkness, the sound of a woman crying could be heard. Jane tried to reconcile the weeping in her altered state but awoke to the sound coming from within the bedroom. Opening her eyes, she noted the four candles, nearly extinguished in their saucers. Jane tilted the bedside clock to see the time—*3:11 am.*

Her heart began to race as the pungent scent of gardenias swept through the room. She turned to find Hank asleep beside her, the covers pulled close to his face. This *had* to be a dream. She pinched her flesh in an attempt to wake up but the woman's cries continued unabated. Jane carefully tossed back the covers and picked up one of the candles on the bedside table in its wax-pooled saucer. She stood up, naked and exposed, and peered into the corner of the room where the sobbing seemed to originate. Jane slowly walked around the bed, allowing the dying candlelight to direct her path. She stopped after several steps, horrified by what she saw.

There in the corner, curled up in a naked and bloody ball from the waist down, was her mother. Her black mascara left ghoulish streaks down her weathered, young face while her once-pristine fire engine red lacquered manicure had been bitten down to the fleshy nubs. Jane knelt down, holding the candle in front of her to cast more light toward her mother, but Anne waved the candle away.

"No!" Anne cried. "You can't see this!"

"My God," Jane whispered. "What happened?"

Anne shook her head and grabbed her lower gut. "I didn't want to lose her...but I had no choice..."

"*Her?*" Jane asked, her eyes wide with shock.

"What was I supposed to do?" Anne sobbed. "He killed himself! That son-of-a-bitch! He left me! What was I supposed to do?!"

The candlewick sputtered in the melted wax. "You...had

an abortion?"

Anne gazed up at Jane. "*I lost her!*" she screamed. With that, Anne reached out and grabbed Jane's arm.

The wraithlike connection sent an electric shockwave through Jane's body, driving an ungodly shock of pelvic pain into Jane, followed by the awareness of profound grief that Jane realized did not belong to her. The candlewick continued to spit its dying light between them. Jane tried in vain to pry Anne's fingers from her arm. "It doesn't belong to me!" Jane screamed. "It's *your* grief!"

Anne released Jane's arm and all the sorrow melted from her face. A calmness and wisdom that belied her youthful countenance replaced it. It was as if the soul within shone through her eyes. "Have the courage to see what follows, Jane."

"What follows?"

"I love you."

With that, the candlelight extinguished.

Jane turned and felt the bed beneath her skin. She opened her eyes and sat up with a shot. Hank was gone. Checking the clock, it was 8:09 in the morning. Streaks of sunshine angled into the bedroom. Jane looked over into the corner and saw nothing. She ran her shaking fingers through her tangled hair and grabbed the terry cloth robe to wrap around her.

Walking into the living room, she called out to Hank but got no response. Her clothes from the night before were carefully laid across the couch while her boots warmed up in front of an electric space heater. She called out to him again, walking closer to the kitchen counter in search of a note. But there was nothing. That familiar feeling rose up in her again. Whether it was because she was coming off one of the most disturbing encounters she'd ever imagined, or whether it was because she expected to be let down, the feeling was palpable and the familiar anger simmered on a slow burn. She heard the sound of a woman's laughter outside the kitchen window. Jane walked into the kitchen and peered outside. There she found Annie Mack touching Hank's arm in a comfortable way and smiling at him with those innocent young eyes. To Jane, his body language was receptive, although she could only see his back.

Pulling back from the sink with umbrage, she accidentally knocked over a glass, shattering it in the sink. The sound got Hank's attention and he quickly excused himself and walked inside. Jane was already halfway across the room, clothes in one hand, and still wet boots dangling from the other.

"Chopper!" Hank called out.

"I'm leaving!" Jane yelled back, turning the corner into the bedroom. She threw her clothes on the bed, tore off the robe and started dressing in a fitful manner.

Hank quickly appeared in the doorway. "What in the hell's going on?"

"Sorry about breaking that glass. Send me a bill." She never looked at him once.

"Jane, what are you doing? I have breakfast in the oven."

"Great. When the next shift moves in, you'll have something to feed her."

"This is about Annie? Jane, I've already told you…"

She turned to Hank, staring him straight on. "Please. Don't bullshit me anymore. There *is* something between you two… something deep." She could see Hank clearly connect with what she said. But still he hesitated. "Exactly…you know what? Chalk this up to just another fucking mistake of mine. Live and learn, right?" She finished dressing and he stood there speechless. He didn't say a word until she started out of the room.

"Jane…*please* don't leave like this. I've got something to show you…"

She dug his truck keys out of her jean pocket and threw them at him. "Fuck you," she muttered under her breath as she stormed out.

Back in front of the B&B, her Mustang had returned to its former self, minus the bloody message on the trunk. Released as part of a crime scene, she could now regain her freedom. Yes, this is what felt normal to Jane Perry. She was alone again, but she was back in charge of her predictable life. She headed up the stairs and met Mollie midway, who was headed down with a basket of dirty clothes.

"You didn't come home last night," Mollie said, with a pensive look.

"Yeah?"

The kid looked at her shirt on Jane and smiled. She leaned closer and whispered. "Did my shirt get lucky last night?"

The sound of a door opening and closing was heard upstairs. Mollie quickly skipped down the steps as Jane stepped aside for Edward Butterworth to make his way downstairs.

"Morning," he curtly offered, brushing past her with his meticulous three-piece suit and monogrammed attaché case in hand.

"Mr. Butterworth," Jane quickly said. Butterworth turned around, looking irritated that someone had the gall to stop his forward progress. "I need to talk to you."

"Why?"

"It's about Jordan Copeland."

"Well, it'll have to wait. I'm heading over there now and then I'm leaving for Denver to catch my plane."

"I just need a second of your time."

"Funny about that. When someone asks for a 'second,' it's invariably longer and usually an imposition." With that, the old guy continued down the stairs and out the door.

Shaking her head in disgust, Jane bolted up the stairs and into her room. The first thing she saw was the photo of her mother and Harry she'd slid under her laptop. She brought it out and looked at it. The possibilities were too stark and she quickly lifted her laptop and hid the photo underneath it.

She took a quick shower and washed her hair, all the time working hard to keep Hank out of her head. She told herself that she'd lost precious time by hanging out with him and silently berated herself for allowing herself to become weak and vulnerable. As she'd always suspected, vulnerability was a sharp sword onto which one impales oneself and suffers needless wounds to the heart. By the time she got out of the shower, she'd resolved to never let it happen again and began the proverbial process of locking up her heart against any further gatecrashers.

To that end, she didn't hesitate when she reached for her standard navy blue poplin shirt. She told herself how ridiculous she'd looked in Mollie's youthful garb and that she was, back on familiar ground and back in charge of her reality again. Yet, Jane wasn't really paying attention as she buttoned the shirt because one-by-one, the white buttons popped off the fabric. It wasn't until the third one hit the floor that she realized that the shirt was useless. She stripped it off and grabbed the remaining poplin shirt off the hanger. This one buttoned up just fine. But as she straightened the collar, she was met with an unforgiving sharp prick in her neck and across her back. It felt as if tiny needles were impaling her flesh. Quickly removing the shirt, she examined the collar and back material. Her eyes could see nothing but when she ran her fingers across the fabric, she was met with what felt like knife-like daggers that drew several drops of blood from her fingertips. This was truly insane. "Fuck!" she screamed, flailing the shirt against the wall.

Whatever was conspiring against her would not win, she decided. She *had* to revert to the safety of what she knew, no matter how much that journey would validate her suffering and belief that she only attracted shitty situations and shittier men. But she was left with the option of wearing her nightshirt again and that didn't seem reasonable. She reluctantly looked through the hangers of remaining shirts that Mollie loaned her. All that was left that she hadn't worn were dressier numbers, brimming with lace collars and embroidered hems. Jane let out a tired sigh and chose the only one of the group that she knew she could strap her Glock across without ruining the fabric.

She turned to the mirror above the desk to comb out her

hair when she looked down at her laptop. There, sitting *on top* of the computer, was the photo of Anne and Harry. She'd put it underneath the computer. At least, she thought she had. With all the confusion in her head, she was probably mistaken. So, this time, she opened her laptop, flung the photo on top of the keyboard and slammed the top shut. *Focus,* she told herself. *Bury your feelings. Bury the hurt.* She would systemically erase the events of the last fourteen or so hours. It wasn't just Hank. She'd expunge the brutal visual of her young mother's naked and bloody body crying about how she lost "her."

Even when she told her mother that "It's *your* grief" and she felt it like a shock of understanding after awakening from a long coma, she would bury it.

Even when her mother let go of her and told her to "have the courage to see what follows," she would ignore it.

The walls would once again be built around her.

Jane pulled on her jeans and boots, strapped her holster gingerly across the delicate fabric of the shirt, grabbed her cell phone and turned to the door. "Holy shit!" she exclaimed as she looked down on the carpet. It was that damn photo again. And with it, came the enveloping aroma of gardenias that was determined to get her attention. As stubborn as Jane was to hold an unknown future at arm's length, another force was surprisingly more intractable to prevent that from happening. There was only one way to put this to rest. And while the thought of it scared the hell out of her, she knew she had no choice.

CHAPTER 31

Jane arrived at the County Recorder's office on the outskirts of Midas just as they opened the doors for business. She stood and waited while the heavyset woman waddled across the room and slid the glass open at the counter.

"You keep the records here of birth and death records?"

"That's right."

"How about a stillborn? Would that be recorded?"

"That depends how the mother wanted to handle it. What year are we talking?"

Jane couldn't believe she was doing this. "1967. The name is Anne LeRóy." Jane spelled it out, including the accent over the o.

The woman saw the holstered Glock. "Is this related to a case?"

"No. It's my mother." When Jane said those words, the reality hit hard. The woman crossed over to a long line of grey file cabinets and spent a good five minutes searching before she revealed a thin green file. The woman opened it and silently read through the few papers before walking back to the window.

"You can't take the file," the woman advised.

Jane's heart raced. "Yeah. I know," she said, pulling the file toward her and opening it. She suddenly felt light headed as she stared at the page.

"Are you all right, honey?" the woman asked, clearly concerned by Jane's reaction.

Jane read the few telling lines on the page again before closing it and handing it back to the woman. Without saying a word, Jane turned and left the building.

The stream of smoke curled precipitously out of the stretch of sheltered green space that sat at the rear of the B&B property. She didn't hear the footsteps approaching until it was too late.

"What are you doing?" Mollie asked in a slightly stunned tone.

Jane took a hard puff on that last cigarette she'd been holding back. "Sedating myself. What does it look like?"

Mollie kneeled down to where Jane was seated. Jane hadn't

noticed the thin book in her hand up until then. "Did something happen?" she asked, her chin trembling. "Did you find Jake?"

Jane pulled out of her self-imposed destruction and put a reassuring hand on Mollie's thigh. "No. It's got nothing to do with Jake."

"So, why are you screwing up your life again after five days of staying off those things?"

"Habit." Jane took another meaningful drag, holding the nicotine in her lungs.

Mollie sat across from Jane cross-legged, laying the book on the ground. "I looked on that website you told me about." Her face was subdued. "You know, *mysecretrevelations*? I read the posts by the fifteen-year-old boy like you asked me to."

Jane took a hit. "And?"

"You're right. That was Jake's writing. It sounded just like him." Mollie drew circles in the dirt with her finger. "What do you think he meant on that last one? The one where he wrote, *I saw you but you didn't see me, you fucking pervert! Which one of us will hang in hell?*"

Jane's restrained manner mirrored Mollie's. The events of her life and this case were starting to take their toll. "I don't know."

"I was thinking about that sketchpad of Jake's you showed me…the one of the old man hanging himself in that prison cell? I couldn't get it out of my head. I've been reading this book that Jake gave me. He told me it had a lot of answers to a lot of questions." Mollie drew the book toward her and opened it to a page of highlighted text. "I don't understand a lot of it, but on some level, it kinda speaks to me, you know? Like here, when he says, *Suffering with a problem is easier to bear than a resolution. That has to do with the fact that suffering and continuing to carry a problem are deeply bound to a feeling of innocence and loyalty at a magical level.*" Jane sat up, letting her cigarette ember die. Mollie turned the page. "This one I liked. *People don't become ill as a result of repressing anger, but as a result of repressing action that would lead to resolution.* He talks a lot about *entanglements* with family members who are dead. I don't know why, but that just put a shiver down my spine!" Mollie searched through the thin book. "I can't find the page, but he was talking about how we unconsciously get entangled with the dead family member and take over their fate and live it out without even realizing that what we're doing isn't coming from *us* but *through them.* A lot of it has to do with family secrets. Like, if a child is given away, even way back in your family tree, and no one talks about it, then a future member of that family starts acting as though they've been abandoned." Mollie leaned forward. "It's wild, you know? But without knowing about that entanglement, the future person in the family tree can't find a resolution in their life. It's like, whoever's been left out or ignored or hidden away, has to be brought back into the picture. And that person then becomes a kind of...*protector*...yeah, that's the word he used, for the person who lives today and has been entangled in the other one's fate. It's all about restoring order out of chaos. One or more family members will repeat the fate and patterns of another who's dead and gone without knowing why these things are happening to them." Mollie found the page she was looking for. "Here. Listen to this: *When an injustice has occurred in an earlier generation, a future group member will suffer in an attempt to restore order in that group. There is a sort of systemic drive to repeat the occurrence.* But what he says later is that it never brings order. The only thing that stops the unconscious patterns and makes one stop struggling is to tell the dead, *I honor you, you have a place in my heart. I'll speak out and name the injustice done to you so it can heal.*"

Jane grabbed the book from Mollie's hands. She glanced through it. "Why was Jake reading this kind of book?"

"I don't know. He read lots of books that were outside the norm."

"With *this* kind of intellectual subject matter? He just

happened on it?"

Jane's behavior worried Mollie. "What's wrong? You're saying it's all bullshit?"

"I didn't say that. I said I wanted to know where he got
this book!" Jane turned the pages one after the other until she
reached the inside back cover. It was the second time that morning that her jaw dropped from something she read.

On the lower edge of the cover, written in pen, in small
print and in virtually indecipherable letters were the words,
Property of Jordan Copeland.

Jane took the book and bolted from the tree-cloaked strip
of greenery. As she rounded the front of the B&B, she met Edward Butterworth as he was getting out of his car and heading
back inside. "Mr. Butterworth!" Jane called out to him but the
old man kept walking.

"I can't talk to you, Miss. I've got to retrieve my bag, get to
the post office and drive to the airport."

Jane stood in front of him, barring his progress. "I can run
up and get your bag faster than you can. And in the time you
save, you can spend one minute talking to me." Butterworth
eyed her Glock and reluctantly nodded. Jane raced up the stairs
and entered Butterworth's room—the only other room up there
besides Weyler and Jane's. She grabbed his small suitcase and
dashed back down the stairs, meeting him on the sidewalk in
front of his rental car. "You said you came here to make an assessment on Jordan," Jane stated, slightly out of breath.

"That's correct."

"As an officer of the law, you are compelled to tell me what
that assessment is." Jane was bluffing and hoped the Copeland
clean up man would fall for it.

Butterworth opened the back door of his sedan and slid his
suitcase onto the seat. "I've known that boy since before he was
born. He was trouble from the second the doctor smacked him
on the ass." He slammed the back door of his sedan and opened

the driver's door. "Nothing has changed."

Jane held the driver's door open. "So, what you're saying is that in your opinion, Jordan Copeland killed Daniel Marshall and is responsible in some way for the disappearance of Jake Van Gorden?"

He sat in the driver's seat. "That's exactly what I'm saying! I'm finished with this son-of-a-bitch! This is the last time my shadow will dim his doorstep. I'm turning my duties over to my son who works in our firm." Butterworth retrieved a small stack of mail from the visor and used it as a prop to make his point. "And when I return to New York, mark my words, I am going to make sure that he finds any and all loopholes in this trust so that it *immediately* becomes revocable. That worthless felon is not going to have the Copelands' money as a goddamned cushion any longer! He needs to suffer," Butterworth exclaimed, waving the stack of mail toward Jane, "and I'm just the bastard who can make that happen!" He jabbed the stack of mail one more time in Jane's direction to make his point crystal clear before he slammed the door. Yet, before the door closed, one of the letters in the stack fell out and landed on the asphalt. Butterworth backed out of the parking space as Jane picked up the letter. She called after Butterworth, waving the envelope at him to get his attention but he was quite done talking to her.

Jane folded the letter in half and stuffed it in the book she took from Mollie. She noticed that Hank's truck was no longer parked in front of the B&B. *Good*, she thought. The man listened when he was told to back off. Looking down at the book, she resolved to find Weyler and fill him in on what transpired with Mollie. She spun around and started inside when the sound of squealing tires rang out behind her. Jane turned to find Hank sitting in his truck in the middle of Main Street. He leaned across the front seat and swung open the passenger door. "Get in, Jane!"

I guess the man didn't listen after all, she thought. "I've got nothing to say to you!" Jane turned back to the B&B.

"Jane! If you want to make a scene, that's fine by me. But one way or the other, you and I are going to talk!"

Jane turned and strode to the truck. "I'll give you five minutes," she said, getting into the car and slamming the door.

"I'll take them," Hank replied, gunning the truck down Main Street. "You're one stubborn woman, Jane!"

"Is that what you wanted to tell me? Because if it is, you're not the first person to figure that out!"

"Yeah and you wear it like a goddamn badge of honor!"

"You're eating up your five minutes. Get to the point!"

"I've never told you the name of my band, have I?"

Jane rolled her eyes. "Jesus, are you kidding me?"

"'No Regrets.'" He turned to her. "That's the name of the band. You know why?"

"Because you have no regrets starting a cover band?"

"Funny. *But no.* I have no regrets...period. Even though I've done a lot of stupid shit in my life, I don't regret one damn thing because they all got me to where I am today. Not the drinking, not the recreational drugs, not the fooling around..."

"Ah, so you admit you're a player. Thank you."

"I was never a player, Jane. But I did make my share of relationship mistakes."

"Well, add me to the long list."

"Dammit, Jane!" Hank quickly turned into an abandoned gravel lot and brought the truck to an abrupt stop. He turned to her. "You're not one of my mistakes! And neither was Annie, no matter how much her mother tried to convince me!"

There was silence. "Annie Mack is your *daughter*?"

"Yes. Mack is her mother's maiden name."

There was that look that Jane had seen between them. It *was* meaningful but her skilled detection of body language failed to be specific as to what type of meaning she was witnessing. "Why didn't you tell me?"

"Well, for one, you never gave me a chance and for another..." Hank hesitated and turned away. "Annie doesn't know she's my daughter." Jane's mouth fell open. "Now, before you go postal on me, there's a reason why she doesn't know. Her mother and I never married. This was back when I lived in Michigan. The relationship was complicated, but Annie was the only decent thing that came out of it. However, her mom decided to leave me when she found out she was pregnant. I fought her tooth and nail because I wanted to be part of the kid's life. But I was drinking pretty hard at the time and I understand now why she made that decision. I told her I'd pay child support, but she wouldn't accept it. She made me promise that I would stay out of Annie's life. So, I did. But I also started a fund. I called it, *Annie's Fund*. All the money that I would have given her for child support, I stuck in that fund and I invested it. They kept moving, but I kept track of them. I got pretty good at figuring out how to find people who wanted to stay lost working in fraud and just applied it to my kid and her mom. In the meantime, I got sober. They moved again and then to Midas. Ten years ago, I finally got the nerve to show up here. I was going to walk up on their doorstep and introduce myself. But when I showed up, I found out Annie's mom had just died of cancer and the kid was heartbroken. Didn't seem like the right time to throw my story on her. Besides, I made her mother a promise. But I never said I wasn't going to look out for her. I bought The Rabbit Hole and she moved in with a family in town who took good care of her. When they'd come by the place for dinner, I always made a point of finding out what was going on in her life. When she was twenty, she told me her dream was to open a diner and she had her eye on the café in town, but she couldn't afford the down payment. That was $35,000. Well, it just so happened that all that child support I invested for her had appreciated quite well."

"You're the anonymous benefactor who left her the check," Jane said, recalling Bo's enthusiastic re-telling of the story.

"You got it."

Jane looked out the window. "So, how does she see your relationship?"

"We're friends. I gave her a lot of business advice when she opened up the diner and it paid off for her. She still asks me for advice. That's exactly what she was doing this morning when you saw us out in front of the house. I didn't have her come in because I'm a private person and I know you sure as hell are. I wasn't about to advertise us to anyone."

Jane turned back to Hank. "*Us?*"

"Sorry. I forgot. It was a one-night stand. We made no connection. We don't think alike. We don't feel comfortable with each other. I don't think you're smart and I'm an idiot. And the lovemaking? Well, that meant nothing to either of us. You also hate my cooking. So, yeah, there's no *us.*" Hank backed his truck out of the lot. "You know what you're problem is? You don't think it's a real relationship unless you feel like shit because, in your book, happiness is a four-letter word."

Okay, that one stung. Jane tried to figure out a decent retort, but she had nothing. She was right back on that *Life's a struggle and then you die* highway and the road was getting rocky. The hard and brutal trail was wearing thin. There was always that fear that if she attained happiness—whatever in the hell that was—there was nowhere to go from that point. Nowhere but death. Thus, happiness equaled death. She realized it was one of those suppositions that a brain trust could deconstruct and show the falsehoods within it. But it was a dogma she'd carried her entire life and one doesn't just throw off dogma without a fight. Dogma must be wrestled and then cut from one's grip. One just doesn't wake up one morning and decide that their tenets are useless. Or do they? Isn't that possibly what Jake Van Gorden did?

They drove back to the B&B in silence. When Hank parked at the curb, he looked at the clock. "Look at that…five minutes on the nose. I guess I do keep my word." Jane sat still, looking straight ahead. "Aren't you getting out?" She opened the door, stepped outside and shut the door. "Before I forget…" He pulled a piece of paper out of his breast pocket. "I was finally able to translate that *Patois* saying you asked me about." He handed her a folded piece of paper.

Jane opened the paper and read the words:

I HOPE FOR THE ONE WHO CAN MAKE MY TENDER HEART WHOLE AGAIN.

"I don't know where you got that from," Hank said, motioning to the translation. "But I find it just a little too ironic, don't you?" He put the truck in gear. "It's too damn bad you decided not to keep me around, Jane. I could do a lot of the heavy thinking for you." Hank slowly drove away.

Jane thought she was confused before, but now it was magnified by the shame and hell she was feeling. She stood there in a daze until the sound of her cell phone slammed her back into the world. She checked the number and didn't recognize it.

"Hello?" There was an onslaught of loud music in the background.

"Hey, it's me!"

Jane didn't recognize the voice. "Me who?"

"Candy! Candy Cane from the club?"

Jane jumped to attention. "Candy! What's up?"

"You told me to call ya if that guy ever came back? Well, he's here by himself, but when I told him we weren't open for another hour, he gave me a hundie if I'd let him wait inside."

"Did he say who he was waiting for?"

"Yeah, sure, *riiiiight*," she said with a sarcastic laugh. "All he said was he had an important appointment."

"Don't let him leave, Candy!" Jane yelled before hanging up and jumping into her Mustang. She tossed the book onto the passenger seat as the envelope Butterworth dropped slid out from the book and onto the passenger floor. Jane peeled out of town, calculating it would take at least forty minutes to get to the strip club, and that was if she drove like a bat out of hell. The mountain roads were mostly clear as she easily flew by cars and trucks and took the curves too fast. Thirty-eight minutes later, she skidded into the parking lot of The Cat House Lounge. A smattering of cars were in the lot, including Bailey's black SUV. Jane removed her holster and Glock and stuck it under the front seat before getting out of her car and walking inside. The place pounded with too much bass as Don Henley's recording of "Get Over It," punctuated the darkness. It took several seconds for Jane's eyes to get used to the drastic change in light. She peered over to where Bailey had been seated on her first visit but saw no one.

"Hey!"

Jane turned around. There was Candy wearing an exceptionally tight, loose knit top with no bra. A short pink skirt that barely covered her ass and chunky, four-inch Lucite heels completed the tawdry ensemble. "Where is he?"

"Taking a leak. That guy standing by the far booth," Candy pointed discreetly, "just showed up about ten minutes ago."

Jane tried to make out the man in the semidarkness. Based on her memory, it wasn't the same one as before.

Candy stuck out her chest, showing off her top. "Hey, what do ya think?"

She turned back to Candy. "About what?"

"You gave me money to buy a sweater, remember?"

Jane looked askance. "That wasn't the kind of sweater I had in mind."

"It's made of yarn, right? Anyway, I wanted to say thanks again. *Because this sweater worked.*"

Jane snuck a look back at the men's room but Bailey was still inside. "Worked?"

"Yeah!" Candy said, her eyes wide with enthusiasm.

Behind her, a stocky man, mid-fifties appeared. His comb-over was inexcusable and his oily skin matched his greasy vibe. "Let's go, baby!" he said, locking his right hand around her neck. His gold pinky ring screamed *creep.*

"See what I'm talkin' about?" Candy quietly said to Jane. "*He's a doctor!*"

Jane grabbed Candy and took her aside. "Yeah, he's a doctor and I just split the atom. Candy, or whatever the hell your name is, don't do this! *Go home*."

The girl's doe eyes lost their glimmer. "I can't. I don't exist anymore as far as they're concerned."

The guy spun Candy around, gave Jane the evil eye and disappeared out the door.

Jane shook her head in disgust and turned back just as Bailey emerged from the bathroom. But instead of crossing to a booth with the other man, they exited the back door. This time, Jane wasn't going to let him slip away. She raced out the front door and got into her Mustang before Bailey could see her. Hunkering down in her front seat, she watched as the two men had a seemingly somber conversation as they walked around the club. Bailey motioned several times up the road, pointing and turning his hand right and left as if he was giving directions to the other man. They nodded and each got into their own vehicle. She watched Bailey slide into his black SUV and roll to the edge of the parking lot while he waited for the other guy to drive up behind him in his sedan. Bailey rolled down his window and gave the thumbs up sign before turning right onto the two-lane road that headed further away from the club. The man followed him closely. Jane gradually got behind the sedan, making sure to stay far enough away so as not to attract Bailey's attention.

They drove for several miles, passing the occasional convenience store and gas station on the rural roadway. As Jane looked around the somewhat desolate area, she envisioned it being the perfect place to dump a body. Gradually, more houses rose up and the topography gained a few signs of an active, albeit, pissant town. She followed behind the sedan, easily hidden by several other cars as they made their way down the main drag of the nameless community. At the far end of the town, they turned left onto a short side street and slowed. Jane backed off a bit, not knowing when the two cars were going to stop.

Watching in the distance, she saw them turn into the

parking lot of a one-story motel. She followed and parked on the street behind a tree for adequate cover. Jane watched as Bailey got out of his SUV and furtively looked around the parking lot in an apprehensive manner. The other man joined him but didn't have the same body language that indicated concern. They talked briefly before Bailey pulled a large envelope out of his shirt pocket and handed it to the man. Jane had a perfect line of sight as the man opened the envelope and counted the cash. The man nodded, replaced the money in the envelope and stuffed it in his jeans. Bailey then took the assertive lead and walked to a door, opened it with a key and ushered the man inside. He closed the door and Jane watched as they appeared in the window together, highlighted by an auspicious shaft of sunlight. Bailey aggressively pulled the man toward him and locked lips with him in a passionate kiss. He chaotically stripped off his starched white shirt, continuing their ardent affection before drawing the curtains on their covert tryst.

Jane sat back, staggered. She never saw this one coming. Bailey was indeed working a backend deal. The only difference was, it was Bailey's backend that was getting worked. In seconds, everything shifted for Jane. The entire case took on a new and curious patina of possibilities. Jane's eyes drifted to the nondescript motel sign, located above her head. Suddenly, one of the mysteries was solved.

This back-road motel was strangely called, *Fourteen O-One Imperial*.

CHAPTER 32

The pieces started to click for Jane, although, there were still a helluva lot of missing chunks. Her mind raced with the various connections. Jake obviously suspected his father was up to no damn good and that's why he ripped off Bailey's mono-grammed pad with the words, *1401 Imperial*. At some point, Jake decided to slide down the rope outside his bedroom and follow his dad furtively in Bailey's second car to this remote location where he must have witnessed his dad's sexual addiction. This also finally explained Jake's last post on March 6th on the *secret revelations* website when he wrote, *I saw you but you didn't see me, YOU FUCKING PERVERT! Which one of us will hang in hell???*

Jane's frantic mind jumped to the YouTube video simply titled, *Bailey Van Gorden*. She rewound the self-indulgent video in her head and recalled some of Bailey's comments. More pieces fell into place. It wasn't an advertisement for Bailey's architectural services; it was a covert visual ad Bailey constructed to solicit men. Rather like, "Come check out my package before agreeing to sell me your skin." The opening shot with him wearing that tight-fitting black T-shirt that exposed his muscular arms was an exemplary start. And the statements that Jane now understood with their double entendre meaning carried more weight. Bailey jabbered about how he loved to create "magic and passion," how he had "enthusiasm for the lifestyle," that it was important that clients "came to the table with that same passion" and that if they only "collaborated on one project to-gether" he knew that it would be memorable. In the end, it was all an elaborate profile piece and the project *de jour* climaxed with a "collaboration" behind a grimy curtain at the *Fourteen O-One Imperial* no-tell motel. All the sundry asides—the shots of his unused Weber grill or his three-tiered Italian fountain, both of which he stupidly misspelled in the tags to the video—might have been there to either raise his profile in the eyes of prospective partners or create a look of legitimacy for someone who came upon the video and didn't realize the audience it was intended for. Jane had to make the assumption that somewhere out there in the cyberworld of gay websites, Bailey inserted the link to his YouTube video. Just how many gay sites featured the link was unknown. But he was certainly eliciting enough email traffic and follow-up phone calls to make it worth his while.

Phone calls, Jane thought to herself. *Of course. Now it makes sense.* Suddenly, the implication of the two rings followed by a hang up on the Van Gorden's phone was evident to Jane. That had to be a code Bailey gave his prospective partners to use to let him know they were on their way to the motel. As Jane recalled, he seemed to be more anxious to leave once he heard that phone code. Another thought crossed her mind. Bailey was eager to release the officers from his house who wiretapped his phone in hopes of receiving and tracing a call from Jake's kidnapper. Of course he didn't want them there! It was interfering with contacting his tainted trysts as well as receiving the ringing alerts that signaled when his conquest was ready to meet him. Yeah, that demonstrated a lot of heart on Bailey's part, Jane deduced. Nothing like having your priorities straight when your only child has been taken and feared dead. That act alone warranted a new addition to the definition of *egoistic.*

Bailey had been unable to curb his sexual addiction throughout the entire case. Jane *was* on the right trail when she checked his SUV on the first visit to their home and found his rear view mirror flipped for nighttime driving. He'd probably been out the previous night knocking boots with an anonymous "Andy." *Ah,* she realized, in a somewhat disgusted revelation. That funky odor she smelled in his SUV was sex.

She glanced at the curtained room where the two men were undoubtedly getting busy. Jane couldn't care less what people did behind closed doors. What she *did* care about was the way some people manipulated their transgressions and wrongly projected them onto someone else when they got caught in an effort to take the spotlight off of themselves. That's exactly what Bailey did to his own son. Jane felt the anger building within her. It was so clear now. Jake witnessed the sexual deception, confronted his father with it and his dad's response was to project the flagrant indiscretion onto him. Maybe Bailey made the kid believe that the apple didn't fall far from the tree? Perhaps Jake looked, acted and dressed just *odd* enough to make him question his identity after his father laid a *gay* trip on him. Whatever happened, it pushed Jake over the edge and to a bridge where he intended to end it all. Jane prickled at the thought of how Bailey boldly told Aaron with impunity that his son was obsessed with gay porn and regularly snuck out of the house to meet with male prostitutes that he met online. *Jesus*, Jane concluded, Bailey used *his* story to sully his kid's reputation after Bailey got caught with his bum in the *nookie* jar.

Jane's visceral reaction to Bailey's treatment of his only child was to bound across the parking lot and kick in the door on the illicit love shack and bring all kinds of hell raining down on Mr. Van Gorden. The more she thought about literally catching Bailey with his pants down, the more she realized the kind of ass-kicking leverage she could finally have with the SOB. *Yes.* This could be the ticket she needed to finally get Bailey to answer her questions. Jane reached under the front seat and pulled her Glock out of the holster. Getting out of the Mustang, she shoved the gun in the back waistband of her jeans, covering it with the dressy shirt. The closer she got to the door, the more satisfaction she felt. But fifty feet from the room, her cell phone rang out. "Shit!" she whispered, ducking behind a parked truck to ensure she wasn't seen by anyone. Checking the number, it was Weyler.

"Yeah, boss?"

"Jane, where are you?"

"Out and about. Why?"

"All hell's breaking loose here. Carol Van Gorden called Bo about half an hour ago. She found another note from the kidnapper in their mailbox. He cut letters out of magazines and pasted them on the page to form words."

Jane sprinted back across the parking lot to her Mustang. "What does it say?"

"*Listen to me now. If you don't, it'll be so sad, too bad.*"

Jane stopped in her tracks. "'So sad, too bad?' Those words exactly?"

"Yes. Why?"

"That's the same fucking term Louise Van Gorden used when I talked with her."

"Good God. That's worth noting given the second part of my news."

"What?"

"When Carol showed the clue to her mother-in-law, Louise became highly agitated and collapsed. She's in the local ER and it doesn't look good, Jane. To cap it off, Bailey's gone and not answering his cell."

Jane put the pedal to the metal and barreled back to Midas. It was as if the veil had been ripped off her eyes and she was quickly seeing what had been staring her in the face all along. All the nervous eye shifting, all the hesitations, all the excuses that didn't make sense, and all the obscure comments were suddenly making a little more sense to Jane. But there was no way she was going to let one of the players leave this world without gleaning vital information that could save Jake's life.

Jane got directions to the local hospital from Weyler and squealed to a halt in front of the place in less than half an hour. She blew through the doors of the ER and into the wide hallway where curtained partitions separated the wheeled cots. The only area curtained off was at the far end. Jane strode in that direction as the beeping sound of a heart monitor and a doctor's urgent voice rang out from behind the cloth wall. She slipped between the sliver of curtain and stood behind Carol who nervously tugged on her sweater hem as the doctor and nurse hovered over Louise's face, attempting to rouse a verbal response from her. "Louise! Louise!" they kept repeating. Her eyes were open and alert, but she seemed unwilling or unable to speak.

"Louise!" the doctor yelled. "Can you tell us what occurred before you collapsed?"

Louise pursed her thin, wrinkled lips and looked as if she

would spit nails at the good doctor.

"Louise?" the nurse interceded, "did you eat anything that may have caused an allergic reaction?"

Again, Louise eyed the nurse with venomous intent and remained taciturn.

Out of sheer desperation, Carol managed a breathy interruption. "We've been extremely stressed…"

"*Carol!*" Louise growled, sounding like her vocal chords had been dragged across the pavement. "*Shut up!*"

Carol turned and jumped when she saw Jane behind her. "How did you…"

"You gonna shut up, Carol?" Jane whispered to her. "How's that working out for you?"

"Get…*out*…" Louise said, struggling for breath.

Jane quickly crossed to the nurse's side. "Don't take it to the grave, Louise," Jane urged. "Tell me what you know!"

"Who are you?" the doctor asked with a tinge of anger.

"Do you know where your grandson is, Louise?" Jane asked, her voice rising an octave.

The nurse glanced down at Jane's Glock still tucked into the waistband of her jeans. "She's got a gun!"

Jane spoke to the nurse. "I'm a cop!" Turning back to Louise, Jane leaned closer. "Louise…tell me what you know! Help me save your grandson's life!"

"Officer," the doctor intervened, "I've got to ask you to leave!"

Jane was undeterred. "*Louise,* for God's sake, don't sacrifice Jake!" The heart monitor rang with a code alert.

Louise arched her back in pain and turned her dying, steely eyes to Jane. "*Fuck you, Jane!*" she snarled with a chilling sneer.

The nurse pushed Jane outside the curtain, leaving only a few inches of an opening for Jane to watch the final tortured seconds of Louise Van Gorden's miserable life.

They called her death at 12:12 pm. Jane left the ER and walked outside into the suddenly chilled spring air. Within twenty minutes, she saw Bailey's black SUV speed into the parking lot. He raced to the doors of the ER but stopped when he saw Jane.

"What in the fuck are you doing here?" he asked, fighting a severely congested nose and wearing a flushed face.

"I'm like the wind, Bailey. I'm everywhere you don't want me to be."

"*Get the fuck away from us!*" he yelled before crossing through the automatic doors.

Jane sniggered, realizing that Bailey's classical symptoms of flushed skin and stuffed sinuses coincided with his *client meetings*. It wasn't the little blue flowers that made him wheeze; it was the original *little blue pill's* side effects. She sauntered back to her Mustang but took a detour toward Bailey's SUV after she spotted something amiss from across the parking lot. While she couldn't be certain, Jane hadn't previously noticed the striking front-end damage to the vehicle's front bumper.

Jane sat in her Mustang, her head spinning and her body exhausted. She glanced down to the thin book on the passenger seat and turned to the inside back cover with Jordan's handwritten name. She opened the book and found various passages highlighted in yellow. Was it Jake who did that or Jordan? One particular line caught Jane's eye:

You don't come from your parents, but rather, through them.

She turned back toward the ER, thinking about the woman Bailey passed through and realized that, now, another ghost would remain tethered to generations not even born. In that same jarring moment, Jane spied the envelope Edward Butterworth had mistakenly dropped and that she rescued. She leaned across the seat and swept it up, figuring she'd gain a few points in heaven and mail it for him.

But when she turned it over and read the name on the front, two words fell from her stunned lips. "Dear God…"

She carefully opened the envelope and withdrew a letter written on gold-embossed parchment letterhead from Butterworth's legal firm.

I'm sorry to hear about your recent health scare, Butterworth handwrote. *I understand that you are doing much better and that you are back in the swing of life. Until next time, Edward Butterworth.*

Attached was a personal check for $10,000 made out to the addressee.

"Son-of-a-bitch," Jane whispered.

CHAPTER 33

Jane felt a need to lay low the rest of the day. She returned to The Gardenia Room at the B&B and sat in silence on the bed as the clothesline of clues continued its daily taunt. Weyler called three times to check in, the first time after getting wind of her dramatic confrontation with Louise Van Gorden. "We're going to be blacklisted from every joint in town if you keep this up," he warned her. When she told him that she'd followed Bailey to the no-tell motel and what she witnessed, there was a long pause on the other end of the line, followed by "What in the hell are we dealing with here?" Given the day's events, Weyler felt it was best that Jane stay where she was so she wouldn't risk running into Bo. She agreed, although it would be difficult for Jane to strike back at the man, knowing now what she did about him.

She stared back to the clues. The person behind these mystifying messages wasn't just clever, he was driven by a need that overwhelmed his reason—*Control.* The word had already come up twice and now it rang like a siren in Jane's ears as she committed the pages to memory again. It first arose when Jane hypothesized to Bailey and Carol that the M.O. of the kidnapper was about control. "It's kind of connected to revenge, but it has its own flavor," she remembered telling Bailey. "Such criminals have lost their ability to feel validated, and so their action, whatever that might be, seeks to control a situation that they feel they are powerless to contain." Jane recalled how Bailey swallowed hard and turned away—a visual *tell* that he deeply related to what he heard.

The second time control became an issue was when Bailey, himself, railroaded Aaron into believing Jake was gay. Bailey knew it would destroy his son's relationship with Mollie and, therefore, he controlled the outcome of their certain demise. If Jane was correct, it seemed that that *C* word was powering and instigating another *C* word—*Chaos.*

Jane closed her eyes momentarily and ran her fingers through her tangled brown hair. In that moment, the nascence of a foreboding sensation wrapped around her being. The same unsettling, yet elusive awareness had imprinted itself on Jane's psyche in the past. When it did, it was the harbinger of a portentous event that would shake the foundation of her existence. Others might call it "that queasy feeling" or "something ain't right." But this was more than just an ominous shadow hovering in the ether; she could taste the fear on her tongue. Jane opened her eyes, hoping to assuage the vague impressions, but it lingered on the edges just enough to make her shift off the bed.

Her gut rumbled, and she realized she hadn't had a bite to eat all day and it was pushing four o'clock. Downstairs, she hunted for something to eat, but there were no breakfast leftovers and she wasn't about to raid the Green's refrigerator. And frankly, the only thing she really wanted was a hot dog.

It took an hour for Jane to work up the courage, but there she was, seated at the bar of the just re-opened Rabbit Hole after their two-day cleaning holiday. The place was pretty busy, and Jane thought she could easily blend in with the crowd if she sat at the end of the bar and ignored the world by escaping into the local town rag. Her plan was to get her dog *walkin'* and beat feet back to the B&B. After ten minutes, the barmaid still hadn't come over to get her order and Jane glanced back to the paper. Then the smell of a hot dog with everything on it wafted toward Jane. A generous basket of cheesy fries followed along with a tall glass of sparkling ice water. She didn't look up. She didn't have to. She could feel him standing there. Somehow, he knew exactly what she wanted to eat.

"You want your dog walking or sitting?" Hank asked.

Jane still kept her eyes pinned on the newspaper. "It's already sitting, so I'll take it like that."

"Oh, I can easily make it walk," he said offhandedly, leaning closer to her. "It wouldn't be the first thing I made walk today."

This was fucking brutal. Jane couldn't understand why in the hell this was so hard for her. She still couldn't look him in the eye and that wasn't the way she operated. There was a minute of the most awkward silence imaginable as she took a bite of the dog and chewed it into a mash before swallowing.

"How is it?" Hank asked, never moving from his perch.

"It's very good," Jane replied, eyes now focused on the food.

"That's all? Just 'very good?'"

"It's a fucking masterpiece," Jane said, without looking up.

He slid the basket of fries toward her. "Try the fries. You look like you haven't eaten since morning."

Jane put down the dog and shook her head. "Jesus, how do you get inside my head like that?"

"It's easy. You think you're so complicated, but to the right person, you're fairly transparent."

That got her back up and earned him direct eye contact. "The hell I am!"

"Like I said, *to the right person*, you are. To everyone else, you're a bloody enigma."

"And you think that you're the right person?"

"No. I don't *think* it. I *know* it." Hank turned to pour a customer a beer from the tap. He returned to Jane and decided to change the subject. "I heard about Louise Van Gorden. I know a guy who works in the ER and he mentioned your brief but memorable appearance this afternoon."

Jane motioned for Hank to move several feet down, away from prying ears. "Whoever took Jake, left another clue in the Van Gordens' mailbox. The wording seemed to connect with Louise on a deep level. I guess I just thought that she might tell me whatever she was hiding."

"What about Jordan? Where does he fit into this?"

"Every time I think he's *not* involved, something happens to change my mind. And every time I think he *is* involved, something happens to change my mind."

"What were you hoping to hear from Louise?"

"I'm not sure. Maybe part of it I already know. I uncovered a fairly substantial lapse in judgment by one of the family members."

Hank shook his head and let a snort of contempt. "And his first name starts with a *B*? I told you he was no damn good. I don't need to know what you found out. You can tell me all about it over dinner when this whole thing is over." Jane had to admire Hank's clever way of manipulating a conversation. "There's an old saying, Chopper. *The only way three people can keep a secret is if two of them are dead.*" Jane considered the statement with grave concern. "Looks like you got one down and at least one to go." It was obvious that Hank took no pleasure in making that observation.

Jane's mind wandered and she considered it carefully before she asked Hank for a piece of paper and a pen. He obliged and she wrote down the pertinent information she had before handing him the page. "Are you still good at finding people who like to stay lost?"

"For you? Sure."

Jane finished her hot dog and wolfed down half the fries. She was about to discard the local newspaper when she was reminded of how Jordan said he "felt" into Jake's vibe by looking at his photo in the local rag as well as the *Denver Post*. "Do you have old copies of the local paper?"

"Yeah, I probably have some in the back. Why?"

"Do you have the one with Jake's photo?"

"Jake's photo?"

"Yeah, the one they published after he was kidnapped."

He looked at her with a quizzical eye. "They never published his photo."

"Are you certain?"

"Yes."

She pretty much knew the answer to the next question. "And there was no photo in the *Denver Post*?"

"No photo."

And the doubt started once again.

That night, sleep came hard for Jane. The persistent sense that something malevolent was on the horizon continued to crowd into her troubled mind. She'd shared her sentient feelings with Weyler. He listened thoughtfully and filed it away in the "wait and see" department. But each time Jane stirred that night, she awoke with a growing sense of urgency and unrest. The only solace was that she didn't awaken at 3:11 am and have another nocturnal visit with her mother.

Sunrise broke forth as fingers of light touched The Gardenia Room and illuminated every dark corner. Jane woke and studied the silence. She was now able to smell the fear she had tasted on her tongue the day before. There wasn't a cloud in the sky but Jane could feel the storm above the town. She got out of bed and crossed to the window, opening it wide. Outside, it looked calm, but the air around her was drenched in a *knowing* that a deed had been done. With her heart in her throat, she showered and dressed, donning the *Groovy* T-shirt, jeans and her boots. After strapping her Glock to her shoulder holster, she headed downstairs, dragging the cloud of doom behind her.

She greeted Sara and Aaron with a perfunctory "Good

Morning" and served herself breakfast as Weyler joined her at the table.

And she waited.

She waited for the confirmation of what she was feeling. She waited like a death row prisoner waits for the gallows floor to drop and the noose to tighten.

The B&B phone rang out like an alarm bell. Jane jumped slightly and then swallowed hard as Sara answered it in the hallway. She heard Sara's footsteps walk back into the kitchen.

"Sergeant Weyler?" Sara said, her voice shaking. "It's Bo. He doesn't sound good. He said he needs to talk to you immediately."

Jane exchanged a troubled glance with Weyler. He folded his napkin and walked into the hallway, picking up the phone.

"Oh, Jesus, *no*," he whispered, before telling Bo that he and Jane would be right over.

Jane looked up at Sara and Aaron. Tears streamed down Sara's face as her hand clasped her mouth in shock. She was sobbing in Aaron's arms by the time Jane and Weyler left.

It was like slow motion as they walked into Town Hall. The few faces present, including Vi and a couple tech guys, looked shell-shocked and grey. When they turned into Bo's office, he was seated behind his cluttered desk, head bowed. Anguish and defeat strangled him. When Weyler approached the desk, Bo never looked up. He simply slid the large, plain envelope across the desk toward Weyler who opened it and pulled out the gruesome color photo. Jane moved closer and stared at the nude, dead body of a teenage boy lying on a sheet, bloated and blackened by decomposition. The head was turned enough to see the single bullet hole in his forehead. The starkness of the photo was made even worse by the contrast of the blond hair against the blackened, slightly mottled flesh. A piece of paper was taped to the bottom of the photo. In black pen, it read, *May the Saints forgive me. Malo, Malo, MALO.*

"Leave me," Bo murmured, never once lifting his head.

Photo in hand, Weyler walked out of Bo's office with Jane. Minutes passed before anyone could speak and when they did, it was colored by disbelief and the sense that this wasn't really happening. It was the same incredulity that all victims felt when the stark reality was too harsh to accept.

"He just wanted someone to listen to him," Jane quietly confided to Weyler.

Weyler looked at her. "Which one are you talking about? Jake or his killer?"

She was about to reply when one of the tech guys called out to them.

"Hey! I think you need to see this!" The techie quickly motioned Jane and Weyler toward his computer. "I was going through some screen captures from the speed camera by the bridge between the first of February and the date your kid went missing." He brought up images as he spoke. "Before the new computer software, you couldn't distinguish the darker backgrounds. But now…" He brought up an image with a date stamp of *February 2nd.* "…you can select the formerly blurred or dark spots, highlight them and bring them forward with pretty incredible results." The image showed the rear of a passing car in front of the speed camera and a clear shot of the bridge. To the naked eye, there was nothing there. The techie selected a far corner beyond the end of the bridge, moving toward the forested area on Jordan's property. "I can basically take any section, highlight it and tell you the leaf pattern on a specific tree. Or, I can show you two faces. Like these…" With that, he sharpened the focus and the clear profile of Jake Van Gorden materialized standing on the opposite side of Jordan's fence while the crystal image of Jordan stood sheltered in the trees.

"Jesus Christ," Jane whispered.

The techie pulled up three more images he had found and repeated the same process, clarifying the darkened spaces into the defined images of Jake and Jordan locked in what looked like a deep conversation.

Vi quickly went into Bo's office and urged him to review the images. He stood and watched in staggered silence as the techie positioned the four screen captures on his large screen.

"He stayed one hundred feet away from kids, my ass!" Bo erupted.

Jane thought back to the red metal rod she'd nearly tripped on twice when she was on Jordan's property. Judging the distance between that rod and the bridge, she was willing to bet it was one hundred and one feet. Hank was right when he said that the "smart ones always figure out a loophole." But it was also clear to Jane that while Jordan may have used that red marker to guide his first conversations with Jake, in these computer-enhanced photos, he was far closer to Jake than one hundred feet. And he was certainly close enough to throw him a book or two. As to whether Jake got close enough for Jordan to do anything more nefarious, she couldn't be sure. But the fact was he lied. He lied about seeing Jake's photo in the newspapers and he lied about not having verbal or physical contact with the boy. Suddenly, the psychic connection Jordan bragged about having with Jake took on a more sinister cast. There were only four photos the tech could find because the camera only tripped when a speeder was photographed. Who knows how many more face-to-face encounters the two shared?

Bo turned to Weyler. "We're taking him down!"

Within ten minutes, Bo had called in two deputies. The five of them left in three patrol cars, with Bo leading the way down the highway to Jordan's property. There were no sirens, but the show of force and the righteous anger brimming from Bo would be enough to scare the hell out of anyone. When they entered the property, Bo instructed Jane to scan the perimeter of the property to see if Jordan was hiding in the woods. One deputy was told to secure the back of the cabin, while Weyler, Bo and the remaining deputy stormed the cabin, kicking in the door.

Jane removed her Glock from its holster and headed

toward the fence. She crept cautiously, patently aware of Jordan's penchant for blending into the scenery and staying silent. When she came upon the fire pit, she stopped and observed the cold ashes. Remnants of burned remains that weren't completely consumed by the flames caught her attention. She spotted what looked like black cloth and grabbed a nearby stick, lifting the charred item into the air for closer examination. All she could decipher was that it was formerly a black T-shirt and it was possibly far too small to fit Jordan's monstrous physique.

Jane heard a frenzied pitch of commotion coming from the cabin. She dropped the shirt and raced in that direction. As she sprinted up the front steps, the sound of glass breaking and tables and chairs being overturned rang out. She stood in the front doorway and watched as two of the deputies held Jordan, chest against the wall, with one hand tightly wrapped around his back. Weyler methodically went through the cabin, checking for anything that stood out while Bo threw Jordan's books across the room, kicked over chairs and verbally assaulted Jordan with every degrading remark he could muster. "You like diddlin' little boys, you bastard?!" Bo yelled. "We know you talked to him! What else did you do to him, you sick son-of-a-bitch?!"

The whole time, Jordan's right cheek was pressed against the wall. And he was staring at Jane with eyes a mixture of wildness and terror.

Bo bound up the steps to Jordan's single bed. With one enraged kick, he flipped the frame onto its side, exposing more stacks of books under the bed. Bo crossed into the kitchen, spotting the sacred blue lily growing in the glass container. "What in the fuck did you do with him, Jordan?!" Bo screamed as he swept his arm across the kitchen sill and sent the glass container crashing onto the floor into a million pieces. The blue flowers dislodged from the tangle of leaves and scattered across the cabin floor. With his anger reaching an apex, Bo proceeded to grind the heel of his boots into the flowers, pulverizing them into a mash. "Where is he, Jordan?!" Bo bellowed, taking another sweep across the kitchen table and scattering the stacks of books everywhere. Looking down, Bo saw the strewn playing cards. He kneeled down and turned one over after another. "I don't see the Ace of Spades, Jordan! No, I don't! What are the chances that bloody fingerprint is gonna come back to you?" Bo moved closer to Jordan as the deputies continued to manhandle him, shoving him repeatedly into the wall.

Jane crept across the room, stepping over the chaotic mess and scanned the area.

"I found two phones," Weyler announced, removing a rotary dial phone from the far corner of a kitchen cabinet along with a push-button model.

"Well, what do you know?" Bo screamed in Jordan's face. "The man assured us he didn't own a phone! How far are we gonna have to toss this place before we find the voice disguiser you used to leave the messages on my voicemail?"

Jane noticed a pair of boots tucked underneath the couch. She grabbed the right one and turned it over. As she feared, a nail had been driven into the sole. When Jane gingerly felt inside the boot, she easily detected the sharp point poking inside the sole. It was perfectly placed to press his toe down onto during the lie detector test in an effort to throw off the results.

Bo continued to verbally assault Jordan but it was eliciting nothing from him. Jane crossed to the bureau on the landing near the loft. As the chaos ensued behind her, she opened the top drawer and withdrew the leather diary. She wasn't sure why she was doing it. The time for sympathy was over. On the surface, this was the possible starting point of a grisly kidnapping and murder. But even knowing that, Jane tucked the diary into her back waistband and covered it with her long shirt. When she turned around, she saw the rage swell around Bo and then erupt as he started pummeling Jordan mercilessly in the kidneys and across his neck, all the while screaming, "Child killer!"

Jordan never made a sound. It was as though he knew his

fate was already sealed.

CHAPTER 34

After Bo threw Jordan into a holding cell in the small but airtight jail back in Midas, Jordan still hadn't let one word escape his bruised lips. Weyler went with Bo to inform the Van Gordens of the death photo. Jane hung back with one of the deputies to root through the clutter at Jordan's cabin in an attempt to uncover more damning evidence. But after several hours of coming up with nothing significant, she bagged the charred black T-shirt she unearthed from the fire pit and returned to Town Hall to drop off the evidence to Vi. She asked Vi for the death shot so she could take it back to her room and examine it more closely with her photo loupe. Perhaps she could decipher something in the shot that would help determine where the body might be located. A type of grass, a mark on the cement... anything that might help them unearth Jake's body and the bevy of evidence that the remains would provide law enforcement.

Once Jane returned to the B&B, she wasted no time in her investigation. She dragged every light in the room to the desk to shed as much illumination on the grisly photograph. Digging her photo loupe out of her satchel, she held it tightly on the photo paper while aiming a light against the back of the shot. Inch by inch, she canvassed the blackened nude body. She was reminded of a comment one of her forensic professors made in school so many years ago. "All dead bodies look the same after three days in the heat." It was true. Once the maggots started their feeding frenzy, it was often difficult to make an accurate visual determination between a male and a female victim. And the longer or faster the decomp, the trickier it became until dental records or DNA confirmed the identity. But having just a photo and not a body made the investigation exponentially more complicated.

Jane painstakingly scanned the edge of the photo with the loupe, searching for any indication of what the sheet under the body was lying on. Inch by inch, she slid the loupe across the film but nothing stood out.

Her eyes ached from the intense work and she sat back in the chair to take a quick break. Standing up, Jane stretched and then reached around to her rear waistband, releasing the leather diary of Jordan's mother from where she hid it. She set it on the desk and dug her hand into her front pocket. She withdrew the handwritten note that Jordan had left on the door for her two days before. MEET ME NEAR THE BRIDGE, JANE, he wrote. She tossed it onto the desk and ignored it but then her eyes glanced back to it. Jane hadn't paid it much notice before, but she looked at the way Jordan wrote the *J* in her name. It was obviously a first letter he was quite used to writing and, thus, the character he gave it was unique. Instead of striking the top line in a perfect horizontal stroke, Jordan made a point of arching the line dramatically toward the right and even including a purposefully pointed tip that resembled a backward, lower case *L*.

Jane pulled her cell phone from her back pocket and located her short file of photos. She found the one she'd snapped of the *Fuck You, Jane!* written in deer blood on her trunk of her Mustang. This *J* was written completely differently and, in fact, had its own distinctive flair. It was tighter, with the bottom of the *J's* lower hook exceptionally controlled and ending with a slight flourish that almost looked like a fish hook. Furthermore, the horizontal line at the top of the *J* was thick and compact to match the angular descent of the lower part of the letter. One could argue that writing in blood and writing with a pen impacts the graphology. Jane knew that while there might be slight variations, the pattern of the writer adding a hook to the bottom of the *J* was akin to their personal calling card. Yes, one's handwriting could change throughout one's life. But in the space of mere hours when these two samples were written, the drastic difference between the two signaled to Jane that Jordan was not responsible for defacing her car.

Jane paced back and forth in front of the clothesline of clues. She stopped at the first section of the line and stared at the bright green sheet of paper hanging there. It read, *JACKSON JAKOB VAN GORDEN* and it was penned at the request of Bo when he asked Bailey to write out his son's full name. Jane held her cell phone image next to the page. There were two *J's* on that green sheet of paper and they *both* displayed the same *fish hook*.

"What the fuck…" Jane murmured to herself. Her mind began racing again. It was written in deer blood. How do you get deer blood? You hunt the animal or you kill it accidentally. Jane flashed to her own high-speed accident due to avoiding a deer on the road. "Oh, shit," she said, recalling the front-end damage she saw on Bailey's SUV the previous afternoon in the ER parking lot. Jane played back the sequence of events over the last few days, paying special attention to what occurred between her and Bailey that could have inflamed him. It was the visit to their house when Bo, Weyler and she laid out the Ace of Spades, Chesterfield cigarette, note and knife with Jake's severed pony-tail. Bailey turned and threw a crystal vase across the room in anger and screamed, "Fuck him!" Bailey was supposedly on the phone talking to a "client" when they left which would mean he possibly had a scheduled dalliance at the *Fourteen O-One Imperial* dive that night. Based only on hypothesis, Jane deduced that Bailey could have easily been driving home later that night, hit the deer on the highway and in his anger over the day's events *and possibly* in an attempt to confuse his son's case, he drove into town, located Jane's Mustang in front of the B&B and using the blood—still warm under the bumper of his damaged vehicle where the blood had pooled—wrote the three-word insult on the trunk of the car. While she had nothing but her gut instinct driving her at that moment, the knee-jerk reaction fit Bailey's narcissistic personality to a T. Jane knew that when a narcissist feels anger or is cornered, he strikes out at whomever he feels has injured his tender ego. Because the narcissist believes that the world revolves around him, any perceived affront is in direct violation of his very existence and must be punished. And, often, the acts done to the offender can be ridiculously petty and even childish—both in keeping with the, *Fuck You, Jane!* assault.

As Jane considered this even further, it seemed just a tad coincidental that Louise's last words on this earth were the same ones left on Jane's car. And she said it with an evil smirk to boot. Was that the old broad's way of warning Jane not to fuck with their lives?

Jane took another look at the bright green sheet of paper. *JACKSON JAKOB VAN GORDEN.* Her eyes focused on *Jackson Jakob.* She located the sympathy card that was included with the first clue, stuffed into page 243 of *You Can't Go Home Again. So sorry for your loss. JACKson sends his regards*, the cryptic message inside the card stated. *JACKson. JACK.*

Jane walked down the line of clues, regarding them with fresh eyes. "Jack…Jack…" she repeated until she stood in front of the Chesterfield cigarette advertisement, featuring actor, Jack Webb.

Jane ripped the page off the clothesline. The story was building, just as she had believed from nearly the beginning of the case. Each clue built onto the next and told a story. Maybe it was a story within a story? Jane looked at the advertisement. "Jack Webb," she said out loud. If *Jack* led to *Webb*, she figured, what did *Webb* lead to? Jane considered the Chesterfield cigarette in Jack's hand. The next time a Chesterfield cigarette appeared again was with the Ace of Spades, the knife, the ponytail and the note. The only clues from that day that weren't sent to CBI were the single cigarette and the note that read: *Who Ever Believes Bad Eventually Resolves.* Jane unpinned that note enclosed in plastic off the line and laid it on the bed. The sentence never made sense to her. There was no question mark at the end and the words *Who Ever* should have been one word. The author of the clues never made a grammatical mistake to Jane's knowledge. She looked at the page again. Each letter of each word was initially capitalized. "Holy shit," she muttered when she formed the first four capital letters of the first four words and spelled *WEBB*. Adding the *E* and the *R*, and the name *WEBBER* emerged.

Webber? Jane wondered. That was the last name of the main character in Wolfe's novel. Jane recovered the novel from the line and turned again to the dog-eared page 243. She'd damn near committed the single page to memory as she attempted to uncover any significance. She'd been so focused on the more metaphorical passages that she had completely ignored the bottom of the page and the sentences that now stood out like a beacon:

That fellow there, for instance! With his pasty face and rolling eyes and mincing ways, and hips that wiggled suggestively as he walked—could there be any doubt at all that he was a member of nature's other sex?

Four lines below, she read,

Was it something in the spirit of the times that had let the homosexual usurp the place and privilege of a hunchbacked jester of an old king's court, his deformity become a thing of open jest and ribaldry?

Jane read it over and over. Was this a direct attack on Bailey's secret homosexuality? Surely, this whole nightmare wasn't solely driven by disgust for a man's sexual preference. The high intellectual capacity Jane garnered from the kidnapper's clues seemed to infer, at least for now, that the ultimate goal was not to judge Bailey's sexual bent, but to *reveal* it.

Uncover. Reveal. Expose. Bring into the light that which has been hidden in the darkness. The words crashed against each other in Jane's head. *Yes.* What hung in front of Jane on the clothesline was a series of revelations, possibly long buried but now thrust into the light in order to be dissected with the skill of a surgeon's blade. "A story of revelations," Jane said out loud. "A story of a man named Jack Webber?"

There was another place she'd seen the word, *Webber*—on Bailey's misspelled tags from his YouTube video. *Was it just a misspelling?* Jane wondered. Or was Jordan right when he mentioned that a secret has a life of its own and wants to be revealed through the unconscious actions of those who are trying to keep the secret buried? "As much as we work to hide our secrets," Jordan stressed, "the unconscious mind prods our soul to reveal all."

So, the question begged, was it just a strange coincidence that Bailey included the word *Webber* in his video tags and that the kidnapper hid *Webber* in a character's name of a classic novel *and* in the cryptic note left with the Ace of Spades? The only thing Jane could figure was that the name resonated somehow with Bailey. Could it be that Bailey Van Gorden was actually Jack Webber? If that was the case, why did his mother continue to go by the name of Van Gorden? Unless…Van Gorden was Louise's maiden name… Jane had certainly run into enough people in this town who had either changed their name…Aaron and Sara Green…or had kept their mother's maiden name… Annie Mack… Was it stretching the seam of possibility that in a town known for attracting people who had secret lives or blemished pasts that they would operate under an assumed name?

If Bailey Van Gorden was really Jack Webber, what kind of hell did Jack Webber instigate to create a situation where his son was kidnapped? Was it a spurned male lover of Bailey's? That thought didn't seem to hold water with Jane as the tone of the clues seemed to indicate a feeling that leaned toward both exposure of a sin and, within that revelation, a chance for revenge from the person who was hurt. Since the name *Webber* was featured so prominently, perhaps, Jane thought, it had something to do with Bailey's past.

Jane re-read the transcripts of the two voicemail messages. Both talked about a child and how, "He *cried like a baby* and will never be a real man."

The first transcript grabbed Jane. "Do you know what it's like to feel as if you're two seconds from your last breath? *DO YOU?* It feels just like this..." This was followed by the whimpering of what sounded like a child crying and then the words, "He pounds on the window and you do nothing."

Jane wasn't certain, but she wondered if the kidnapper-turned-killer was talking about someone *else* besides Jake in that clue.

"Webber," Jane said to herself. If she was going to link that name to the Van Gordens, she needed something solid to prove it. Her mind flashed on a very *solid* item—the silver cigarette case in Bailey's office. The ornate *VG* lettering on top seemed very elaborate to Jane when she first saw it. While she didn't have a perfect memory of the engraving, she now realized that it was in actuality a flamboyantly carved *W*. And the way that Carol grabbed the cigarette case, holding it to her chest and not wanting Jane to see it? Jane thought it was because of what was *inside* the case, not what was written on the *outside*. For whatever reason, when Bailey assumed a new identity, he couldn't let go of that silver cigarette case. Maybe when you willingly lose so much of who you were, you need something tangible from the past—especially if killing that past wasn't of your own making. Jane glanced to the lone Chesterfield cigarette protected in a plastic evidence bag. "Of course," Jane realized. You have cigarettes, you need a place to put them. Chesterfield was a brand closely associated with the 1960s and before, and it was quite common back then for the upper class to serve cigarettes to their guests out of a case rather than the pack they came in.

But Bailey was forty-eight, which meant he was born in the early 1960s. The specific Chesterfield cigarette featured in the clues was the *101* brand. And Jane's research showed that

that specific brand was launched in late 1967 and then faded into obscurity years later. In fact, the person behind the clues made a point of carefully outlining each cigarette with a black pen exactly one millimeter from the tip to stress that *101* brand. As Jane regarded the cigarette with new eyes, it was as if the kidnapper was also pointing with authority to either 1967 or 1968 when the *101* was first marketed. And since Bailey was born five to six years prior to that, Jane highly doubted that *he* was the one puffing on the Chesterfields.

Jane stood back and checked out the line of clues. She looked at the stack of pages she'd copied off the microfiche viewer from the *Millburn Township Register*. Unpinning the pages from the line, she checked the date on the first article—*January 5ᵗʰ, 1968*. The headline, SEARCH IS ON FOR MISSING BOY appeared beneath the date. Why in the hell was the year 1968 continuing to show up? It was the year Jordan was arrested, when David Sackett moved into the house across from the Copelands, when an eight-year-old boy went missing in the area and when Chesterfield 101 cigarettes had their first wave of popularity. The serendipitous dovetailing was far too much to ignore. The question for Jane was where did Jordan Copeland fit into it?

Jane carried the stack of pages copied from the Millburn paper to the bed and thumbed through them, in search of the second article. Page after page of advertisements fell to the floor and Jane kneeled down to collect them. One advertisement caught her eye. It was a quarter-page ad, bordered by a thick black line. At the top was a mock-up of a playing card—the Ace—but instead of the traditional symbol for the spade suit, there was a drawing of a digging spade in its place. The line below read,

Ace Builders
Family Owned and Operated Since 1926
Let Ace Builders design your dream home.

And their slogan? *It's in the cards that we're the right*

builder for you!

There was a phone number listed. Jane dialed the number, expecting to get a message that it was no longer in service. But instead, a man answered. "Holgate Construction, John Holgate speaking."

"Hello," Jane said, not sure how to approach this. She introduced herself and gave her title, which instantly seemed to make Holgate take notice. "We're working a cold case out here and your phone number looks like it's associated with a company called Ace Builders that operated there in Short Hills in the late 1960s?"

"Ah, hang on, would you?" Jane heard Holgate close a door and sit back down. "I thought that was all behind us. We did our best to distance ourselves from the Ace name."

"Could you please elaborate, Mr. Holgate?"

"We had to keep the number in order to maintain the customer base, but it took years to bury all the gossip…"

"Sir, I need you to be more specific. What gossip are you referring to?"

"I'd have to assume your cold case has something to do with Jack Webber."

Jane felt her mouth go dry. "Yes," she quickly recovered. "That's exactly it. But I need you to tell me what you know before I proceed."

"Shit," he whispered, clearly uncomfortable. "I bought Ace Builders back in '68 from the Webbers after they left the area…"

"Could you please verify for me the names of those family members?"

"Well, there was Jack, of course. And his wife…uh…it started with an *L*."

"Louise?"

"Yeah, Louise Webber. They had one kid…a son…he was around six, I think."

"Bailey?" Jane offered.

"Yeah, Bailey Webber. Small kid for his age. Really puny

looking."

"Why did they leave?"

He hesitated. "What do you mean?"

Jane glanced down to the article in the *Millburn Township Register*. "The missing boy? The red-haired kid?" she asked, trying to remain as vague as possible.

"Yeah." Holgate sounded suspicious. "But why are you calling him *missing*? They found him a couple weeks later."

"Sir, I can't go into a lot of detail about the angle we're working here. That's why you'll have to bear with me and tell me what you remember."

Holgate seemed more relaxed. "Yeah, okay. As I'm sure you already know, it couldn't be proven that there was a connection between the Webber family cutting out of town and the Russian kid also leaving. But you know, there were a few whispers of what might have happened."

Jane's gut clenched. "This Russian kid? He lived in the back house at 43 Warwick Road in Short Hills?"

"I think that's correct. I know it was right near where that crazy teenager lived who killed that retarded boy."

"Jordan Copeland?"

"Yeah! Copeland. Must have been some bad *juju* going on in that neighborhood to have all three of them live there."

"*Three?*"

"Well, yeah? The Russian kid, the Copeland boy and the Webber family."

Jane felt the floor drop out from beneath her feet. She opened her computer. "Sir, could you hold one second please. I've got to take this call." Jane buried the cell phone underneath a pillow on the bed and quickly entered the Russian kid's address into the MapFind search engine. The page displayed, depicting a much more detailed overview than the artist's illustration in *Time* magazine. Jane clicked on the boy's address to include the immediate area around it. "Son-of-a-bitch," she whispered as she noted the name of the street that ended in a cul-de-sac and

T-boned right into 43 Warwick Road. It was *Wentworth Drive.* Jane grabbed the phone from under the pillow. "You said people whispered? What exactly did they whisper?"

Holgate sighed, not comfortable with the conversation. "Well…you know? That Jack Webber took the Russian kid and…you know…" His voice trailed off. "Hurt him?"

Jane thanked Holgate and hung up. She was just about to dial Weyler's cell when he called her.

"Jane!" he said urgently. "I'm back here with Bo at town hall. I just got a call from CBI. They got a hit on the bloody fingerprint on the Ace of Spades. This doesn't make any sense. It comes back to a missing boy from over forty years ago. His name is Samuel Kolenkoff."

"Russian…" Jane murmured.

"Yeah. I did a quick background check using different aliases and I found a Sam Cole in the system…same heritage, same hair color, same birth date, same place of birth. He lives in Chicago and he drives a black Nissan pickup truck. He was picked up on several vagrancy charges ten years ago. But here's where it gets macabre. On his employment history, it states that he worked exclusively at mortuaries and cemeteries."

Jane looked at the photo of Jake's dead body. She saw his blackened upturned fingers, his maggot-eaten feet and his mottled chest…His chest. She grabbed the loupe and held it close to the photo. "Jake…"

CHAPTER 35

The shades were drawn in Bailey's office, lending a funereal mood to the room. It had been several hours after Weyler and Bo left the Van Gordens' house. Bailey took off in his SUV to clear his head at the Midas gym, leaving Carol alone at home to roam the massive house in shock. With such a large house, it was easy for someone to sneak in and sit in Bailey's office chair, cowboy boots propped on his pristine desk and wait. And that's just what Jane was doing when she heard Carol's footsteps descend the stairs and cross to Bailey's office to close the doors.

"Hello, Carol," Jane quietly said.

Carol jumped and stepped into the room.

Jane rested her Glock on her right knee. "Close the door, Carol."

"Please put the gun down," Carol whispered.

Jane didn't move an inch. "*Close the door.*" Carol did as she was told. "Sit down!" Jane's voice was harsh.

Carol slid into the chair on the opposite side of Bailey's desk. She looked like a trapped deer during hunting season. "What do you want?"

"When you look in your husband's eyes, Carol, what do you see?"

Carol seemed taken aback, not expecting such a question. "I...ah..."

"Do you see love?"

Her chin quivered as tears welled. "No."

"Compassion?"

"No," she whispered.

"Trust?"

The tears streamed down. She shook her head.

"What *do* you see?"

Her eyes brimmed with agony. "Distraction."

"How does that make you feel?"

She lowered her head. Tears welled and fell to the carpet. "Forgotten...ignored...," she whispered as a deep ache swelled in her heart.

Jane swung her feet off the desk, still holding the Glock. "How about when you looked at Louise? What did that feel like?"

"I'm not sure..."

"You never felt like you were looking in the mirror? Like you were the fresher version of her, dutifully acting out your appointed role of the passive, blind, numb mother and wife?"

Carol looked up at Jane. "We...we had an understanding."

"Oh, I bet you did. You were perfect for the part. I bet she handpicked you for the job. She looked for the woman who could be her substitute. Someone who knew how to block out the obvious and turn away at the appropriate moments, pretending that everything was fine." Jane leaned forward. "Isn't that what *she* did when she was a young wife with her little son, Bailey? When her husband's sordid indiscretions reared up, she just turned away. You know what I'm talking about. If I don't see it, it ain't there?" Jane got up, moving around the desk slowly in the dim light. "But her husband, Jack *Webber*, made it difficult to keep turning away." Carol looked at Jane in shock when she heard the name, *Webber*. "Isn't that right, *Mrs. Webber*?" Carol looked apoplectic. Jane drew the silver cigarette case toward her and tapped on the embellished engraved *W* on top. "Take a look at the only vestige of your married name, honey! *Right there!*" Jane emphasized, forcing Carol to really look at the case. "That's where Jack *Webber* kept the Chesterfield 101s. And that..." Jane pointed to Bailey's out of place, rough-at-the-seams desk chair, was the ol' man's office chair. I can see the pervert sitting in that chair, smoking his Chesterfields and reading his dirty European kiddie porn magazines. I bet he ordered them from one of those slimy little catalogs they used to have back in the day...the ones that promise you plenty of photographs of naked boys romping in the grass or playing in the stream. So innocent, right? To the untrained eye, it's not obscene." Jane stood behind Carol and leaned closer to her. "But to a pedophile like Jack *Webber*, it's cotton candy, a bag of peanuts and a home run." Carol turned away from Jane and covered her right ear with her hand. Jane leaned against Carol's left side. "Does the word *pedophile* disturb your delicate senses, Mrs. Webber?"

Carol turned away again. "*Please...*"

"*Pedophile*, Carol! Your husband's father was a pedophile! And your mother-in-law knew it, but she didn't do anything about it! She just kept turning away because that's the kind of dirty family secret you don't talk about. She had her money, her nice house in Short Hills...no need to upset the applecart just because ol' Jack has a compromising compulsion. So, Jack starts with photos and then...*then* it's time for the first conquest." Jane pulled up a chair and sat knee-to-knee with Carol. "Now, I wonder who he practiced on? Any ideas?" Tears fell from Carol's eyes but she stayed silent. "Come on, Carol. The days of you keeping your damn mouth shut are over. Who do you think Jack used first?"

It took Carol almost half a minute before she whispered, "Bailey."

"If the stats are correct, then you're right—*Bailey*. Now, I don't know what Jack did to Bailey. I don't know how far it went with him. But I do know that Bailey either pissed him off, or he was done with him because Jack decided to look for another little boy. You see, that's the way it works. They go just so far with the first one before their courage is bolstered and feel they can take it to the next level with the second kid. *Patterns*, Carol. The devil is in a criminal's known patterns. Discover the pattern and you'll know the next step of the crime, *unless* he gets caught. And Jack got caught, didn't he? But as luck would have it, Jack was obscenely rich and the kid he stole and held in some location for...what...a couple weeks? *That* kid wasn't rich. He was just a fuckin' immigrant...and a *Russian* immigrant at that! In the late 1960s, no one gave a shit about a Commie immigrant. Maybe the kid's mama wasn't a citizen. Maybe ol' Jack threatened her. Or, maybe...*yes*...his family paid the kid's mother off and they left. Disappeared. Gone. If you can't see it, it doesn't exist." Jane leaned closer. "But sometimes, Carol, those pesky little ghosts from the past who we like to pretend aren't there, decide that they don't like being ignored anymore. And they come out of the shadows and turn our lives upside down until we finally acknowledge them."

Jane reached over into the darkness and pulled the stack of plastic-covered clues across the desk. She laid Wolfe's book down on the desk in front of Carol. "And they start to tell us their story." Jane slapped down the first transcript. "They use words," she said, following this with the magazine cutout of the boy wearing a red cap being dragged by his arm, "and they use pictures." Jane angrily slammed the fourth clue of the second transcript on the desk. "Words!" She pounded her fist on the wood as she revealed the graphic drawing that implied sodomy. "And then more extreme pictures!" Carol turned away, but Jane reached over and turned the woman's face back to the desk. "This is *real*, Carol! Don't turn away!" Jane showed Carol the riddle about the Packard. "Sometimes they tease us with riddles," Jane said before reaching across the desk to reveal the stuffed bear. "Or toys that meant something to them." Jane pressed the front of the stuffed bear to Carol's face. "You smell that, Carol? That's vomit from a *long* time ago. That's vomit from fear when that poor little Russian boy was being raped by Jack *Webber*!"

Carol weakly pushed the bear away and sobbed. "*Please… please* don't…"

Jane stood up, towering over Carol's submissive frame. "But you already know that, *don't you*?! Because when Bailey found this clue in his mailbox, he knew *exactly* who in the hell it belonged to! He understood the story that was being told because he was there! He stupidly believed that if you don't see it, it doesn't exist! But there, right there…" Jane said shaking the bear, "in three-dimensional reality was his worst fucking nightmare! The ghost he thought was long dead had resurrected and was regurgitating a past he thought his family had buried. All these clues that had arrived in your mailbox and didn't make any sense, suddenly fell into place. Now I understand when Bailey slipped and referred to that 'little shit,' he wasn't talking about Jordan or Jake. He was talking about the little kid from a long time ago because that's the last time he saw him, so he's still a 'little shit' in Bailey's mind. And, later, when Bailey smashed the vase against the wall and said, 'Fuck him' *again*, he wasn't talking about Jake!" Jane hovered over Carol's chair. "So, *he* knew and *you* knew within days of Jake going missing who had him! And *that* is when Bailey made the decision to ignore everything! To pull the reward fund! To not deal with this pesky, buzzing creature who refused to stay dead. That's when Bailey called in his mama…his frontline, old-guard defense. Maybe he was feeling a little unsure of himself, and he knew that mama Louise could be depended upon to remind him how important it was to bury the past." Jane forced Carol to look at her. "And when she told him that some sacrifices had to be made and that those sacrifices included losing his only child, he accepted that, didn't he?"

Carol collapsed on the desk, burying her face in her hands. "Oh, God, please, stop!"

Jane was relentless. "And you went along with it!" she screamed.

Carol raised her head. "What was I supposed to do?" she asked in a weak voice.

"I gave you every opportunity to talk to me! You and I were alone more than once. You could have used *me* to save Jake! But instead, you decided to keep playing the dumb, ignorant, victimized wife!"

"And I will suffer the rest of my life because of it!" Carol said, her voice finally showing some modicum of anger.

Jane sat back. "Well, you're good at suffering so you shouldn't have any problem handling that!"

"Why are you talking to me like this? What did I ever do to you?"

Jane shook her head. "Jesus, Carol. You really do have that victim mentality honed to perfection, don't you?"

Carol reached out to Jane, clutching at Jane's arm. "If I had Jake back for one minute, I'd tell him that I loved him more than life itself and that I was so sorry…"

Jane believed her. "You know, it's too damn bad you can't love yourself as much as you loved your son. If you did, you would have saved him." Jane sat back. "But little Jake was pretty far gone before fate intervened. He could hear his ancestor screaming from the other side and he thought he was going crazy. But he kept being drawn to books and people who he thought might help shed some insight into all the questions that remained unanswered in his troubled head. His battle cry became, *Truth!* He even got a poster with that word and he put it up in his room so he would always be reminded of his ultimate objective. That poster must have pissed the shit out of Bailey. But the more Jake dug and tried to work out his feelings through his art, the more confused he became. The demons that were unleashed didn't match the pretty little box that he lived in. And when he *really* started digging…to follow the trails and see where they led, he sure got one fucking eyeful." Carol stared at Jane, obviously confused. "Oh, you didn't know about that? He caught his daddy dipping his wick in unfamiliar territory."

Carol's mouth dropped open. "*Oh my God!*"

"I know that *you* knew about it. That was another one of those *understandings* you had. But it just didn't set too well with Jake. I mean, he's fifteen years old. He's questioning his own sexuality and he looks in the mirror and he's not exactly developed or masculine-looking. So, now, Jake is a mess. His entire reality is shot to hell and that damn ghost keeps haunting him from the past. Until one day, he thought that his only recourse was to hang himself. But I understand why he felt that way. It was programmed into his bloodline." Jane leaned over the desk and slid Jake's sketchpad to Carol. "And as long as we bury past deeds, we run the risk of unconsciously repeating those deeds over and over again" Jane opened the pad and flipped the pages in front of Carol several times. The woman's eyes shone with astonishment and shock. "Just like Jake's grandfather ended up stashed away in a mental hospital…it *was* a mental hospital, wasn't it? I thought it was a prison cell at first, but I did a quick check and there's no record of Jack Webber going to prison. And of course, he didn't! Because the crime was never reported! But that didn't mean that the family wanted him around. He was a liability and so the decision was made to stash him away in an asylum because, remember Mrs. Webber…if you can't see it, it doesn't exist." Jane continued to flip the animated pages showing the old man stepping onto a chair and hanging himself. "So one day, Jack Webber, wearing his Palm Beach shirt and his fedora, stood up in his room in the asylum and tied his belt around a beam and hung himself." Jane snapped the book shut. "Problem solved!" Carol jumped, startled.

"But, you know what, Carol? Patterns…patterns…patterns…They stalk us. Wonder how long it'll take before Bailey hits rock bottom and finds a good piece of rope?" Carol looked at Jane incredulously. "Oh, yeah. It wouldn't shock me one bit. Jake certainly got acquainted with a strong rope before he was rescued."

"Rescued?" Carol asked.

"Yeah, rescued from the rope only to be held against his will. From the frying pan and into the fire. That's pretty bad karma, wouldn't you say?"

"But…how would he know where to find Jake?" she whimpered.

"His name is Samuel Kolenkof. He goes by Sam Cole. Did they ever tell you his name?" Carol shook her head. "Well, they probably figured the least said to you the better. So, how did Sam find Jake? I'm not sure. But I do know that when you want something badly enough, you figure out how to get it."

Carol started to think. "What about Jordan Copeland? You arrested him."

Jane pursed her lips. "It's still up in the air as to how that one plays out." Jane got up, gathering the clues together and stuffed them, save for the teddy bear, into Jake's sketchpad. "You know, the best gift you can ever get is a good night's sleep. How many years has it been since you've had one of those, Mrs. Webber?"

Carol stayed silent as Jane moved to the office doors.

"It's crazy, isn't it?" Carol said, her voice hardly above a whisper. "The way you keep trying to make someone happy and you can't do it. No matter how hard you try, they're never satisfied. And the only reason you keep trying is because you want to be loved and feel safe."

Jane considered her words. "Get off the cross, Carol."

It was obvious that the town's Twenty-first Century improvements hadn't reached the Midas jail yet. Located behind Town Hall, the building housed three small cells and one interrogation room with an observation area on the other side. A tiny, secured front room held a desk and computer and a deputy whenever the cells were occupied. When Jane arrived in that front room, the deputy greeted her and asked if she wanted him to accompany her. She declined his offer, but before he buzzed her through the large door, she asked him one question.

"This area here, it's still low-tech, right? No cameras on the cell block?"

"No, ma'am. Only camera is in the interrogation room."

Jane followed the deputy down the short hallway that led to the first of the three cells. In her hand, she carried a small plastic trash bag filled with items. When she saw Jordan, her heart ached. He was seated on the cot with his back braced against the cement wall. He wore his usual oilcloth duster and still had the same unkempt appearance. But his face was bruised and his lip bloodied by the beating that Bo had given him. He wasn't broken, but he was on the road to that location.

Jordan refused to look at Jane. She instructed the deputy to let her inside the cell. He vehemently tried to dissuade her, worried that Jordan was "half-cocked" and would harm her.

"I need to go into the cell, please," Jane stressed. "If he tries anything," she said in full voice, "I've got a gun and I'll just shoot him." The deputy was too stupid to realize that her tone of voice was purely sarcastic. But Jordan got it. She looked out the corner of her eye and saw Jordan smirking.

The deputy unlocked the cell and let Jane inside, locking it behind her. He told her to call out whenever she needed him. Once the deputy was out of the area, Jordan broke the silence.

"I read once that the minute sheep are born, they're looking for a place to die." He turned to Jane, his face awash in a life that knew no soft edges. "I never thought of myself as a lamb before. But now that I've had a chance to think about it, I can see that, like a lamb, I'm headed to slaughter." He looked at Jane with hard eyes. "And you're gonna take me there, aren't you?"

Jane pulled up a folding chair from against the wall and set it in front of the cot. She sat down and placed the trash bag beside her.

"Let me ask you a question, Jane. Do you attend Women's Empowerment Workshops?

"No, I do not."

"And why is that?"

"Because no businesswoman worth her salt is going to give another woman the secret to success or any competitive edge when the playing field is clearly overcrowded."

Jordan smiled broadly. "Oh, Jane. You are such a cynic."

"I'm a realist. I understand how most people think. And I'm pretty good at figuring out people's motives."

"Well, we are just two peas in a very strange little pod, aren't we?"

Jane opened the trash bag and pulled out Jordan's boot with the tack in the sole. She held the boot sole up, pointing to the tack. "You know all the little tricks, don't you?"

Jordan smiled a mischievous grin. "You never know what they're gonna ask you. It helps to have something in your back pocket that you can quickly put in your shoe… just in case."

"In case they ask you something simple like if you're the son of Richard and Joanna Copeland?"

"Exactly."

She set the boot on the floor. "You checked out Thomas

Wolfe's book, *You Can't Go Home Again* at the Midas Library."

Jordan shrugged his shoulders. "I check out a lot of books. What's the problem? Did I not return that particular one? You going to add a library fine to the charges?"

Jane rooted through the trash bag and pulled out the two telephones Weyler found in his cabin. "You said you didn't have a phone."

"I guess I should have been more specific. There is no *phone jack* in the cabin. Therefore, I don't have a phone that operates in my domicile."

"Why do you have these?"

"When *Eddie* sent my belongings to me after I got out, he included those phones in the boxes. But I've never used them and I just stuffed them away in the farthest corner I could find."

Jane nodded, checking off the points in her head. She withdrew the charred black shirt protected in a plastic bag, that she found in the fire pit on his property.

Jordan furrowed his brow. "What in the hell is that?"

"A black T-shirt, small size. Similar to the type that Jake was known to wear. Found it in your fire pit."

"Oh. So, you assume that because it's *like* a shirt he might wear, it belongs to him? That would be thrown out of court, and you know it. Because once they got the DNA back from that *shirt*, they'd find out that it was a navy blue shammy cloth that I used to sop up grease from the kitchen. I discovered they made wonderful fire starters due to the oil in the material. Can't you just hear the *Greenies'* collective assholes puckering at that thought?"

Jane lay the cloth to the side. "No Ace of Spades in that deck back at your house."

"Did you count the cards, Jane?" She shook her head. "There were probably around seventy or eighty cards in that deck on the kitchen table. I don't use them for playing cards. I use them for bookmarks. I use the face cards for history text and the Aces for books I especially enjoy."

Jane removed the next item. "Like this book?" She handed him the thin volume that she got from Mollie. "Is that one of your favorites?"

He let out a long sigh. "Yes, it is."

"Was it easy for the wind to carry it when you tossed it to Jake over the fence?" Jane removed a manila folder and laid the four highlighted photos of Jordan and Jake by the bridge in front of him.

Jordan examined the photos. "We're all gonna get fucked by technology one day, aren't we?" He sat up. "To answer your question, I didn't throw the book to him. I handed it to him and he said, 'Thank you.'"

"And therein lies the problem, Jordan. You always told me that you never had contact with him."

"I never said that, Jane. I simply evaded the question when asked."

"You said you read his thoughts by looking at his photo in the two newspapers. That was a lie."

"Guilty," Jordan freely admitted. "I felt a need at that particular moment to validate my intuitive feelings to you in a way that you could accept. So, I lied. But I didn't lie when I told you that I could read his thoughts. He's an open book. He's tortured. I could relate. He had a million questions and he wasn't afraid of me the way everyone else is. He found my truth-telling refreshing which, frankly, I found quite odd but also intriguing." Jordan traced the edge of the cot with his finger. "He told me he hated his father, and I told him that I understood how he felt because I hated my father for what he did to my mother. But I also told him that the more you reject your parents, the more like them you'll become."

"You told him that?"

"It's true, Jane. The more you say you don't want to become like someone who gave you life, the more you attract their fate to you."

Jane nodded. However, she realized that while this gem

of insight held water, Jake most likely took it to mean that *he* would become gay like his father.

"Emerson wrote, *People only see what they are prepared to see*. But sometimes when they see it, it's too overwhelming for them because the truth—while necessary and enlightening—can destroy you if you're still locked into your pretty illusions. I tried to warn him, Jane." He looked at Jane with a sorrowful eye. "*Honestly, I did*. I tried to explain to him that he was too wrapped up in his ego and that his depression didn't belong to him. But I kept forgetting he was too young to understand. I told him to start slowly and dig around his own family tree and maybe he'd find answers to his uneasiness there. But sometimes the uneasiness is so far back—sometimes, it's been buried for so long that its expression is warped. But I said that often a simple act of illumination can trigger a domino of energy that shines the light on the greater Truth." Jordan looked up at Jane. "I feel that he did find the truth and it destroyed him."

Jane reached into the bag and removed another manila folder. She slid out the photo of the bloated, blackened dead body and handed it to Jordan. "That was delivered a few hours ago."

Jordan took the photo and showed an obvious repulsion. "This can't be, Jane."

"Why is that?" She leaned forward, waiting.

"Because I still hear him."

She nodded. "Like you hear the little kid you call, *Red*? The one who you've been seeing in your dreams these last couple weeks? The curly-haired, red-haired boy who stood at the back fence and never said a word but told you with his mind how no one listened to him. How he cried but no one cared?"

Jordan's eyes filled with tears. He looked down at the photo, reading Jane's thoughts. "Oh my God...I...I don't understand..."

"Magnets, Jordan. That's what you told me. We're drawn to each other in the electric haze and, with a synchronistic aim, we shoot into each other's lives. The more we try to run from our secrets and hide our past, the more we encounter it and are forced to reconcile our sins."

Jordan stared at the photo in disbelief. "Yes...that's it exactly. Magnets."

"I have to find him, Jordan. I have to find that little red-haired kid so I can find Jake and bring him home." She pointed to the writing on the edge of the photo that read, *May the Saints forgive me. Malo, Malo, MALO.* "You told me that you only needed to meet a person once and they were forever imprinted on your psyche. I need you to remember that little boy at the back fence and I need you to get inside his head and tell me where he is right now."

Jordan turned to the side, eyes open but traveling to a distant plane of awareness. He looked back at the message on the bottom of the photo. "Saints...he emphasized it. Saint...Malo... Saint Malo. It's Celtic. *Maclou.*" Jordan looked at Jane. "It has something to do with light. Shedding the light in the darkness." He glanced at the photo. "That's where *Red* is...but not for long."

"He's where?"

"There's a church on the Highway, about twenty miles from here. It's known as *The Chapel on the Rock.* But it's called the St. Malo Retreat."

Jane quickly gathered everything she brought with her and stuffed it back into the trash bag. But before she secured the bag, she removed one item and handed it to Jordan. It was his mother's leather diary. His eyes shone first with surprise and then with gratitude. She called for the deputy and turned to Jordan.

"I got a riddle for you. What can you keep only after giving it away to someone else?"

He thought about it. "Your word."

The deputy unlocked the cell. "And you have that, Jordan."

CHAPTER 36

Jane rolled into the small rock-walled parking area outside the St. Malo Chapel and got out of her car. She removed her Glock from the holster and stuffed it into the rear waistband of her jeans. She crested the uneven steps to the chapel and walked inside the tiny church. "Sam?" she called out, but her voice echoed back to her. Walking outside, Jane followed the flagstone pathway around the chapel that led to a wide-open forested area. Parked under a tree was a black Nissan pickup truck with Illinois plates. A soft mist fell from the sky as Jane walked into the wooded enclave, dotted with Ponderosa pines and the sporadic patch of old snow that lingered at this higher elevation. Along the path, she found the occasional picnic table or bench where people could sit and meditate with God. But as she approached the first bench, she found a small white envelope propped up addressed to, *To Whom It May Concern*. She opened it and read the handwritten suicide letter. It became clear to Jane that it was written by a man who was so deeply traumatized that he regressed at times into the body of the tortured child that still cried out in pain.

```
Dear Bawy,
    You can't go home again and neither
can I.
    Do you know what it's like to feel
as if you're two seconds from your last
breath? Do you? I DO.
    I pounded on the window of the old
Packard and you did nothing as you
watched him take me and drive away. I
screamed your name. BAWY! And you never
told anyone.
    He stole my innocence. I cried like
a baby and will never be a real man.
    Why you piss me off, Bawy?
```

I only had my red cap and my bear.
You remember? And now I bare my soul and
you still ignore me.

He smoked Chesterfields 101 and he
left them burning in the ashtray when
he raped me.

His name was WEBBER. JACK WEBBER.

His family owned Ace Builders. Ace
with a spade like the card.

And they all knew what he did to me
and still, they did nothing.

LISTEN TO ME NOW!!! But no one ever
did. The bitch just said, "so sad, too
bad."

So I hope the Saints forgive me because I am finished with this life. Malo,
malo, malo.

But you WILL hear me from the grave,
Bawy. I will haunt you like his memory
still haunts me.

Sam

Jane folded the letter and stuffed it into her back pocket. She quickly trod through the forested landscape. "Sam!" she called out. "Where are you? *Sam!!*" The pathway rose slightly in elevation. To the side was a patchwork of snow with fresh footprints leading off the main trail. Jane followed the prints until the snow disappeared. From there, she followed the shallow imprints in the wet ground until she came into a smaller clearing. A picnic table stood in the center. A man was seated on the table with his back to Jane, slumped forward. She fought the flashback from so many years before that was still etched in her memory. Standing still, she called out to him. "Sam?"

There was slight movement.

"Sam?" Jane moved to the right and forward. "You still with us, Sam?" Jane cautiously crept closer. "Sam?" The mist turned into a soft rain. She stayed ten feet from the table but was finally able to see his face. He wore a long leather coat that skimmed his calves. Underneath, was a pair of black jeans and a navy blue turtleneck sweater with small holes dotted around the fabric. Even though Jane figured Sam was in his mid-forties, he still had a bright shock of red curly locks that he'd let grow into a wild mane down his back. Jane moved a few feet closer. In Sam's right hand, he held a knife, similar to the one he lodged in the front door of Town Hall. The blade was pressed against his right thigh. In systematic motion, he'd been rocking it back and forth, cutting through his black jeans and slicing into his flesh. Blood seeped through the open fabric and dripped down his pant leg. She took another step around the table and saw a revolver clutched in his left hand with the business end lodged in his trembling mouth. His, pale, almost ghostly white, freckled complexion stood out against his dark clothing, lending a stark look of death to his mien. Sam seemed to be in another world, although he was aware of Jane's presence as he turned his head slightly to her and spoke in a tortured whisper. "Go away..."

Jane pushed the death scene from fifteen years ago to the back of her mind. "Sam," she said gently, "my name is Jane Perry. I'm a cop. I'm trying to find Jake. You have my attention. I have your note and I want to hear your story."

He turned to her, gun still in his mouth as tears rolled down his pasty cheeks. "It's too late," he choked out.

"I promise you, it's not."

"My life is ruined now because of what I did."

"Please take the gun out of your mouth, Sam." It took about a minute but Sam finally removed the tip. "Could I ask you to set the gun on the table, Sam?" Sam complied, tears flowing freely now. "And the knife? Please stop cutting yourself and let go of the knife?" Sam looked down at his leg as if it didn't belong to him. He released his grip and let the knife fall to the seat of the picnic table. "I'm going to walk in front of you but I'm not going to touch you or hurt you." Jane slowly moved around the table so she could face Sam. She leaned against a tree about six feet from the table and gradually slid down onto the earth, taking a seat on a bed of pine needles.

"How did you find me?" he asked in a quiet voice.

"You told me…on the photo of the body? I'll admit I had some help deciphering it. But I did figure out some of what you sent us. You took a lot of time to put all that together. I know how smart you are."

"I'm not smart," he said, hanging his head.

"*Yes*, you are. Maybe a little ambiguous but you're very smart. I understood it was a story from almost the beginning but nobody would believe me. The police chief basically ignored me."

He looked at her. "Why?"

"People want simple answers to complex questions and if they can't get that, they don't pursue it further." Jane extended her legs demonstrating an easy, comfortable, nonthreatening posture. "And then there's denial. You know? It can't be real. It can't be true? It's all in your imagination."

Sam hung his head as her words rang in his heart. "Yes, yes, yes, *yes*." He sobbed like a child. Jane realized at that moment that the crying on the two voicemail clues was indeed Sam, reverting to his childhood alter. "No one pays attention to you, no matter how much you tell them you were hurt." His lip curled in a sudden show of anger. "They just throw money at you and tell you to leave…dirty, filthy money! They tell you to shut-up and never breathe a word of what happened to you."

"I know what happened to you, Sam. And I know who did it."

He looked at her with pleading eyes and leaned forward. "You believe me?"

"Yes. Absolutely."

"It *did* happen! He *did* take me in his Packard! And I was crying, 'Bawy! Bawy!' because I didn't know how to say Bailey. But he just stood there. And I had my hand pressed against the glass of the car and I was screaming, 'Bawy! Help me!' But he just turned away. He was eight and I was six and he could have said something. 'Tell her what you saw!' I yelled at him before we headed toward the road that led to the highway. He knew that son-of-a-bitch was taking me to their vacation house on the coast of Maine. It was January and nobody would be looking there." Sam shook as the flashback overwhelmed him. "And he did things to me that no man should ever do to a child. When he raped me, he would grab my throat and choke me until I thought I was a breath from death. But then I'd always wake up and he'd be looking at me with those cold, crazy eyes and the hell would start all over again. I'd puke on my bear and he'd laugh at me. He'd call me a baby. But I was just six for God's sake!! I *was* a baby!" Sam looked off in the distance. "When he finally took me home, we first went to his house. And his wife saw me. He told her to give me a bath and clean the shit and piss out of my clothes. She did exactly what she was told. But all she said to me while she was doing it was, 'So sad, too bad. So sad, too bad.'" His tenor rang with an eerie, singsong quality. "She was as weak as he was crazy. And then, he had her drop me off in front of my house and she just left me there...shattered, lost, terrified. When I told my mother what had happened, she was scared to say anything and refused to go to the police. Being from Russia, she didn't trust the police and she didn't want to get in trouble. Everyone was making sure they were taken care of...everyone except me! When the couple my mother worked for showed concern about where I'd been, I blurted out Mr. Webber's name to him. The next day, my mother found an envelope on our stoop. Inside was a thousand dollars and a note that said, *Leave or be deported.* It was Mrs. Webber's writing. So, we left and I was told by my mother to forget about everything...*to pretend it never happened.* That we had to move on and that, thanks to that thousand dollars, we could move far away. We ended up in Chicago and I could never speak about what happened to me again. As far as she was concerned, the book was closed." Sam looked at Jane. "But *I* never closed that book! I never forgot! I was obsessed! The anger ate away at me until I knew I had to do something about it. When my mother died, I was finally free to take action. I wanted revenge and I wasn't going to stop until I got him and got him good."

"How did you find Bailey since he changed his last name?"

Sam grinned. His body relaxed slightly. Finally, there was someone in front of him who was willing to listen to him. "I figured the little cocksucker would change his name. Don't we all do that, thinking it's going to give us a fresh start? I changed my name from Kolenkoff to Cole so I could fit in. I got to thinking of all the possibilities. He could have shortened it to Webb but that was too close to the real name. And then I remembered his mother's name because the Van Gordens were a fixture in Short Hills. I put the two together and did some searching on the Internet and even added *Webber* just for kicks and then… Wow! Bingo! *Jackpot!* There he was in all his glory on that damn video!"

Jane realized at that moment that Bailey unconsciously created the perfect storm of words within the text of his video by using the tags, "Bailey Van Gorden" and "Webber"—albeit mistakenly for "Weber"—making it easy for someone savvy like Sam to locate him.

"I searched the video link to see if it appeared anywhere else. That took some creative thinking but I eventually found several other websites where it was linked and I quickly figured out what Bailey was *really* after."

"Gay websites?"

"Yeah." His eyes shone with mischief. "So, I knew how to play him. I contacted him via email using a fake name. He liked what he heard, I guess, because he asked to meet me at this strip club. I was in Chicago so I told him I needed a few days to get time off work. That seemed to excite him to think I would travel a distance just to meet him. It stroked his ego."

"I bet it did."

"I had a lot of vacation time built up from the funeral home I work at and so I decided to take it. And we met. I decided I would play a role so I wouldn't let my anger take over until the right time. It was easier than I thought. He took my nervousness as excitement. But I told him I liked to get to know my customers before I agree to the final deal. And since he likes to hear himself talk and he talks even more when he's drinking, I got to hear a whole lot of important information." Sam's eyes narrowed. "When he said he had a son, his *only child*, I couldn't believe it! My plan for revenge started at that moment! It was perfect! I followed him back to his home one night and he didn't even notice. For one week, I sat in the shadows and I watched who came and went from that house. It didn't take more than a day for me to see his kid sneaking out and walking into town or heading over to the bridge. The more I watched his son, the more he reminded me of Bailey. And I hated him even more for that! But I couldn't let him know that yet. I knew I had to act like a friendly face to draw him into my web. So one day, when Jake was on the bridge, I just *happened* by and we struck up a conversation. Nothing important. Just chatter. But it worked. It was obvious that the kid was hungry for someone to talk to. And I was more than happy to give him exactly what he wanted." Sam patted his bloody leg, pressing the open wound back and forth with his fingers. "I was gonna take him that day, but I knew I needed at least one more visit with him to make him feel safe. I didn't want him to fight me until I could control him. And then, fate intervened. I was waiting on the bridge for him one night, and there he shows up with a goddamned rope. I couldn't believe it. My whole plan was imploding in front of me. He swung that rope over the bridge beam and stood up on that rail. I bolted from my car and grabbed him. I told him we'd go somewhere and talk. I could see he was desperate, and I knew that he'd do whatever I told him. Desperation is a manipulator's best friend, don't you know?" Sam sat back on his hands. "And the rest…well, you know the rest."

"The clues."

"It was *my* time! Like Thomas Wolfe, I published my

revelations about the Webber family for all to see in hopes that they would finally acknowledge what happened to me!" He forced his hand through his thick, tangled red locks. "But nothing happened! There was one news conference. *One!* And nothing in the papers! Not even two sentences! You think that if you take a man's son and you let him know that you mean business, that he's gonna say or do something! *But he does nothing!*" Sam screamed. *"Nothing!!"* He buried his head in his hands. "All I wanted was for him to feel a little bit of what I felt over forty years ago! *And he won't even give me that!!*" Sam looked at Jane, weariness painted on his face. "So, I do what I have to do. I tell his son everything. For several days, I tell him every dirty little secret about his family. But it gave me no pleasure. It just made the pain come back and hit me harder. And so, this morning, I gave up. I took that photo into town and left it where I knew it would be found." He turned away. "And then I came here."

Jane leaned forward. "Where's Jake?"

Sam eyed her with suspicion. "What do you mean? You saw the photo."

"Yeah. And I know it's not Jake."

"Of course, it is."

"No, Sam. Jake has a tattoo of a dragonfly over his heart. That body has no tattoo."

"It's black and bloated. The tattoo must be obscured..."

"If you look very carefully through a loupe, you can see the outer edge of the stainless steel table underneath the sheet. You took that photo of a dead body in the morgue where you work." Sam looked like a deer in the headlights. "That was all part of your advance plan, wasn't it? Your clues were so well thought out. Every second was planned, including the climactic photo, should the need arise. You might have fantasized about torturing Jake and making him suffer, but I don't think you did." Sam hung his head. "I think you realized he was already tortured, especially when you saw him trying to hang himself." Jane stood up. "I've never met Jake, but I know that kid pretty well now.

And I imagine you and he hit it off pretty damn well." Sam's face gave him away. "So, I just need to know where he is."

"He told me he doesn't want to be found anymore."

"I understand that. But do you want him to get hurt?"

Tears flowed down Sam's face. "No."

"Then tell me where he is." Sam hung his head. "Look, I know what it feels like to be fifteen years old and all alone and abandoned. I know what it did to me, Sam. I know what it did to you. And I don't want that to happen to Jake."

Jane drove back toward Midas with Sam seated in the passenger seat. She dialed Weyler's cell number and told him in the vaguest of terms to get into a patrol car *alone* and meet her in front of the Sunshine Mountain Lodge cabins just off the highway, which was located twelve miles from town. He arrived just minutes after Jane pulled up to the high mountain hideaway. She got out of the Mustang and walked around to the passenger side, opening the door. Sam's injured leg was wrapped in the poplin shirt Jane had tossed into her car several nights before. Weyler took in the scene, not sure what was going on.

"Sam," Jane said, "this is Sergeant Morgan Weyler." She turned to Weyler. "Boss, this is Sam Cole." Weyler's eyes widened. "Before you bust a gasket, you gotta trust me on this one." Jane started up the steep hill that led to the cabins.

"Jane!" Weyler called out. "What in the hell..."

"*Please!* You gotta trust me!" she yelled back as she ran up the hill and turned right. She jogged to the last cabin on the dirt lane. Sam said the door would be unlocked and he was telling the truth. Jane walked inside the low-ceiled, sparse bungalow. Just as Sam described, there was a bathroom to the left, next to a small kitchen. To the right was the living room and then a yellow door which led to an attached bedroom and bathroom. "Jake?" Jane called out. She tried the door and found it locked. "Jake?" She put her ear to the thin door and thought she heard movement. "I'm coming in," she yelled as she stood back and gave the door a hard kick, busting the lock and swinging the door wide open.

She held back, taking a quick glance of the tiny room and seeing no one. "Jake?" she said with urgency. She noted a trashcan near the single bed. Inside was one of the vintage shirts, shredded to pieces. A plaid fedora lay on top of the shirt, also destroyed. Jane was almost positive she could hear the breath of another person close by. She hunkered down and tried to see if there was movement under the bed. "Jake? My name's Jane. I'm a cop and I want to help you." She stepped into the room, but when she cleared the small bathroom on the right, she was tackled from behind. She fell forward, stunned, as she felt her Glock being stripped from her rear waistband. Jane flipped over on her back and looked up into the eyes of Jake Webber.

CHAPTER 37

Jake's hands shook as he grasped the Glock and aimed it at Jane's chest.

"You shouldn't have come here!" he screamed.

"Jake, put down the gun!"

"Fifteen more minutes and I would have been gone!"

"Where are you going?"

"Away!" he yelled, still training the Glock on Jane with an unsteady hand.

"How are you going to do that?"

"I'll hitchhike."

"How far?"

"Far enough!"

"What are you gonna use for money, Jake?"

"Sam gave me five hundred bucks."

"That was decent of him." She sat up and Jake jerked the

Glock forward. "Hey, hey, hey…take it easy! That gun's got a hair trigger. Can I please just get up and sit on the bed?"

Jake nervously watched her. "Okay. But don't you try anything with me."

"Don't worry," she said, methodically standing up and sitting down on the single bed. "Five hundred bucks won't last you long, Jake."

Jake moved across from Jane, holding the Glock on her the whole time. "I'll get a job. I'll wash dishes, do odd jobs, whatever it takes."

Jane noticed the jagged line in the back of his hair where Sam cut off the kid's ponytail. "Sounds good, but you look real young for your age. How are you going to explain why you're alone and need work?"

He clearly hadn't thought of that. "I'll figure that out when it happens. I'm changing my name, too, just in case anyone heard about me from the TV."

Jane turned away. "Oh, shit…"

"What?"

"Change your name? And the beat goes on, Jake. Hey, I got an idea. Use your mother's maiden name. That worked real well for your dad!"

He took a shaky seat in a chair, still keeping the gun on Jane. "I can't go back there and live with those people."

"I agree. But running is not going to fix your problem either. You read those books, Jake…the ones that Jordan gave you? If you run away, you'll just play right into the family pattern. And everything you despise today, you will repeat in the months and years to come. *Guaranteed.*"

The kid started to cry, still holding the Glock, but his intention dimming as his emotions took over. "Do you have any idea what it's like to find out the darkest secrets about your family history?" He glanced to the trashcan and the tattered shirt and fedora.

"Yeah. Actually, I do. It sucks. And it sucks worse when

they're dead. But you're the one who bought the *Truth* poster. You're the one who wanted to know it all." Jake dissolved into a flood of tears. Jane reached forward and gingerly removed the Glock from his trembling hand and stuffed it in the rear waistband of her jeans. "You know, somebody recently told me that awareness is a demanding mistress. Once she wakes you up, she won't let you go back to sleep."

"Sounds like something Jordan would say."

"That's because he's the one who said it. And it's true, Jake. Once you discover the truth, you can never go back to the way it was before. Life…" She considered her own personal predicament. "God, life is forever changed. And it's gonna take a while to see that life through new eyes. But give yourself some time and you can do it."

Jake buried his head in his hands. "My bloodline has cursed me!" he cried. Suddenly, in a wave of rage, he stood up and kicked the trashcan hard against the wall.

Jane reached over and grabbed his hands. "No, Jake. The curse ceases to operate once you bring it into the light and expose it."

He looked at her with beseeching eyes. "For real?"

She nodded. "For real, Jake."

He thought about it. "How do you know for sure?"

"Because I feel it in my heart. You should understand that more than anyone. You chose to have the dragonfly tattooed over your heart so you'd always remember to be the light in the darkness. But before you can do that, you said you'd have to bust through the illusions. That's what Liora told me, at least."

"God, I miss her," he said, choking on tears.

"I can fix that." Jane said, standing up. "You coming?"

"I'm not pressing charges against Sam. I'll stand up in court for him and I'll be a hostile witness if I have to."

"I'd expect nothing less from you, Jake."

He stood up and walked toward the front door, glancing back at Jane's *Groovy* T-Shirt. "Liora's got a shirt just like that."

"Is that right?"

Weyler's eyes widened as Jane walked Jake down the dirt path and toward the two cars.

"Holy mother of God," Weyler said. "You think you might have shared this with me, Jane?"

Jake reunited with Sam, touching him softly on his shoulder.

"It all happened pretty fast," Jane admitted, standing back and staring at Sam and Jake. "Well, boys, this is what we call a predicament." She turned away, considering the possibilities. "But I'm in the mood today to give everyone what they want and maybe a little bit of what they need as well." She turned to Weyler. "And I mean *everyone.*" Jane thought her plan through. "Maybe if I can get you guys to cooperate and maybe another guy…maybe we can close out this day on a better note than it started." Sam and Jake nodded. Jane sidled up to Weyler. "First thing I have to do is send a text to Bo's cell phone. You have his number?"

"Sure." Weyler brought out his phone. "What are you going to say?"

"This has got to be his catch."

"Agreed."

"So I'm going to tell him to meet us at the jail in thirty minutes."

Bo looked taken aback when he got out of his patrol car and met Jane and Weyler. He hadn't even seen Jake and Sam yet.

"Which one of you texted me?" he carefully asked.

"I did, Bo," Jane said.

He looked at her with fearful eyes.

"We need your help, Bo," Weyler broke in. "Jane's got a plan but we need you to help make it happen."

Bo still looked shell-shocked.

"Bo?" Jane said quietly.

"What?" Bo asked, his mind elsewhere.

"Can you help us?"

He nodded. "Whatever you need."

"Well, first, old friend," Weyler said, putting his arm around Bo's shoulder and walking him around the back of the jail complex, "we need to introduce you to two important people."

Bo looked up. "Holy shit."

It took Weyler and Jane half an hour to work out an agreement between Bo and Sam. After that, they parted and Bo called Bailey to come down to the jail immediately. "Come alone," Bo insisted to Bailey.

Bailey arrived ten minutes later, freshly coiffed, flush-faced and obviously congested. He was agitated with Bo, telling him that he had an important client he had to meet. But Bo explained to Bailey that Jordan Copeland asked to see him and make an on-camera confession regarding the kidnapping and murder of his son. When Bo insisted that this could wrap it all up, Bailey acquiesced. He led Bailey down the short hallway that led to the interrogation room and assured him that he and others would be on the other side of the mirrored wall watching and capturing the statement on video. Bo opened the door and Bailey walked in. As the door closed, Bailey heard the lock click loudly.

He turned and saw Jordan standing with his back to him, his trademark oilcloth duster covering his body and a hood covering the back of his head. Bailey brusquely pulled out a chair and plopped down, checking the camera with the red light on in the corner of the room so he could feature his best side. He folded his arms across his crisp white shirt and leaned back in the chair so that it balanced precariously on the back two legs. "Okay, old man. You said you wanted to see me. Tell me your confession."

The man turned and removed the hood, revealing his face.

"You're not Jordan Copeland," Bailey said, dropping the chair back on four legs.

"Remember me?" Sam asked, his tenor confident.

Bailey was clearly confused. He looked toward the mirrored

wall, seeing only his reflection but knowing that Bo and others were behind the wall watching. "What in the hell is going on here?" He glanced nervously at the camera with the red light. "Who are you?"

"You don't remember me? We sat across from the back table at The Cat House Lounge and had some drinks a few weeks ago."

Bailey's eyes froze. "What in the hell are you talking about?" he asked with a nervous laugh.

"I never called you back like you asked me to, so we could close the deal. You're just not my type."

Bailey got up, angrily shoving his chair into the table. "What in the fuck is going on here?!"

Sam moved a few steps closer. "But I'm glad we have a chance to talk again, face-to-face. Just so I can say...long time, no see, Bawy."

It took Bailey several seconds to figure it out and, when he did, the look that Jane saw on his face from behind the glass was like none other she'd ever witnessed. It was a combination of someone seeing a ghost and their worst nightmare all wrapped up into one. Even though there was the thick pane of glass between them, Jane could smell the fear in that tiny room where the two men faced off. Jane turned to her right and put a comforting arm around Jake's shoulder. "Are you positive you want to watch this?" she whispered to Jake.

The boy nodded, never taking his eyes off the scene playing out in front of him.

Bo and Weyler leaned against the mirror, both equally captured by the unfolding drama.

Bailey spun around and reached for the doorknob, but it was locked. "Open this door!" he screamed.

"It's scary as shit to be locked in a room with someone you're afraid of, isn't it?"

Bailey gave the heavy door several kicks and turned the locked knob repeatedly. "Open this door *now*!"

"I screamed like that too forty-one years ago but it didn't do any good. It just made your father crazier!"

Bailey paced to the mirrored wall. "*Get me out of here!*" he yelled, his voice rising several octaves in fear.

"Yeah, I paced like that. I sure did, Bawy. I shit and pissed my pants too, but none of it mattered. He still fucked me!"

"You're insane!" Bailey screamed. "I don't know you!"

The flip switched in Sam's head. All the years of holding the pain inside erupted. He threw a wooden chair across the room, splintering it in half as it hit the cement wall. "*Excuse me?!* Don't you dare call me insane, you fucking weasel! *You don't know me?!* You son-of-a-bitch! *Who am I?!*"

"Get away from me!"

Sam grabbed another chair and flung it across the room, nearly hitting Bailey. "*Say my name!*"

"You are nobody!" Bailey screamed at him.

Sam strode across the room and clamped his hands around Bailey's neck. "Say my name, motherfucker!"

Bo started to leave the observation room to intervene but Jane held him back. "No, Bo. Let this happen."

Bailey gasped for breath, trying in vain to peel Sam's fingers off his throat.

"How does it feel to be one breath away from death?!" Sam growled at Bailey, spitting in his face as he spoke. Bailey struggled, his eyes turning helplessly to the mirrored wall.

Jake regarded his father on the other side of the glass with a reserved front.

Sam continued to shake Bailey's neck, pressing his fingers tighter around his throat. "Say my name, Bawy! *Say my name!!*"

Bailey fought for breath and gasped two words. "Samuel… Kolenkoff."

Sam released his grip and slammed Bailey into the wall. "Yes!"

It took Bailey a good minute to recover and when he did, his ego took over. "You will pay dearly, you crazy bastard!"

"*Pay?* Pay for what?" Sam goaded.

"For everything you've done to us for nearly two weeks!" Bailey staggered to the table. "I should have given them your name and helped them find you! When I saw that fucking bear, I knew Jordan Copeland had nothing to do with this! There was only one man who couldn't let the past go! You had to fuck everything up, didn't you? Jesus Christ, you didn't have to *take* Jake, you stupid son-of-a-bitch! *You could have let him hang himself and saved us all a fucking lot of trouble!!*"

Jake stared at his father, his worst fears realized.

Bailey started to laugh. "Think about it, Samuel. You could have let him die by his own hand, but you chose to take him and *then* kill him! So, which one of us is the fool?"

Jake heard enough. He stormed out of the observation room and pressed the button on the doorknob to unlock the interrogation room door. Swinging the door in, he stood in front of his father. Bailey fell backward into the only chair left in the room. "Which one of us is the fool now, Dad?"

CHAPTER 38

By the time the dust settled on the long, soul-baring day, Jane sat in her Mustang and felt exhaustion set into her bones. Because Jordan had violated his probation by talking with Jake, he would have to stay another night in the Midas jail until Bo could sort out the mess. Sam joined him, occupying an adjacent cell. From the few moments Jane spent with the two of them, she figured their reunion would be nothing short of ironic.

Bailey returned home, canceling his "client meeting" for that day. While Jane wasn't sure, she surmised his revelation to Carol that their son was still alive and that Bailey had been used to support Sam's future court case, fueled more tension between them. Carol sent word that she wanted to see Jake, but the kid refused, choosing instead to reunite with Mollie and her parents. He would spend the first night of many under their roof.

Jane stared at Bo's office window from her Mustang checking for any movement in the room. Her cell phone rang. Recognizing the number, she answered.

"Hello! Thank you for calling me back…..Yes…..Very good…..Tomorrow? That would work out very well…..I'll arrange for your transportation…..Goodnight." Jane hung up and quickly dialed Weyler, giving him the news. After making arrangements with him, Jane clicked off her phone. She let out a long sigh and felt her nerves shudder. She wasn't sure whether it had to do with the phone call or what she was about to do.

She saw a dim light go on in Bo's office and slight movement around his desk. Bo's demeanor had remained cautious around Jane ever since she sent him the text message. When he and Weyler left to get dinner at Annie's Diner, she could feel the tension building around Bo. He was waiting for the other shoe to drop and Jane was about to drop it.

Vi was heading out of the building, just as Jane walked up to the door. She buzzed Jane inside and wished her goodnight. The air felt thick with trepidation as Jane made her way to Bo's door and gently knocked. When he didn't answer, she pushed the door open. He was seated in his chair, his feet propped up on the desk and finishing off a bottle of Jack Daniels, which he'd poured into his coffee cup. He never looked up at Jane.

She set the trash bag filled with the items she'd taken into Jordan's cell on Bo's desk. "The stuff inside belongs to Jordan. You can give it to him when you let him out."

Bo nodded, still not looking at Jane.

"I figured," Jane continued, resting her leather satchel on a chair, "that with all the mess around here, it made sense to put Jordan's stuff in a trash bag. I could put it in a box and label it but that wouldn't work for you, would it?"

Bo turned away, his face sweaty and his lower lip quivering.

"Look, Bo, I'm not going to tell anybody about this, okay? There are only three people on this planet who know you can't read. You, me and Vi. Oh, and Vi doesn't know I found the text codes in her drawer. So please don't blame her for giving me the secret symbols you two used." Jane had to applaud Vi's creativity in coming up with that one. Her text to Bo of, *! ... # ///* —meaning, *Emergency. Come to jail in 30 minutes* — was nothing short of brilliant. "But you know," Jane was careful in her tone, "you really did get Weyler...Beanie...up here on pretext. All those years he thought he owed you something for breaking in that door when you were rookies, and it turned out it was your fault because you couldn't read the address. Was that the incident that forced you to start memorizing text so well?" Bo shifted nervously in his chair and took a slug of whiskey. "I imagine your wife was a great help to you. Did you take home documents and have her read them to you and memorize what you heard? Her death must have been one helluva blow for a lot of reasons. You obviously trusted Vi with your secret. I thought her idea of putting pictures on the files was brilliant. You're a man who is very visual. Jordan looks like a trash bag to you so there's a picture of a *trash bag* on the front of his file, just in case someone asks for the file and Vi's not here, right? *Juice Box Jake,* same thing." Jane walked to the doorway and looked out into the main room where all the new computer equipment was set up. "This must have scared the shit out of you. Writing emails, navigating the Internet, digital files...Jesus, it was too much." She turned back to Bo. "So when Vi said she was retiring, you had no choice. Your only backup was leaving you. You had to retire."

Bo turned his chair around and faced the window. Jane walked around his desk and pulled out the front drawer. "But it's not just that you can't read." She removed his appointment book and opened it. Page upon page was filled with scribbling and odd drawings that lacked form. "You've had something else going on for quite some time. Maybe since you were a kid?

Something wonky in your brain?" Jane turned to the last page of the book. On the left side, Vi had written his name in cursive down the page. On the right side, Bo had tried desperately to replicate the lines he saw. But if a letter leaned to the right, Bo's attempt leaned to the left; if a letter rose above the line, Bo's letter dipped below the line. "It's like your brain is firing things backward." She turned to Bo. "Did your father have the same problem?" Bo took another sip of whiskey from his coffee cup and hung his head. "Okay. Maybe he did and you didn't know it. Maybe he kept it a secret just like you." Jane set the appointment book back in the drawer and touched the yellow folder on his desk. "It's tough to keep your son a secret though, isn't it?"

Bo spun around in his chair, tears welling in his eyes. "How much?!"

Jane stood back. "How much what?" she asked softly.

"Money? I don't have a lot but I can call Vi and she can come in and sign my name on a personal check. *How much*?!" Bo was shaking and desperate.

"That's funny you should ask that question, Bo," Jane replied, walking around the desk and opening her leather satchel on the chair. "Because I was planning on giving this to you..." Jane brought out a check. "Let me make sure I spelled the name of your son's facility correctly." She leaned across the desk and opened the yellow folder. Inside was the cover letter from the director of operations at the MacIntosh Center for the Severely Handicapped in Tampa Bay, Florida. The letter explained that Bo's mentally disabled, twenty-eight-year-old son would be relocated to a residential apartment in preparation for Bo's arrival and permanent guardianship of the young man. Jane laid the check in front of Bo. "I made it out for a thousand bucks and asked that it was allocated for your son's needs."

All the emotion Bo had bottled up inside, burst out. He cried, covering his face in shame.

Jane waited several minutes while Bo contained himself. "I checked into the facility online. Did you know they sponsor an outreach program for adult literacy? You should ask them about that, Bo." Jane stood up, grabbed her satchel and headed to the door. "You know, you told me that when you take away everything, a man is left with two things…his integrity and his reputation. As far as I'm concerned, Bo, you're walking out of here with both of those."

Jane grabbed a bite of leftovers Sara had prepared for her and then headed to bed. Outside her window in the garden below, she heard the soft conversations between the Greens—Mollie and Jake. It took Jane five minutes to pack her clothes and wrap her mind around the fact that tomorrow was Thursday and the day she expected to hear back from the doctor. She lay her weary body in the honeymoon bed and watched the night swallow the light. Slumber overtook her and for the first night of many, she slept the sleep of the innocent.

As the morning light pierced the veil between the worlds, Jane hovered peacefully in that middle ground, aware of her surroundings but still floating where dreams and spirit dance. She heard no footsteps approach but she felt the gentle hand stroking her forehead in that familiar rhythmic motion that always soothed and calmed her as a child. Jane was aware of the presence suspended over her but she kept her eyes shut. She felt the cool breath come nearer and whisper in her ear.

"I had no choice. Now you know. Please forgive me."

Jane opened her eyes. She saw no one there. But the room sparked with an electric buzz for several seconds before dissipating.

She got up and showered and dressed in the same shirt she showed up in six days before. Gathering together the clothes that Mollie loaned her, Jane started down the hallway when Weyler stepped out of his room.

"When are you leaving?" she asked him.

"About half an hour. That should give you enough time."

"You know the drill, right?"

He put a reassuring hand on Jane's arm. "Jane. I can handle this. I'll call you when I'm heading back."

She nodded and they walked downstairs. The kitchen was alive with laughter and conversation. Jake and Mollie sat at the table while Sara pulled a tray of blueberry muffins out of the oven and urged Jane and Weyler to have a seat. Jane set Mollie's shirts on an empty chair.

"What are you doing?" Mollie asked.

"Thanks for the loan," Jane replied, pouring herself a cup of coffee.

"You keep those!" Mollie insisted. "It'll give you a good start until you can buy a new wardrobe. Use that..." She motioned to Jane's poplin shirt. "...to wash your car."

Jane handed the kid her clothes, "I can't take your clothes..."

"Don't be a *yutzi*. You want to look like a *meeskite*?"

"Liora!" Sara exclaimed. "Don't call her stupid and she's certainly not unattractive! Jane's a true *mensch* and a *hamish* person!" She turned back to her baked goods, suddenly realizing what she just said. Mollie looked at her mother in stunned silence. Sara recovered. "Eat your breakfast!"

Jane carried her cup of coffee outside into the backyard. She checked her cell phone, in case she'd missed the call from the doctor.

"Thank you," Aaron said.

Jane turned. Aaron was seated on the bench with a writing pad. "You're welcome. Working on your next sermon?"

"Yes...for Easter Sunday. I'm sorry you won't be here to join us."

Jane made a point to obviously look under the bench. "I don't see your little red photo album of inspiration."

"I don't need it this week," he said with a warm smile. "This is on the resurrection."

"Ah, yes. I can relate. I've brought the dead back to life this week myself."

He motioned for her to sit down next to him. "I always

found the idea of being reborn and discarding the old and dead ways so elegant. To have the chance to reinvent yourself and live a life that felt true and reflective of what you truly were inside… how could anyone not find power in that?"

"I get what you're saying. But reinventing yourself and not acknowledging who you were is a halfway birth. It's one thing to become someone new and another to hide who you came into this world as."

He nodded. "I understand what you mean, Jane."

"Will you give Jake a new life?"

"That's his wish. We always looked on him as the son we never had."

"You think his parents will fight you?"

"His father won't. But Carol…she still needs contact."

There was a moment of contemplation. "Maybe Carol could move in too," Jane offered with a smile, patting Aaron's shoulder. "I'm glad Jake has you and Sara. He could use a family that's a little more secure and open."

Aaron's face tensed up. "Yes. Regarding that…Sara and I talked and we're going to figure out a way to tell Mollie the truth."

"Good."

"I still have a lot of a fear, though."

"I know about fear, Aaron. But it could be worse. You could be a recovering alcoholic, who's desperately trying to quit smoking and who is terrified that she's dying of cancer." He looked at Jane with compassion, realizing the intent of her statement. "But every time I go there, I just say to myself, 'I will be all right and one day I *will* die. I can believe the first part and it calms me to the inevitability of the second part."

Jane pulled up to the Midas jail and waited. Weyler had called and let her know he was driving back into town. The front door opened and Jordan walked out, carrying the trash bag of his belongings. She honked the horn and he strolled to her car. "Get in. I'm driving you home."

"I can walk," he assured her.

Jane leaned over and pushed open the passenger door. "Get in, Jordan."

They drove in silence along the highway that led to his house. But about a quarter mile from the property, he turned to Jane with a questioning look on his face. "What's happening?"

She glanced at him. "It's okay, Jordan."

He looked off into the distance. "No...it's not..." His hand began to shake, gradually at first and then with profound movement. He looked at Jane, fear in his eyes. "Jane? What's going on? Where are you taking me?"

"It's all right, Jordan. You're going home."

Jordan looked at Jane. "Oh, God. It's that something you have that I desperately need...you're the one who can bring me my life..."

She turned left onto his road and crossed the bridge over the roaring river. Jordan grabbed his chest, as his breathing labored. "What's happening, Jane?" he asked, struggling for breath.

Jane parked the Mustang twenty feet from the front door of the cabin. A rental car sat unoccupied next to the cabin. Jordan shook, canvassing the area around his house. Jane got out of the car and walked around to the passenger side. She opened the door and helped him out of the car. He stood there, staring at the front porch, his heart aching. The memory of a dream floated into his consciousness. But this was real. He turned to Jane, confused. "I feel like I'm in my dream."

"You're not," Jane said. "But sometimes dreams come true." She turned him around to face the front porch.

Weyler walked out onto the porch and held the front door open. There was a second of suspended time before a woman walked out and joined him. She was in her early eighties with a Creole complexion and dressed in an elegant suit and hat. Weyler helped her down the steps. Jordan stared in disbelief and shock.

"Mama? Is that you?" he cried.

"Yes, baby. It's me." She walked to him and held him tightly. "I love you, child."

They held each other for what seemed like forever, speaking from their hearts but saying no words. And then, Maureen pressed her lips against Jordan's ear and whispered the words he'd already heard in his dream. "And in the quiet it comes. Not from a shout. But in a whisper."

Later that day, when the timing was right, Jane would tell Jordan the truth that had been kept from him for over fifty years.

The truth was that Maureen only spent one brief night in the hospital after leaving the Copeland's house fifty-one years ago. Jordan's father had an immediate change of heart and arranged for Maureen to move into her own home in upstate New York, which he paid for outright, along with a generous monthly allowance.

The truth was that Maureen remarried a light-skinned black man several years later, suffered two miscarriages and divorced at age thirty-eight. Two and a half years later, Richard Copeland came back into her life. Unbeknownst to Jordan, his father suffered great guilt, believing he was responsible for his son's felonious behavior by taking Maureen away from him. The Copelands separated and Richard continued his love affair with Maureen until his death twenty-two years later.

The truth was that Richard Copeland set up a multi-million-dollar trust for Maureen LaFond, administered by Edward Butterworth, that would continue until her death. At that point, the beneficiary would become Jordan Copeland.

Jordan would also learn that Maureen's life almost ended the night of March 22nd when she suffered a heart attack. Somehow, through the feathers of consciousness, Jordan's connection to his blood mother remained sentient and he absorbed what she was experiencing on the same stormy night that Jake was rescued from death by Sam.

And finally, Jordan would now understand why he could never contact his mother when he sought her on the other side. But it would take him longer to accept that his father was not the prefabricated scoundrel he imagined him to be and that, while Richard may have been unable to show his son affection, his devotion and love for Maureen was unending. Just as Jordan contended that Jake was too wrapped up in his ego to comprehend his situation on a broader scale, the same could be said for Jordan when it came to appreciating his own family's private battles.

But all that would have to wait. Because at this moment, the world was stopping briefly so that a mother and son—separated for over four decades—could each find the elusive peace that had been missing from their lives. When they finally released from their embrace, Jordan looked at Jane with blue eyes of gratitude.

Maureen turned and walked over to Jane, who was leaning against the side of the Mustang. She stared into her eyes with a gaze that dove into Jane's soul. Maureen clasped Jane's hand with her two palms, never taking her eyes off her. A smile crept onto her face as she recognized Jane. "You?" she whispered. "It's *you.*" She leaned closer to Jane. "Mwê ni èspwa pou la yonn kilès ki sa fè mwên tjè feb antyè ankò. I hope for the one who can make my tender heart whole again." She pulled Jane toward her and held her tightly. "Thank you."

Maureen moved her hand down Jane's spine until it rested in the small of her back. Jane felt a shock of heat enter her body that burned into her bloodstream and exploded beneath her waist. There was a second of pain in her pelvis and then a cooling sensation that permeated her bones. When Maureen pulled back, there were tears welled in her eyes. "You'll soon know what you have to do, Jane."

CHAPTER 39

Jane and Weyler drove to the edge of Jordan's property, each in their own vehicle. Weyler rolled his window down. "You still need that week off?"

"I don't know yet. I'm still waiting for the call."

"Let me know." Jane nodded.

"Oh, I almost forgot. Bo asked me to give you this." Weyler leaned outside his window and handed Jane several pieces of torn paper.

"What is it?"

"The speeding ticket he gave you." Weyler started to drive away.

"Hey, wait a second." Weyler stopped. "I gotta know. Your luggage says *M.E.W.* What's the *E* stand for?"

"Oh, Jane. Some secrets are never revealed." He rolled up his window and headed onto the road that led back to Denver.

Jane stared out the window—for the first time in a long time, feeling calm. She didn't even jump when her cell phone rang. Checking the number, it was the doctor's office.

"Hello, doc."

"Hello, Jane. I have your results. Curiously, the pathology appears to be more likely a mild dysplasia. There must have been a false positive on your last test. These things can happen...although it's rare. I want to take a wait-and-see approach. Come back in three months and we'll do another test to be on the safe side."

Jane could still feel Maureen's hand in the small of her back. "Sure. But you won't find anything in three months, doc."

She could have headed back to Denver, but she turned back toward Midas. She called Hank and told him to meet her behind The Rabbit Hole. He was waiting when she arrived. Jane got out of the Mustang and walked over to him. "His name was Mark," she said. "I was twenty-two. He was my first true love. He was an alcoholic and a drug addict. He shot himself sitting in a wingback chair while he listened to Puccini's "O Mio Babbino Caro." He set it up so the song would repeat and that's what I heard when I found him. He left me his car, his collection of Pavarotti CDs and his leather satchel. I live with the ghost of his memory and his regret. And I'm scared to death of loving someone like that again because when they go, part of me will die another death. And I'm afraid if that happens, I'll be destroyed and I will spend the rest of my life in a daze and unable to function until I finally leave this world."

Hank touched Jane's cheek. "Oh, Chopper. All we have for sure is right now. This moment. We have this stupid illusion that we have control over the future. But that's just an illusion. All we know is this second. Death is inevitable, sweetheart, but the life that leads up to it doesn't have to be built on bricks of tears." Jane listened to him for the first time. "You think that around every corner there's a dark body lurking, waiting to strangle you. So, before you turn that corner, you've got your fists clenched, ready to strike. What I'm telling you is that around *this* corner here…there's peace and whatever freedom you need. Around *this* corner, you don't have to clench your fists because there's no one to fight or fear." He took her hand in his. "Maybe I understand you better than anyone else. I happen to think you need someone like me in your life. I'm not fresh out of the factory box. I'm road tested but I'm not road weary. The warranty isn't up yet and the insurance hasn't expired. I know there's a bit of an age difference between us. But I think if you can have a little patience…you'll be able to keep up with me." He smiled. "Oh, hell, Jane. You need an older man. You'd weaken a younger one." Hank leaned forward and kissed her. He looked into her eyes and grinned. "It's really okay to be happy, you know?"

Jane nodded. "That's the rumor."

He looked her in the eye. "Think with your heart, Jane." Hank tenderly kissed her. "Hang on a second." He ducked into his house and returned with an envelope in his hand. "You asked me to do a search on that woman?"

Jane's mouth went dry. "Yeah?"

"I found her. All of her information is in there." Jane tentatively took the envelope. "Has this got anything to do with your next case?"

"Why?"

"I don't know. The circumstances, maybe?" Hank said, motioning to the envelope. "You heading back to Denver tonight?"

"No. But I'll need a place to stay."

Hank smiled. "I'll make a couple calls." He winked. "I've got a hot dog sitting inside with your name on it."

"I'll be in. Give me a second."

Hank kissed her passionately before heading back into the sports bar.

Jane stared at the envelope, opening it slowly.

The truth was staring at her in black-and-white, and with a color photo.

She had an older sister named Wanda LeRóy, age forty-two.

According to her birth certificate, she was born at exactly 3:11 am.

And Wanda LeRóy was just about to be released from prison.

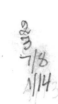

CPSIA information can be obtained at www.ICGtesting.com

265278BV00001B/17/P

9 780984 190553